MASH UP

MASH UP

STORIES INSPIRED BY FAMOUS FIRST LINES

EDITED BY
GARDNER DOZOIS

TITAN BOOKS

Mash Up
Mass market edition ISBN: 9781785651052
Print edition ISBN: 9781785651038
E-book edition ISBN: 9781785651045

Published by Titan Books
A division of Titan Publishing Group Ltd
144 Southwark Street, London SE1 0UP

First mass market edition: June 2017
2 4 6 8 10 9 7 5 3 1

CONTENTS

INTRODUCTION

If you are reading this page, you are about to enjoy an anthology that began as a glimmer of a notion way back in 2007. The conceit was simple: each author would take the first sentence of a favorite classic—fiction or nonfiction—and use it as the first sentence in an original short story. The stories could have everything to do with the original source—or nothing at all.

James Patrick Kelly was my first sounding board, and it was he who floated the idea of approaching the Science Fiction and Fantasy Writers of America (SFWA) to partner with Audible. The idea germinated for several years until its next stop at John Scalzi, SFWA's president at the time, who offered great insight into the nuts and bolts of turning the concept into reality. From there, literary agent Eleanor Wood worked her magic, and the project was born.

Ultimately, though, it took the amazing efforts of editor Gardner Dozois to draft a team of writers *par excellence* and to sculpt a collection of wonderful stories, each of which takes a single sentence to unexpected places. "Call me Ishmael" introduces a tough-as-nails private eye—who carries a harpoon; the opening of *The Wonderful Wizard of Oz* inspires the tale of an aging female astronaut who's being treated by a doctor named Dorothy Gale; the first line of *Huckleberry Finn* leads to a wild ride with a foul-mouthed riverboat captain who plies the waters of Hell; and so much more.

The response to Audible's original audio edition was beyond even our highest expectations. Mary Robinette Kowal's story was honored with the Hugo Award for Best Novelette; several other stories were chosen for annual Best-of collections; the audio production was nominated for an Audie Award; and now, thanks to Titan Books, these stories are finding a whole new audience.

Most gratifying, though, was the opportunity to work with writers and an editor I've long admired. My fondest wish is if you encounter an author here for the first time, or rediscover an old favorite, your very next step will be to seek out more of their great work.

Steve Feldberg
Audible.com
January 2016

ROBERT CHARLES WILSON
FIREBORN

I've been writing science fiction since the publication of my first novel in 1986.

I took the opening line of the story that follows from one of the *Rootabaga Stories*, by the American poet and author Carl Sandburg. Sandburg won the Pulitzer Prize no fewer than three times, twice for his poetry and once for his biography of Abraham Lincoln, but generations of Americans remember him best for his children's books, most famously the *Rootabaga Stories*. In these stories, populated with corn fairies and talking skyscrapers, melancholy adults and far-traveling children, Sandburg aimed to create a uniquely American response to the classic European fairy tales. They're written in language that's simple, evocative, vivid, and often wonderfully strange. Sandburg's description of one of his own characters could equally describe himself: "He seems to love some of the precious things that are cheap, such as stars, the wind, pleasant words, time to be lazy, and fools having personality and distinction."

I'm not a poet, and I haven't attempted to duplicate what Carl Sandburg did so uniquely and so well, but it was Sandburg's whimsicality, love of language, and deep sense of place that inspired this science fiction story, called "Fireborn."

FIREBORN
BY ROBERT CHARLES WILSON

Sometimes in January the sky comes down close if we walk on a country road, and turn our faces up to look at the sky.

Onyx turned her face up to the sky as she walked with her friend Jasper beside a mule cart on the road that ran through Buttercup County to the turnpike. She had spent a day counting copper dollars at the changehouse and watching bad-tempered robots trudge east- and west-bound through the crust of yesterday's snow. *Sunny days with snow on the ground makes robots irritable*, Jasper had claimed. Onyx didn't know if this was true – it seemed so, but what seemed so wasn't always truly so.

You think too much, Jasper had told her.

And you don't think enough, Onyx had answered haughtily. She walked next to him now as he led the mule, keeping her head turned up because she liked to see the stars even when the January wind came cutting past the margins of her lambswool hood. Some of the stars were hidden because the moon was up and shining white. But Onyx liked the moon, too, for the way it silvered the peaks and saddles of the mountains and cast spidery tree-shadows over the unpaved road.

That was how it happened that Onyx first saw the skydancer vaulting over a mountain pass northwest of Buttercup County.

Jasper didn't see it because he was looking at the road ahead. Jasper was a tall boy, two breadloaves taller than Onyx, and he owned a big head with eyes made for inspecting the horizon. *It's what's in front of you that counts*, he often said. Jasper believed roads went to interesting places – that's why they were roads. And it was good to be on a road because that meant you were going somewhere interesting. Who cared what was up in the sky?

You never know what might fall on you, Onyx often told him. *And not every road goes to an interesting place*. The road they were on, for instance. It went to Buttercup County, and what was interesting about Buttercup County? Onyx had lived there for all of her nineteen years. If there was anything interesting in Buttercup County, Onyx had seen it twice and ignored it a dozen times more.

Well, that's why you need a road, Jasper said – *to go somewhere else*.

Maybe, Onyx thought. Maybe so. Maybe not. In the meantime, she would keep on looking at the sky.

At first, she didn't know what she was seeing up over the high northwest col of the western mountains. She had heard about skydancers from travelers bound for or returning from Harvest out on the plains in autumn, where skydancers were said to dance for the fireborn when the wind brought great white clouds sailing over the brown and endless prairie. But those were travelers' tales, and Onyx discounted such storytelling. Some part of those stories might be true, but she guessed not much: maybe fifty cents on the dollar, Onyx thought. What she thought tonight was, *That's a strange cloud*.

It was a strange and brightly colored cloud, pink and purple even in the timid light of the moon. It did not move in a windblown fashion. It was shaped like a person. It looked like a person in a purple gown with a silver crown and eyes as wide as respectable townships. It was as tall as the square-shouldered mountain peak Onyx's people called Tall Tower.

Onyx gasped as her mind made reluctant sense of what her stubborn eyes insisted on showing her.

Jasper had been complaining about the cold, and what a hard thing it was to walk a mule cart all the way home from the turnpike on a chilly January night, but he turned his eyes away from the road at the sound of Onyx's surprise. He looked where Onyx was looking and stopped walking. After a long pause, he said, "That's a skydancer – I'll bet you a copper dollar it is!"

"How do you know? Have you ever seen a skydancer?"

"Not to look at. Not until tonight. But what else could it be?"

Skydancers were as big as mountains and danced with clouds, and this apparition was as big as a mountain and appeared to be dancing, so Onyx guessed that Jasper might be right. And it was a strange and lonely thing to see on a country road on a January night. They stopped to watch the skydancer dance, though the wind blew cold around them and the mule complained with wheezing and groaning. The skydancer moved in ways Onyx would not have thought possible, turning like a whirlwind in the moonlight, rising over the peak of Tall Tower and seeming for a moment to balance there, then flying still higher, turning pirouettes of stately slowness in the territory of the stars. "It's coming closer," Jasper said.

Was it? *Yes*: Onyx thought so. It was hard to tell because the skydancer was so big. Skydancers were made by the fireborn, and the fireborn made miraculous things, but Onyx could not imagine how this creature had come to be. Was it alive or was it an illusion? If it came down to earth, could she touch it?

It began to seem as if she might have that opportunity. The skydancer appeared to lose its balance in the air. Its vast limbs suddenly stiffened. Its legs, which could span counties, locked at the knee. The wind began to tumble it sidelong. Parts of the skydancer grew transparent or flew off like evanescent colored clouds. "I think it's broken," said Jasper.

Broken and shrinking, it began to fall. *It'll fall near here*, Onyx thought, if it continued on its wind-tumbled course. *If there's anything left of it, the way it's coming apart.*

It came all apart in the air, but there was something left behind, something small that fell more gently, swaying like an autumn leaf on its way from branch to winter. It fell nearby – down a slope away from the road, on a hillside where in summer wild rhubarb put out scarlet stalks of flowers.

"Come on, let's find it," Jasper said.

"It might be dangerous."

"It might," said Jasper, who was not afraid of the possibility of danger, but all the more inclined to go get into it. They left the mule anchored to its cart and went hunting for what had fallen, while the moonlight was bright enough to show them the way.

They found a young woman standing on the winter hillside, and it was obvious to Onyx that she was fireborn – perhaps, therefore, not actually young. Onyx knew the woman was fireborn because she was naked on a January night and seemed not to mind it. Onyx found the woman's nakedness perplexing. Jasper seemed fascinated.

Though the woman was naked, she had been wearing a harness of cloth and metal, which she had discarded; it lay on the ground at her feet, parts of it glowing sunset colors, parts of it twitching like the feelers of an unhappy ant.

They came and stood near enough to speak to the woman. The woman, who was about Onyx's size but had paler skin and hair that gave back the moonlight in shades of amber, was looking at the sky, whispering to herself. When she noticed Onyx and Jasper, she spoke to them in words Onyx didn't understand. Then she cocked her shoulder and said in sensible words, "You can't hurt me. It would be a mistake to try."

"We don't want to hurt you," Jasper said, before Onyx could compose a response. "We saw you fall, if you falling was what we saw. We thought you might need help."

"I'm in no danger," the woman said, and it seemed to Onyx her voice was silvery, like a tune played on a flute, but not just any old wooden flute: a silver one. "But thank you."

"You must be a long way from home. Are you lost?"

"My devices misfunctioned. My people will come for me. We have a compound on the other side of the pass."

"Do you need a ride, ma'am? Onyx and I can take you in our cart."

"Wait, that's a long way," Onyx said. Anyway it was her cart, not Jasper's, and he shouldn't be offering it without consulting her.

"Yes," Jasper agreed, "much too far for an undressed woman to walk on a night like this."

Onyx considered kicking him.

The fireborn woman hesitated. Then she smiled. It was a charming smile, Onyx had to admit. The woman had shiny teeth, a complete set. "Would you really do that for me?"

"Ma'am, yes, of course, my privilege," said Jasper.

"All right, then," the woman said. "I might like that. Thank you. My name is Anna Tingri Five."

Onyx, who knew what the "Five" meant, gaped in amazement.

"I'm Jasper," said Jasper. "And this is Onyx."

"You should put on some clothes," Onyx said in a small voice. "Ma'am."

Anna Tingri Five twitched her shoulder and blinked, and a

shimmery robe suddenly covered her nakedness. "Is that better?"

"Much," said Onyx.

On the road to the fireborn compound, as the mule cart bucked over rutted snow hard as ice, the three of them discussed their wants, as strangers often do.

Onyx was expected at home, but her mother and father and two brothers wouldn't worry much if she was late. Probably they would think she had stayed the night in Buttercup Town, detained by business. Onyx worked at the changehouse there and was often kept late by unexpected traffic. Her parents might even hope she had stayed late for the purpose of keeping Jasper company: her parents liked Jasper and had hinted at the possibility of a wedding. Onyx resented such talk – she liked Jasper well enough, but perhaps not well enough to contemplate marriage. Not that Jasper had hinted at any such ambition. Jasper wanted to sail to Africa and find the Fifth Door to the Moon and grow rich or immortal, which, Onyx imagined, would leave him little time for wedding foolishness.

Anna Tingri Five perched on a frozen bag of wheat flour in the mule cart, saying, "I am, as you must suppose, fireborn."

No doubt about that. And how astonished Onyx's parents and two brothers would be to discover she had been consorting with the fireborn! The fireborn came through Buttercup County only on rare occasions, and then only one or two of them, young ones, mostly male, riding robots on their incomprehensible quests, hardly deigning to speak to the townspeople. Now here Onyx was right next to a five-born female – a talkative one!

"Was that you in the sky, dancing?" Jasper asked.

"Yes. Until the bodymaker broke."

"No offense, but you looked about five miles tall."

"Only a mile," said Anna Tingri Five, a smile once again dimpling her moonlit face.

"What's a skydancer doing in Buttercup County, if you don't mind me asking?"

"Practicing for the Harvest, here where there are mountain winds to wrestle with and clouds that come high and fast from the west. We mean to camp here through the summer."

Without so much as a by-your-leave, Onyx thought indignantly, though when had the fireborn ever asked permission of common mortals?

"You mean to dance at the Harvest?" asked Jasper.

"I mean to win the competition and be elevated to the Eye of the Moon," said Anna Tingri Five.

The Eye of the Moon: best seen when the moon was in shadow. Tonight the moon was full and the Eye was invisible, but some nights, when only a sliver of the moon shone white, Onyx had seen the Eye in the darker hemisphere; a ring of red glow, aloof and unwinking. It was where the fireborn went when they were tired of living one life after another. It was what they did instead of dying.

Since Anna Tingri Five had divulged an ambition, Onyx felt obliged to confess one of her own. "I'm nineteen years old," she said, "and one day I mean to go east and see the cities of the Atlantic Coast. I'm tired of Buttercup County. I'm a good counter. I can add and subtract and divide and multiply. I can double-entry bookkeep. I could get a city job and do city things. I could look at tall buildings every day and live in one of them."

Spoken baldly into the cold air of a January night, her desire froze into a childish embarrassment. She felt herself blushing. But Anna Tingri Five only nodded thoughtfully.

"And I mean to go east as well," Jasper said, "but I won't

stop in any city. I can lift and haul and tie a dozen different knots. I'll hire myself onto a sailing ship and sail to Africa."

He ended his confession there, though there was more to it. Onyx knew that he wanted to go to Africa and find the Fifth Door, which might gain him admission to the Eye of the Moon. All the world's four Doors, plus perhaps the hidden Fifth, were doorways to the moon. Even a common mortal could get to the Eye that way, supposedly, though the fireborn would never let a commoner past the gate. That was why Jasper dreamed about the hidden Fifth. It was his only hope of living more than one life.

Skeptical Onyx would have bet that the Fifth Door was a legend without any truth at the heart of it, but she had stopped saying so to Jasper, because it made him irritable. Lately, he had begun to guard his ambition as if it were a fragile secret possession, and he didn't mention it now.

"This is my fifth life," Anna Tingri Five said in her silver flute voice, "and I'm tired of coming through the juvenation fires with half my memories missing, starting out all over again with nothing but the ghosts of Anna Tingri One, Two, Three, and Four to talk to when I talk to myself. I want to live forever in the Eye of the Moon and make things out of pure philosophy."

Onyx didn't comprehend half this peroration, but she understood the yearning in the words of Anna Tingri Five.

"Both of you want to leave this place?" Anna Tingri Five asked.

Yes. Both.

"Come into our encampment then," said Anna Tingri Five. "It's warm inside. Let me repay you for your interesting kindness."

They came to the place the fireborn had made for themselves. No one in Buttercup County had seen the fireborn arrive, and their camp was over the rim of a hill where no one went in the leafless winter. But the camp itself was not leafless. A mortal commoner passing by, Anna Tingri Five explained, would see nothing unusual. Some ensorcellment kept the campground hidden from casual glances. But Anna Tingri Five allowed Onyx and Jasper to see the place and pass inside its perimeter. Inside, the fireborn had undone winter. In their enchanted circle, it was a pleasant summer night. The trees were leafy, the meadow plants flowering. Vast silken pavilion tents of many colors had been staked to the fragrant ground, and hovering radiant globes supplemented the pale moonlight. It was late, and Onyx supposed most of the fireborn were asleep, but some few were still passing between the tents, talking in unknown languages, as lean and tall and perfect as flesh can be. Supple robots moved silently among them, performing inscrutable robot tasks. Onyx marveled at the warmth of the air (she shrugged out of her woolen coat, loosened a button on her hempen shirt), and Jasper's eyes grew big with awe and eagerness.

"Spend the night with us," said Anna Tingri Five.

Anna Tingri Five had never been out of contact with her compound even after her bodymaker failed; at the first tickle of a wistful thought a robot would have flown her home through the January sky. But she had been intrigued and interested by the helpful commoners who appeared out of the darkness. She had met few real commoners and was curious about them. She thought that this pair might be worth keeping. That was why, a few days later, she offered them jobs in the encampment and a free ride, come the end of summer, to the continent's great Harvest Festival.

Onyx's parents begged her not to accept the offer. Her mother wailed; her father raged; but they had known they were raising a rover ever since they named their restless baby girl Onyx. And they had two stout and unimaginative sons who were bound to remain in Buttercup County and lead useful and sensible lives.

Jasper's father had milled grain all his life, had continued to mill grain after the death of his wife ten years ago, and would mill grain until the day he died. He had once harbored his own ambition to see the world outside Buttercup County, and was pleased and terrified in equal parts by the prospect of his son's departure. "Write me letters from foreign places," he demanded, and Jasper promised to do so. When father and son said goodbye, both wept. They knew that life was short and difficult and that, as a rule, commoners only lived once.

It was soon obvious to Onyx that the fireborn had no real need of hired help. It was not that she and Jasper did no work – they did – or that they were not paid for their work – they were, in genuine copper dollars. But the carrying of water and the serving of food had previously been conducted by robots, and Onyx felt embarrassed to be doing robot work, even for generous wages. The fireborn said please and thank you and smiled their thin, distant smiles. *But we're pets*, Onyx complained to Jasper one day. *We're not good for anything.*

Speak for yourself, said Jasper.

It became increasingly clear that Anna Tingri Five favored Jasper over Onyx.

Onyx assigned herself the task of learning all she could about the fireborn. The first thing she learned was that there were greater and lesser ranks among them. Some of the fireborn in the skydancer camp were firstborns, who had never passed through the rejuvenating fire and who had trivializing Ones attached to their names. As old as some of them might seem, the firstborns were novices, junior members of the troupe. They watched, listened, kept to their own circles. They were not skydancers but apprentices to skydancers; they managed the small incomprehensible machines that made the dances possible.

The dancers themselves were many-born: some Fives, some Sevens, a couple of Nines. And despite her reservations, Onyx loved to watch them dance. Whenever they danced she would leave her unimportant work (folding ceremonial silks, crushing seeds to flavor soup) and study the process from its beginning to its end. The dancers' apprentices helped them don the harnesses they called bodymakers, and in their bodymakers the dancers looked like some robot's dream of humanity, perfect coffee-colored flesh peeping out between lashings of glass and sky-blue metal. But there was nothing awkward about the way the harnessed dancers moved. They grew buoyant, they stepped lightly to the launching meadow, they flexed their supple limbs as they assembled. Then they flew into the air.

And once they were aloft, still and small as eagles hovering on an updraft, the bodymakers made their bodies.

Onyx understood that the bodies were projections of the dancers' bodies, and that the projected bodies were made of almost nothing – of air momentarily frozen and made to bend light to create the illusion of colors and surfaces. But they looked real, and they were stunningly large: one mile or more top to bottom as nearly as Onyx could calculate. Because they were insubstantial, the bodies were not affected by even the most powerful winds, but they touched and rebounded and gripped one another as if they were real things. In the rondo dances, vast hands held vast hands as if air were flesh.

"I'll bet I could do that," Jasper said yearningly, on one of the mornings when they sat together at the edge of the flying meadow and watched until their necks ached with up-staring.

"Bet a copper dollar you couldn't," said Onyx.

"Someday you'll die of not believing."

"Someday you'll die of dreaming!"

The greatest of the dancers – a category that included Anna Tingri Five – were rivals, and they danced alone or with single partners selected from among the lesser dancers. During the Harvest festivities, a single Finest Dancer would be selected, and that individual would be offered transit to the Eye of the Moon. Only two dancers in the troupe were eligible to compete for this year's Moon Prize: Anna Tingri Five and a man named Dawa Nine.

Both danced beautifully, in Onyx's opinion. Anna Tingri Five danced as a blue-skinned goddess with bells on her wrists and ankles. When she flirted with the white clouds that climbed the sunlit mountains from the west, her bells tolled sonorously. Dawa Nine danced as an ancient warrior, with silver armor and a silver sword on his hip. Often in his practice, he rose to impossible heights and swooped like a predatory bird to within a feather's-breadth of the treetops.

But Jasper had eyes only for Anna Tingri Five, an attention the fireborn dancer enjoyed and encouraged, much to Onyx's disgust. Jasper pleased Anna Tingri Five by befriending the apprentice who maintained her gear, helping him with small tasks and asking occasional pertinent questions. On idle days he folded Anna Tingri Five's silk and poured her dinner wine. What he hoped to accomplish with this foolish fawning was beyond Onyx. Until it became clear to her.

One cloudless night in spring, when the fireborn were gathered under a great pavilion tent for their communal meal, Anna Tingri Five stood and cleared her throat (*like the sound of a silver flute clearing its throat*, Onyx thought) and announced that she had revised her plan for the festival and that she would teach the commoner Jasper to dance.

The fireborn were startled, and so was Onyx, who nearly dropped the pitcher of wine she was carrying. Last month, she had been given a device the size of a pea and the shape of a snail, which she wore behind her ear, and which translated the confusing languages of the fireborn into words she could mostly understand. In that startled moment, the device conveyed a tumult of dismay, disapproval, disdain.

Anna Tingri Five defended her decision, citing examples of novelty dancers who had been admitted to tournaments in supporting roles, citing the elevation of certain commoners to near-fireborn status for certain sacred functions, citing Jasper's fascination with the dance. A few of the fireborn nodded tolerantly; most did not.

Jasper had been training in secret, said Anna Tingri Five, and tomorrow he would make his first flight.

Jasper wasn't present in the tent that night, or Onyx would have given him her best scornful glare. She was forced to save that for the morning, when she joined a crowd of the fireborn for the occasion of his ascent. She watched (he avoided her eyes) as Jasper was strapped and haltered into a bodymaker by Anna Tingri Five's sullen apprentices. She watched with grim attention as Anna Tingri Five escorted him to the launching meadow. She watched as he rose into a mild blue sky, bobbing like a paper boat on a pond. Then he engaged his bodymaker.

Jasper became a mile-high man. A man dressed like a farmer. A flying peasant. An enormous gawking rube.

The false Jasper flexed its county-wide limbs. It turned an awkward, lunging pirouette.

Now the fireborn understood the nature of the dance; they laughed in approval.

Onyx scowled and stalked away.

* * *

"It's a silly custom," Onyx said, "skydancing."

Perhaps she shouldn't have said this – perhaps especially not to Dawa Nine, the troupe's other keynote dancer. But he had come to her, not vice versa. And she guessed that he deserved to hear her true and honest opinion.

"You only say that because you're jealous."

Dawa Nine was a tall man. His skin was dark as hard coal, even darker than Onyx's skin. His head was well-shaped and hairless. He had lived nine lives and that was enough for him. He aimed to dance his way into immortality, and the most immediate obstacle in his path was Anna Tingri Five.

"I am not jealous," Onyx said.

It was noon on a spring day and the sun was shining and he had come to her tent and asked to speak with her. Onyx had agreed. But what could Dawa Nine have to say that would interest Onyx? She cared very little about the fireborn or their ambitions. In five days, the troupe would leave Buttercup County for the windswept granaries of the Great Plains. Onyx planned to leave them there and make her own way to the cities of the Atlantic Coast. She had saved enough copper dollars to make the journey easier.

"Be honest," Dawa Nine said. His voice was not a flute. His voice was the wind hooting through the owl-holes of an old tree, and his smile was soft as moonlight. "With yourself, if not with me. You came here with Jasper, and he was your everyday boyfriend, and now he's flying with a beautiful fireborn dancer. What sane woman wouldn't be jealous?"

"It's not like I ever would have married him," Onyx protested.

"In that case, you should stop paying him such close attention."

"I'm not! I'm *ignoring* him."

"Then let me help you ignore him."

I'm doing fine in that department, thought Onyx. "What do you mean?"

"Work as my apprentice."

"No! I don't want to fly. I don't want to be some dancer's clown."

"I'm not suggesting that you learn to fly, Miss Onyx. But you can husband my machinery and harness my bodymaker. The boy who does it for me now is a mere One, and you're smarter than he is – I can tell."

Onyx took this for fact, not flattery. And – yes – Jasper would be gratifyingly annoyed to find Onyx working for Anna Tingri Five's bitter rival. "But what do *you* get out of this, Old Nine? Not just a better apprentice, I'll bet."

"Of course not. You're a commoner. You can tell me about Jasper. Who he is, what he wants, how he might dance – what Anna Tingri Five might make of him."

"I will not be your spy," Onyx said.

"Well, think about it," said Dawa Nine.

Dawa Nine's offer was on Onyx's mind as the troupe packed its gear and left Buttercup County.

The fireborn all rode robots, and robots carried their gear and supplies, and even Onyx and Jasper were given robots to ride. The troupe found and followed the road that ran through Buttercup Town, and Onyx was able to wave to her parents from the comfortable shoulder of a tall machine. They waved back fearfully; Jasper's father was also present, also waving and weeping; and Onyx burned with the pangs of home-leaving as they passed the hotel, the changehouse where she had worked, the general store, the barber shop. Then Buttercup Town was behind them, and her thoughts moved differently.

She thought about commoners and the fireborn and the Eye of the Moon.

Now that she had dined and slept and bathed with them, the fireborn were far less daunting than they had seemed to her in stories. Powerful, yes; masters of strange possibilities, yes; rich beyond calculation, surely. But as striving and envious as anyone else. Cruel and kind. Thoughtless and wise. Why then were there two kinds of people, commoners and fireborn?

Legend had it that commoners and fireborn had parted ways during the Great Hemoclysm centuries ago. But not even the fireborn knew much about that disaster. Some said the Eye of the Moon had watched it. Some said the Eye of the Moon had only just come into existence when the world began to burn. Some said the Eye of the Moon had somehow *caused* the Hemoclysm (but Onyx kept that notion to herself, for it was a heresy; the fireborn considered the Eye a holy thing).

Onyx cared little about the Eye. It was where the fireborn went after they had lived their twelve allotted lives – or sooner, if they tired of life on Earth and could claim some worthy achievement. In the Eye, supposedly the fireborn wore whatever bodies they chose and lived in cities made entirely of thought. They could travel across the sky – there were Eyes, some claimed, on other planets, not just the moon. One day the Eye would rule the entire universe. Or so it was said.

As a child on a pew in Buttercup County's Church of True Things, Onyx had learned how Jesu Rinpoche had saved wisdom from the Hemoclysm and planted the Four Doors to the Moon at the corners of the Earth. The story of the Fifth Door, in which Jasper so fervently believed, was a minor heresy much favoured by old pipe-smoking men. What was the truth of it all? Onyx didn't know. Probably, she thought, nine-tenths of these tales were nonsense. She had been called cynical or atheistic for saying so. But most of everything people said was nonsense. Why should this be different?

All she really knew was that there were commoners and there were fireborn. The fireborn traveled at will and played for a living and made robots that mined mountains and cultivated harvests. The commoners lived at the feet of the fireborn, untroubled unless they *made* trouble. That was how it had been since the day she was born, and that was how it would be when she left the world behind. Only dreamers like Jasper believed differently. And Jasper was a fool.

Jasper's foolishness grew so obvious that Onyx gave up speaking to him, at least until they argued.

The troupe descended in long robotic marches from the mountains to the hinterland, where the only hills were gentle drumlins and rolling moraines, and where the rivers rippled bright and slow as Easter ribbons. Some days, the sky was blue and empty. Some days, clouds came rolling out of the west like gray monsters with lightning hearts.

The road they followed was paved and busy with traffic. They made their camps by the roadside where wild grass grew and often stayed encamped for days. A month passed in this lazy transit, then another. Where the plains had been farmed, a vast green bounty mounded and grew ripe. The Harvest approached.

Jasper's dancing skills improved with practice, though Onyx was loath to admit it. Of course, he wasn't as good as the fireborn dancers, but he wasn't supposed to be. He was a foil, as Dawa Nine explained to her; a decorative novelty. The theme of Anna Tingri Five's dance was the misbegotten love of a fireborn woman for a young and gawkish commoner. It was a story the fireborn had been telling for centuries, and the tale was always tragic. It had been set to music many times, though Anna Tingri Five would be the first to dance it. Jasper was required only to clump about the sky in crude yearning poses, and to adopt a willing stillness while Anna Tingri Five beckoned him, teased him, accepted him, loved him, and forsook him in a series of highly symbolic set-dances. The rehearsals were impressive, and with her head turned to the late-summer sky, Onyx even felt a kind of sour pride: *That's our Jasper a mile high and another mile tall*, she thought. *That's the same Jasper who walked behind a mule cart in Buttercup County ten months ago*. But Jasper was as stupid and bemused as the peasant he portrayed in the dance.

And then, one night as she served wine, Onyx discovered Jasper with Anna Tingri Five in a dark corner of the fireborn pavilion, the two of them exchanging bird-peck kisses.

Onyx left the pavilion for the bitter consolation of the prairie night. Jasper guessed what she had seen and followed her out, calling her name. But Onyx didn't stop or look back. She didn't want to see his traitorous face. She went straight to Dawa Nine instead.

Jasper caught her the next day, as she passed along a row of trees where a creek cut the tabletop prairie. The day was warm. Onyx wore a yellow silk skirt one of the fireborn women had given her, and a yellow silk scarf that spoke in gestures to the wind. The troupe's lesser dancers rehearsed among clouds high above, casting undulant shadows across the wild grass.

"Don't you trust me?" Jasper asked, blocking her path.

"Trust you to do what? I trust you to do what I've seen you doing," said Onyx.

"You have no *faith*!"

"You have no *sense*!"

"All I want is to learn about the Eye of the Moon and how to get there," Jasper said.

"I don't care about the Eye of the Moon! I want to live in a city and look at tall buildings! And all I have to do to get there is walk toward the sunrise!"

"I'll walk alongside you," said Jasper. "Honest, Onyx!"

"Really? Then let's walk!"

"After the dance, of course, I mean…"

"Hah!"

"But I owe her that much," he said, not daring to pronounce the name of Anna Tingri Five for fear of further provoking Onyx. His big eyes pleaded wordlessly.

"She cares nothing for you, you mule!"

These words wounded Jasper in the tender part of his pride, and he drew back and let his vanity take command of his mouth. "Bet you're wrong," he said.

"Bet how much?"

"Ten copper dollars!"

"*It's a bet!*" cried Onyx, stalking away.

The Harvest Festival came at summer's decline, the cooling hinge of the season. The troupe joined a hundred others for the celebration. Onyx marvelled at the gathering.

There were many Harvests in the world but only a few festivals. Each of the world's great breadlands held one. Prosaically, it was the occasion on which the fireborn collected the bounty of grain and vegetables that had been amassed by their fleets of agricultural robots, while commoners feasted on the copious leavings, more than enough to feed all the mortal men and women of the world for the coming year. That was the great bargain that had sealed the peace between the commonfolk and the fireborn: food for all, and plenty of it. Only overbreeding could have spoiled the arrangement, and the fireborn attended to that matter with discreet lacings of antifertility substances in the grain the commoners ate. Commoners were born and commoners died, but their numbers never much varied. And it was a custom of the fireborn to bear children only rarely, since each lived a dozen long lives before adjourning to the Eye of the Moon. Their numbers, too, were stable.

But the Harvest Festival was more than that. It was an occasion of revelry and pilgrimage, a great gathering of people and robots on the vast stage of the world's steppes and prairies, a profane and holy intermingling. The fireborn held exhibitions and contests, to be judged by councils of the Twelve-Lived and marvelled at by commonfolk. Jugglers juggled, poets sang, artisans hawked their inscrutable arts. Prayer flags snapped gaily in the wind. And of course: *skydancers danced*.

Several troupes had arrived at the site of the North American festival (where the junction of two rivers stitched a quilt of yellow land), but the troupe Onyx served was one of the best regarded and was allotted the third day and third night of the festival for its performances.

By day, the lesser dancers danced. Crowds gawked and marvelled from below. Warm afternoon air called up clouds like tall white sailing ships, and the skydancers danced with them, wooed them, unwound their hidden lightnings. The sky rang with bells and drums. Sunlight rebounding from the ethereal bodies of the avatars cast rainbows over empty fields, and even the agricultural robots, serene at the beginning of their seasonal rest, seemed to gaze upward with a metallic, bovine awe.

Onyx hid away with Dawa Nine, who was fasting and praying in preparation for his night flight. The best dancers danced at night, their immense avatars glowing from within. There was no sight more spectacular. The Council of the Twelves would be watching and judging. Onyx knew that Dawa Nine was deeply weary of life on Earth and determined to dance his way to the moon. And since the day she had discovered Jasper and Anna Tingri Five exchanging kisses,

Onyx had promised to help him achieve that ambition – to do whatever it was in her power to do, even the dark and furtive things she ought to have disdained.

She could have offered Dawa Nine her body (as Jasper had apparently given his to Anna Tingri Five), but she was intimidated by Dawa's great age and sombre manner. Instead, she had shared secrets with him. She had told him how Jasper worked Anna Tingri Five's gear, how he had learned only a few skydancing skills but had learned them well enough to serve as Anna's foil, how he had mastered the technical business of flight harnesses and bodymakers. He had even modified Anna Tingri Five's somatic generator, making her avatar's vast face nearly as subtle and expressive as her own – a trick even Dawa Nine's trained apprentices could not quite duplicate.

None of this information much helped Dawa Nine, however; if anything, it had deepened his gloomy conviction that Anna Tingri Five was bound to outdance him and steal his ticket to the Eye. Desperate measures were called for, and time was short. As the lesser dancers danced, Dawa Nine summoned Onyx into the shadow of his tent.

"I want you to make sure my bodymaker is functioning correctly," he said.

"Of course," said Onyx. "No need to say, Old Nine."

"Go into the equipment tent and inspect it. If you find any flaws, fix them."

Onyx nodded.

"And if you happen to find Anna Tingri's gear unattended…"

"Yes?"

"Fix *that*, too."

Onyx didn't need to be told twice. She went to the tent where the gear was stored, as instructed. It was a dreadful thing that Dawa had asked her to do – to tamper with Anna

Tingri Five's bodymaker in order to spoil her dance. But what did Onyx care about the tribulations of the fireborn? The fireborn were nothing to her, as she was nothing to them.

Or so she told herself. Still, she was pricked with fleabites of conscience. She hunched over Dawa Nine's bodymaker, pretending to inspect it. Everything was in order, apart from Onyx's thoughts.

What had Anna Tingri Five done to deserve this cruel trick? (*Apart from being fireborn and haughty and stealing kisses from Jasper!*) And why punish Anna Tingri Five for Jasper's thoughtlessness? (*Because there was no way to punish Jasper himself!*) And by encouraging this tampering, hadn't Dawa Nine proven himself spiteful and dishonest? (*She could hardly deny it!*) And if Dawa Nine was untrustworthy, might he not blame Onyx if the deception was discovered? (*He almost certainly would!*)

It was this last thought that troubled Onyx most. She supposed that she could do as Dawa had asked: tamper with the bodymaker and ruin the dance Anna Tingri Five had so carefully rehearsed – and it might be worth the pangs of conscience it would cause her – but what of the consequences? Onyx secretly planned to leave the festival tonight and make her way east toward the cities of the Atlantic Coast. But her disappearance would only serve to incriminate her, if the tampering were discovered. The fireborn might hunt her down and put her on trial. And if she were accused of the crime, would Dawa Nine step forward to proclaim her innocence and take the responsibility himself?

Of course he would not.

And would Onyx be believed, if she tried to pin the blame on Dawa?

Hardly.

And was *any of that* the fault of Anna Tingri Five?

No.

Onyx waited until an opportunity presented itself. The few apprentices in the tent left to watch a sunset performance by a rival troupe. The few robots in the pavilion were downpowered or inattentive. The moment had come. Onyx strolled to the place where Anna Tingri Five's bodymaker was stored. It wouldn't take much. A whispered instruction to the machine codes. A plucked wire. A grease-smeared lens. So easy.

She waited to see if her hands would undertake the onerous task.

Her hands would not.

She walked away.

Onyx left the troupe's encampment at sunset. She could not say she had left the festival itself – the festival was expansive; pilgrims and commoners had camped for miles around the pavilions of the fireborn, crowds to every horizon. But she made slow progress, following the paved road eastward. By dark, she had reached a patch of harvested land where robots like great steel beetles rolled bales of straw, their red caution-lights winking a lonesome code. A few belated pilgrims moved past her in the opposite direction, carrying lanterns. Otherwise she was alone.

She stopped and looked back, though she had promised herself she would not.

The Harvest Festival smoldered on the horizon like a grassfire. A tolling of brass bells came down the cooling wind. Two skydancers rose and hovered in the clear air. Even at this distance Onyx recognized the glowing avatars of Jasper and Anna Tingri Five.

She tried to set aside her hopes and disappointments and watch the dance as any commoner would watch it. But this wasn't the dance as she had seen it rehearsed.

Onyx stared, her eyes so wide they reflected the light of the dance like startled moons.

Because the dance was different. The dance was *wrong*!

The Peasant and the Fireborn Woman circled each other as usual. The Peasant should have danced his few blunt and impoverished gestures (*Supplication, Lamentation, Protestation*) while the Fireborn Woman slowly wove around him a luminous tapestry of Lust, Disdain, Temptation, Revulsion, Indulgence, Ecstasy, Guilt, Renunciation and eventually Redemption – all signified by posture, motion, expression, repetition, tempo, rhythm, and the esotery of her divine and human body.

And all of this happened. The dance unfolded in the sky with grace and beauty, shedding a ghostly rainbow light across the moonless prairie…

But it was the Fireborn Woman who clumped out abject love, and it was the Clumsy Peasant who danced circles of attraction and repulsion around her!

Onyx imagined she could hear the gasps of the crowd, even at this distance. The Council of the Twelve-Lived must be livid – but what could they do but watch as the drama played out?

And it played out exactly as at rehearsal, except for this strange inversion. The Peasant in his tawdry smock and rope-belt pants danced as finely as Anna Tingri Five had ever danced. And the Fireborn Woman yearned for him as clumsily, abjectly, and convincingly as Jasper had ever yearned. The Peasant grudgingly, longingly, accepted the advances of the Fireborn Woman. They danced arousal and completion. Then the Peasant, sated and ashamed of his weakness, turned his back to the Fireborn Woman: they could not continue together. The Fireborn Woman wept and implored, but the Peasant was loyal to his class. With a last look backward, he descended in a stately glide to the earth. And the Fireborn Woman, tragically but inevitably spurned, tumbled away at the whim of the callous winds.

And kept tumbling. That wasn't right, either.

Tumbling this way, Onyx thought.

It was like the night so many months ago when the January sky had come down close and Anna Tingri Five had fallen out of it. Now as then, the glowing avatar stiffened. Its legs, which could span counties, locked at the knee. The wind began to turn it sidelong, and parts of the skydancer grew transparent or flew off like evanescent colored clouds. Broken and shrinking, it began to fall.

It came all apart in the air, but there was something left behind: something small that fell more gently, swaying like an autumn leaf on its way from branch to winter. It landed nearby – in a harvested field, where copper-faced robots looked up in astonishment from their bales of straw.

Onyx ran to see if Anna Tingri Five had been hurt. But the person wearing the bodymaker wasn't Anna Tingri Five.

It was Jasper, shrugging out of the harness and grinning at her like a stupid boy.

"I doctored the bodymakers," Jasper said. "I traded the seemings of them. From inside our harnesses everything looked normal. But the Peasant wore the Fireborn Woman's body, and the Fireborn Woman appeared as the Peasant. I knew all about it, but Anna Tingri Five didn't. She danced believing she was still the Fireborn Woman."

"You ruined the performance!" exclaimed Onyx.

Jasper shrugged. "She told me she loved me, but she was going to drop me as soon as the festival ended. I heard her saying so to one of her courtiers. She called me a 'dramatic device.'"

"You could have told me so!"

"You were in no mood to listen. You're a hopeless skeptic. You might have thought I was lying. I didn't want you debating my loyalty. I wanted to show it to you."

"And you're a silly dreamer! Did you learn anything useful from her – about the Fifth Door to the Moon?"

"A little," said Jasper.

"Think you can find it?"

He shrugged his bony shoulders. "Maybe."

"You still want to walk to the Atlantic Coast with me?"

"That's why I'm here."

Onyx looked back at the Harvest Festival. There must be chaos in the pavilions, she thought, but the competition had to go on. And in fact, Dawa Nine rose into the air, right on schedule. But his warrior dance looked a little wobbly.

"I crossed a few connections in Dawa Nine's bodymaker," she confessed. "He's a liar and a cheat and he doesn't deserve to win."

Jasper cocked his big head and gave her a respectful stare. "You're a saboteur too!"

"Anna Tingri Five won't be going to the moon this year, and neither will Dawa Nine."

"Then we ought to start walking," said Jasper. "They won't let it rest, you know. They'll come after us. They'll send robots."

"Bet you a copper dollar they can't find us," Onyx said, shrugging her pack over her shoulder and turning to the road that wound like a black ribbon to a cloth of stars. She liked the road better now that this big-headed Buttercup County boy was beside her again.

"No bet," said Jasper, following.

MIKE RESNICK
THE EVENING LINE

I created Harry the Book a few years ago as my tribute to the immortal Damon Runyon – and I wasn't the first science fiction writer to do so, either. Robert Bloch's Lefty Feep stories, half Runyon and half groan-out-loud puns, pre-date Harry by more than half a century. I remain convinced that if Runyon were alive today, and interested in imaginative literature, his guys and dolls would be stopping by Joey Chicago's 3-Star Tavern to lay their bets with Harry.

This was the twelfth Harry the Book story, and the first where I was required to use an opening line from a classic novel. All any Harry story needs is a sporting event, a dance contest, *something* that people can disagree and wager on, and it occurred to me that the opening line of my wife's favorite book, *Pride and Prejudice*, set up just such a situation. A plunger has won big at the track, so of course he becomes the most desirable husband material around. Will he marry or not – and if he does, who will be the lucky woman? And as quick as that, I had a conflict that took Harry 7,500 words to resolve. So enjoy "The Evening Line."

THE EVENING LINE
A HARRY THE BOOK STORY
BY MIKE RESNICK

"It is a truth universally acknowledged that a single man in possession of a good fortune must be in want of a wife," says Benny Fifth Street.

"I don't want to hear this," replies Plug Malone.

"I do not think that what you want enters into this," says Benny.

"What is this all about?" asks Joey Chicago, who is polishing glasses behind the bar. Well, not really polishing them, but at least flicking a semi-damp towel over them.

"I hit three long shots in a row when I am at Aqueduct this afternoon," explains Malone, "and no matter what Harry's stooge says, I plan to enjoy my winnings on my own."

"I am his flunky, not his stooge," replies Benny with dignity.

"Big difference," snorts Malone. "Either way, I am not in want of a wife."

I am sitting in my office, which happens to be the third booth at Joey Chicago's 3-Star Tavern, sipping an Old Peculiar and minding my own business, which at the moment consists of doping out the odds for the fight card at the Garden that night, when Benny turns to me. "What do you think, Harry?"

"I think Kid Testosterone lasts about thirty seconds of the first round against Tidal Wave McTavish," I say. "Forty-five if he's lucky."

"No, I mean about all the women who will soon be pursuing Plug Malone with a single-minded intensity."

"How much did you win today?" I ask Malone.

He looks furtively around to make sure no one else is listening. "Fifty-three large," he answers.

"That is nothing," says Gently Gently Dawkins, munching on a candy bar as he enters the tavern. "I myself am a fifty-eight large."

"We are talking about money, not pants sizes," said Benny. "Our friend Plug Malone has had a remarkable run of luck at Aqueduct."

"Spend it fast," said Dawkins, "before some filly spends it for you."

"No one knows except you three, and Joey Chicago here," says Malone. "No one *will* know."

"That's like saying no one will notice an earthquake because it happens on the next block," says Dawkins.

"Then no one will care," says Malone. "I will share a confidence with you. My real name is Jeremiah Malone. I know you think Plug is for the chaw of tobacco I usually have in my mouth except when I am in classy establishments like this one" – he glares at Joey Chicago – "*where they do not even have the courtesy to furnish a spittoon,* in truth it is short for Plug Ugly, which is a nickname they gave me back at P.S. 48 and which has stuck with me ever since. I am the ugliest, least attractive husband material in Manhattan, maybe in all of New York. You have never seen me with a woman. Women take one look at me and run in the opposite direction."

"Which direction is the opposite direction?" asks Dead End Dugan, who has been more than a little confused ever since he became a zombie, and is standing in the farthest, darkest corner of the tavern.

"Do not bother yourself with such trivialities," I tell

him. "Go back to staring peacefully at a wall and thinking dead thoughts."

"You're the boss, Harry," replies Dugan, and suddenly he is as still and silent as a statue again. Benny and Gently Gently do most of my errands for me, but every now and then, when someone is reluctant to make good his marker, it is nice to have a six-foot ten-inch zombie on my team.

"So what are the odds of Malone's looks frightening away potential brides?" asks Benny.

"Yesterday, three thousand to one no one will give him a second look," I answer. "Since he won the fifty-three large, half a million to one that they will."

"But nobody knows!" wails Malone.

"It goes out on the wind, like news of antelope drinking at a waterhole goes out to a hungry lioness," I say. "They'll start showing up any minute now."

No sooner do the words leave my lips than Mimsy Borogrove walks in. She slithers right past my two flunkies and sidles up to Malone, who acts like he has never been sidled up to before.

"Got a light, Big Boy?" she half says and half breathes.

"A light *what*?" asks Malone.

"Come back to my place and we'll talk about it," she says, reaching out for him.

"Unhand that man!" says a voice from the doorway, and we all turn to see Almost Blonde Annie standing there.

"Unhand me?" repeats Malone, staring at his hands in horror and then trying to tuck them into his pockets. "But I *need* them."

"Of course you do," says Almost Blonde Annie. "After all, you have to sign the marriage license."

"I beg your pardon," said Mimsy Borogrove, "but I got here first."

"And I got here last," says Snake-Hips Levine, entering the tavern and undulating right up to Malone. "Come on, sweetie," she says. "We don't want to have anything to do with these other broads."

"Do I know you?" asks Malone.

"Wouldn't you like to?" says Snake-Hips. "Look at me," she continues, running her hands over her body just the way any healthy male of the species would like to. "Isn't this worth fifty-two thousand, two hundred and twelve dollars?"

"Fifty-three thousand," says Mimsy.

Snake-Hips shakes her head, and everything else she has just naturally shakes with it. "Fifty-two thousand, two hundred and twelve. The other seven hundred and eighty-eight dollars was the money he bet that was returned to him when he cashed in." She stares compassionately at Mimsy. "You'd better get a new source of information."

Gently Gently Dawkins leans over to me. "Perhaps we should do a little something to save him from this veritable plague of potential fiancées," he whispers.

"I am a bookie, not a marriage counselor," I say. "Plug Malone's pre-marital problems are his own."

"I think Mimsy may take a poke at Snake-Hips," says Dawkins. "What will we do then?"

"I will practice my trade and offer eight-to-five that Snake-Hips takes her out in straight falls," I answer.

As we are conversing, four more women have entered the tavern, and now it is Joey Chicago who approaches me.

"Harry," he says, "we have to do something. All these women are taking up space at the bar, and none of them are buying any drinks."

"I hope you are not suggesting that I should buy drinks for the house," I reply. "Along with everything else, I have long suspected that Almost Blonde Annie has a hollow leg."

"Can't Milton cast a spell that either makes them buy drinks or go home?" he asks. "I will tear up your tab if he does."

"All right," I say, because my tab has reached almost six dollars, and I hate spending my own money. "I will talk to him."

"Good. Where is he?"

"Where else?" I say. "In his office." I head off to the men's room, which is where Big-Hearted Milton, my personal mage, has set up shop for the past two years. I find him, as usual, sitting cross-legged inside a pentagram he has drawn on the floor just next to the row of sinks, and there is a black candle burning at each point of it.

"Milton," I say, "I need you to cast a spell."

He holds a finger up to his lips. "In a minute."

He began chanting in a language that bears a striking resemblance to ancient Mesopotamian, or possibly French, and finally he snaps his fingers and all the candles immediately go out.

"Hah!" he says, getting to his feet. "*That* will show her!"

"Mitzi McSweeney again," I say. I do not ask, because these days it is always Mitzi McSweeney.

"We are sitting at a table in Ming Toy Epstein's Almost Kosher Chop Suey House, and she remarks that one of her garters is pinching her, so I reach under the table to adjust it, and she hits me in the face with a plate of sweet and sour pork." He frowns. "Me, who hasn't had pork since he was bar mitzvahed!"

"So what kind of terrible curse did you put on her this time?" I ask in a bored tone, because somehow Milton's curses never seem to wind up bothering anyone but Milton.

"Oh, it's a good one," he assures me with an evil smile. "Since it is her garter that causes this humiliation, I curse every garter she owns. Now none of them will work!"

"That is very brilliant, Milton," I say. "Now whenever she is out in public…"

"…her garters will unsnap…" he laughs.

"Right," I say. "And she will have to stop right there on the street and lift her skirt and try to re-snap them, and of course some handsome man will see this lovely lady with even lovelier legs in distress and will come to her aid, and try to help attach her stockings and doubtless introduce himself and tag along with her in case the garters give her further trouble, which of course they will."

"Damn!" growls Milton. "Why didn't *I* think of that?"

He relights the candles, stands in the middle of the pentagram, chants something in another unknown language, makes a mystical gesture, and then rejoins me by the door.

"All done," he announces. "Now, what can I do for you?"

"Not for me," I say. "It seems that Plug Malone made a big score and is being whelmed over by women."

"What is wrong with that?" asks Milton.

"They are taking up space at the bar and not buying anything, and Joey Chicago wants them to spend money or go home."

"Hell, have Plug Malone treat 'em all."

"There is a school of thought that opines that Plug Malone has never so much as spoken to a woman, except perhaps for his mother," I say.

Milton cracks open the door and takes a peek at the bar.

"Her?" he says. "And her too? And is that Sugar Lips Sally? And…"

He studies each of the dozen women who have gathered so far, and shakes his head in wonderment. "I have not seen such an outstanding field since the 1997 Belmont Stakes," he says at last.

"So can you do one or the other?" I say. "Send them home or get them to part with some money?"

"I will not send them home," announces Milton. "There

is always a chance Mitzi McSweeney will refuse to see me again. She complains that she is getting arthritis in her hand after the last forty times she bloodies my nose."

"All right," I said. "Then cast a spell that makes them spend their money."

"Look at all those skin-tight dresses, Harry," he says. "They cannot possibly be hiding three dollars between them. I will hex Malone into buying drinks for all of them."

"Yeah, I think Joey Chicago will go for that."

So Milton mutters a spell, and suddenly Malone gets the strangest, most puzzled expression on his face, and announces that he is buying for everyone in the house.

"Everyone?" repeats Joey Chicago with a happy smile.

"Every man and woman in the place," Malone assures him.

"What about zombies?" asks Gently Gently.

"Do zombies drink?" asks Almost Blonde Annie.

"I don't know," admits Malone. "Hey, Dugan!" he shouts. "Do zombies drink?"

Dead End Dugan blinks his eyes a couple of times, and frowns. "I don't know," he answers. "It's been so long…"

"Besides, even if he started, it would probably all pour out through those holes in his chest," says Benny Fifth Street.

"Probably," agrees Dugan unhappily. "Or maybe where I got my throat slit. That was… let me think… the fourth time."

"How many times have you been killed?" asks Malone.

"Five that I can remember," says Dugan.

"That's horrible!" says Snake-Hips Levine with a shudder that attracts the attention of every man in the place.

"It hardly hurt at all after the third time," Dugan assures her. He makes a face. "I really hated it when they dumped me overboard though. You think they'd have been more considerate, what with all the ice in the East River."

45

While all this high-brow discussion of life and death is occurring – or to be totally accurate, death and more death – word seems to have gone out on the wind that Malone is paying, because suddenly almost a dozen men enter the tavern and ask for drinks.

Brontosaur Nelson, who is a midget wrestler, asks for a tall one, which cracks everyone up, and the laughter attracts Loose Lips Louie, who is just walking by, and Impervious Irving, who is between bodyguard jobs, and Charlie Three-Eyes (who has a scar where he claims his third eye used to be, though word on the street is that it is simply where his ever-loving wife bites him when she finds he has been watching Bubbles La Tour's Dance of Sublime Surrender at the Rialto every night, and try as he will he cannot convince her that he goes for the music, which any ever-loving spouse will agree is like buying *Playboy* for the articles.)

Everyone keeps drinking and having a good time, and finally Loose Lips Louie says, "So who's the lucky lady, Plug?" and two seconds later you can hear a pin drop. And this is not a figure of speech; Gently Gently is loosening the pin that is holding his shirt together where he has popped a button after his fourth hot fudge sundae of the day, and so silent does the tavern become that I can hear it hit the floor fifteen feet away.

"I'm not the marrying type," says Malone.

"Are you the type who buys drinks for the house?" asked Loose Lips Louie.

"Certainly not," said Malone.

"Well, there you have it," says Loose Lips Louie. "Now, who's the lucky lady?"

Malone looks like a deer caught in the headlights, except no deer ever looks so frightened, even when surrounded by a pack of elephants or whatever it is that has a taste for freshly killed deer, and suddenly he frowns and points a finger at Milton.

"This is your doing!" he yells. "I would never stand for drinks unless I was hexed, and you're the only mage here. *You're* the reason all these gorgeous man-hungry women are after me!"

"If I am the reason all these women are here," answers Milton calmly, "then I am also the reason you won fifty-three large at Aqueduct, and I would like my fee, please."

"Never, you foul fiend!" screams Malone.

"I thought *I* was the foul fiend," says Dead End Dugan, who looks puzzled for a moment and then goes back to thinking dead thoughts.

"It is not Milton," I explain. "Not only does Milton not have a way with women, but he cannot go through a single day without Mitzi McSweeney bloodying his nose and threatening his life. It is the money that has attracted all these women."

Of course every woman in the place denies it, and Stella Houston, who claims to be Stella Dallas's better-looking sister, slinks up to Malone and offers to hold his money before Milton or I can steal it.

"So tell us, Malone," says Loose Lips Louie. "Who's the lucky woman?"

"I keep telling you," replies Malone, looking even more exasperated than terrified, "I am *not* getting married."

"Of course you are," says Brontosaur Nelson. "You don't think these lovely frail flowers are going to let you leave the place un-engaged, do you?"

"Hell, even Impervious Irving couldn't make it out the door if he was in your place," says Loose Lips Louie. "So who's your choice?"

"I am not getting married!" screams Malone. The nearest men jump back, startled, but the women merely look amused.

Benny Fifth Street walks over to me. "I smell a profitable enterprise here," he says.

"That thought has not escaped my notice," I say, turning to the room at large. "Let me make up a morning line, and then the book is open for business."

"It is ten o'clock at night," notes Gently Gently. "Unless you want them to stay here until daybreak, what we need is an evening line."

"The man's got a point," agrees Benny Fifth Street.

"All right," I say. "Bring me the blackboard on which Joey Chicago advertises the day's special, and a piece of chalk."

The place has fallen silent, as each of the men is studying the field and trying to decide where to put his money. It is not without incident. Almost Blonde Annie decks Charlie Three-Eyes when he tries to examine her teeth, and Mimsy Borogrove kicks Brontosaur Nelson almost to the ceiling when he tries to examine things down at his eye level.

"How's it coming, Harry?" asks Bet-a-Bunch Murphy after a few minutes.

"I'm working on it," I tell him.

"Who's the favorite?"

"That is the one thing that requires no work at all," I answer. "I make Bubbles La Tour the top-heavy favorite, you should pardon the expression."

Impervious Irving nods his head in agreement. "She is truly the Secretariat of women."

"Better," adds Short Odds MacDougal.

"Now just a minute, Buster..." begins Stella Houston ominously.

"What are the odds on her, Harry?" asks Loose Lips Louie.

"I make it one-to-eight-thousand."

"So if I bet eight thousand dollars on Bubbles La Tour and she wins what I think we shall call the Plug Malone Sweepstakes, all I win is a dollar?" continues Loose Lips Louie.

"That's right," I say.

"An underlay," remarks Gently Gently Dawkins. "I make her one-to-ten-thousand, minimum."

"If he proposes to Bubbles La Tour, there won't be enough of him left to bury," vows Mimsy Borogrove.

"We'll kill him with such skill and dexterity that a jury will award us both ears and the tail," chimes in Snake-Hips Levine.

"You know," says Benny Fifth Street, "I never thought of it until just now, but I'll bet all the other superheroes who came equipped with just one or two super-powers apiece didn't like Superman any more than these delicate feminine blossoms like Bubbles La Tour."

"Shut up about her!" snaps Stella Houston.

"Right," says Short Odds MacDougal. "Mentioning her in front of these lovely ladies is like mentioning Babe Ruth to a bunch of minor leaguers."

Even Impervious Irving can't pull the women off Short Odds MacDougal as fast as they pile on, and I call Dead End Dugan over to help.

After about three or four minutes MacDougal is uncovered and helped to his feet. Both of his eyes are blackened, what's left of his nose is bleeding, and he spits out three teeth. Both knees and an elbow are exposed where his suit has been torn, and his face seems much larger than usual. Then Benny Fifth Street loosens his tie and suddenly he can breathe again and the size of his face goes back down to normal. He is about to say something, but then he looks into the unforgiving faces of the assembled ladies, sighs once, and trudges off to a corner.

In the meantime Gently Gently Dawkins has been whispering into his cell phone, and finally he puts it back into his pocket.

"Bubbles La Tour has scratched," he announces.

"Why?" asks Brontosaur Nelson.

"She must have thrown a shoe," muses Bet-a-Bunch Murphy.

"She says she remembers Malone, and would not marry him if he was the last man on Earth."

"This is unheard of," says Murphy. "When has a horse ever rejected his jockey?"

"Well, that makes it a more competitive field," says Loose Lips Louie. "What is the evening line now?"

"I will have to re-compute it," I say. "Losing Bubbles La Tour in the Plug Malone Sweepstakes is like doping out the odds in a golf match where Ben Hogan, Arnold Palmer, Jack Nicklaus and Tiger Woods all fail to make the cut. It is clearly a wide-open race."

But in just a handful of minutes we are given to realize that it is not as wide-open as it had seemed, because who should walk into the tavern than Morris the Mage. He walks right up to Mimsy Borogrove and holds out his hand. She puts a couple of C-notes into it, he pockets them, nods, and shakes her hand.

"What is going on here?" demands Milton, who does not like having his territory encroached upon.

"I have been retained by this lovely spinster here," announces Morris as Mimsy kind of growls deep in her throat at the word 'spinster', "to help her nab – uh, to help her *wed* – the man of her choice." He looks at Mimsy, smiles, makes a mystical sign in the air, and says, *"Presto!"* – and suddenly instead of wearing what looks like an exceptionally wide black satin belt and not much else, Mimsy is decked out in an elaborate wedding gown.

"Lacks a little something," muses Morris. "Ah! I have it! *Abracadabra!*" And just like that, Mimsy is carrying a huge bouquet of flowers.

Almost Blonde Annie frowns. "Is that fair?"

"Don't worry," says Bet-a-Bunch Murphy. "She is still nowhere near as heavy a favorite as Bubbles La Tour was before she scratched."

The other women aren't paying much attention to Murphy *or* Mimsy. Each of them is speaking into their cell phones, and we know what is coming next, just not in what order.

Spellsinger Solly is the first to arrive. He pauses just long enough for Snake-Hips Levine to fork over some cash. Then he snaps his fingers, and Mimsy Borogrove's gorgeous wedding gown has suddenly turned into some severely tailored widow's weeds.

"Get me outta these things!" she screams, tearing at the clothes, and Impervious Irving and Gently Gently Dawkins help her, and suddenly she is standing there in nothing but her lacy underthings, and there's not much of *them*, and she is glaring at Morris. "*Do* something!" she bellows.

Morris takes a good look at her, of which an awful lot is exposed for looking at, and applauds.

"Something *else*, damn it!" she snaps.

Morris mutters a spell, and she is back in the dress she entered with.

"That's a relief," says Benny Fifth Street.

"Is it?" asks Joey Chicago curiously.

Benny nods. "Another ten seconds and I'd have proposed to her myself."

The other mages start showing up, each finds his client, and I am hoping that we are about to have a Mexican standoff, because as far as I can see the alternative is a Mexican shootout.

The mages each have a drink, and then I assume that they begin mentally bombarding Malone with marriage proposals, because he claps his hands over his ears, scrunches up his eyes, and screams, "I *ain't* getting married!"

"What are *you* doing?" demands Morris, as I work on the blackboard.

"I am adjusting the odds," I reply.

"How?" asks Bet-a-Bunch Murphy.

"I had Mimsy Borogrove as the nine-to-five favorite," I answer, "but now I put her at six-to-one."

"Why?" demands Morris, who is clearly concerned for his client.

"She gets dressed," I answer.

"Is *that* all?" he says, muttering a spell and pointing to her – but just as he points she turns to the bar to order another drink, and the spell hits Gently Gently Dawkins full force, and suddenly he is standing there in his colorful boxer shorts and his undershirt and not much else.

"Petunias!" giggles Loose Lips Louie, pointing to the flower design on Dawkins's shorts. "Ain't that sweet?"

"He may not be much," I whisper to Milton, "but he's one of ours. Do something."

"Right," Milton whispers back. He mumbles a spell and a bumblebee crawls out of one of the petunias, flies across the room, and stings Loose Lips Louie on the nose.

Louie bellows in pain, and Stella Houston, who is standing beside him, laughs.

"Lady," says Louie, dabbing his wound with a napkin, "you might as well go home. You ain't ever gonna get a husband with an attitude like yours."

Well, there is one husband she is never going to get, and that is Loose Lips Louie, and she starts pummeling him with such intensity that it looks like no one else is ever going to get him either, unless they are heavily into necrophilia, but finally her mage, Willie the Wizard, pulls her back.

"Why are you stopping me?" she demands.

"You only give me three C-notes," he says, "which is fine for a wedding, but nowhere near enough to get you out of stir after you have been arrested for murder. Let us concentrate on marrying you to this poor unassuming bozo who has no idea what misery is in store for him."

It is entirely possible that he is going to say more, but suddenly Stella Houston starts pummeling *him* instead. He gets loose and runs out into the street with Stella in hot pursuit.

"Another scratch," says Benny Fifth Street. "This field is getting smaller and smaller."

"Right," says Gently Gently, who actually looks more comfortable without his suit and shirt, which are about four sizes smaller than he is. "I figure we are down to maybe only a million eligible women."

"Let us eliminate all those women who are not attracted to Malone because of the money he is carrying around with him."

"Right," says Dawkins. "Now we are down to nine hundred and ninety-nine thousand, nine hundred and ninety-seven, give or take."

"Let's be reasonable," suggests Bet-a-Bunch Murphy, which I personally think would make a pleasant change. "There are so many mages on the scene that there is no way, now that Bubbles La Tour has scratched, that any woman without a mage has a chance."

"You know, he's got a point," says Brontosaur Nelson.

I find that I have to agree with him, and shortly thereafter I come up with the evening line, which reads as follows:

> Snake-Hips Levine, 9-2
> Bodacious Belinda, 5-1
> Mimsy Borogrove, 6-1
> Almost Blonde Annie, 6-1
> Penelope Precious, 8-1

Lascivious Linda, 8-1
Bedroom Eyes Bernice, 10-1

And the rest go up in odds from there.

"Harry, you must be out of your mind," whispers Benny Fifth Street. "You've got Lascivious Linda down there at eight-to-one. Why, she can take Snake-Hips Levine in straight falls."

"They are all utterly charming morsels of femininity," I say, "and I would never try to rank them in order of desirability, at least not without a set of body armor. But I am not ranking the ladies so much as I am ranking their mages."

"Aha!" says Benny. "Now it makes sense."

"You are forgetting something vitally important," says Malone.

"Oh?" I say. "What is that?"

"*I ain't marrying* none *of them!*" he bellows.

"Please do not interrupt us when we are having a serious discussion," says Benny. And he goes on to tell me which mages he thinks I am ranking too high.

"Milton," says Malone, with just a note of panic in his voice, "you're the resident mage here. Make them all go away."

"All the other mages?" asks Milton. "That will leave you at the mercy of the very people you wish to have nothing to do with."

"Not the mages," says Malone. "The *women*."

"Probably their mages would object," says Milton, "and looking around the tavern I see twelve… no, fourteen of them."

"That is no problem," says Malone. He takes my chalkboard away and lays it on the far end of the bar. The mages all gather around it, studying the odds and arguing about whether their prices are too short or too long. "You see?" continues Malone. "They are only concerned with where Harry ranks them. Their interest in the women starts and stops with their fees."

Milton takes a good hard look, and sure enough, none of the mages is paying any attention to the women.

"What the hell," says Milton. "Give me ten large and I'll vanish them all."

"Forever?" asks Benny Fifth Street, who seems to have taken a liking to, or at least an interest in, Mimsy Borogrove.

Milton shakes his head. "Not for a lousy ten thousand dollars. But I'll vanish them long enough for Malone to take what remains of his stash and head out into the wild, untamed wilderness of New Jersey."

"It's a deal," says Malone, and he peels off the ten large and hands it to Milton, who stuffs it into a pocket.

"Now I'm only going to have time to cast this spell once before the other mages notice what is happening, so I need to gather all the women close together."

Having said that, Milton starts leading each of the women over to the farthest part of the bar from where the mages are. He has twelve of them standing together and is just leading Lascivious Linda over when we hear a female voice bellow from the doorway: "Since when did you become a collector?" and in walks Mitzi McSweeney with blood in her eye.

"You misunderstand, my dear," says Milton nervously, backing away a few steps as she approaches him with her hands balled up into fists. "I am just doing a service for Plug Malone here, who has no desire to be near any of these women."

"So you're carting them all off as a favor to him?" she screams.

"Certainly not," says Milton. "Women don't interest me at all. I prefer you."

"*WHAT?*" she bellows.

"I didn't mean that," says Milton, his hands stretched out defensively in front of him as he begins backing away toward his office.

"Just don't let him vanish all your clothes," says Mimsy Borogrove as Mitzi McSweeney walks by her in pursuit of Milton. "I didn't realize how cold it was in here until—"

She does not get to finish the sentence.

"You vanished her clothes?" demands Mitzi.

"Never!" protests Milton, his back to the door of the men's room. "That was Morris the Mage's spell. I cannot vanish anyone's clothes unless I say *barota nictu*!"

And as quick as the words leave his mouth, Mitzi McSweeney's clothes disappear.

Milton's eyes widen, more in terror than lust. He swallows hard and leans back against the door, which starts giving way. "You're looking... uh... *well* today," he says, then turns and races hell for leather into the interior of his office.

Mitzi is one step behind him as the door swings shut and they vanish from sight. There follows a great deal of noise, a few shrieks of pain and terror, a crash, and a lot of words I never knew existed, all screamed in a feminine voice.

"Now magic them back – or else!" yells the voice.

There is a brief pause, and then a fully dressed Mitzi McSweeney emerges from Milton's office. She pauses and turns to him just before the door swings shut.

"I'll talk to you *later*!" she snaps and walks out of the tavern.

I head toward the men's room, with Benny and Gently Gently falling into step behind me. Just before I get there I call Dead End Dugan over, in case the carnage is so great that only a zombie can endure it on an empty stomach, and then the four of us enter.

"Any sports fans see this and they will never talk about Muhammad Ali again," says Benny.

"Who would have guessed that there was that much blood in a body?" asks Gently Gently.

"It's not *in* him," notes Benny. "It's *on* him."

"And there wasn't a mark on her," adds Gently Gently in awestruck tones.

"Thad's because I ab a gendulmad," says Milton, holding a blood-soaked handkerchief to his nose. "Helb ged me on my feed."

We help him up. He sways a bit, but then Dugan steadies him.

"Thag you," he says, blowing some more blood out of his nose. "Thad woman has a left you wouldn't believe."

"I think we're missing a bet here," says Gently Gently.

"Oh?" I say.

"Have Milton cast a spell to marry Mitzi McSweeney off to Malone. No one's bet on her, so you'll win all the money, and this way Milton will at least live 'til his next birthday."

"No!" says Milton. "She is the love of my life, or at least the goal of it. I will give her time to cool off and then throw myself at her mercy."

Last time you throw yourself at her mercy you miss, I remind him, and she is somewhat less than pleased with what you hit.

He winces in pain at the memory. Maybe I had better just extend my hand in friendship.

And the last time you do that, adds Benny, she is bending over watering her flowers, and you know what happened.

"I am the greatest mage in Manhattan," groans Milton. "In all of New York City, even. How can this keep happening to me?"

"Luck," suggests Dead End Dugan.

"Luck?" repeats Milton uncomprehendingly.

Dugan nods. "With a left like she has, you should have been as dead as me months ago."

We escort Milton back to the bar, where all the other

mages are still arguing over the evening line, and all the women are eyeing Malone not unlike the way a healthy cat eyes a crippled mouse.

"The women are still here!" snaps Malone, reaching into Milton's pocket and taking back his ten large.

"You are having your usual fine luck with the opposite sex," noted Morris the Mage.

Milton, whose nose has started bleeding again, mutters a curse. It comes out as "*Blmskph!*"

"Let us be charitable here," adds Spellsinger Solly. "You have to admit that Mitzi McSweeney is about as opposite as sexes get."

"You are speagig aboud the woman I love!" growls Milton. "Well, lust for," he amends.

"Let us get back to the man we all lust for," says Almost Blonde Annie. She turns to her mage, Sam Mephisto, who does most of his magicking in the Bronx. "I paid you good money for a husband. I want him."

"I am working on it," says Sam Mephisto. "These things take time."

"Work faster!" she snaps.

"Not to worry," he says. "If worst comes to absolute worst, I'll marry you myself."

That is when we learn that interacting with the female of the species is not a problem unique to Big-Hearted Milton, but may very well affect *all* mages. Dead End Dugan and Impervious Irving wait until she pauses for breath and lift him up to the bar, where Joey Chicago douses his face with water.

Sam Mephisto blinks a few times, then slowly sits up. "That was a most amazing experience," he says. "For a minute there I dream I am back in Egypt, mounted on my camel and leading my men into battle against General Sherman." Which is when we know he is not entirely recovered, unless General

Sherman went further astray than most history books would have us believe.

He gets down off the bar, blinks his eyes a few more times, and finally speaks. "It has been a long, hard night," he says. "I think I am going to take a little nap." And with that he slides down to the floor and lies there, snoring up a storm.

"Some mage!" snaps Almost Blonde Annie, making the same kind of disgusted face I make whenever I see Gently Gently Dawkins pour Tabasco sauce on his oatmeal. She glares from one man to another, and finally says, "I am a woman alone, without representation. Isn't *anyone* going to do something about it?"

I decide that she has a point, so I walk over to the blackboard where I have posted the evening line and raise her odds to forty-to-one.

She takes a glass of beer off the bar, throws it in Sam Mephisto's face, and stalks out into the night, leaving him licking his lips while still snoring.

"Well, that's one less to worry about," says Malone with a sigh of relief.

"Two," says Benny. "Stella Houston's probably still chasing Willie the Wizard all over Manhattan."

"Right," adds Gently Gently, surveying the tavern. "Twelve more and you're out of the woods."

"Well, 'til tomorrow, anyway," agrees Benny.

"I hadn't even thought about tomorrow," says Malone.

"Well, you had better be prepared for it, because how long do you think you can keep something like fifty-three large a secret?" says Gently Gently. "Why, even now, I'll bet women are approaching from Connecticut and New Hampshire and New Jersey, maybe even from as far away as Delaware." He furrows his brow in thought. "It must be borne on the wind, like phera… phero… those things that perfume tries to copy."

Even as he speaks three more women enter the tavern, looking neither right nor left, but eyes trained straight ahead on Malone.

"Milton, *do* something!" says Malone, his voice shaking.

"I *ab* doing subthig!" snaps Milton, still holding his handkerchief to his face. "I ab bleeding!"

One of the three newcomers notices all the mages, and immediately pulls out her cell phone and speaks to it in low tones. The other two soon follow suit.

"Well, whatever the result," says Joey Chicago happily, "at least we are doing some business."

"Why don't they all want to marry *you* then?" asks Malone.

"Because I lose all my money betting with Harry on everything from horses to politics," answers Joey. "Why, just last night I bet on Horrible Herman to win a steel cage match at the Garden."

"And does he?" asks Malone.

Joey Chicago shakes his head. "The steel cage beats him without drawing a deep breath."

Two mages walk in the front door and a third materializes by the jukebox, so I walk over to the chalkboard and adjust the evening line again.

Suddenly I am confronted by Morris the Mage.

"You really think my entry is no better than a six-to-one shot?" he says pugnaciously.

"It's a well-matched field," I say. "And unless it comes up mud, I still make Snake-Hips Levine the favorite."

"Maybe we should make her carry extra weight," suggests Gently Gently.

"Shut up!" snaps Morris. He turns back to me. "Six to one, that's your final odds?"

"Not necessarily," I reply. "The starting gate is far from full yet."

"But you don't expect her odds to go any lower?"

"Not unless Snake-Hips Levine or Bodacious Belinda scratch," I say.

"All right," says Morris, pulling out his wad and peeling off a dozen hundred-dollar bills. "I'm putting twelve C-notes on her to win the Plug Malone Sweepstakes."

This makes all the other mages look like they lack confidence, and soon they are all lined up, putting bets down on their entries, and when they are all done the purse is up over fifteen large and one or two of the women are looking at me the way they look at Plug Malone, but then they remember I will have to pay most of it to the winner, and I am back to being a wallflower again.

"Well, Plug baby, where shall we go on our honeymoon?" asks Lascivious Linda.

"We don't need a maid coming along with us, Plug honey," says Bedroom Eyes Bernice. "Tell her we want to be alone."

"Tell them both," chimes in Bodacious Belinda. "It's me that you love."

"I don't love anyone!" yells Malone.

"It's me he'd *better* love," says Bodacious Belinda, glaring at her mage.

"Harry, this is becoming intolerable," says Malone. "Hell, I'd almost marry the woman who tried to kill Milton if that would make the others go away."

"You can't!" says Milton, who has finally unclogged his nasal passages. "She's mine!"

"She sure didn't act like it," says Malone.

"It was just a lovers' spat."

"If the Third Reich could spat like that we'd all be speaking German," says Malone.

"Just keep away from her," says Milton. "She's *mine*." Then he pauses and adds: "Potentially."

"All right, all right," says Malone. "It was a silly thought to begin with."

"What's so silly about sharing a bed with Mitzi McSweeney?" demands Milton pugnaciously.

"I get the feeling that the bed is a hospital bed," answers Malone. "And that Mitzi McSweeney isn't sharing it, but is signing the papers about not using extraordinary means, like giving me food and water, to keep me alive."

Milton is about to object, but then he realizes that he agrees down the line with Malone, and just nods his head instead.

"It is getting near midnight, and the object of our affection still hasn't made his choice," announces Mimsy Borogrove. "I don't know about the rest of you, but I am getting tired of waiting."

"Me, too," says Lascivious Linda. "But what do you propose to do about it?"

"I say if he hasn't chosen one of us by midnight, we draw straws for him," says Mimsy.

"We could have a nude mud-rasslin' tournament, with Malone going to the winner," suggests Joey Chicago. "At least we'd get to charge admission."

The mages all nod their heads in approval, but Bodacious Belinda points out that the wrong kind of mud could ruin their complexions and did anyone really trust Joey Chicago to supply the right kind, and they spend the next five minutes arguing about what kind of contest to have, but there is no question that they plan to resolve the problem before morning and a whole new crowd of women shows up.

"Damn!" mutters Malone. "I wish I'd never won that money to begin with."

Which is when I begin to get truly profound inspiration.

"Do you really mean that?" I ask him.

"Yes," he says. "Look at these women. Now I know how a seal

feels when he finds himself in the middle of a flock of sharks."

"I think it is a pride of sharks," says Gently Gently.

"No, it is a school," says Benny.

"Don't be silly," says Gently Gently. "Sharks don't go to school." Suddenly he frowns. "Well, not in this hemisphere, anyway. I can't say anything about African sharks."

"Shut up!" I snap at my flunkies. I turn back to Malone. "Well?" I say.

"Yes, I really mean it."

"Bet me the fifty-three large that twelve plus twelve equals seventy-three," I say.

"But it doesn't," replies Malone.

"I know," I say.

Suddenly his face lights up. "That's brilliant, Harry!" he exclaims. He raises his voice so it can be heard throughout the tavern. "Harry the Book, I will bet you fifty-three large that twelve plus twelve equals seventy-three."

"No!" cries Snake-Hips Levine. "Do not make that wager!" Everyone turns to her. "Twelve plus twelve is sixty-seven."

"I think it is forty-one," says Mimsy Borogrove.

Even Spellsinger Solly gets into the action, opining that it is ninety-four.

"I am sticking by my guns," says Malone. "Fifty-three large says that the answer is seventy-three."

"The answer is twenty-four, and I will thank you for my money," I say.

Everyone pulls out their pocket computers, and they finally admit that I am right, and suddenly I am surrounded by women.

"Good," I announce in a loud voice. "This will just about pay off the money I owe Hot Horse Harvey for that Daily Double he hits this afternoon."

"But Hot Horse Harvey is tapped out and hasn't laid a bet

since— *Ow!*" says Gently Gently as I kick him in the shin while all the women and their mages are stampeding out the door.

Finally there is just Joey Chicago, Plug Malone, my flunkies and me, and then Malone walks up and shakes my hand.

"Thank you, Harry, for saving me from a fate worse than death."

"You've really never spoken to a woman since you were a kid?" I ask.

"Well, except for Granola Gidwitz," he says. "She seemed less intimidating, what with her cock eye and her triple chin and…" His voice trails off and he stares wistfully off into space for a minute. "You know, it's strange, but I miss her. I wonder if she still lives over on West 22nd Street?" He heads off toward the door. "I think maybe it's time I paid her a visit."

Then he is gone, and no sooner does he leave than Mitzi McSweeney re-enters the tavern.

"You came back!" says Milton excitedly.

"I have decided to forgive you this one time," says Mitzi.

"And I will never give you cause to regret it," says Milton, reaching his arms out to her and walking forward to embrace her. But he forgets that Sam Mephisto is still sprawled out on the floor, and he trips over him, and he reaches out his hands to grab hold of something, anything, to stop himself from falling, and as you can imagine Mitzi is somewhat less than thrilled with what he grabs hold of, and a moment later he has retreated to his office, she had followed him in, and the rest of us conclude that World War III will sound pretty much like the sound coming from Milton's office, only less violent.

ELIZABETH BEAR
NO DECENT PATRIMONY

I am a Sturgeon, Campbell, and multiple Hugo Award winner who divides her time between Massachusetts, which is where my dog lives, and Wisconsin, which is where my partner, fantasy author Scott Lynch, lives. I've been interested in Elizabethan literature for years, and for my story, I've chosen to rip off Christopher Marlowe's *Edward II*, a play about a bad king who comes to a notorious end.

It's hard to remember that Marlowe died when he was only twenty-nine years old, an age at which many modern storytellers (myself included), and in fact Marlowe's contemporary, Shakespeare, have only just begun their careers and are more or less fruitlessly pursuing publication or production, depending on their goals. It is important to remember that when we consider Marlowe as an artist, we only have access to his juvenilia.

Chronologically speaking, Marlowe's *Edward II* is probably his final play. It's certainly his most mature. It's the story of a king who destroys himself, his wife, his lovers, and very nearly his kingdom through self-absorption, selfishness, and obsession. It's the best of Marlowe's histories, replete with complex and realized characters and featuring a nuanced thematic arc.

The canon of Shakespeare's works and development makes obvious what he learned from Marlowe. If *Titus Andronicus* is Shakespeare's attempt at Marlovian blood and thunder, then *Edward II* reflects what Marlowe was learning from Shakespeare. As artists, we are all strongly influenced by our contemporaries, our peers and colleagues; the conversations we have with them and the techniques we steal—ahem, learn—from their efforts.

This piece is not an homage to Marlowe, precisely. But it is certainly influenced by his work. I offer for your consideration, "No Decent Patrimony."

NO DECENT PATRIMONY
BY ELIZABETH BEAR

My father is deceased.

Gravel gouges my palms, my knees. I crawl across the smoking ground from where I was thrown. I'd say I take his hand, but it's not—not his anymore, and not really a hand. I take the remains of his hand, bloody and raw. Splintered things grind inside, as if I had clutched a bag of broken glass. His face is—

His face isn't. The hulk of his car smokes beside him. My own hand burns where I touched his skin; the burning echoes all along my shoulders, my spine, in my hair. I had turned, begun walking away—

Acid. The fuel cell exploded.

That doesn't happen.

Thickly, as if through feet of water, sirens tremble in my ears.

It's five days in the hospital. Would have been two, but I have private insurance and can pay to keep the healthcare income unit out of my private room. Two might have been better, because after day three I've had exactly enough of daytime dramas that have been on the air since my father was a kid, as unchanged and as unchanging as their core market. The old adage was that it took three generations for a social more to change; how different now, when the generation in power never needs to let go of it. They'd never have gotten same-sex marriage or right-to-gender rules through Congress in these days when the longest-serving senator has been there for a hundred and fifty years.

The press are waiting for me on the day when I am released—a mad whirl of bloggers, journalists, cameras, tweeters scattered all over the steps and stretching down Seymour Street. Behind a police cordon stand the protestors. A clump of Anonymous, hooded and masked. Professional protestors with fluid placards and crowd-sourced distributed funding paying their bills. There are even a few of the old-school paint and plywood variety.

I particularly like *Please Die So I Can Have Your Job*.

It's a circus, and of course it's not for me. Not really. Not at all. It's for my father, and for the people who might be influenced by these performances. It's sort of comforting to look down there and think, this isn't about me. I stand watching it from a sixth-story window when Marna comes in.

"Edward," she says, coming over to take my hand. "You'd think somebody important had died."

Marna never approved of my father. She's not alone in that. At a certain level of fame, everyone feels entitled to have an opinion of you.

"Fuel cells," I say. "They don't just explode like that."

She shrugs. "Maybe it was all his tinkering."

My raw palm burns when she squeezes. She says, "I got the hospital to agree that you could sneak out through the children's wing. A car's waiting."

"Will you have to push me in a wheelchair?" They always say it's liability issues. But I think it's about control.

"There's a steam tunnel. I think they expect you to walk." She pats me on the shoulder. "Come on, Eddie. Get your pants on."

* * *

The steam tunnel is actually kind of fun. It connects the two hospitals—adult's and children's—and I'm pretty sure it's mostly only used by staff members. It probably dates from when they got hard winters here. Now there are tornado shelter signs posted. Marna and I walk through as fast as I can manage. I have to lean on her, and I have to pause frequently. The weight of my arm doesn't seem to trouble her. She's also carrying my bag. She wears tailored slacks. A white sleeveless top lies open across her collarbones, displaying an athlete's shoulder development.

As we wait for the elevator on the other end, the sweat beaded on my forehead trickles into my eyes. My back still tingles, despite the anesthetic cream. They told me I got lucky. Lucky not to need skin grafts. Lucky I was as far away as I had been. Lucky that my back was turned. Lucky it wasn't much worse.

They said my father got the reverse. Fuel cells… just don't blow up that way. And he was just about to get into the car when it happened.

The tunnel was cool; the children's hospital is passively temperature-controlled and quite comfortable. When we step out of the revolving door onto the sidewalk, the tropical heat of New England in April hits us like a steam towel slapped across the face. But the car is right there, one of my father's, a self-driving model. He had half a dozen, some retrofitted antiques, and damn the tax penalties for owning multiple automobiles.

There were a lot of things about which William Jacobin, my father, said damn the tax penalties. Such as creating me. And putting me through the process that his investment capital had supported, a hundred and fifty-odd years before.

That's one of the reasons Marna hated him. Hates him.

I hesitate by the car. "What if this one blows up, too?"

"It won't."

"What if my father was assassinated?"

She sighs and opens the door. "Eddie. It won't blow up. It was a freak accident. Let's roll."

Her head-tilt and glare are three parts concern, one part affection, one part exasperation. What the hell do I have to do to get this woman to sleep with me?

We climb into the cool interior. Air conditioning dries the sweat on my neck, sends chills across my scalp. Marna insists that I ease into the back and stretch out. I'd fight her but I know from the nauseated tingle that I'm pale from walking, and the sweat challenging my wicking shirt's ability to keep up isn't just from the heat. In fact, I'm cold as hell, and the glare of the sun on pavement slices right through me.

The windows are tinted; between that and my eyelids, it's almost bearable. The pressure of the seat against my scalded back is as nauseating as the walk was. As we pull away from the curb, the electric motor silent, the tires hissing on pavement, Marna reaches back between the front seats and pats my knee. I try not to notice… at least not viscerally.

My father's RFID gets us through the checkpoints without so much as a hesitation. It's all security theatre, though we're supposed to believe it serves some useful purpose for the public safety.

Somehow, I make it home without vomiting all over the interior of the car. My father's car. My car now, I guess, when against all expectations I have somehow… inherited something.

Inherited everything.

I know I can only escape for so long—but I'd hoped the respite would last longer than the brief ride from the hospital to my father's house. I try to concentrate on catching up with inboxes, keeping my eyes lowered, ignoring the scenery. As the car whirs through the automatic gates and up the curving driveway, though, I am distracted from my feeds by a woman who waits beside the steps to the front door. When I lift my head to peer through the window, I see her just clearly enough through the blurriness of injury, exhaustion, and painkillers to wonder how she scaled the estate wall in those shoes. She looks tightly professional in her beige suit jacket, her hair done up so severely I know she's trying to seem more mature than she is.

I'm familiar with the problem of being underestimated due to my apparent age. That she's trying so hard to look older—rather than flaunting her dewy olive skin and slick, inky hair—tells me she's not one of us. Not elect. Just another natural wearing a feed and shifting nervously from foot to foot.

"I'll get rid of her," Marna says from the front. "You keep your head down—"

"No," I say, as Marna's door cracks open. Her shoes crunch on the drive. I have to raise my voice and repeat myself, which takes more energy than it should.

She pauses half out of the car. Her hair's as black as the trespasser's but silvering at the temples. Her clothes are considerably more casual. Marna doesn't try not to look like a natural. For her, it's political. "Eddie?"

"I'll deal with her," I say, not really sure why. Pity. Exhaustion. The urge to talk about my father to somebody who will be excited to hear it, because it's the scoop of a young career.

"You feed one, you'll never get rid of the rest of them." Marna turns back in to talk over her shoulder.

"I'll call it an exclusive." The young trespasser is picking her way toward us. She's trying to look confident and managing something more like a hesitation march. The suit isn't tailored, but it's meticulously pressed. From the way she holds her arms, I guess there are half-moons of sweat concealed beneath it. There's no telling how long she's been standing in the sun.

I bet she's just starting out. She's got the hungry look of an independent, running her own feed, no real following. I look at the three stories of violet, green, lemon, salmon, and white Queen Anne Victorian rising behind her. The extravagant retrofits to bring it up to modern code, to make inhabitable a house built in an era when coal and oil furnaces kept people warm in bitter winters, are invisible under gracious 19th-century wood and stone. It looks as it always must have, the green forested hills rising behind it. No insulative foamed ceramic siding coarsens its outline; no habitat frame dripping greenery conceals its elegance; no turf, turbines, or panels have been thrown up willy-nilly to muddle the line of that colored slate roof, the slender turrets.

My father would say he earned the money and the privilege. But he handed it to me, along with the anti-aging process that his venture capital funded the creation of and that his paid-for politicians worked to keep exclusive.

"Eddie," Marna warns.

"You keep wanting me to speak out against the elect and the geritocracy." I'm not playing fair. She shoots me a look that tells me she knows it. "Help me out of the car."

Marna stands, turns, passes her hand across the sensor to open the rear door. It pops for her and she reaches in to help me slide across the seat. The clothes she brought for me to come home from the hospital in are just khakis and a cream-colored, short-sleeved shirt. I smooth the collar with my thumbs. Too late to do anything about the hair, burned and bleached by acid, patchy and greasy and uncombed.

"Mr. Jacobin," the trespasser says, one hand extended.

Despite the sun, I can pick out the shimmer of her feed across her irises. She's spending her money on tech, not clothes.

I could fix that for her. I wonder if she's got the ethics to say no.

I guess I should probably feel guilty, but you don't grow up in my father's house without understanding intimately that everybody has a price.

Facewreck tells me her name and a quick link gives me an idea of her provenance. I show her the bandages on my right hand and say, "Pardon me if I don't shake, Ms. Garcia."

She winces an apology. Time will grind that out of her: I just wrong-footed her reflexively, gaining the advantage in the conversation, and she'll need to get over it if she's going to succeed in her chosen career.

She is Sandra Garcia; she is just as young as I thought. She runs an investigative blog out of Brooklyn, so she's come a couple of hours by solar train to get here, and then either hired a share-car or found a rideshare out to my father's house. One of the advantages of living where I live is that it's expensive for people to get to you—unless they already have the money to maintain a private vehicle. So she's smart enough to know I'd never consent to a remote interview, and bold enough to hope that a pretty woman showing up at my door might have the edge in getting me to talk.

"Mr. Jacobin, you probably know why I'm here." Wrong-footed or not, she's not a coward. She glances at Marna and holds out a hand again, although there's a little tremble in the gesture this time. "I'm sorry, ma'am, but I don't think we've met."

Marna smiles. She's a privacy hardliner, and keeps herself off Facewreck and the paparazzi sites with lawyer letters she's endlessly qualified to write. "Marna," she says, and takes Ms. Garcia's hand. It's a cool, professional handshake. I know what it feels like, because Marna gave me one just like it the day we met. "I'm Mr. Jacobin's counsel."

Give Ms. Garcia this—she takes it without a flinch. She nods politely, says "a pleasure," and turns back to me. "I was hoping I could interview you for my feed."

"You're not feeding now?"

"That would be illegal without permission," she says. "If you agree, we'll start, and I'll allow a thirty-second delay and recall."

Pain, grief, shellshock are retreating in the practiced businessman's mindset that my father pounded into me. "A word of advice, Ms. Garcia?"

She leans forward.

"Don't offer the concessions until people ask for them. Please flash Marna the contract. She'll look it over, and then we can have a chat."

Ms. Garcia blinks, her face stilling for a moment as she checks what I said for the trap. Her mouth is half-open; she was ready to argue her case.

I kill my feeds, my inbox notifications. This deserves my full attention.

"I'll offer you an exclusive, ma'am."

Ten minutes later, we've walked around back and the ducks have come running—or waddling—to greet us. It's not actually affection; they're hoping to be fed. My father's gardener—*my* gardener—Olivia is down in the vegetable patch tending the tomatoes, which explains why she didn't notice the journalist hanging around the front steps. The mower is leaned up against one of the yellowing legacy evergreens—trees my father fought to keep alive, but even he couldn't make a temperate conifer endure the new normal—blades freshly sharpened and shining, but Olivia hasn't started the grass yet. There's an acre and a half of lawn back here; keeping it mowed is job security at its finest. The hedge roses around the borders are wilting. We can pay to exceed our graywater ration, and my father often did—a form of conspicuous consumption. From the sidelong glance Marna shoots me, she's wondering what I'm going to do about those roses now that they're my problem. Her neck curves like a sculpture. I'd swallow my tongue for permission to lay my palm against it.

Some of them are over two hundred years old, planted by my father's mother. It seems a shame to destroy them—and a shame to keep pouring resources down the hole of their non-adaption. Marna doesn't feel my ambivalence about the whole thing. Maybe I should just let her rip them out, and then hate her for it.

That would be my father's solution… would probably have been my father's solution.

You're supposed to bring a woman roses when you court her. I wonder how Marna would react to the uprooted corpses of five hundred rose trees that have endured since the twentieth century.

Marna leads Ms. Garcia over to the table under the ponderosa lemon dominating the yard, flanked and supported by fat-trunked fan palms. Its branches hang heavy with fruit the size of footballs. Garcia gives it a quick visual scan; she's got to be filtering its cultivar and approximate age for her feed. My father planted it just around the time New England really started warming up, about when Bridgeport was inundated. It's older than all three of us put together, and it required serious protection during the wild years of the climate swing.

Camilly has noticed I'm home. She brings out the kitchen scraps for the ducks and asks if I'd like refreshment for Ms. Marna and the other guest. The ducks recognize the bucket and respond by pushing and shoving around my feet. They're small, black. They have uneven white bands around their necks. Jade-green iridescence shimmers across their feathers when the sun strikes them.

I wriggle my unburned hand into the glove Camilly tucked into the bucket handle, hook that handle awkwardly over my wrist so it doesn't press bandages against tender flesh, and start broadcasting the scraps. Ducks pile over one another, webbed feet pedaling. I feel the unwilling smile curve the corners of my mouth.

They were a boyhood project, and my father never liked them—though he liked the eggs well enough. It was more political than personal for him, raising some of our food here. A way of saying we weren't nouveau riche, we didn't need to perform as consumers by letting other people grow everything we ate. It was a kind of conspicuous consumption via refusing to participate in conspicuous consumption, as it were. I never quite figured out how it meshed with roses, but as a wise person once said, the mystery is not that human beings don't make sense, it's that they ever do anything non-contradictory at all.

"Cayugas," Ms. Garcia says on my right. She must have skinned them, unless she has some weird reason to know a lot about ducks.

"A heritage breed," I confirm. "They started off in upstate New York. I like them because they're quiet. As ducks go. And pretty."

"As ducks go."

When I glance at her, there's a sparkle. More than I anticipated. I match her smile. A dim red light flickers in a corner of her iris. "Are we recording?"

"Is this a photo op?"

"Oh, definitely. I keep ducks around for ops with the journalists I strongly discourage from coming to my home."

"Touché." No rancor. "Are they good layers?"

"Supposed to be very tasty, too, but I'm too sentimental to eat acquaintances."

76

Marna is watching from a few feet off, outside of Ms. Garcia's pickup range. "You'd never have made it as a farmer."

"Or a cutthroat venture capitalist," I agree. "I've the privilege of living off the legacy of someone else's ruthlessness."

If it took her aback, she finds her feet again and presses on. "Tell me about your father."

"My father is deceased. I've been in the hospital since the… explosion." Behind Ms. Garcia, Marna lifts her chin in warning, like a restive mare. But I can't make myself say *accident*.

Fuel cells just don't explode like that.

When Garcia is gone, I'll put Marna on the police. I was interviewed in the hospital, but I want to be kept apprised of the state of the investigation, and cops are like anybody else. You get exactly as much attention and consideration as you ride them for—until you don't want it, and then they're over you like butter on toast.

"I'd rather talk about his life than his death." Garcia has a nervous tic of miming pushing hair off her face, even when it's all tied back sleekly. She says, "That surprises you."

"It's not every day the world loses one of the elect. It's not every day—"

I pause. She waits. So much of the art of the successful interview lies in an inviting silence. She could be good at her job someday…

But maybe I've gotten lost in my own chain of thought again. Or maybe I'm just pretending. I don't re-emerge until she clears her throat and says gently, "Congratulations."

It puts my head back. The ducks scatter as my body jerks, then reconvene at my feet. They're still skirting Garcia. The pail is almost empty. "I'm sorry?"

"On your inheritance. On… being out of your father's shadow. Were you distracted by your feed?"

Does she think I'm checking the stock ticker? The

headlines? Texting with a lover?

"Just my thoughts." Is she really going to take the interview confrontational this quickly?

She says, "Can you tell the ducks apart?"

I huff through my nose and toss more scraps. "Inevitable, I suppose."

"The death?"

"The congratulations. Thank you, of course. And of course I am relieved."

"You were about to say?"

Hide the frown. You're recording. Marna is chewing her lower lip, but letting me play my game.

I don't look any older than Ms. Garcia. But unlike her, I'm at least a little older than I look. "I was about to say… 'It's not every day the world loses a Jacobin.' But then I thought we might be better off if it did."

She tries to hide the eye stutter as she triple-checks to make sure she got that on media. When she looks back, I've managed to arrange my lips in a tolerant smile.

She says, "I'm sorry if my congratulations were out of line."

We're struggling for control of the interview, now, and both of us are trying to look like we're not doing it. I bite my lip against a giggle as I imagine a fist-fight in the cockpit. I wonder if she has developed the instincts yet to feel the weight and trajectory of the conversation, the way it has a life of its own. The fact that I mean to take it away from her.

I find my dilettante pose and smirk. "Oh, no. There's no need to lie about it. Isn't everyone a little relieved when one of those superannuated fuckers kicks it? *Sliiiiiiiiiides* off this mortal, as it were? No matter how ugly that sliding is. Especially the kin, who can finally get down to the serious business of scrabbling over the inheritance without worrying that Grampa is going to outlive the moon. No. No… *apologies* are necessary."

"But *you* cared," she says. "He was your father. He wasn't just William Jacobin, filthy-rich elect, legendary investor behind the Maddox Process, founder of the geritocracy, notorious rich guy, impediment to your inheritance. He created you, didn't he? Raised you? You knew the private man."

A little too well. "You have a way with words. Are you always this plainspoken, Ms. Garcia?"

"You mean confrontational."

"I said what I meant."

"Usually people read a blog before they consent to the interview."

"That's why you show up on doorsteps, huh?"

She cracks first, face breaking in a smile. But she doesn't look down. "Are you saying you didn't have any warm regard for the old man?"

"William Jacobin…" I sigh. "Everything was a trophy to my father. This house. Me. His money. Living forever. Assorted members of Congress and the occasional megastar. The car that killed him. It's not that he didn't care about things—but what he cared about was owning them."

"But you loved him anyway," Garcia says, persistent.

"Yes," I tell her. "I loved my father. After a fashion."

A note of admiration keeps coming back into her voice as she talks about my father. Of course—she's young, and although she thinks of herself as a hard-nosed investigator, it's difficult for the young not to be swayed by power. It's difficult for *anyone* not to be swayed by power. The young are just less likely to notice it happening.

She's not setting out to be a starfucker, this Sandra Garcia. But if she's not careful, it's an easy slide into hagiography and becoming a wholly owned subsidiary. Wealth has a gravity well.

"A fashion?"

"You'd think that archaic emotions like filial piety would have long since burned away in the fires of the old man's unrelenting *existence*. His *presence*. His sheer unwillingness to die." I can't stop my gloved left hand, unburdened by bandages or the bucket, from making a brief, helpless gesture. I hope it's effective. "But that's not how it happens in real life, is it? The situation gets… complicated."

She's all syrup and sympathy as she says, "His death was unexpected."

"No one ever expects to get blown up. Except for maybe soldiers in a war zone."

From the look on her face, her reblogs and uplinks must be going through the roof. I imagine the distraction of skyrocketing comments and pings. We're going viral: *Bereaved Son of Exploded Geriocrat Loses Shit at Pushy Interviewer.*

I hope she has an escalator clause with her advertisers.

I toss another handful of scraps. Olivia quits hand-pollinating tomatoes—apparently this was all much easier before the bee colony collapse—and wanders over to collect her mower. The creak of the wheel carries through lazy insect-drone. Turning blades flash in the sun.

Marna flashes me a quote from Garcia's liveblog: *There is a striking incongruity to this man—elect, immortal, wealthy, attended by servants in his gorgeous home—tossing filthy garbage to a gang of birds with his own hands.*

Funny. I never looked at myself that way.

She makes me sound like my father.

The ducks still throng around me, even though the bucket is empty. They avoid Garcia's neighborhood, however. Garcia says, "The birds can tell us apart."

"Birds can," I reply. "They recognize facial features." I lead her back to the house, Marna still flanking, and turn away to rinse my hands and the bucket under a metered spigot. "What can I tell you about my father that you don't already know, if you've done your research?"

The ducks squabble over the scraps of sweet potato on the ground.

She says, "I'm here for your words, your perspective. Not for facts. Facts are cheap." She holds up a finger and the red gleam in the corner of her iris dies. "And my followers aren't going to bother doing the research. That's what I'm for."

She drops the finger, and we're back on the record again. Lazy people—or busy people—have been keeping journalists employed since the business was invented.

I say, "My father, William Jacobin, was two hundred and thirteen years old on the day of his death. Which was last Sunday. I assume you and your proxies and followers have heard the Jacobin name, which is why you're here—or have linked it by now. Even if you hadn't, a little simple math would tell you he was one of the first elect."

She's young—so desperately young that she actually says, "What was his exemption?"

I can't let my smile look pitying. "The exemption laws hadn't been passed yet. He got the Maddox Process as soon as it entered second-stage human trials, before laws could be passed limiting it. He made his money in pharma. So he was Noruco's primary investor, and he... got in on the ground floor. So to speak."

"And were you a child of his youth?"

I bet she knows the answer. But half of a good interview is seeing how people navigate questions you know the answers to. And her followers won't know. Not unless they link it, or somebody like me—or her—tells them.

The kitchen door opens beside us. I can see over Garcia's shoulder the source of that grassy rustle of steady footsteps, the clink of a spoon against a glass. She does not turn.

Camilly, now in her white company apron, sets a tray holding three sweating glasses of pale yellow liquid on the table under the lemon tree. At that sound, Garcia glances over.

I say, "Actually, I'm a good deal younger." I pause while Camilly withdraws, escaped brown curls sticking to the sweat at the nape of her neck. "Lemonade?"

This is the second year we've had a commercial citrus crop in the northeast, now that the weather is settled enough. My father's tree is a good deal older. Citrus doesn't come cheap, especially since the failure of large-scale production in Florida and California—and the end of the era of inexpensive long-distance shipping. But we always had lemons, and there are limes and blood oranges and grapefruits growing in the conservatory behind the house.

"Please," she says. It's hot. And her uplinks will want the experience. I imagine she speaks from one part greed, one part dehydration, one part looking for ways to bond with her subject. Me, in this case, though I've watched journalists hone these tricks on my dad since the beginning of time.

It's a reason the best interviewers support the cost of going to meet their subjects. You learn a lot more about a person *in* person. I would bet Sandra Garcia travels more than most people, possibly even all around New England and the Mid-Atlantic.

Her followers would want to smell the air—or a bottled facsimile of it—on their uplinks. They'd want to feel the virtual grass between their toes.

If I hadn't been my father's son, I might be doing what Garcia is doing. If I hadn't been my father's son—

—am I really just the old man come again? Caught a little bit younger this time, before the wrinkles and the aching joints set in? Of course we're not really immortal, we elect—

we get injured like anyone else—but the Maddox Process means our bodies repair themselves a hell of a lot better. Given time... our bodies can repair almost anything from failing cartilage to demyelinating neurons.

We sit at the old painted iron picnic table beneath the tree, Marna on the far side of Ms. Garcia so as to be edited out of the pickups. The lemonade tastes fresh. Tart, sweet, complicated. Ice floats in it. It is cold enough to hurt my teeth.

Camilly's left a curl of rind in each glass to show that it's the real thing, and to perfume the drink with oils. A little more of my father's subtle brand of ostentation. As if Garcia would not have noticed that she's sitting under a mature lemon tree.

I catch myself trying to show her that I'm not my father, slowing down to savor the flavors and calories. Of course, in so doing I only ape him; William Jacobin, self-made man, would have considered it too revealing of his upbringing to squander food like some jumped-up petit bourgeoisie.

He'd have kept Garcia waiting forever, though. I answer her hanging question as soon as I've swallowed. "No, William was already in middle age when the Maddox Process became available, but he'd frozen semen as a younger man and chose to go ahead with life extension immediately despite the reproductive side effects. His theory was that he could reproduce any time he liked. By the time he got around to it, the semen was no longer viable—and it didn't matter.

"He got his cheek scraped, had some stem cells made, and grew his own gametes in a jar, then in a surrogate. Not quite in his own kitchen, although I'll show you what it's like before you go. You wouldn't doubt it was a facility adequate for genetic engineering while simultaneously catering a wedding dinner for seven hundred guests."

"This was his house?"

"A trivial expense to keep it habitable through peak and

post. Just as it was a trivial expense to put me through the process as my eighteenth birthday gift—even though, by then, the tax penalties were exorbitant."

Those penalties exist to keep the immortality process exclusive. A club inhabited by the richest and most powerful—those able to afford a process and maintenance treatments that are already expensive beyond the means of most.

The taxes can be waived by government order—and are, in the case of certain scientists, statespersons, and other "indispensables." But Garcia will never be one, and neither will Marna—unless I talk her into letting me pay for it, which would take a bigger miracle than getting her to go to bed with me—and neither will any of Garcia's followers. Not unless they're on track to win a Nobel, and I doubt most of those people follow gossip blogs.

Although… people can surprise you.

The ducks have gotten bored with us and wandered off to pick among the tomato plants. Unlike chickens, they will not damage most vegetables. But they're hell on soft fruits like strawberries. We still grow strawberries—fall and winter—but we grow them in hanging baskets around the edge of the porch. It's too hot in the spring and summer, anyway.

Marna's glass clicks on the table. She holds up a finger, and the light in Garcia's eye dies away.

Marna says, "Did you know that William Jacobin was one of the people most instrumental in bringing about the exemption laws? He liked his little club exclusive."

Apprehension tingles in my fingertips. Garcia leans forward. "Tell me more."

Marna lifts her glass from a sharp, moist ring on the table top. Excitement or emphasis makes her gesture a little too sharp; the lemonade splashes over her fingers. She pauses to suck them clean. She scoffs and says, "We couldn't have five hundred million undying middle managers cluttering up the landscape. You think housing situations and opportunities for promotion are limited now! Much better to make it too expensive for anyone who isn't *our kind of people*, isn't that right, dear?"

She glances at me. Is she trying to make us look like lovers?

Could we be lovers, with my father gone?

What do I have to *do* to get this woman to sleep with me?

Garcia's glossed lips thin. I wonder if she tried to do anything else before taking herself into business as a member of the so-called creative class. (Is interviewing rich people creative? I'm surely the last person anyone should ask.)

Marna continues, "Besides, think of the costs in terms of divorce litigation if *nobody* had any hope of outliving the bastard."

I bite my lip, fighting to maintain my deadpan. I succeed… for whole moments. Then I snort, my lip curls, and I begin to laugh hard and sharp while Garcia looks from Marna to me and back again, her angelic brow revealing the shadows of lines that will eventually crease it whether she's puzzled or not. It's a tiny little window through time, a glimpse of an unavoidable future.

Marna leans back and lowers her hand. *Resume transmission.*

Garcia's still struggling with it while I stand, as hard and sharp as I laughed. I snatch up my glass and say, "Let's take this inside, shall we?"

We troop across a sandstone patio and through the sliding doors, where I introduce Ms. Garcia to the house. "Charmed," the house says. It begins a series of offerings that I have to interrupt to silence. I'll have to get Camilly to reprogram that. I prefer my domiciles unobtrusive.

Inside, it's dim and airy. The living space is high-ceilinged and white-walled, with solar shades drawn across the windows. This old house stays cool in the heat, with its deep porches and lazily rotating ceiling fans. The windows have been sealed and the place is silent enough that I can hear the soft creak of wide floorboards beneath the pile of thick Oriental carpets older than all three of us added together. Older than my father, too, if he were here.

I usher my guests into a small sitting room, touch the wall to let the house know to let Camilly know where we are, and make sure the ladies are seated before I drop my own butt on a couch.

"Where were we?" I ask rhetorically. "Oh, the elect. And my history with my father. You know what they call us in the streets? The Parasites. And I'd feel the same if our positions were reversed. Hell, our positions *aren't* reversed, and I'm pretty sure they're right about us."

"All right," Garcia says. "I'll play. Do you want to open up the Maddox Process to everyone? How would we afford it? How would we support it? What about the population curve? What about opportunities for the young?"

"That wouldn't be as much of a problem if people stopped having babies. Since the process results in sterility, that should be effortless."

But she's on to my deadpan now, no matter how much bitterness I steep my tone in. She smirks; the chase is *to be continued*. "As your father did?"

"It's two primal and conflicting human urges, isn't it? The desire to reproduce yourself, and the desire to live forever. What I'm saying is that maybe evolution had it right, and we shouldn't be living forever."

Marna's leaned back, an arm draped across the back of the loveseat upon which she half-reclines. She's looking at me with pursed lips, a speculative expression.

It occurs to me that I've never actually said any of this stuff out loud in front of her before. Possibly not in front of anyone. I feel brave. A little giddy.

Congratulations, Garcia said. *Congratulations*.

I'm so busy remembering what she did a few minutes ago that I miss what she says now, and have to replay it before I can answer. And once I hear it, and actually register it, I'm too stunned to gather my thoughts.

She has drained her lemonade and set the glass down decisively on a coaster. What she asked is, "So, at least on an ideological level, you're saying you support the assassination of people like yourself and your father?"

"*Assassination*?!"

And just like that, she's won. I sit gaping; Garcia leans forward eagerly. She flashes me a link; I'd filtered out my feeds. And been doubly concerned with ignoring them once my attention wandered that first time.

Federal Bureau of Investigation Takes Over Jacobin Murder, the headline says. *Anti-Terrorism Squad Confident of Imminent Arrest*.

Marna holds up her finger. "They just say that to try to flush out the perpetrator."

"There's not *supposed* to be a perpetrator!" It's a second before I actually realize what I said. That I said anything at all. It bursts out in a kind of channeled explosion, rage and frustration. *Fuel cells don't just explode*.

Marna stands. "Ms. Garcia? I'll show you out. The interview is at an end."

When she comes back, she sits down on the sofa beside me. She reaches out and takes my unbandaged hand. She says, "Eddie…"

"They killed him?"

She shakes her dark ponytail. "I think that's still up in

ELIZABETH BEAR

the air. But if they've called in the FBI, they must think they have—at least—something. Or maybe they're getting pressure from somebody with a political agenda."

I gather myself sufficiently for sarcasm. Atypically, it's an effort. "Have you ever met somebody *without* a political agenda?"

"It's an East African Plains Ape thing to have," she agrees.

Somebody blew up my father. And they nearly blew up me. "Marna. You're from a good natural family. Surely one of your many siblings or cousins or aunties must have a pronounced opinion on our relationship?"

I'm not sure I've ever seen Marna look awkward before. "I let it bounce off me."

"Well, I guess those must be no uncertain terms. I know you have your own opinions…"

"I think your dad and those like him are a blight. That's not a surprise to you."

"But you work for me."

"We all work for the geritocracy one way or another, Eddie. In my case, it's just a little more direct than most. And it's not like you asked to get cloned." She pats my knee. "I was surprised by and proud of what you said today."

The look she gives me is a hell of a lot less exasperated than the last one. I can't stand the curl of anxiety that rises in my gut under the steadiness of her regard. *Does that mean you might consent to sleep with me?*

For the love of all that's holy, Eddie. Get over it. An unwelcome attraction isn't pretty on anybody, man.

I say, "It's not like we can escape from them. Like you can escape from us, I mean."

"Not without a revolution," she agrees. Tiredness and frustration crease her face. The lines on her brow never smooth entirely away.

"Christ," I say. "I need a drink. You want one? This place

makes a great Bohemian. I hear they grow and squeeze the grapefruit themselves."

"Hah!" she says. And, "Should you be mixing alcohol and painkillers?"

As I drop a text to Camilly, it occurs to me that I might be spoiled. That doesn't stop me from wanting the drink. I'm still thinking about it, letting my head fall back against the divan and damn the soreness where it presses my healing neck and shoulders, when the house says, "Edward Jacobin, this is the police. We have a warrant; you will facilitate our immediate entry!" in a voice I'm used to hearing only on TV.

"House?"

"They appear to be legitimate," the house says. "They used a valid override to pass the gate."

Marna has jumped up off the divan, an unfocused look on her face. She says, "The warrant's genuine. Eddie, I'm—"

"Edward, open the door!"

They could override, and I could override, and then they'll just break it down. And it's not as if we have anything to hide. Lemonade's not a controlled substance yet, as long as there's under nine grams of sugar in it.

I think about waiting to see if they'll actually say *We know you're in there*, but some things aren't worth experimenting with. They must think I had something to do with my father's death. Isn't that the way it always goes? They look first at the family.

Fortunately, I have a really good lawyer.

Marna beside me, I start walking toward the door. "House, let them in."

The door doesn't crash, because House opens it. And then my father's Oriental carpets are trampled under a dozen black boots as men and women broad with body armor pour into my front parlor. They have weapons. They look official.

I'd shoot a quick text to Camilly to let her know not to risk coming out of the kitchen, but I'm not getting any signal.

That's the sickest-making, most disorienting thing of all.

I put my hands up and keep walking toward them. "Officers," I say to a forest of face shields, "I think this is a little extreme. If you'll just explain the nature of the complaint, I'd be happy to come in and discuss it with you—"

"Sir!" an officer—or an agent, I guess? They could be the FBI—shouts, "Get down!" She grabs me by the elbow and tosses me aside, a sort of whirl and a sling. I expect somebody to tackle me, hands wrenching my arms behind my back.

Instead there's more shouting, but nobody touches me. I cover my head with my hands reflexively; when I collect myself enough to peek out again, two men in body armor are patting Marna down. One of them says, "Marna Davies, you are under arrest for conspiracy to commit murder, murder in the first degree, conspiracy to commit terrorism, and carrying out acts of terrorism on US soil. You have the right to remain silent. If you choose to remain silent, you may be subject to enhanced interrogation techniques. You have the right to an attorney but you do not have the right to private consultation with that attorney…"

Nobody is paying any attention to me. I push myself to my knees. Her head cranes as they're leading her out. She's looking for me.

She did it. She really did it. Maybe not with her own hands, but she was involved.

"Marna?"

She opens her mouth as if to say something. Thinks better of it. Closes it again and just smiles. She winks at me, and she smiles.

If they dragged her out of the house, if they were rough with her, I might have hurled myself at somebody. Probably gotten myself shot. But she strides along like a queen in chains, and they… escort her.

I follow down the steps to where cars are waiting, long and black with tinted windows. They stuff her into the back of one. An officer places her hand on Marna's head to guide it into the car without striking the doorframe.

She catches my eye once more before the door thuds shut between us. An officer is left standing beside me. He says, "We'll want you to come with us, Mr. Jacobin. We have some questions."

I can't make myself look at him. "You really think she killed my father?"

He says, "You know I can't discuss that with you."

But she didn't look surprised.

She looks too small in that big black car ever to change the world. And she is—too small alone. As are we all.

But she's not alone, is she? I like to think *I* wouldn't stoop to murder. But I'm not sure she was wrong.

So Marna will go to jail. And my father is dead. But I'm just getting started.

I wonder how hard it will be to contact Ms. Garcia.

ALLEN M. STEELE
THE BIG WHALE

According to some, there's a clear distinction between literary fiction – that is, the novels and stories that belong to the canon of great literature – and popular fiction, the stuff that belongs to mass culture. However, I don't believe there's really that much difference. Many novels now considered to be literary classics were bestsellers in their time. Likewise, quite a few novels which came out of popular culture are now considered classics.

I've always admired the works of Herman Melville... particularly *Moby Dick*, for which I gained an appreciation after visiting the historic district of New Bedford, Massachusetts, where that novel is set. I'm also a big fan of pulp fiction from the 30s and 40s, especially mystery thrillers by writers like Raymond Chandler and Dashiell Hammett. So I think that, had Melville been living in the early twentieth century, he might have been writing for pulp magazines like *Argosy*, *Black Mask*, or *Adventure*. For me, the first line of *Moby Dick* – three simple, direct words – sounds like the opening of a hard-boiled detective story. Based on that notion, I decided to rewrite Melville's masterpiece the way he might have, had he collaborated with someone like Mickey Spillane or Norvell Page.

I had fun with this story, and I hope you do, too.

THE BIG WHALE
BY ALLEN M. STEELE

Call me Ishmael. That's what everyone does, down on the New Bedford waterfront: the longshoremen and wharf rats and sailors who've been away from sea for too long and are drowning their sorrows in a jug of grog. They don't call me unless they're in trouble, though. Trouble is my business. I carry a harpoon.

I'd just returned from a trip to New York. The Bartleby case had been tough, but I got it done. Not that the client was grateful. When I asked him to pay me for helping him keep his job at a Wall Street law firm, he'd said that he'd prefer not to, so I stuck his nose in his ledger book and slammed it shut a few times until he finally coughed up. Never trust a scrivener.

I was pretty wrung out when I got back to Massachusetts. I tried to sleep during the long ride home, but the carriage I'd hired needed a new set of wheels, and by the time the driver put me off in the middle of town, I could have used my spleen for a doormat. If I'd had any sense, I would have gone straight home. Instead, I decided to drop by the office first. I told myself that it was just to check the mail, but the truth of the matter is that I missed the place. For all of its seediness – the stench of cod, the drunks passed out on the sidewalks, the painted women lounging in tavern doorways – the waterfront still has its own bleak, salt-crusted majesty. New Bedford may not be in the same class as Boston, but it's home.

My office was on the second floor of the Customs House, a one-room loft with a view of the wharf. As usual, the door was blocked by a small hill of mail that had been dropped over the transom, most of it bills that would have to be covered by the handful of gold I'd managed to frisk from Bartleby's pockets after I smeared his meticulous handwriting with his face. I transferred the mail from the floor to the desk, and was searching the drawers for the bottle of Jamaican rum I kept stashed in there, when there was a knock at the door. Thinking it was the landlord dropping by for the rent, I told my visitor to come in… and that was when *she* appeared.

The moment I laid eyes on her, I knew the dame was trouble. The beautiful ones always are. A vision in crinoline and wool, her lavender dress covered her from neck down, but as she levitated into the room, I caught a glimpse of a well-turned ankle, the kind of *lateral malleolus* that keeps lonely men awake at night. A lock of lustrous chestnut hair fell from beneath her fringed pink bonnet; I found myself wondering what it might be like to run my fingers through it. Yeah, somewhere beneath three layers of store-bought clothes was a woman with the body of a ship's figurehead. And not a mermaid, either.

"Pardon me," she said, "but are you Mister…?"

"Ishmael. Just call me Ishmael." I beckoned to the chair on the other side of the desk. "Have a seat, will you, Miss…?"

"Ahab… *Mrs.* Ahab," she added, emphasizing her marital status a little more than necessary. If she knew my name, though, then it was a good guess that she also knew my reputation. "And thank you, but I'd rather stand."

She didn't have a choice. Her dress had a bustle in the rear big enough to hide a navy crew. Not that they'd mind very much. I thought about offering her a drink, but I could tell she was the sort of lady who never had anything more than a dainty little glass of sherry once a week on Sunday. So I left the rum in the drawer and refrained from putting my feet up on the desk.

"How can I help you, Mrs. Ahab?"

"I understand you solve people's problems, Mr. Ishmael."

I shrugged. "Depends what they are, ma'am. I can recommend a good doctor."

She frowned. "I don't require the services of a physician. My problem is... shall we say, of a delicate nature."

A high-class dame, all right. I could tell from the way she spoke that she'd had some schooling. Which was good. The ones with class have money. "Perhaps you can tell me about it."

"It involves my husband, Mr. Ishmael... Captain Ahab, master of the whaling vessel *Pequod*. Perhaps you've heard of him?"

I shook my head. "Name doesn't ring a bell, sorry. A lot of ships come and go out of New Bedford, and you can't throw a rock without hitting a captain."

"Certainly you'd recognize my husband if you saw him. He is older than I, his hair and beard already white with age. But his most noticeable feature is his left leg, which has been replaced by a wooden peg from the knee down."

"You've just described half the sailors in town. The other half have pegs on their right legs."

A smile flickered uneasily at the corners of her full lips. "Yes... quite so," she said, putting a clamp on her amusement. "Nonetheless, my husband is quite distinctive, not only in appearance, but also by his recent behavior, which has lately become rather strange."

She nervously looked down at the bare wooden floor. I'd once had a nice oriental rug there that had come all the way from China, but I had to throw it out after one of my former clients bled all over it. The room was warm, so I stood up to open a window. From outside came the morning sounds of the wharf: the creak of sail lines, the curses of workers loading and unloading heavy crates, wagon wheels rattling across cobblestones.

"Tell me about Captain Ahab," I said.

"You know how sea captains are, Mr. Ishmael. They're home for only a few weeks, maybe a month or two, then they're off to sea again. Although I wasn't expecting this when I married my husband, I've become accustomed to his long absences. He has accumulated some small measure of wealth from his voyages, which has allowed us to live in comfort."

She wasn't telling me anything I didn't already know. The mansions of sea captains were among New Bedford's most stately homes. They often had so-called widow's walks, and sometimes the lady of the house got tired of standing out there, watching for the sails of her husband's ship to appear upon the horizon. I'd entertained the wives of more than a few captains, in a discreet way that involved entering and leaving through the kitchen door. They were rich, young, bored, and eager for the company of a gentleman who didn't smell of whale oil and blubber.

But Mrs. Ahab didn't fit the type. One look at her solemn brown eyes, and I knew that she hadn't come here to see if I'd scratch an itch. "I take it that his behavior has become unusual even for someone in his line of work."

"Yes, it has, Mr. Ishmael." She shifted from foot to foot, the frilled hem of her bustle whisking the floor like a broom. How she'd managed to climb a flight of stairs in that thing was beyond me. "When he returned from his last voyage, it was obvious that he had changed. And it was not just that he now had a wooden leg, which he told me he'd lost while climbing up a topsail. My husband has always been a serious man, but this time he was aloof, distant. As if his mind was elsewhere." She hesitated. "He's become obsessed with someone named Moby."

"Moby?"

"Yes. Moby… Moby Dick."

"Sounds like a woman." I was thinking of someone I knew with the same surname: Crazy Phil, who hung out in grog shops, raving about things no could understand. Perhaps Moby was his sister…

"This is what I've come to suspect, yes. I know women aren't usually allowed aboard whaling vessels, Mr. Ishmael, but a sea captain can bend the rules if he so desires. If my husband were to take a mistress…"

"All captains have a mistress, ma'am."

"I'm not talking about the sea!" Her dark eyes flashed. "I'm talking about a woman who is sharing my husband's cabin aboard the *Pequod*. He's going on another voyage very soon, and if he has a… a hussy… who has become his secret lover, I want to know who she is."

I was startled by her anger. Yes, Mrs. Ahab definitely strolled her widow's walk alone. "I understand. So you want me to…"

"Find out who this Moby Dick is, Mr. Ishmael. I don't want the *Pequod* to leave port without knowing whether my husband will have a woman in his cabin."

"My fee is ten dollars a day, plus expenses." That was more than what I usually charged, but she clearly wasn't going to have to sell the household silver.

"You'll have it, Mr. Ishmael… along with my gratitude, if my suspicions are confirmed." It may have only been my imagination, but something in her eyes hinted that she'd express her gratitude in an interesting way.

That made me smile. "Very well, then, ma'am. I'll take the case."

* * *

Mrs. Ahab had just left my office and was beginning to hobble downstairs when the front door slammed and someone started coming up. A shriek of horror, then the clatter of patent leather shoes running the rest of the way down the stairs. I closed my eyes, shook my head. She'd just met my partner.

"You need to stop frightening people like that," I said as he came in. "We can't afford to lose any more clients."

"Wang dang doodle." Queequeg rested his harpoon against the wall, then removed his beaverskin stovepipe and hung it on the hat rack. As tall and solid as a mainmast, his walnut-brown skin was etched with so many tattoos that he looked like a lithograph. Queequeg was from somewhere in the South Seas – Samoa, Tahiti, Fiji; I was never quite sure – and he was probably too weird for even that place. I guess that's why he came to America; here, he fit right in. He was big and scary, the best goon in New England.

"Yeah, that's our new client. Some looker, huh?" Queequeg shrugged as he sat down and reached into his overcoat pocket for his pipe. "She wants us to see if her husband is cheating on her. Ever heard of some guy named Ahab?"

"Poppa poppa ooh mow mow mow ooh mow mow mow."

"Yeah, I know he's a captain. She told me that already. The *Pequod*'s his tub. What I'd like to know is whether he's knocking boots with someone who isn't his wife."

"Ooh ee ooh aah ahh." He lit his pipe, blew a smoke ring at the ceiling. "Ting tang walla walla bing bang."

"Yeah, I was thinking the preacher might know something. He's pretty sharp about stuff like this." I stood up and walked around the desk. "By the way, did you manage to shake down that deadbeat Hawthorne? He owes us some serious bucks."

Without a word, Queequeg reached into his other coat pocket and pulled out a gnarly object about the size of an apple. He handed it to me, and I looked down to see two tiny eyes and a mouth that had been sewn shut. I sighed. No one was going to read a sequel to *The Scarlet Letter* any time soon.

"Great," I muttered. "Just great." I gave the shrunken head back to my partner. "I didn't mean for you to take me literally. A threat would have sufficed."

"Bum bum bubbagum bum bum."

"All right, never mind. Can I borrow your harpoon, at least? I left mine in New York." Stuck in someone's chest, I might have added, but didn't. No sense in encouraging my partner. He was bloodthirsty enough already.

"Wamma bamma ding dong."

"Thanks. I'll bring it back." I picked up the harpoon, slung it over my shoulder. "See you later."

"Shaboom shaboom." Standing up, he walked over to a wall cabinet, opened it, and added the head to his collection. I was glad he'd remembered to shut the cabinet the last time he was here. If Mrs. Ahab had seen how he treated clients who didn't pay on time...

The Whaleman's Chapel was located a couple of blocks from the waterfront. You wouldn't think that a church would get much business in that neighborhood – hell, the best whorehouse in town was just up the street – but I guess a lot of sailors wanted to get right with the big guy before they shipped out again, because Father Mappel held services there every morning. I'd never had much use for religion, but the preacher and I weren't strangers. He was one of my best sources for what was happening on the street.

Father Mappel was winding up the daily sermon when I arrived. The door was open, so I stood in the foyer. The

Whaleman's Chapel looked pretty much like any other run-down, working-class church on the outside, so it wasn't until you went in that you saw that it wasn't the place where your folks dragged you every Sunday. The first time I saw Father Mappel's pulpit, I thought it was pretty clever that he'd had one built to resemble a ship's bow, complete with a rope ladder dangling from its side. It wasn't until later that I learned that the pulpit really was what it looked like. After a schooner ran aground on a sandbar in the Boston harbor, the preacher had it salvaged and towed to New Bedford, then removed its bow and installed it in his church. Pretty impressive, even if it was overkill.

As usual, the sermon was the one about Jonah and the whale, retold in a weird amalgam of Jonathan Edwards-style hellfire-and-damnation and seaman's vernacular that bore only a faint resemblance to the Old Testament version. It was the only sermon I'd ever heard the preacher deliver. I don't think he'd changed his schtick in years. It went down well with the toothless wonders in the pews, though, and they never seemed to mind hearing it again, so the good reverend had never bothered to write something new.

So I leaned against the door and watched while he wrapped things up. The offering plate was passed – a handful of coins, along with the occasional gold tooth someone no longer needed – and an off-tune recital of "The Old Rugged Cross" soon followed. The preacher waved a hand in a desultory sort of benediction, then everyone got up and shuffled out the door, either off to work or the nearest tavern for their own brand of communion.

I waited until Father Mappel climbed down the rope ladder from the pulpit, then I left my harpoon in the foyer and walked down the aisle to meet him. "Nice sermon. Ever thought of buying a new one?"

He'd just bent over to pick up one of the spittoons placed in front of the pews. "Careful, my son," he murmured, standing up to glare at me. "The Lord dost not tolerate blasphemy. In the words of the prophet Ezekiel…"

"Knock it off, padre. Save it for the civilians."

He sighed. "Sorry, Izzy. Get carried away sometimes." He bent over again to pick up the spittoon, then grimaced. "Oh, for the love of… can't these guys ever hit the thing?"

"Are you kidding? How many eye-patches can you count when you're standing up there?"

"You got a point." Father Mappel took a seat in the nearest pew. "Man, when I took this gig, I thought it would be easier than fishing. Kind of wish I was still working the lobster boats."

"Naw, you're good at it." I nodded to the offering plate on the altar. "Besides, look at all the tips you get."

"Sure. Two bits a day and all the leftover hardtack I can eat." He ran a hand through what little hair he still had. "So what's on your mind. Don't tell me you're here for confession… guy like you, that'll take all day."

"Funny. Very funny. Ever hear of someone named Ahab? Captain Ahab, of the *Pequod*?"

"Maybe. Name kinda rings a bell." He squinted a bit, rubbed his forehead. "Y'know, I've always got a lot on my mind. Like collecting donations for the widows and orphans fund…"

I fished a couple of coppers from my watch pocket and dropped them in the offering plate, then came back to sit down next to him. "Uh-huh, now I remember. Yeah, I've heard of him. Strange dude, even for this place."

"I know about the peg-leg…"

"That ain't half of it." He lowered his voice. "The captain never set foot in here, but I get his wife in my confessional every Sunday. Man, if I could marry a woman, that's the one I'd want… but from what she tells me, he's been cold-cocking her since day one. I hear about it because I'm always having to give her penance for what she does to make up for it."

"She's on the loose? I had the impression that she wasn't… sort of."

"You're right. She ain't… but that doesn't keep her from looking. She's a walking Tenth Commandment violation, only in reverse. I'm tellin' ya, Izzy, beneath that prim and proper exterior is one very repressed lady. If she ever got a guy in bed, she'd probably break his back."

"She hired me to see if her husband was fooling around. She thinks he is… someone named Moby."

"Yeah, she's told me that, too. But you know as well as I do that women don't go aboard whaling ships… they're just not allowed, period. And believe me, if there was a slut in town who goes by the name of Moby, I would've heard about her. So there's something else going on around here, and it ain't no girl."

I was beginning to think that the preacher might be right. Whatever Ahab was obsessed about, it wasn't a dame. But my client wasn't paying me to tell her that her suspicions were wrong; Mrs. Ahab wouldn't be satisfied until she found out who Moby Dick was. "Maybe his crew knows something," I said.

"They might." Father Mappel shrugged. "Their hangout is the Spouter Inn, so you might check there." He paused, then dropped his voice again. "Just be careful of Starbuck, their chief mate. He and his pal, second mate Stubb, are two galoots you want to avoid."

"Thanks, padre. I'll keep it in mind." I stood up to head for the door. "Blessings?"

"Yeah, yeah." He made the sign of the cross. "May the Lord bless you and keep you, yada yada. Now get out of here."

I retrieved my harpoon from the foyer and stepped out into the street. It was almost noon; the first winos would be showing up at the Spouter Inn to get a head-start on their drinking. Some of them might be *Pequod* men. Time to buy a few drinks and strike up a conversation or two.

I hadn't walked a hundred feet from the chapel before someone took a shot at me.

It didn't even come close. The lead ball chipped a cedar shingle off the corner of the tackle shop I happened to be walking past; it missed me by about six feet. A half-second later, I heard the bang of the gunshot from across the street.

Looking around, I saw a little guy with a mean face standing at the mouth of an alley. He'd lowered the flintlock pistol he'd just fired and was pointing the other one at me. If he'd bungled the shot so badly when he'd fired with his right hand, his aim probably wouldn't improve when he fired with his left. I wasn't taking any chances, though, so I dove behind a row of wooden kegs on the sidewalk in front of the shop. I'd barely taken cover when his second shot shattered a window pane behind me. Damned if he didn't get better the second time…

All around me, townspeople were either running for their lives or finding some place to hide. This wasn't the first time shots had been fired in the streets of New Bedford; now and then, a couple of guys would settle an argument this way, usually after they'd had a few pints. The town constable would be here soon, but not soon enough. Whoever that character was, he wanted me dead. When I peered between the barrels, I could see that he hadn't run off, but instead was standing behind a stack of old lobster traps. Probably reloading, which meant that he was carrying only two pistols.

I began to count to fifteen.

There's three reasons why I carry a harpoon instead of a pistol or a musket. First, it looks tough. Second, carrying a harpoon in New Bedford is much less conspicuous than carrying a brace of pistols. The latter means you're looking for trouble; the former means you're looking for a job. My line of work requires a low profile, so it behooves me to appear to be just another harpooner searching for his next billet.

And third, guns are for losers. They can be fired only once before you have to reload, and that means half-cocking the hammer, pouring a dose of block powder into the muzzle, dropping in the ball, packing it down with the ramrod, priming the flash pan with a little more powder, closing the pan, then cocking the hammer all the way. If you don't make any mistakes, the pistol won't blow up when you fire it and leave you picking your nose with a hook for the rest of your life. And if you're really fast, you can do all this in about fifteen seconds.

Takes only a second to throw a harpoon.

When I got to fourteen, I stood up from behind the barrels, raised my harpoon, and waited. A couple of seconds later, the killer stepped out from behind the lobster traps. Since I hadn't returned fire, he probably figured that I was unarmed, hence a sitting duck if I remained where I was, or little more than a moving target if I tried to run for it. He hadn't even bothered to reload his second pistol, that's how confident he was that he'd get me on his third try.

Wrong. Wrong. Wrong.

The instant I saw his face, I let fly with the harpoon. I'd had lots of practice with the thing, so I knew just how to chuck it. There was a look of dumb astonishment on the killer's mug as he caught a fleeting glimpse of what was coming his way, but there was no time for him to duck before it slammed into him. The harpoon's iron barb, which Queequeg kept nice and sharp, went straight through his chest, entering the solar plexus and coming out through the middle of his back.

I didn't wait for him to finish dying before I strolled

across the street to the alley. He lay on his side in a red pool that had already spread far enough to enter the sidewalk gutter, and his wide eyes and gasping mouth reminded me of a brook trout that some Indian had just speared. But he was still breathing when I crouched down beside him.

"Hello, sweetheart," I said.

"H-h-h—" he coughed up some blood "—how d-did…?"

"How did I nail you? You made a mistake. You brought a gun to a harpoon fight. Your turn… Who are you, and who sent you?"

"St-St-St…" Pink froth bubbled upon his lips. "Stubb. S-s-s-sent by Sta-Sta-Star…"

"Starbuck?" I finished, and he managed a weak nod. "Both of you work for Ahab. Did he order you to…?"

A low rattle from somewhere deep in his throat, then a stench as something foul left his body. Stubb sagged against the harpoon's wooden shaft, and that was it. He'd told me enough, though, so I found a couple of pennies in my pocket and carefully placed them upon his unseeing eyes. He'd tried to kill me, sure, but I always pay my informants. At least he'd have something for the boatman he was about to meet.

I'd just stood up when I heard a voice behind me. "St-st-st-stop right th-th-there, Ishma-ma-mael, and p-p-put your h-h-h…"

"Hands up? Sure." I raised my mitts, then slowly turned around. "'Bout time you got here, Billy. What took you so long?"

Constable Budd stood just outside the alley, pistol pointed straight at me. He wouldn't miss if he fired, but I knew he wouldn't. Billy and I went way back, when we'd both served on the same ship in the navy. He was a pretty handsome guy, with the kind of angel looks that make the girls swoon, but he was a lousy foretopman and had never been able to do anything about his speech impediment. Now he was just a stuttering flatfoot who was never around when you needed him.

"I-I-I w-w-w-" Billy stopped, counted to ten, and then went on. "I was handling another call when I heard about what was happening here. What made you kill this guy?"

"He tried to kill me first. You can ask anyone." A small crowd of bystanders had come out of hiding and were beginning to gather around us. I had no shortage of witnesses. And, indeed, when Billy turned to look around, he saw a lot of heads nodding in agreement with what I'd just said.

"Uh-huh." Billy wasn't completely convinced. "And w-why w-would he do something like th-that?"

"Beats me. I was just defending myself." Ignoring the pistol pointed at me, I planted a foot against Stubb's body, grabbed the harpoon with both hands, and gave it a good, hard yank. The harpoon made a wet sound as it came loose.

"Yeah, I'm s-s-sure that's all you w-were do-do-doing." Billy remained skeptical, but at least he lowered his weapon. "Y-y-you don't th-th-think it has anything t-to do with something y-y-you m-might be working on, do y-you?"

I wiped the harpoon clean on the corpse. "I haven't the foggiest what you're talking about."

"Oh y-y-yes you do." Billy stuck his pistol back in his belt. "I-I-I've t-told you m-m-many times, Ish-Ish-Ishmael... st-st-st-stay out of p-p-p-police b-b-b-business!"

"I'll keep it in mind. Want some advice of my own? You really need to make another appointment with your speech therapist."

Constable Budd cast me a cold glare, but he knew he wouldn't get anything out of me. "G-g-get out of h-h-here. C-come d-down to the st-st-st-station later s-s-so w-w-w-we can get a... a... a..."

"A statement. No problem." I shouldered my harpoon

again, stepped around him. "C-c-catch you later."

"J-j-j-jerk," he muttered.

Making my way through the crowd, I continued walking down the street. Time to drop by the Spouter Inn and learn why Starbuck had sent Stubb on an errand that would've left me dead if only he hadn't been such a lousy shot.

It was happy hour at the Spouter Inn, which meant that the proprietor had just opened the doors and let the drunks in. If it hadn't been for local ordinances, I don't think Pete would have ever bothered to close up; he probably would have just hired another bartender to handle the graveyard shift, rented cots to the chronics, and mopped the floors every other week. On the other hand, perhaps it's just as well that he gave the regulars a chance to sober up. They'd only come back again the next day, anxious to damage their livers with the nasty swill Pete made from fermented apples and rubbing alcohol. Pete's last name is Coffin. Don't get me started.

It was half past noon when I walked in, yet the tavern had this perpetually lightless gloom that made it seem as if midnight never went away. Sailors and derelicts were sitting around tables, using wooden spoons to slurp up bowls of that reeking foulness that Pete called clam chowder; if you ever find a clam in there, please carry it back to the ocean and let it go; the poor thing got lost. The regulars were gathered at the bar, where Mr. Coffin himself was holding court. He noticed me almost as soon I found a vacant stool and sat down.

"Hey, Izzy... I hear someone took a shot at you." He grinned as he spit into a beer stein and wiped it down. "What's the matter? Someone's husband upset with you again?"

One day, a smart fellow is going to invent a rapid means of communication. I'd be willing to bet that it might have something to do with electricity. Whatever it is, though, it won't be half as fast as the waterfront grapevine. The guys at the bar laughed and I faked a smile.

"Wouldn't know, Pete." I rested my harpoon against the bar. "Why don't you ask your wife?"

More laughter. Pete picked up another stein. "I will, soon as she gets back from giving your sister swimming lessons so she can catch up with troop ships."

"You win," I said, and as a consolation prize he filled the stein with ale and slid it down the bar to me. "Thanks... say, you wouldn't happen to know someone named Starbuck, would you?"

Pete's grin faded. "Over there, corner table. The guy with his back to the wall." He lowered his voice. "Careful, Izzy. He doesn't look it, but he's one tough hombre."

I dropped a silver piece on the bar, then picked up my ale and sauntered across the room, leaving my harpoon at the bar. There wasn't enough room in the tavern for me to use it effectively; besides, the management frowned on customers killing each other. Starbuck spotted me before I was halfway there; although he didn't stop talking to the sailor sitting across the table from him, his dark eyes regarded me steadily as I approached. His sun-darkened skin told me that he'd spent his life at sea, and the way his pea jacket bunched around his biceps was evidence that he'd never been a passenger. Other than that, he looked fairly ordinary... and it's the ordinary ones who are often the most dangerous.

"Mr. Ishmael, isn't it?"

"Just Ishmael. And you're Mr. Starbuck?"

"Uh-huh... and don't forget the mister." He didn't bother to introduce his companion, a muscle-bound pug who couldn't have been anything else but another seaman. Without a word, the sailor stood up and walked away.

Starbuck pointed to the vacated chair. "Have a seat."

"I'd prefer not to." A line I'd picked up from Bartleby. The scrivener may have been weird, but he was an expert at the art of passive aggression. "Met a friend of yours just a little while ago. Mr. Stubb."

"Oh? And how is he?" As if he didn't know already.

"Aside from the heart trouble he's been having lately, just peachy."

Starbuck's eyes narrowed, but otherwise his expression remained stoical. "Stubb's a good man. It would be a shame if anything happened to him. I might get upset."

"Really?" I took a swig of ale and put the stein down on the table; I needed to keep my hands free, just in case he tried to start anything. Beneath his open jacket, I could see a big, bone-handled knife stuck in a scabbard on his belt. Starbuck's right hand never strayed very far from it. "If you'd wanted to send me a message, maybe you should've asked someone else to deliver it."

"A message?" Starbuck's head cocked sideways just a fraction of an inch. "Now what sort of message could I possibly want to send you? We've only just met."

"Perhaps a warning to stay away from your captain's wife."

"Mrs. Ahab?" A corner of his mouth ticked upward. "Pray tell, friend Ishmael… what possible interest could I have in the spouse of my commanding officer?"

"If not her, then the woman she'd like to find." I gave it a moment to sink in, but all I could see was bewilderment. "Moby," I added. "Moby Dick."

Starbuck stared at me in disbelief, then suddenly burst out laughing. "Surely you jest! You think Moby Dick is… is a woman?"

Only one way to clear this up: lay my cards on the table, let Starbuck know what I was holding. "She does. That's why she hired me… to find the lady with whom Mrs. Ahab believes her husband is having an affair. Moby is a name her husband has frequently mentioned, so…"

Starbuck laughed even more loudly, a hilarious roar that caught the attention of everyone in the room. "Oh, *really*," he yelled, slapping his knee, "this is too much! I mean… my God, when one of my crewmen happened to spy her leaving your office early this morning in a rather furtive fashion, he believed that she might have been having a tryst with you!" He chuckled, shaking his head. "That's why I dispatched Mr. Stubb to… shall we say, attend to you. The captain has always been wary of unmarried men taking an interest in his wife… and you, sir, have a reputation."

"Oh, boy…"

"Yes. One error, compounded by another." His grin disappeared. "But now it seems as if I'm down one crewman, on the very day that the *Pequod* is about to set sail again."

"You're leaving today?" Mrs. Ahab had told me the ship was leaving soon, but not *that* soon. I wondered if she even knew.

"The whales are running, Mr. Ishmael, and the *Pequod* is a whaling ship." His gaze shifted to the harpoon I'd left leaning against the bar. "You're good with that thing. I could use another harpooner."

"Thanks, but I've got a job already."

A malicious glint appeared in his eyes. "You misunderstand me, Mr. Ishmael. I'm not offering you a billet… I'm giving you one." His gaze shifted past me. "Dough Boy…?"

I'd forgotten the sailor who'd been sitting at the table. I was about to look around to see if he was behind me when something crashed against the back of my head. The next instant, I was face-down on the unvarnished floor.

I wasn't unconscious yet. Dough Boy's boot made sure that I was. The moment before it connected with my ribs, though, I heard Starbuck say one more thing.

"Now you'll get to meet Moby Dick," he said. And then Dough Boy kicked me into oblivion.

The creak of oak boards; the mingled odors of salt and fish and sweat. The brown-tinted light of an oil lamp swaying from the rafters of a low ceiling. A narrow bunk that rocked beneath me. As soon as I woke up, I knew I was at sea.

That wasn't my only surprise. I opened my eyes to find a tattooed face hovering above me. "Queequeg ... what the hell are you doing here?"

"Iko iko." My partner's black eyes regarded me from beneath his beaverskin hat.

"You signed up? Why would you...?" My headache wasn't so bad that I couldn't put two and two together. "We're on the *Pequod*, aren't we? And you took a billet when you'd heard I'd been shanghaied. Right?"

"A whop bop-a-lu a whop bam boo."

"Yeah, okay... the pay's better, too." I started to sit up, and the sharp pain from my ribs told me that I might be rushing things. Dough Boy had done a number on me. I was in the crew quarters aft of the main hold; there were no portholes below decks, so I couldn't tell whether it was day or night. "Have you seen Ahab? Do you know who Moby...?"

A deck hatch swung open, and I heard booted feet descending the ladder. Queequeg stepped aside to make room for my visitor; a second later, Starbuck came into view. "Very good. You're awake." There was a copper mug in his right hand. "Like some coffee?"

I stared at him. "You abduct me, and then you offer me coffee. You're a real piece of work, Starbuck."

"It's good coffee. Made it myself. And I told you... it's Mister Starbuck to you."

"It's going to be Mister Dead Meat when I get through with you."

"Uh-huh. You and what navy?" He slapped a hand on Queequeg's shoulder. "Your pal here is the only friend you have aboard, Mr. Ishmael. There's forty men on the *Pequod*, and they all take their orders from me. I'd think twice about making idle threats. The captain usually lets me give twenty lashes for insubordination… and you know, of course, that mutiny is punishable by hanging."

Yeah, I knew. Old scars on my back were proof that I was no stranger to a bullwhip, and I'd once seen a sailor do the dead man's jig from the end of a noose. So I accepted the mug from him and took a sip. Not bad coffee, for a creep. "I don't get it. Why did you bring me along? If you've got Queequeg, you're no longer short a harpooner. Hell, he's better than I am."

"He signed up after we brought you aboard. Someone on the dock must have recognized you when Dough Boy and I hauled you down from the Spouter Inn." Starbuck grinned. "We knew that he's your partner, of course… but you're right, he also has a good rep as a harpooner, and we need all the spearchuckers we can get."

Queequeg scowled at him. "Bang shang a lang," he growled.

"What did he say?"

"Don't call him a spearchucker. He doesn't like that." I didn't give him an accurate translation; it was something Queequeg's victims often heard just before he shrunk their heads. "So when are you going to tell me what's going on here? Who the hell is Moby Dick, and why is he so important to Captain Ahab?"

"You can ask him yourself. He sent me down here to fetch you." He stepped back, made a beckoning gesture with his hands. "C'mon now… time to get up."

It wasn't until we came up the ladder that I realized that night had fallen. A cold wind slapped at the mainsails; Orion was rising from the east, and when I looked to the port side, I spotted the Nantucket lighthouse upon the western horizon. The *Pequod* was several miles off the Massachusetts coast, heading north. It must have set sail shortly before dusk; I'd been unconscious for quite a while.

A group of sailors were gathered on deck, eating beans and drinking rum. A guy with an eye-patch sat on a pickle barrel, playing an accordion. All the scene lacked was a talking parrot and some guy in a striped shirt singing "What Shall We Do With A Drunken Sailor?" Now I remembered why I left the navy. God, I hate sea chanteys.

Queequeg and I followed Starbuck to the aft cabin. The chief mate knocked twice on the door, then opened it and walked in. The captain's quarters were larger than the crew accommodations, of course, but it was still a cold and uncomfortable little room that made the rudest hovel in New Bedford look like a luxury suite. Not that its occupant would probably mind. One look at Captain Ahab, and I knew that he was a hard-boiled egg no one would ever crack.

"Mister Starbuck? Is this our new crewman?" Ahab turned away from the window, the wooden peg of his left leg thumping against the deck. Cool gray eyes regarded from a leathery face framed by a white jaw beard. He reminded me of every bad teacher I'd ever had, the kind who'd break your fingers with a ruler for chewing tobacco in class.

"Yes, sir. Woke up just a few minutes ago." Starbuck unnecessarily pushed me forward, as if I was a prisoner being brought before the warden. "Name's Ishmael."

"Ishmael." Ahab stamped closer to me until our faces were only a few inches apart. "Mister Starbuck tells me my wife hired you to check up on me. Is this true?"

"That's pretty much the shape of things. She thinks you're having an affair with a woman named Moby."

"Does she now?" A smirk danced on his lips. He glanced over his shoulder at Starbuck. "Moby Dick is a woman… did you get that?"

"Sure did, Captain. I'm just as amused as you are."

"Indeed." Ahab turned away from me, hobbled over to his desk and sat down. "Moby Dick took my leg, Mr. Ishmael, but my wife would take all my money if she could. I suppose that's why she hired you. If she could prove in court that I'm having an affair…"

"Hold on. She told me that you lost your leg when you fell off a topsail."

"I know. That's what I told her." His eyes rolled toward the ceiling. "If I'd let her know the truth, I would've never heard the end of it. 'You lost your leg to a whale? What kind of idiot loses his leg to a—?'"

"Moby Dick is a *whale*?"

"Of course it's a whale. Have you ever heard of a girl named Moby?" Ahab stared at me in disbelief. "The biggest sperm whale anyone has ever seen, and as white as an iceberg. Mean, too. My leg got caught in a harpoon line when we fought it a year ago, yanked it right off. Not that I'm going to tell this to my wife." He sighed and made a talking motion with his hand. "Nag, nag, nag…"

"Might have saved us all a lot of trouble if you had."

"Yeah, well… she wants a divorce that bad, I might just give it to her. When I catch Moby Dick, I'm gonna saw off its head, take it home, and drop it on the front lawn. 'Here's the lady I was having an affair with, bitch. Now gimme a divorce so I can have my life back.'"

"I take it that you're going after Moby Dick for the sake of revenge."

"Revenge is such a harsh word, Mr. Ishmael. I prefer to think of it as aggressive fishing. Anyway, I need another harpooner, and since you took out my second mate, you and your partner are going to replace him."

"Diddy wah diddy," Queequeg said.

"Diddy wah diddy?" Ahab scowled at him, then looked at Starbuck and me. "Can somebody tell me what diddy wah diddy means?"

"He's asking about bennies. Y'know… medical insurance, stock options, retirement plan…"

"Three bucks a week, a cup of rum every day, and a promise to keelhaul either of you if you ask me that again. But you can have my wife after I dump her, Ishmael. God knows I never slept with the skank."

"So I've gathered." No wonder he hadn't ever been his wife's monkey. He was too weird for sex. At least I had something to look forward to once we got home.

I didn't know it then, though, but that was going to be a problem.

I'll make a long story short. Ahab didn't get the whale. The whale got him.

The *Pequod* spent the next week roaming the waters off Nova Scotia, watching for whale pods making their seasonal migration from the Arctic waters further north. We saw quite a few sperms and right whales, but the captain wasn't interested in any cetacean that wasn't an albino.

In the meantime, Ahab stomped around the poop deck, raving like a loon while everyone else hoisted up sails and battened down hatches and all that other sailor stuff. There was a coffin on the main deck. I don't know why it was there, but Queequeg and I used it as a card table while we played poker and waited for this whole stupid trip to end.

Which it finally did, and not well. Seven days after the *Pequod* left New Bedford, the guy up in the crow's nest caught sight of something big and white breaching the surface about a half-mile away. We chased it down, and sure enough, it was Moby Dick. When we were close enough, the captain ordered all the harpooners into the boats. As luck would have it, he picked me to be the bowsman for his boat.

Moby Dick was as big as Ahab said he'd be, and twice as mean. First, he took out two other whalers, crashing straight into them and sending everyone straight into the water. Then he came after my boat. I threw my harpoon, missed, and decided that was all for the day, but Ahab wasn't giving up. When the whale got close enough, he began hacking at it with his harpoon. "From hell's heart I stab at thee, for hate's sake I spit my last breath at thee…" Crazy as hell, but man, he sure knew how to rant.

The whale had other plans. Moby Dick capsized my boat, and when that happened Ahab got tangled in a harpoon line. Again. How anyone can let the same thing happen to him twice is beyond me, but the whale was still taking the captain for his own personal Nantucket sleigh ride when it charged the *Pequod*. Moby must have decided that he'd had enough of that damn ship, because he slammed into it hard enough to open a hole in its side.

So the *Pequod* went down, taking everyone with it. Funny thing about Queequeg; he never learned to swim. Nor did anyone else aboard, I guess. All that was left behind was that stupid coffin, which I clung to for the next couple of days until another ship happened to pass close enough for its crew to spot me.

When I got back to New Bedford, I went to see my client and gave her the good news: she was now a rich widow. She paid my fee, and then she expressed her gratitude in a different way. The preacher was right; I could barely walk after I left her place.

After that, I visited a friend of mine, a customs inspector whose office was just down the hall. Herman is a writer, the starving variety. Who knows? Maybe he might find something useful to do with my story. There might even be a novel in there.

Naw. No one would ever believe it. I mean… a whale named Moby?

DARYL GREGORY
BEGONE

Sometimes I get asked where I get my ideas. I usually give some vague answer. But because this is the Mash Up Anthology, I thought I'd finally admit the truth: I steal them.

For this story, it was *required* that we steal from a great work of literature, and I burgled from one of the best, Dickens' *David Copperfield*. The first line is, "Whether I am to be the hero of my own life, or whether that station will be held by anybody else, these pages must show."

It's my favorite opening line of a novel. It hints at the scope of the story. It establishes the character's voice. And it raises a question that has a metafictional bent to it— something you wouldn't expect from a fine upstanding realist like Dickens. How can you be replaced as the hero of your own life, your own story?

That idea reminded me of a TV show I'd grown up watching. One of the stars of the show was replaced mid-series by another actor. Even as a kid, I felt sorry for the guy. Not the actor, but the original character. Did he miss his wife? His daughter? And what did he think of the man who replaced him?

Which put me in mind of a close friend who recently went through a hellish divorce. You know the kind. Property fights, child custody battles, the sudden appearance of the ex's new "lover"—who immediately begins to pop up in family photos posted online.

When it came time to write the story you're about to read, I tapped into the hurt and confusion my friend had experienced. Then I added the line from Dickens, a few details from old TV shows, and bits and pieces from a dozen other sources, including my own life. Your honor, I grabbed everything in sight. I only hope you enjoy the story that came from it. Here's "Begone."

BEGONE
BY DARYL GREGORY

Whether I shall turn out to be the hero of my own life, or whether that station will be held by anybody else, these pages must show. The issue is not yet decided. The axe can fall any day. There are powers in the world, I have learned, who can replace you with the snap of their fingers. One more bastard is always waiting in the wings.

In my case, he was a blow-dried, empty-headed puppet of a man. He answered to my name, and wore my suits, and carried the keys to my house in his pocket. He slept with my wife. When my daughter went to bed, it was the Fake who read her to sleep. In the mornings, when he kissed them goodbye on the front porch, my wife called him Dear and my child called him Daddy.

I knew what I had to do to win my place.

The morning I had chosen for the deed, I was parked down the block, hunched over the wheel of a battered Plymouth that did not belong in my upper-middle-class neighborhood. Neither he nor my wife noticed me. The Counterfeit jogged with a runner's bounce to the new Chevy Corvair I had purchased only months ago. He moved like the athlete I once was. Every Thursday, he met his *pals* at the country club I paid for. On Saturdays, he golfed with my former clients. None of them noticed that he was an imitation, an inexact copy of the man they knew and respected. Oh, there was a superficial resemblance. We were both trim, good-looking men with brown hair. But he was taller than I, his hair more full, his teeth a shade of white that begged for kicking.

I reached for the ignition and my lower back seized, a spike of pain that jerked my body and held me, jaw clenched. You'd think I'd have been used to it by then, but no. Experience had taught me that there was nothing that could hurry the seizure away. I waited, hissing through my teeth. When I thought I could move my arm without triggering another jolt, I dipped a blind hand into the pocket of my suit jacket, uncapped the bottle with my thumb, and tilted a few pills into my palm. I threw them into the back of my throat without chewing.

The Imposter had driven away. But I wasn't worried. After a week of surveillance, I knew where he was going, where I could find him at the time I had decided upon. I had hours to kill. I lit a cigarette, my fourth of the morning, and put the car into gear.

Years ago, before my banishment, before I had even met my wife, I was in an accident. The muscles along the right side of my back snapped like banjo strings. I spent three weeks in the hospital, and two months in bed after that. I climbed out of that bed on a Jacob's ladder of Hycodan and Dilaudid.

When we met, at a party held by the advertising firm I had recently joined, I hid my infirmity from her. How could I not? She was beautiful. No, more than that—a mathematical proof that solved my desire. That blonde hair, those hazel eyes, those legs! I brought her a glass of Scotch and said with mock confidence, You have to try this. I feared she would have nothing to do with me if she knew how fragile I was. I'd been to bed with women who knew about the accident. Who *took care*. Is that all right, they'd ask? Does that hurt?

My every grunt, even in pleasure, became an alarm.

Of course, I did not understand what *she* was hiding from *me*. Her age, for example. I suspected that she might be older than she appeared. Something in the frank appraisal of her gaze almost sent me running. Would I measure up? Would I provide what she needed?

She swirled the Scotch glass, and sniffed. One twitch of that nose and I was in love.

Oh, a shallow kind of love, a fairy glamour, though I didn't recognize it then. I only understood true love when my daughter was born.

I spotted her immediately by her white-blonde hair. She moved among her fellow first-graders as if lit by a followspot.

I was parked too far away to make out her face. Any closer would have been a mistake. Each morning since my banishment, I had driven here, and each morning, a few minutes after ten, her class entered the yard for their first recess of the day. The children ran for the swings, the grassy yard, the four-square block painted on the cement. This morning, my daughter made for the eagle's nest, a dome of monkey bars. She's a climber, my girl. A brave one. She reached the top and lifted her hands, balancing on her knees. Her face turned in my direction.

Did she see me? Had she ever noticed my car, the familiar hand hanging outside the window, the smoke signal of my cigarette? Some days I thought so.

The night I was cast from my home, the night of my banishment, we had a terrible fight. I was not at the top of my game. My back was killing me. The usual before-dinner cocktail had turned into dinner itself, then dessert. The pain pills could find no purchase.

"Don't let her see you like this," my wife said, referring to our daughter. "Go up to bed." But I would not go up; the staircase was insurmountable. Sitting was impossible. I paced the first floor of the house, smoking, holding my spine at the particular angle that kept the pain to a manageable level.

Early bedtime for everyone else, then. My daughter, in her pajamas, ran to me for goodnight kisses. She slammed into my hip, and pain lanced up my spine. My drink went flying. "Jesus Christ!" I yelled.

My daughter looked up at me with a shocked expression. She didn't know that she could hurt me. Then she turned and ran up to her bedroom.

My wife attacked. "You're ruining it," she said.

"Ruining what?"

"*Everything.*"

You see, she had pictured for herself a perfect life. Picture perfect. A two-story house in the suburbs, a handsome husband with a job in the big city, an adorable daughter. Or perhaps, I began to realize that night, it was only the daughter she needed, and I was the prop required to make that happen.

I did not go gentle. I yelled. I asserted my ownership of the house, its furniture, and lawns. Also the lawn furniture. I accused her of withholding support when I really needed it.

"I *try* to help you," she said, "But you refuse every—"

"*Normal* help!" I shouted.

I continued my—let's call a spade a spade—my rant. It wasn't as if I hadn't delivered it before. Even drunk, I hit all my marks, and nailed the key lines. My wife, however, had departed from the script. She was no longer looking at me. She sat on the couch (*my* couch) and stared at the floor. I went on for another minute, then finally interrupted myself.

"*What?*" I asked.

"You're not the man I imagined you to be," she said. "And you're not what we need right now."

She looked up at me. Her eyes, as I had often noted during our courtship, were changeable. Sometimes blue, sometimes dark green. At that moment, they were hazel. Her nose twitched in what could have been disgust.

A wild, cold wind sprang up out of nowhere. I could feel a vast emptiness open behind me, and the wind rushed past me, then into me, ripping me to tatters.

She said a single word that was lost in the roar.

I left my daughter's elementary school with plenty of time to make my appointment in the city. Before my banishment, I paid no attention to the commute from the suburbs to the city, and I cannot remember those trips now. They were interludes between the important scenes in my life. But after my reappearance, after I began trailing the Counterpart, each trip was a gauntlet. The stolen car, an ancient Plymouth, transmitted every bump and pothole to my spine.

Oh, but the city still thrilled me. For an hour, I leaned in a doorway on Madison Avenue, smoking, and regarded the building where I once worked, a gleaming tower planted like a flag at the dawn of the sixties to lay claim to a decade of prosperity, stability, and brand management. Yes, I was a Madison Avenue Ad Man. A cliché. Or more charitably, an archetype in a city of metonyms, one with the Wall Street bankers and Broadway actresses. Is that what my wife first saw in me? Was I merely the *type* of man she was looking for?

At 12:05, the Successor exited the building with a flock of other toothy men. My former colleagues. My former friends. They walked uptown, heading to the same restaurant as always, Maxi's on 6th.

I went into the lobby, seeing no one I recognized, and

rode the elevator to the fifteenth floor. Just as the elevator opened, a wave of anxiety swept over me. For the first time in weeks, I was worried that someone *would* recognize me.

The door opened, and Betty, the receptionist, was not at her desk. I had planned this, knowing that she took her lunch in the break room, but still I was relieved. I walked quickly to my office and shut the door behind me. My heart beat fast. I'd soaked my shirt with sweat.

But I was safe now. I had plenty of time. The Pretender and my former officemates would return in an hour and a half with ties loosened, suit jackets rumpled, bodies thrumming with companionable warmth. Not drunk—we knew how to hold our liquor—but well lit.

I had not been in my office since my banishment, and I realized that I missed it more than I did my house. The view of the city, the cherry panel walls, the polished desk as wide as a car… the wet bar. I poured myself a double shot of Jameson and used it to wash down a couple of pills. Just enough to keep the pain from clouding my head. I needed to stay sharp.

The Mock Me had not taken my CLIO award from the shelf, nor had he removed the three paintings I had acquired in the past few years, modern pieces that demonstrated that I was a creative person engaged with the zeitgeist. Perhaps he was afraid to arouse suspicion that he was not the man who had acquired them. Or perhaps he had no taste of his own.

Certainly his latest project indicated that he had not stolen my creativity along with my life. An easel in the corner held story boards for a commercial for a new TV dinner called "Mom's in a Minute." I flipped through the boards, growing more appalled with each panel. Not an inspired thought in the presentation. But it was with my colleagues, and my boss, that I grew angry. Did none of them notice the lack of originality? Did none of them think, he's better than this? It was one thing to be taken in by the Doppelgänger when in close proximity to my wife—her influence was powerful. But alone with him, how could they not suspect? Would this stand-in know how to use the word "metonymy" in a sentence? I think not.

A while later, the Bogus Me stepped into the room and closed the door behind him. He saw that the Grossholtz abstract had been removed from its place near the window, and now sat on the floor. I stepped from my hiding place behind the door. I swung the CLIO with a firm, two-handed grip and connected with the back of his head. A solid, base-clearing line drive. He collapsed onto the thick Berber carpeting.

I suspected that he was already dead, but half measures would not do. I set the CLIO well outside the spreading pool of blood and knelt on his back. Then I removed from my pocket the length of hanging wire—good name, that—and passed it under his neck.

The morning after the fight with my wife, I woke before dawn with the taste of ashes in my mouth. I say *woke,* but it is more accurate to say that I *appeared.* A moment before I was not conscious, and then suddenly I was wide awake, my eyes open.

I stood on a lawn, staring up at a row of arborvitaes as symmetrical as the miniatures in a model railroad. These evergreens, I realized, were the same ones I had stared at from my breakfast table for years. They were mine, now seen from the other side. I was just outside the border to my property, in my neighbor's backyard.

Through the trees, past the patio furniture collecting dew, past the Weber propane grill with electric start and two auxiliary burners, rose the two-story house I had bought and paid for. (Partially. Twenty percent down-payment, plus five years on a thirty-year mortgage.) The kitchen was dark through the sliding glass door, as were the bedroom windows above.

I had no memories of the previous night. I'd had blackouts before. I admit it. But this was something different. An erasure, not just of memory, but of myself.

There is a disappearing trick common in film and television. The camera stops rolling, a character steps out of the frame, and filming resumes. Perhaps the disappearance is accompanied by a sound effect—say, the glissando of a harp. *Sha-riing!* A quick edit and the character reappears.

My absence from the scene, however, had lasted at least through the night.

I stepped between the trees. When I reached the edge of my yard, my feet stopped. A hairsbreadth from the toe of my shoe was an impenetrable border. I did not have to touch it to know that it was there.

I could not cross. I leaned forward, or rather tried to lean. My body shook with the effort. Finally, I stepped back, and into a depression in the mulch. The misstep sent a spasm through my back.

I circled the house, seeking a gap in the barrier, and could find none. The house was off limits to me. Or rather, not to me alone. My wife had told me that she had sealed the house against strangers. Our daughter would be safe here, she said.

And now I was a stranger.

I did not understand the full extent of what she had done—I had not yet seen my replacement—but I recognized that a crime had been committed upon my person. I stood in my neighbor's backyard and screamed. I called my wife terrible names.

On the second floor a light winked on—my daughter's

bedroom. A shadow moved behind her gauzy curtains. I recognized her tiny shape.

Then a porch light flicked on behind me. A moment later another light sprang up, and another, like a bank of Klieg lights. I was struck by a feeling of intense embarrassment, as if I were naked before an audience. I did not belong here. I did not know my lines. At any moment, the authorities would yank me from the stage.

Before another light went on, I lurched away.

I should have been flush with triumph. My rival lay dead, killed by my own hands. My life was again mine to command. I was a hero.

Instead, a cold dread filled me. But why? He was a golem. A construct with as much soul as a cardboard cutout. It made as much sense to weep over a dismantled lawnmower.

I was briefly disappointed that his body did not disappear in a puff of smoke (with or without sound effect), but I was grateful to have a corpse to loot. The car keys were in his right front pocket. I drove out of the city behind the wheel of my Corvair, radio loud. My back, aggravated by the torque of my skull-bashing swing, throbbed. I needed a drink.

I pulled off the freeway at a bar I'd visited before, an oasis on the way to the suburbs. I'd never seen women there, or any man younger than thirty. It was a place for divorced men, or those in the midst of divorce, or those contemplating it. In other words, a bar for men.

I took a seat at the bar. The Diner's Club card slid from my wallet like the sword from the stone. A double Scotch, I told the bartender, and keep it coming.

Ah, to have my own wallet again! My credit cards, country club membership card, the plastic photo album—all exactly where I had left them. True, the Surrogate's face still clung to my driver's license, and his horsey smile still beamed from the pictures of me alongside my wife and daughter. That persistence worried me, but I decided that I would think no more of it until morning. Night was a fade-to-black that allowed the stage to be reset. One spin of the earth to right all wrongs.

"Tough day, huh?" a voice to my left said.

He was about my age, perhaps a few years younger, and dressed in the uniform of an air force officer. He had a famous face. Had I seen him on television? In the papers? It looked as if he'd been in the bar a while. His shirt was rumpled, his tie loose. His blue jacket draped the back of the bar stool.

I waved down the bartender. "And one for my friend here," I said.

We drank for a while, and I signaled for another round. "My wife is a witch," I said.

"I hear you," my friend said.

"Our whole marriage," I said. "It's just been one crazy thing after another. Reality derangement on a weekly basis."

He nodded in commiseration.

"I tried to restrain her," I said. "Demand that she act like a normal person. By God, I told her, we will live as ordinary citizens, obeying the laws of physics and the rules of polite society."

He laughed into his drink. When he smiled I remembered where I'd seen him. He was the astronaut. The one who'd come down on the wrong beach. He said, "That never worked for me—restraint. She'd promise to do better, but—"

"Exactly!" I said. "Something comes up, some *emergency*, then it's back to her old tricks. Just like her crone of a mother. Runs in the family, my friend. The old woman pops in at all hours, doesn't even knock. Can't even call me by my real name. If I'd known what I was getting into with that family— but you're married, right?"

"Thought about it," the astronaut said. "I don't know, though. My girl worships me, but..." He winced. "She's impulsive. It's a full-time job just to keep a lid on her."

We drank to our misery. I shook a pair of Dilaudid into my hand and chased them with another shot. The astronaut raised an eyebrow.

A thin red line ran across my palm, the cut from the hanging wire.

"An accident," I said. "But the pills are for my back. If it wasn't for these babies I couldn't get out of bed in the morning. My wife would say, Do you *really* need those? No, only if I need to be in pain every God damn day. But that's her, always trying to change me. But you know who's changing? Them. Your girl may worship you now, but she'll start to get ideas. Oh, it's 1969, and suddenly you're not good enough for them. The next thing you know, the locks are changed and you can't see your kids."

"You've got kids?"

"A daughter," I said. I showed him the picture in my wallet.

"Beautiful," he said. Something wistful in his voice.

"All women are witches," I said. "But daughters? Daughters are angels."

The next time I awoke—again, wrong word, but my vocabulary for these events is inadequate—it was morning, and I was lying in a familiar bed of cedar mulch, staring up at those same damn trees. Unseen birds sang overhead.

I stopped myself from sitting up. My back was at that moment free of pain, but I was sure that the next move would be agony. I had been drinking, I remembered that. Drinking with the astronaut. I'd showed him a picture of my daughter, and he'd showed me a picture of his girlfriend, a beautiful blond Persian girl. And then?

Fragments floated up from memory. That drive home in the dark. Coasting down Mockingbird Lane, aiming for the driveway. I don't remember why I'd decided to come home then. My plan was to wait until morning, but at some point bar logic had asserted itself. Midnight then. The spell of the Trickster would be broken like Cinderella's charms.

Too late, I remembered the force field. I gripped the wheel, bracing for impact, but then suddenly I was through it. I braked before I hit the garage door. The Corvair, it seemed, was my passport into the castle, my Trojan horse.

I don't remember entering the house. Suddenly, I was in the living room. A voice spoke to me, and I turned.

My wife stood on the darkened stairs. She wore a white gown. There should be no moon indoors, but she seemed to glow in the moonlight. "Sweetheart?" she said. Her voice was soft, filled with concern. Once, a tone that had been reserved for me.

I issued the traditional greeting of men of my station. "Honey, I'm home!"

She recognized me then. "How did you get here?" she said. I remember the shock in her voice. The way she suddenly reached for the bannister. She had not expected to ever see me again. I felt a hot flush of triumph. You're not as powerful as you thought, are you?

"I'm back now," I said. "Let's just go to bed."

She released her grip on the bannister and pointed at me. She spoke a word that vanished into the sudden wind.

And then? The void.

I lay on my back in the stiff grass, staring at the blue sky between the tree tops. I had returned from that timeless dimension a second time. I had fought my way back. True, I had no memory of the fight, but that meant that it must have been an unconscious struggle, an action of the soul, not the intellect. My spirit had instinctively returned me to my home, and these trees. Arborvitae, I remembered, means "tree of life."

The birdsong became repetitious, as if on a continuous loop. I began to prepare my body to move, when I heard the patio door scrape open. From the far side of the trees came my wife's voice. "Don't you worry, dear. I'm sure they'll love your presentation. And I'll just whip up something for the barbecue."

"Whip up?" a man's voice said, worriedly. "You don't mean…?"

I sat up, and stifled a yelp of pain.

My wife said, "Relax, dear." She could have been speaking to me. But no, it was the Usurper. Alive.

Had I imagined the murder? I looked at my right hand, then my left. There were no wounds. The cuts had disappeared. But I remembered so clearly wire biting into my flesh, and into his…

I leaned back and peered between the trees. My wife and the Fraud stood on the back patio. She had her hands on his chest, calming him. She wore tight capri pants that showed off her lovely calves. Her blonde hair was tied back. And the Ringer looked as good as new. He wore one of my best suits, and if his neck was injured below that collar there was no hint of it. His hair was perfect.

He kept yammering about how important this presentation was, how vital it was to impress the "Minute Mom" clients. Not a word of his recent murder. My wife responded as she always did, cajoling, reassuring. It was a conversation we'd had so many times. But that hectoring tone he used—had I ever been that much of a whiner?

Then my daughter's voice. "Mommy, Daddy, look!" She stepped from the kitchen, a tiny, towheaded girl, holding a plate stacked high with pancakes and topped with a pile of whipped cream. "I made my own breakfast!"

Daddy. She'd called him Daddy.

"You see?" the Ersatz Husband said. "This is exactly what I'm talking about! Poof!"

My daughter's lower lip trembled. My wife stooped to take the plate from her. "He's not angry at you, honey." She looked up at him. "For your information, *I* made the pancakes—the old-fashioned way. She only put on the whipped cream."

The Duplicate threw up his hands and marched into the house.

What an asshole.

I did not stand up. I did not throw myself at the invisible boundary that surrounded the house. I knew what would happen if my wife saw me.

My second attempt on his life required tools. A gun would have made everything easier, but I didn't own one, or know anyone who did. That was not the world we lived in. We were decent people. Instead, I gathered materials available in my local hardware store: a hammer; plastic garbage bags; an ultra-fine point scratch awl with hardwood handle; and duct tape. On my train ride into the city, I carried the supplies in one of the garbage bags like a hobo.

I was forced to take the train. My hands may have been healed, and the bottles of painkillers in my pocket magically refilled, but the Corvair's keys were gone. The wallet as well. They were no doubt back in the Claim-Jumper's pockets. As for the stolen Plymouth, I supposed it was still parked on 10th Avenue, if it had not already been towed. I did not go looking for it. I walked from the Penn Station to the private garage under my office building. The Corvair sat in my reserved space.

It was 3:30 PM, well after lunch, well before quitting time. No one was on this level of the garage. I swung the hammer at the rear passenger window. The window cracked, but did not break. I frowned. How could glass be more resilient than the back of a skull?

I swung again and the window shattered. Very satisfying. I glanced around, but no one shouted, no one came running. And if they did, would they even see me? On the train, no one looked me in the eye. I had moved into another category of existence: not quite invisible, merely beneath notice. More proof that until I reclaimed my life, I would be nothing.

I reached in and unlocked the door. The floor mats glittered with broken glass. I hadn't planned on that. I turned the mats over, then put the garbage bags over them. I lowered myself to the floor, the hump of the gas tank under my belly, and braced myself on forearms and knees. Glass crunched under my elbows.

In thirty seconds, the position became excruciating.

I climbed onto the back seat and lay on my back. I figured I'd be safe there for the time being. I never quit before five, and I bet the Polyester Me didn't either. At, say, 4:30, I would crouch behind the driver's seat. Then when he slipped behind the wheel I would rise up like an assassin and press the awl to his jugular. "Drive me home," I would tell him.

A face appeared at the window. "Napping at your age?" she said. It was my mother-in-law.

I tried to scramble to a sitting position, but scrambling was no longer an option in my condition. Any radical change in position required at least three discrete moves, the stop-action choreography of a steam shovel.

My mother-in-law opened the door and said, "Would you hurry it up and come out of there? If I'm going to be seen rolling about in the back seat of a car, there are younger, handsomer men on that list." Hairspray had fixed her red hair into architecture. Her eyebrows were razor-edged weapons.

With thumb and finger, she extracted a shard of glass from the window frame. "So what is the master plan, Dick?" She never called me by my real name. "You aren't going to strangle him again, are you?"

I pulled myself out of the car, straightened my jacket. "So," I said. "You can see me."

"If only you could see *yourself*. You look ridiculous. How do you expect this to work? Keep killing the man until my daughter forgets to conjure him back? Or until she banishes you for good?"

"She can try," I said. "I'll keep coming back. My soul is strong."

She burst into laughter, a shower of tiny knives. "Oh, Derwood, you have no more soul than an old sweater, and you're unraveling every day. Do you even remember your life before the wedding? Your sports victories in college? Your tragic injury?"

"It was an accident. The muscles in my back snapped—"

"Like banjo strings, yes, yes. That was to give you character. As well as something to talk about—mortal men love their sports injuries, according to my daughter. But you, you took the idea and *ran* with it." She waved a hand dismissively, and began to walk away. The hammer was still in my hand.

"Not that I blame you," she said. "If I were in your situation, I'd be tempted to become a drunk as well, if not one so grandiose and wordy."

"What are you doing here?" I asked. "You can't stop torturing me?"

She realized that I wasn't following her, and turned. "You've never understood me. I have only, ever, wanted what was best for my family."

"You're protecting him, aren't you?"

"Who, the *new* Dick? Nonsense. He doesn't need protection. Though I must admit to cleaning up the mess before my daughter had to deal with it. Really, Durbin—there was blood all over that office! I didn't think you had it in you. You're the Spartacus of Morons."

"Damn it!" The hammer seemed to rise of its own accord. "This is *my* family! Stay out of it!"

She rolled her eyes—and the world rolled with them. The cement floor tilted beneath me, and then I lay on my back, staring up at her bemused face. The hammer was in her hands. She tossed it away, and it struck a nearby car with a thunk. "Look at you," she said. "All bothered and bewildered."

She leaned over me, her hands clasped behind her back. "You are absolutely wrong for my daughter," she said. "A mistake from the beginning."

"Screw you."

"Language, Dundicus. I was about to add that you are also just what my granddaughter needs right now."

"I am?"

"Evidently."

"Wait—you're the one bringing me back?"

She pursed her mouth in mock pity. "Oh, you poor thing. You really did believe that you were doing this on your own, didn't you?"

She straightened, tucked a stray hair into place. "I must be going. I only dropped in to offer you a word of advice: You can't murder your way out of this, as entertaining as I would find that."

I pushed myself to a sitting position. My back was on fire. "What then?" I said. "What am I supposed to do?"

She strolled away from me. "Be the better man, Delwyn."

"I *am* the better man!" I shouted. But she was already gone.

I waited for him in the parking garage, loitering between the cars. The Nemesis emerged from the elevator talking and smiling, leading two other men I didn't recognize. Clients. Men from the Mom's in a Minute account. They walked with him to the car, and I realized that my plan would not have worked. The men were coming home with him for the barbecue.

I slipped behind a delivery van. They expressed shock when they discovered the broken window, the obvious burglar tools left at the scene.

"That's life in the Big Apple," one of the clients said, his voice echoing.

"Not the kind of thing we get in Des Moines," the other said.

The Pseudo Me looked about warily but did not spot me. Did he retain any memory of his recent death? Some subliminal dread? Or had his just-add-water brain been wiped clean by his resurrection? "Probably just kids," he said, and smiled winningly. He used his jacket to sweep the broken glass from the upholstery, and they drove away.

I took the train back to the suburbs.

The sun had set by the time I reached Mockingbird Lane. I approached my house from my neighbor's yard and took up position in the now-familiar spot behind the trees, atop the soft pile of mulch. The party was well under way. The guests were scattered across the patio and backyard: the three clients, my white-haired boss and his bewigged wife, several other men from the office with their wives, laughing and drinking in the flickering glow of the tiki torches. Mr. Ditto mixed gin and tonics on the outdoor bar while my wife chatted up one of the Iowans. Something delicious cooked on the grill, making wonderful smoke.

My daughter went from person to person carrying a

tray of canapés. I could tell she was proud of herself. She asked one of the men from Des Moines, "Would you care for another?" So precocious. Of course they adored her. The client nodded to her supposed father and actual mother, signaling his approval—and then let his gaze linger on my wife. She was easily the most beautiful woman there: blonde, long-legged, otherworldly. No man dared make a pass at her, no woman could hope to measure up to her.

It was fascinating to be an audience to the party and not a participant. The anxiety I felt whenever we allowed visitors into our home was replaced by almost giddy anticipation. Something was bound to go disastrously wrong; my own dinner parties had turned to catastrophe countless times. People and props would line up like dominoes, awaiting the inevitable trigger—a spilled drink, a puff of smoke, a levitating table—making a panicked guest, say, fall back into the grill, which would tumble and set the trellis aflame, which would… you get the idea. And then my wife, unnoticed on the sidelines, would in the blink of an eye set all aright.

I edged forward and my foot sank into the depression I'd found earlier. My shoe crunched against something firm that gave way like cardboard. I stepped out of the hole, and my daughter called, "Daddy!"

I looked up. She was running toward me. She *saw* me, and she was beaming.

"You're home, you're home!"

My first reaction was fear. I was not supposed to be here, I was not to be seen. Then the fear untwisted and I dropped to my knees. She threw herself into me.

"I knew it," she said. She pressed her smooth cheek against my stubble. Her hair smelled fresh and clean. "I knew you'd come back."

Figures ran toward us but I didn't care. I closed my

eyes and hugged her tight. "I sure missed you," I said. "I thought—" Emotion closed my throat. I wanted to say, I thought you forgot about me.

"Get away from the strange man, honey," my wife said.

My wife stood over us, hands on hips. Behind her, the Facsimile charged across the lawn. He was followed by my mother-in-law, gliding along in a green, diaphanous gown that belonged to no identifiable time period. I shouldn't have been surprised that she'd inserted herself into the party.

My daughter pulled away from the hug. "He's not strange, he's Daddy," she said matter-of-factly.

The False Husband swept up my daughter in his arms. He said to my wife, "Do you know this guy?" He didn't recognize me. He had no recollection of my hands pulling a wire across his trachea.

My mother-in-law seemed amused. The other party guests craned their necks to see.

"He's…" My wife summoned a lie. "I know him from the Parent Teacher Association. His son is in second grade."

I opened my mouth to speak, and she flicked a hand at me. Suddenly I was gasping for air, unable to speak.

"Go back to the party, dear," my wife said to my alter ego. "You too, Mother."

I lunged for my daughter. The New Dick drew back and I seized on his double-knit sport shirt. My daughter reached for me—for me!—and I put out a hand to her.

My wife yelled, "Enough!"

A wind with teeth sliced into me. The void sucked me backward. The world disappeared—

And then I was on the ground again, kneeling in the mulch.

My wife looked shocked. She aimed a sharp look at her mother, who put up her hands and said, "Don't look at me."

"Would you two cut it out?" the Replicant said. He thought one of them was doing this, popping me in and out of the world like a jack-in-the-box. And how much had the guests seen?

"Take her inside," my wife said in a flat, ancient voice. She is old, my wife. Centuries old. I've never gotten her to tell me her true age. Or her mother's.

He hesitated, then turned toward the house. My daughter said, "Daddy!"

My wife pointed at me. "Don't move." The command pinned me in place.

My mother-in-law clapped her hands. "Well! I'll go take care of the guests while you two catch up." She followed the Xerox and my daughter, who wailed all the way into the house.

"You've done it again," my wife said.

"Another dinner party ruined. Just like old times." I nodded toward the house. "So him. The Substitute." I smiled tightly. "Is that what you wanted? Taller? Better hair?"

She regarded me for a long moment. "He does have better hair. But no one kept a part as straight as you."

"Damn straight."

She almost smiled. I pressed my advantage. "We can try again," I said. "I've learned some important things about myself during this whole experience."

"Have you," she said.

"Yes!" I tried to think of what I'd learned. That I could kill, if necessary. That I could fight for what was mine. However, my ad-man instincts told me that neither of those were what she wanted to hear.

I reached into my pocket and brought out the yellow plastic bottle. "I don't need these, for one." I threw the bottle to her, and she caught it. She glanced at it, seemed ready to drop it, then held it up to the moonlight.

"Just send what's-his-face back to where he came from," I

143

said. "We'll pick up where we—what are you doing?"

She had opened the bottle. She shook a couple of pills into her hand, squinted at them, and then popped them into her mouth.

"I don't think you should do that," I said.

"Candy," she said.

"What?"

"The little mints we keep by the front door." She tilted her head. "That's odd."

"I don't know how—that's not what—" A spasm wrenched my back. I almost fell, then caught myself. The pills were fake? How could that be?

She dropped the bottle to the ground. "It's time to go."

I held up a hand. "All I'm asking for is a chance. If not for me, then for our daughter."

"*Our* daughter?" She stepped forward, and the shadow of the tree fell across her face. "*Our* daughter?" Her hands moved, making subtle shapes out of the dark. That old black magic.

"Please, honey—"

"I'm tired of 'honey' and 'dear.' From both of you. In fact, I'm beginning to rethink this whole project."

Had she ever loved me? Once I thought we'd been happy, as happy as anyone else. We'd kissed goodbye every morning and made love twice a week—Wednesday nights and Sunday mornings. We'd renovated a kitchen together.

But now? Now I was nothing to her.

I forced myself to straighten. "I'll come back," I said. "I always come back."

"Not this time." Her fingers twisted, and I was gone.

Here is a secret that every man tries to forget: We are made from women, by women, for women. Theirs is the first touch we feel, and we carry that imprint upon our hearts for the rest of our lives. Later we fall in love, and the most beautiful woman in the world tells us that our children will also be beautiful and strong. Then a daughter is born, and we are possessed all over again.

A mortal man doesn't stand a chance.

I awoke in snow. I wasn't cold, but I was sure that I'd lain there for some time, the drift covering me. I sat up. Crystals dropped into my collar and burned down my neck. Above me, the branches of the arborvitaes were laden with snow. The sky was dark, the air clear and clean. I still couldn't feel the cold. I should have been worried about frostbite, but the thought didn't occur to me.

I got to my feet, brushed the snow from my pants and sleeves. Perhaps a foot of new snow lay on the ground, a smooth, unbroken expanse glowing faint blue in the moonlight. The only mar in the surface was the man-shaped hole I'd climbed out of.

Something lay at the bottom of it. I crouched, and pulled it up. It was a shoe box, crumpled by my weight and weather and years underground. I peeled off the lid.

Inside lay a little doll made out of blue and green sticks—plastic swizzle sticks like the kind we used to keep on the credenza—and a construction paper face that wore a blue crayon smile. A swatch of wool cloth was taped to the front of him with a fat wad of masking tape. I picked him up, and the cloth fell off. The box had been out here for a long time.

I turned him between my thumb and index finger. The torso was crimped. I ran my fingers along the stick, straightening him out.

The other contents of the box were an old container of Brylcreem, the Cross pen I used to keep in my front pocket, and a yellow prescription bottle. The mints had turned the inside dusty.

"Hello, Dad."

And there she was. Almost as tall as her mother, wearing a miniskirt that was ridiculous for the weather, and a little green waist-length jacket with a fur collar. She stood with her hands jammed in the pockets. Because of the cold, or was she nervous?

I was too stunned to speak at first. I guessed her age to be fourteen or fifteen. But of course I recognized her immediately. I would recognize her anywhere. Any when.

She said, "I'm so sorry."

I jumped to my feet. "Oh, honey, no. What do you have to be sorry for?"

She stood on the other side of the boundary of trees. The house was dark behind her. I walked toward her, my feet punching awkwardly through the snow. I had the absurd idea that I would spook her. I stopped myself just shy of the border.

"I forgot how to do it," she said. "After the party? Mom put a stop to it. I was so little, I didn't know what I was doing, or how I could get around her. Even with the doll. And later, when I wanted to—"

She was crying. I strode across border of the property and nothing stopped me, no force field, no curse. "It's okay, sweetie," I said. "You did great." I wanted to wipe the tears from her cheeks. But I'd never been the father of a teenage girl. I didn't know what was appropriate. "Look at me—I'm here."

She shook her head. "When I tried to bring you back again, I'd—I'd forgotten what you looked like." She was so upset to admit that. "She didn't keep any pictures of you. Just of—"

She stopped herself, out of deference to my feelings. She noticed me glance toward the house and said, "Don't worry. He doesn't live there. Mom and I don't live there anymore either."

"He's gone?"

She heard the lift in my voice. I'm embarrassed about that.

She said, "He's not a bad person. He was a good father."

I nodded. "I'm glad to hear that." And I meant it.

"Anyway, Mom's kind of had enough of the whole husband thing." She laughed apologetically, then wiped at her cheek with the backs of her fingers, a gesture so grown-up and ladylike. "We move around a lot now. Wherever's interesting."

"That's good," I said. "Seeing the world."

We lapsed into silence. What to say, after such an absence?

"They're expecting me back," she said.

"Sure. I understand."

"I'm not very good at this," she said. She moved her fingers, and suddenly they held a man's leather wallet. "There's money in there. I didn't try credit cards—those are tricky."

I took it from her and opened it. The New York driver's license in the plastic window showed my face.

"You can't use your old name," she said. "He's still got that. But I tried to pick something nice."

"It's… manly." I smiled.

"I can change it," she said, worried.

"Names don't matter," I said. "It isn't names that make us real."

LAVIE TIDHAR
THE RED MENACE

When I was asked to do a story for Mash Up it didn't take me long to settle on Marx and Engels' *The Communist Manifesto*. It has such a great opening line! Such a sense of... menace. I used to go to the Red Lion pub in Soho, in London, where Karl Marx worked in an upstairs room, and later did his drinking. I grew up on a kibbutz – my grandfather was a socialist. I tried to picture him in a different life, one where world history took a slightly different turn...

I went past a demonstration the other day, by the Bank of England, with people wearing those *V for Vendetta* masks. It seems to me the stuff Marx was talking about then is still relevant to us now. Maybe with some added weird SF stuff! So here it is, the story – "The Red Menace." We start in London, and the year is 1936...

THE RED MENACE
BY LAVIE TIDHAR

1.

A SPECTRE IS HAUNTING EUROPE – THE SPECTRE OF COMMUNISM. I was staring at the headline in the *Daily Express*, so often repeated in those days, reading as I walked. The City of London, in autumn. A cold wind. I had pulled up the collar of my coat higher around my neck but it did not help the chill. The wind snatched at the newspaper, trying to tear it from my grasp. The same old thing in the paper: the insurgents, sabotage of French ships in Marseilles, a terrorist attack in the heart of Krakow, and the continuing battle in Russia as the rebels approached ever closer to Moscow. On the same page, the *Express* reported on Jesse Owens winning the one-hundred-metre race in the Berlin Olympics and of American aviator Amelia Earhart's plans for a round-the-world flight. I was on Old Jewry, coming around the corner. A flock of pigeons, startled perhaps by my approach, flew into the air in a cloud of grey wings as I came to the hulking architectural tome that was the Bank of England. The sky was a faint blue streaked with grey clouds. This was when I first met her, and saw the unearthly spectre firsthand.

My name is Mathieu Heisikovitz, of the Heisikovitzes of Transylvania. I had come to London in 1931 to study medicine, yet unbeknown to my parents had soon abandoned my studies at the School of Tropical Medicine in favour of the semi-existence of a student of literature at University College of London, supplementing my income by teaching languages as a private tutor. Though naturally I kept company with the other students at the university, many of them radicals of various stripes, I was not myself a particularly political person. The continuing war between the House of Romanov and the communist insurgents left me, on the whole, indifferent, as did my own people's nationalistic aspirations in Palestine. The stories told in the popular press, of the communists, I naturally found exciting yet outlandish. Could anyone really accept H.G. Wells' *The Space Machine* as a factual account? The truth is that I was happy as I was, living in one of the greatest cities on Earth, in what would always seem to me, later on, as a Golden Age; yet any childhood, it seems to me now, must sooner or later come to an end.

On that day, as I was coming round the corner from Old Jewry, the wind picked up even more and, at long last, had managed to snatch the newspaper from my hands. I could only stand and watch, helplessly, as it tore and tumbled through the air, like a great big bird made of ink and wood pulp. I watched it soar in the wind, rising higher and higher into a sky like a pummeled bare-knuckle boxer's face. The Bank of England was before me, vast columns rising to support its facade, which bore the legend ANNO ELIZABETHAE and ANNO VICTORIAE and above it carved figures in a shape like a Napoleon hat. For a moment, the air seemed perfectly still. It tasted as if it were going to rain, a slight electric shock on the tongue. It was heavy with humidity. Then I heard a shout. A passer-by, someone strolling by on that day; it must have been a Saturday or a Sunday, I no longer recall. 'Look!' he shouted. 'Look at the sky!'

As though in response, in some strange synchronicity,

there was a rumble of thunder. The sound exploded, caught between the buildings of the Royal Exchange circus, magnified like the blast of a bomb. I looked up at the sky. There had been no lightning to precede the thunder. The clouds had amassed over the bank, creating an impregnable wall. Amidst the grey, new colours began to bloom: the purples and lilacs of a heliotrope, the scarlet and blood of rose, the vibrant blue of a forget-me-not. An unearthly glow seemed to penetrate from behind the clouds, and I felt a sudden rise in temperature, a heat as of another sun. Then the clouds seemed to part, like lips, or a wound, and I could see the flash of lightning, like jagged teeth, inside that mouth. The air was hot, oppressively heavy. There was a silence, and I became aware of my fellow passers-by standing still, like myself, all watching the skies. Then there was a second, enormous crash of thunder and the gap in the sky seemed to expand and a red tongue of smoke or flame burst out and licked at the ground before the bank. I heard people shouting and was myself startled into movement, stepping back as though I had encountered a bomb. Then as if it had all been a dream, a hallucination of some sort, the colours were sucked into the sky, the wound in the clouds closed with impossible speed, and the quality of light changed. In moments, the temperature dropped, making me shiver. The light dimmed, and the sky was once again a uniform London grey.

In the place where that red tongue touched, there stood a group of people. They had not been there a moment before.

For a moment, they seemed to be frozen. Then they unfurled, moving with graceful, liquid motions. I heard gasps from the other onlookers. There were around ten people there, moving quickly, with purpose. Some climbed up the stairs to the entrance of the bank. Some went towards us, the watchers, while one, unfurling a flag, climbed up to the Duke of Wellington's statue and stood there, tall and proud, waving his banner in the cold air.

The flag was white. On it, it bore one large red star, shocking in its presence, here, at the heart of the City of London.

The red star of communism.

The red star of the world called Mir.

'Communists!' I heard the cry. 'Insurgents!' The crowd was swelling up. A mixture of horror and curiosity, Londoners drawn to anything out of the ordinary, the promise of street theatre, no matter how dangerous. I watched in fascination, unable to withdraw despite knowing that this could not end well. The – insurgents? radicals? – spread out as if planning to somehow occupy the front of the Bank of England. They all wore Lenin masks, smooth ivory oval shapes decorated with the distinct, carefully cultivated demon-like beard and moustache of the man who had led the first expedition to Mir nearly twenty years before.

'Workers of the world, unite!' the man straddling the Duke of Wellington statue shouted. 'You have nothing to lose but your shackles!'

There were boos and a couple of cheers. Clearly, the communists had some covert sympathisers even in the Square Mile. Two of the masked apparitions unfurled a large banner and tied it to the bank's columns. *Eat the Rich*, it said. I noticed one of the two *Leninistas* on high; for a moment, the mask slipped and a cascade of long, dark hair fell down over slim shoulders. A woman, I realised. A shrill whistle cut through the air and I heard running footsteps approaching.

Someone had summoned the police.

I was shoved from behind and stumbled as burly officers pushed through the crowd. They were traditional bobbies, I saw with relief. They stood for a moment between us and the demonstrators, a human wall, before moving on the masked protesters with single-minded determination, swinging their billy clubs in their hands. The protesters moved as one, in the same fluid, graceful way they had. As if they were used to a heavier world, I suddenly thought. Co-ordinated, they moved to evade the policemen.

'Go get them!' someone shouted.

'Pigs!' someone else shouted. For a moment, I thought that the spectators would begin to fight amongst themselves. I was trapped in a mass of heaving bodies, pushed this way and that, towards the bank's entrance, towards the impending confrontation between the protesters and the bobbies. I began to fight back, to push when I was pushed, to try to escape. The mood, almost jubilant a moment before, had turned ugly. At last, I was almost away from the sway of the crowd. I raised my eyes and looked over their heads and what I saw made my chest constrict painfully in fear.

Blackshirts.

Oswald Mosley's ragtag band of fascists had been co-opted by King Edward, forming, in effect, a second, brutal police force. I watched their impassive faces, their black uniforms, and I felt fear suffocate me. It was difficult to breathe, my heart was beating too fast in my chest, my palms were sweating. I needed to escape. I saw one of the Blackshirts raise his hand in a throwing motion. He was holding something long and black and heavy in his hand. It rose into the air in an arc and travelled high above the panicked spectators' heads, to land between the policemen and the masked protesters.

For a moment, nothing happened.

I saw the protester I had noticed before, the woman, turn her head towards the device. Everything seemed to happen so slowly. I heard a policeman near me say, 'What the—' and begin to move slowly away, and then the black device disintegrated, and a bright ball of expanding flame burst out of it, impossibly fast, rushing at the retreating policemen, the protester on the Duke of Wellington statue, the spectators and me. It blossomed like a flower, petals like shards of molten metal flying in all directions. I was thrown back and fell, painfully, and the sound of the explosion erupted in my ears and was abruptly cut.

All sound ceased.

My eyes felt gummed together. I painfully pushed them open. My vision shifted and swam as if I were watching things from the bottom of a deep, murky pool. Slowly, I pushed myself up. My face burned. A terrible pain seized my head in a vice. I turned my head and saw the body of the policeman lying in a pool of blood, his uniform burned clean off his body. I retched. I had not eaten earlier and now all that would come out was a thin trickle of sour, noxious liquid that burned my tongue. Looking up, I saw a forest of moving legs – and prone bodies. Smoke bellowed into the air, stained fantastical reds and yellows. I saw rather than heard gunshots. I saw a Blackshirt fall down, blood spreading on his chest where he'd been hit. I saw a protester in a Lenin mask run, holding a pistol, and saw him drop to the ground, half his head blown off.

I had to get away. There were people dead all around me, policemen and spectators and insurgents alike. Their corpses lay in grotesque forms on the ground. Blood and smoke and something else, too, a terrible smell that made my eyes burn – some sort of gas, I thought. I stood on unsteady feet, ghostly figures moving through the smoke around me in silent motion. When I looked up, there was a hole in the sky, reaching down. A cone of darkness reaching to where the Duke of Wellington statue had been. A Blackshirt loomed at me out of the smoke suddenly, a billy club studded with nails raised, a sneer of hatred on his animated face.

He swung it at me and I fell back. I felt the hiss of air as the club sailed by my face, narrowly missing me. Someone bumped into me. I turned instinctively, held on to muscled arms. Her mask fell off to one side of her face, her long black hair spilling down to her shoulders. There was an ugly gash on her face, her left eye was a black mess. There was blood on her shirt.

She looked up at me and I pushed her, hard, and turned, too late, holding up my arm as the studded billy club smashed into it. I screamed, feeling the bones in my arm breaking. The Blackshirt grinned and swung back for a death blow. Then she was standing beside me, the girl with the black hair, and she had a gun in her hands. I did not hear the shot. The Blackshirt stared at us, dumbly, then looked down. Blood spreading on his black shirt, turning it muddy. I saw the flash of the second shot and the impact of the bullet in the Blackshirt's belly. He sank to his knees, the club falling from his hands.

The girl took my hand and suddenly sound rushed back in and I could hear the screams of the wounded, the sound of gunfire, and the trill of whistles blowing in futility. Ahead of us, the remaining protesters were huddled with their wounded in the square. The black tongue came down from the sky and licked at them and then, just like that, they were gone. I turned and the girl collapsed into me. I held her with my good arm and cursed. I tore the mask off her and dropped it to the ground. Without it she was just another spectator. I began to drag her away.

2.

Her name was Anastasia.

'But you can call me Anna,' she said.

3.

In the night, I awoke into darkness and the touch of something cold and sharp against my neck, an unfamiliar weight on my chest. I was pinned down. It was early. I could hear my landlord's snores from beyond the thin walls. A cockerel cried out and was abruptly silenced. My bandaged arm shot darts of pain at me. I blinked. Slowly, features resolved in the room, and I saw her face. She was straddling me, leaning over me with a knife pressed against my throat. Her long hair fell down and tickled my face. Her eyes were dark and serious and her face oval, and lovely. 'Who are you?' she said. 'Where am I?'

'You were hurt,' I said. 'At the bank. I carried you away.'

'Where am I?'

'On Brick Lane,' I said, and, at her look of confusion, 'the East End of London. Don't worry, you're safe here.'

Still the knife would not leave my throat. She shifted her position on me. Her touch made me ache… She said, 'Who did this to me?'

'It wasn't me,' I said, quickly. 'A neighbour, a nurse. Mrs Gernsbacher. She came. She removed your clothes and cleaned and bandaged your wound. You were shot in the shoulder. She said you were lucky. Had it hit any lower…'

Her eyes opened wider. For the first time, she seemed to really see me. 'You're hurt too,' she said. The pressure on my throat eased, a little.

'Yes,' I said. She touched my arm gingerly, prodding it with her finger, and I suppressed a groan.

'I remember,' she said. 'The Blackshirts. We did not count on them arriving so quickly…'

'They threw a bomb!' I said. She almost smiled.

'Yes…' she said. 'They would blame us, later. Call us terrorists. It is their method.'

'You are a communist,' I said.

'Yes.'

'From… Mir?'

This time, she did smile. The pressure of the knife on my throat eased further. 'Evidently,' she said.

'Why?' I said.

'Why what?'

'Why did you do it? It was a massacre!'

She examined my face. As if deciding something, she suddenly lifted her arm. The knife glinted in the faint light coming from outside. Dawn was coming. She climbed off me, awkward with one hand, and I realised just how fragile she really was. She tossed the knife away, and then, surprising me, she lay down beside me, as easy and as natural and trusting as though it were the simplest thing in the world. We had shared the mattress in the night, of course. There was nowhere else to lie: the bed was my desk and my dining table when it wasn't used for sleeping.

'It was a diversion,' she murmured. I could feel the heat of her. She lay with her back to me. I expelled breath that I didn't know I was holding. Turned carefully, my good arm against the thin mattress. I stared at her bare shoulders.

'A diversion?' I whispered.

'The British…' she said. She sounded drowsy. 'They have anti-gate technology now… We couldn't open a gate into the bank. We had to break in… the old-fashioned way.'

'You robbed the *Bank of England*?' I said, horrified.

'I… hope so,' she said. Then she began to gently snore.

4.

It was only later, much later, that I realised that I had asked the wrong question.

I had asked why.

I should have asked *what*.

5.

The next morning, we sat awkwardly at my tiny table having breakfast. I had boiled two eggs and gone down the road for fresh bagels. I boiled tea, black. Anna put a sugar cube between her teeth and took a sip of tea. I watched the sugar dissolve between her white, slightly crooked teeth. It was the first time I got to study her properly. Her face was tanned, made almost black by the alien rays of the sun which bathe Mir, or so it is said. Her arms were muscled, strong. She was used to physical work. She seemed to me, in my enchanted state, a true worker, a poster girl for the Socialist revolution. Her eyes were brown, and sparkled with tiny flecks of gold in the wan sunlight coming in through the window. She had a small, old scar on the left side of her mouth. When she smiled, it was as though the Mir sun shone through her, transforming the room into a temple – though I had never seen it, the Mir sun; not then, not yet.

We ate without speaking. I cut a cucumber and served it with some salt. Anna ate quickly, hungrily. She did not waste food. Earlier, I had gone and purchased the newspaper. COMMUNISTS TERRORISE CENTRAL LONDON, the headline read. BOMB ATTACK LEAVES FIFTEEN DEAD. There was no mention of the Blackshirt fascists, and no mention of a break-in at the Bank of England either. I didn't know if it meant the insurgents had been unable to carry out their objective, or whether they had been successful and the news was suppressed.

'Mathieu,' Anna said when she had done eating. I liked the way she said my name.

'Yes,' I said.

'What you did was very dangerous.' She reached over and squeezed my hand. 'Thank you.'

Her hand was very hot. She released her hold quickly. 'I

must sleep now,' she said. Just as quickly she rose, and went to the bed, and lay down. I listened to her breathing change. Sleep came easily to her. I was left alone at the table with my *Daily Express*, but, for once, I could not concentrate on its banalities. Much had been left unsaid between us. One thing we both knew, and wouldn't say, not then: sooner or later, they would come looking for her.

6.

A week later, they came.

I had begun to think we were safe. Why would anyone remember us, or count how many insurgents there were, or note that one, still alive, had been left behind?

'A man was asking for you today,' Menachem, the butcher, told me one afternoon. I had gone out for food. I had been neglecting my pupils but I didn't care. My arm was healing and I had Anna to look after, Anna to replace all that may have meant something to me in my life before.

'What sort of a man?' I said. Menachem just shrugged – the only answer he needed to give.

'There was a government agent asking about me today,' I told Anna that same day. 'He was told I was gone, that I have been gone a week already. A *goyish* man in the East End asking questions is like a Jew asking the Church for forgiveness. In neither case is an answer forthcoming. But they'll be back. Sooner or later, they'll be back, Anna.' I looked at her. To my surprise, she was radiant. Her smile was ecstatic, the smile of the devout at prayer.

'Then we did it,' she said. 'We were successful!'

Her joy made me afraid.

Had the burglary been a failure, I realised, no one would have cared one whiff for a lone rebel on the loose. But if the insurgents were successful... if they had broken into the vaults of the Bank of England, the security forces would stop at nothing, would trace every last insignificant lead.

By assisting Anna, I realised, I had become an enemy of the state.

And I realised that I had known that all along, and that I didn't care.

'We have to leave London,' I said. 'Tonight.'

She nodded, flashed me a quick smile of sympathy. 'I have already made the arrangements,' she said.

7.

Charing Cross Station, at night, and the last train to Dover... The street lamps burned electric and there was a manic, almost forced, gaiety in the air, like a curlicued end to the thirties.

War, Anna had told me.

War is coming.

And it seemed to me that I had known, for a long time, that it was so; and that the people thronging the capital's streets that night, drinking and laughing and puffing on cigarettes, knew it too.

Charing Cross Station and the whistle of train engines, the chuga-chuga of metal wheels on the track, the calls of the newspaper vendors, the smell of pasties and caramelised peanuts, the suggestion of foreign shores. A short and nervous man, balding, with a French cigarette, went past us. His arm brushed Anna's. Then he was gone and she was holding a small handbag that wasn't there a moment before.

'Let's go,' she said.

8.

On the way to Dover, the train stopped in the middle of nowhere and was boarded by men in plain clothes that fooled no one. I sat tense by the window, but Anna beside me was the image of smiling unconcern.

'Tickets, please. Identification.'

A thin man, with round glasses and a trim moustache as thin as he was. I handed over my carte de travail. He barely glanced at it. 'You are from Hungary?' he said.

'Budapest,' I said. 'I am returning home, with my fiancé...' I half-shrugged. He looked at Anna. 'You seem to have both been in an accident recently,' he said.

'Thugs,' Anna said, with sudden passion. 'We were attacked, for being foreign. Is this how your country treats visitors?'

'These are difficult times,' the thin man said. 'Your papers?'

She gave him her documents. Again, he barely looked at them. Instead, he looked at her, and at me. Then he shrugged. 'Here,' he said, returning the documents to us. 'My apologies for your misfortune. Please have a safe onward journey.' For a moment, he hesitated. 'You would be advised not to travel by ferry, mademoiselle. Many eyes are watching the channel, and not all are as friendly as mine.' He spoke low. No one else could have heard him. He smiled at my horrified face, gave us a quick salute, and was gone down the aisle. 'Tickets, please. Identification.'

I sank back in my seat. My heart was beating at a rapid, irregular rhythm. 'He knows,' I said. Anna gripped my hand.

'Sympathisers to our cause are everywhere,' she said. 'But so are our enemies.' We held hands, and did not speak again, until we reached Dover.

9.

We crossed the Channel into France by fishing boat, in the dead of night, and I was sick several times; and that is all that I wish to say on that subject.

10.

You must understand that my story is not one of a hero. I was not responsible for any of the things that transpired on the world stage. I am merely an observer, a man caught, as all of us were caught, in the violent changes then overtaking the world. That I survived, where so many didn't, is enough for me. The fate of two people during that great war is of no significance. This is how I came to Mir:

We beached at a cove beyond the port of Calais…

We were met by a group of insurgents. A diverse group: an old woman in a peasant's shawl, a boy of perhaps fifteen, three men dressed like bankers, others dressed like soldiers, women in the starched uniforms of maids and others in the outfits of upper-class ladies of leisure. It was as if we had gone aground not just in another country but in a sort of fairyland: these people seemed to me an actors' troupe, a disreputable travelling show. I could not for the life of me account for their presence there, though clearly Anna had been expecting them. For the first time, the question rose in my mind: what was I doing here? My old life was gone forever, and I did not know what was to replace it. I felt apprehensive, yet also, strangely, free. Perhaps that is what is meant by *revolution*, I thought. It is an upheaval, an explosion that tears your old life away from you, forever, and leaves you falling free. Where you'd land, and how, is sometimes up to you, but more often a subject to historical process. And so:

'The train will arrive in one hour,' a man in a sombre banker's suit and a wide-brimmed hat – the latest fashion from Paris – said. He seemed to be in charge. 'We must be ready by then. The comrades on the line are ready – we must not let them down.'

Bewildered, I followed Anna and the others. We boarded

automobiles that took us, separately, to the train station in Calais. There were perhaps twenty of us altogether, with nothing in common. Once at the station, we seemed like any kind of crowd waiting on a platform, a group of disparate strangers.

It was there, while waiting for the train to Paris, that Anna first kissed me.

I remember it, even after all those years, so vividly. Her hand was on the back of my neck, she smelled of salt water and sweat and soap, her eyes sparkled, flecked with gold. She pulled me to her and our lips met. She was so warm… 'What was that for?' I said.

'Just in case,' she said.

'In case of what?'

'In case there is no later,' she said, simply.

The train arrived. We boarded it. I noticed, as we walked through, looking for seats, that the train bore a large contingent of military personnel. They were easy to spot: they bore prominent swastikas on their shoulder patches. Germans. Escorting someone high up in Hitler's National Socialist Party? I wondered, uneasily.

A round-faced man in a suit sitting amidst them, neat and proper. 'Herr von Ribbentrop,' Anna whispered to me after we passed and settled into our seats. 'The German Foreign Minister.'

'Shouldn't he be in Berlin, for the Olympic Games?' I said, surprised.

'I believe he has just concluded a meeting with the British,' she said, 'which could not wait.'

About whatever it was the insurgents had stolen from the bank? But Anna said no more, merely gripped my hand. I felt her tension, and felt apprehensive. 'We *are* going to Paris, are we not?' I said; but she only smiled.

11.

In 1908, a vast object crashed into the Earth's surface, impacting in Siberia, near the Tunguska River. The resultant explosion destroyed a forest of some eighty million trees covering an area of nearly a thousand square miles.

A cadre of socialist revolutionaries were sent by Lenin to investigate the crash. They had expected a large meteorite, perhaps. What they found instead was anything but natural.

The train, moving through the French landscape. Flat lands and fields, low-lying villages in the distance. A low, dim sun in a blue sky dotted with clouds.

'Now,' Anna said.

Her good hand went into her handbag. Came out with a small silver gun. All over the train seemingly random people rose as one. I recognised them from the beach, earlier. The three bankers, the young boy, the old peasant woman. They were all holding silver guns. The Nazi soldiers started, reaching for their weapons, but they were too late. I saw the old woman raise her gun and press the trigger. Instead of a gunshot an impossible beam of light burst from the muzzle of the gun and hit the nearest soldier. His head was simply *erased*, leaving behind a stump of a neck, neatly cauterised. The body collapsed to the ground.

'This is a hijacking, don't anyone move!' the old woman screamed.

In moments, it was all over. I saw the German official – von Ribbentrop – look at us coolly. But he stayed in his seat, and said nothing.

'Come on!' Anna said to me. She was radiant then. Her hand tugged at mine and I followed her down the train.

'Where are we going?'

All around us, bewildered passengers were sitting, guarded by armed revolutionaries. 'Here,' Anna said, flinging open the door of a private compartment in first class. It was empty. We went inside and she pulled up the window. Cold air streamed in.

'Where are we going?' I said, and she grinned.

'Look!'

I sat facing the direction of travel. She sat beside me. We held hands. I put my head out of the window and the wind buffeted my face. Fields, flat lands, distant villages...

Ahead of us, the air shimmered.

A thing like a concave mirror made of air and sunlight formed in front of the train. It was a few hundred feet ahead of us and coming up fast. It engulfed the train tracks, and the engine, heading towards it, would hit it head on, I realised. We were going into it. I couldn't see what was beyond. 'Anna!' I said. She squeezed my hand and said nothing. I watched it approach. We were mirrored in it. Then the engine hit it – and disappeared *through*. I gave an involuntary cry and heard Anna laugh beside me. I heard other passengers shouting elsewhere on the train, but their voices were weak and fractured, like bubbles rising underwater. I watched the train being swallowed by the mirror, and then, with a cry, we too were submerged into it.

The world changed.

One moment we were travelling along tracks laid down in French soil, nothing but the countryside around us. The next, a blast of warm air hit my face and I could smell a strong, sweet, almost cloying smell of flowers, a humidity of vegetation, and hear the hum of insects. The landscape changed. The world changed. All around us were thick, alien forests. I saw flowers larger than a man, trees rising impossibly high into the air, twisting and turning in a tangled mass of black branches like octopus arms. A bird the size of a bicycle perched on a branch above the passing train, holding a worm-like thing the size of a human leg. The train continued to run on. I watched the train tracks ahead, cutting through the forest, and then we were out of the trees and a hot sun beat down on my face. I raised my head and saw a massive red sun in the sky. Its light near-blinded me. I quickly ducked my head back into the compartment's relative cool, blinking back tears. The air tasted different. The light was different. And my weight, I suddenly realised, felt different, too, heavier, and it was harder to breathe. 'You'll get used to it,' Anna said, kissing me. When my eyes stopped hurting at last, I looked out of the window again. The forest had disappeared and in its place there was the city.

12.

I had never thought to see such a city. It rose into the air, towers and ziggurats like needles pointing at the sky. Webs of brightly spun metal connected them, high in the air. The city spread out for untold miles, made of dark stone and light metal, with sheer walls rising around it like a protective shield. 'Leningrad…' Anna said. Dark shapes moved in the sky, and one swooped low over the train, calling out in a strange and haunting voice. As it swooped near us, it blocked out the sun and I realised that it was as large as the engine pulling the train. I heard gunshots from a nearby window and the reptilian creature turned, majestically, and swooped away unhurt on leather wings.

The train headed to the city. As we came near, its sheer scale became harder to fathom, the walls rose forbiddingly, and two enormous gates appeared, opening slowly to allow the train passage.

Inside, we arrived at some sort of terminal, an enormous stone building, as though built for creatures far larger than humans. Red flags waved everywhere in the hot wind, and, above the rising arch of the building, I saw the red star of Mir. This was it, I realised. This was the mysterious new world discovered by those early cadres in 1908, as they traversed the gate that had appeared – was created? – in Tunguska. And this was Leningrad, seat of the revolutionary forces, the base from which the insurgents fought for the communist cause back on Earth.

We were taken off the train. Soldiers dressed in khaki uniforms, moving sluggishly through the heavier gravity, escorted away von Ribbentrop and the German soldiers. The rest of us remained, under the heat of that alien sun, captors and captives both. A hush settled on us, slowly. The smell of the city was old, the smell of stone and weathered metal and plants. In the cracks between the walls, the same giant flowers I had seen before grew, and their scent, sickly and sweet, seemed to make my limbs heavy, my head dull. It was so quiet. Anna stood beside me, her eyes closed, her head tilted up to catch the sunlight. Her face seemed so peaceful then. I heard sound: booted feet on gravel. I turned and looked. A man, heavy-set, with thick black hair and a bushy moustache, stood on a stone platform above the tracks, facing us. 'Friends!' he said. He raised his hands as if to hold us. His voice carried. 'Comrades!'

We all looked at him. His raised hands held us, bound, as if by magic. 'I am Stalin,' he said, simply.

'Comrade Stalin…' Anna breathed beside me, her eyes filled with awe.

'Welcome to Mir!' Stalin said. 'Comrades, I will speak to you plainly. You have come a long way to be here, and you are far from home. Impossibly far. And yet so very near, too. It is a paradox.' He laughed, and it made me shiver. 'Our gates open on Earth, allow us to travel instantaneously! Here, on Mir, the socialist revolution has already happened. Ours is a workers' utopia, a true commune. Not so there, on Earth. Comrades, I tell you true: a war is coming. A great war, a world war, a class war. A war that we shall win. And so I ask you: will you join the revolution?'

My heart was beating fast; my hands were clammy. 'Will you join us, with all your heart and of your own free will?'

'What if we don't?' someone at the back shouted. Stalin smiled. His hands, spread out, held us in a steel trap. He made one simple gesture. Indicating the outside. Go, he seemed to say. The gates are open.

We were silent. Exchanging glances. The only true choice is no choice at all.

'Will you join us?' Stalin roared, and before I knew it my good hand was raised in the air, holding Anna's still, and I cried, 'Yes!' and all around me the others were doing the same, caught up in the fervour or acceding to the inevitable, or both.

'Will you join us?' Stalin roared.

'Yes!' we shouted, as one.

'Revolution!' Stalin cried. And we replied, in an echoing, growing wave of sound, threatening to spill and to rise and to drown, there on that alien world, under its alien sun: 'Revolution! Revolution! Revolution!'

13.

There is no true night on Mir. The three moons describe conflicting orbits in the sky, always casting their light. There are periods of gloom, but they are few. On one such, I was patrolling the outer perimeter of the city with Lansky, a Russian and fellow volunteer. Lansky was smoking. There were agricultural collectives beyond the city, and the tobacco, Mir-grown, was harsh and fragrant, and was said to give the user a mild sense of euphoria.

'We won't be staying here forever, you know,' Lansky said. We carried guns, keeping an eye out for the native predators.

'I know,' I said. Moscow had fallen without a fight the previous winter. The Romanovs had escaped to Ekaterinburg, and there they were cornered, and executed. The Soviet Union was formally a reality. I never saw Stalin again after that first day on Mir. Shortly after that day, he departed back to Earth, to lead the revolution and prepare for the coming war.

I knew, by then, that von Ribbentrop, the German official on the train, had met with Molotov, to discuss – so the rumours went – a pact between us Soviets and the Nazi regime. I did not know what was agreed.

Human presence on Mir grew daily. More and more volunteers came through the gates, joining our utopia, working in the collective farms and being trained in combat. I had swapped my London clothes for khakis, my muscles strengthened in labour and the heavier gravity, and my skin was tanned from the burning sun of Mir. I was a new man. I felt that, by crossing the gate, I had been reborn. I was no longer Mathieu Heisikovitz, of Transylvania, a student of literature adrift in the world. I was now Comrade Mathieu, of the Glorious Army of the Revolution, and there was nothing I couldn't do. Those had been the happiest years of my life.

Then, too, there was Anna, always Anna. We had healed on Mir, our wounds and our hearts, and in the summer of 1937 we were married in a simple ceremony, alongside ten other couples in our commune.

'There!' Lansky said. 'What was that?'

In the gloom, it was hard to tell apart shapes or depths. 'A *zmag*?' I said, cocking my gun – it was our name for the great, dragon-like creatures that still lived in the wilds of Mir.

'No,' Lansky said. 'No, I do not think s—' and with that, and with hardly a sound, he fell.

I stared at him, for a moment nonplussed. He convulsed on the ground and then was still. There was blood seeping out from a hole in his forehead.

He'd been shot.

'Attack!' I cried, when I found my voice. 'We're under attack!'

I dropped to the ground and saw tracer fire flash over my head, narrowly missing me. I could see them ahead now, a group of men in dark clothes, moving through the wild forest that surrounded the city. Who were they? How had they come to be here? They moved awkwardly, as though not used to the heavier gravity of Mir, but they were coordinated, efficient.

'Report your position!' My radio came alive.

'Sector five, sub-sector blue,' I said.

'On our way.'

I stayed on the ground. Then there was a burst of light coming from the trees, shooting high into the sky, where it exploded. The gloom turned to daylight, and I could see everything in sharp relief, see the men moving towards me, see their insignia, but not understanding, for some wore the Nazi swastika, while others bore the winged horse of the British Airborne, and others still had the distinctive stars-and-stripes of the United States.

They swarmed towards me, pointing their guns, surrounding me in a half-circle. 'On your feet... Comrade,' one of them said. Above our heads, the flame died, but I could hear the sound of a flyer approaching. 'Take him,' the man – their commander – said. They pulled me up roughly and bound my hands. I was dragged after them. Overhead, more fliers arrived. I heard something fall through the air with a whistle and hit the ground. An explosion tore up earth and trees, flinging them in all direction. 'Retreat!' They dragged me into the woods. Bombs were going off everywhere, but the soldiers seemed to melt into the trees, to disappear in the gloom. Suddenly we arrived at a clearing, and I saw a bubble of shimmering light, growing. A gate, I realised in horror.

'No!' I said. 'Please! Let me go!'

They pulled me with them, into the light –

And we emerged in night-time, a moon overhead, a military base, the air cold, searchlights lighting up the sky. My teeth were chattering. 'Welcome back to Earth,' someone said, unkindly. Then they took me into the building and locked me up in a cell, and for a long time, no one came to see me.

14.

You all know about the war. I spent most of it in a series of prisoner-of-war camps, first in Königsberg, then near Munich, and the last in Dresden. I was locked up in a butchery cellar when the Allies bombed the city. When I stepped outside, the city had been wiped clear; nothing but rubble remained. I wandered its ruined streets like a ghost upon an alien world. And yet I was free!

The raid on Mir, I had soon found out, was only one of many as the Axis powers – that is Germany, Great Britain, and the United States – waded into the great war against our Soviet Union. The Molotov-Von Ribbentrop Accord had been a washout. Adolf Hitler's ambition was to rule the whole of Europe, and the United States and Britain backed him as the only viable alternative to communism. From time to time, we would get news, in the POW camp, from the outside world. An Allied victory in Greece, a country which embraced communism; the Axis annexing Yugoslavia; China entering the war in the Pacific on the Allies' side, Japan on the side of the capitalists, Hitler's Afrika Korps sweeping across Egypt – it was hard to know how the war was going.

But the tide of war was turning. After Dresden, I was picked up by communist partisans operating in Germany. I was given a gun, and, once again, control of my own destiny. Together we roamed the countryside, blowing up bridges, attacking convoys, killing Axis soldiers. The Americans finally committed the bulk of their army to a D-Day attack in Normandy that, for a time, threatened to destroy the advances made by the Soviet forces. But we had a secret weapon…

There is a moment I do not dwell on. We had made camp, somewhere in the Ardennes. Built a fire. I sat with my back against a tree, weary beyond thought. At that time, communication with Mir was difficult; the Axis had gate-disruptor technology as well as their own, however crude, gateway devices. The war was carried out not only on Earth but on Mir, too. That night, however, a gate was opened, for just a moment, and a cadre came through from the other world. He spoke briefly with our commander, a burly Frenchman named Allard, before returning through the gate. Later, Allard came around with post for us. When he came to me, he stopped. 'There is a letter for you,' he said. I took it from his hands. It was a plain white envelope, stamped with the official red star. I did not want to open it, but at last I did.

It was printed on official letterhead. It was from the Department of War and it began, *We regret to inform you.*

'I'm sorry,' Allard said, awkwardly. I nodded, but said nothing. I folded the letter back and put it into the envelope and sat there, through the night, staring at it all the while but not seeing it. I was looking far away, to another world, and another time. And that is all I wish to say on that, now or ever.

15.

I never learned what it was in the vaults of the Bank of England that day so long ago, but I can guess. Let me tell you something about Mir, and about the city we called Leningrad. It was not a human city. Who built it? What comrades from beyond the stars may have fashioned that place, and what strange technology did they leave behind?

The gates, of course – but by the time the war ended, both sides had access to the technology. So it was not that.

On May eighth, 1945, a gate opened in the skies high above Munich. A solitary flyer emerged from it, a Mir flyer, of a type built and designed by Leningrad's former, nameless occupiers. A silver cigar-shaped object, about ten feet in length, dropped from it and fell on the city. At exactly the same time, gates were opened over Birmingham, in England, and over Chicago in the United States.

You have seen the footage countless times. The bright, terribly bright flash of light. The way it engulfed the city and then, in the blink of an eye, constricted upon itself, became a pinprick of darkness, and faded out of existence, taking the entire city with it; buildings, people, bicycles and all. Nothing was left: nothing but earth.

Where did they go? Were they exterminated like so many ants? Or were they shipped, somehow, to some other place; another, desolate world? They are not on Mir. Not anywhere.

Two days after the fall of the Aetheric bombs, the war was officially over. Hitler committed suicide in his bunker. Churchill and President Truman met with Stalin at a place called Potsdam and negotiated a peace treaty.

The war was over.

Though we had not yet won.

16.

Life went on. I travelled to Mir for one last time, and thereafter never returned. In time, I remarried, and with my new bride travelled to Palestine, working and living on an agricultural commune, what we called a *kibbutz*. We had three children and they, in their turn, gave us grandchildren. The world remained divided: capitalism, led by the United States, on the one side, communism and the Great Soviet on the other. But we were slowly gaining. Capitalism carries inside it its own inherent downfall.

One more memory, perhaps:

In 1991, I was watching television, live from Washington, D.C., where a coup had taken place. For three days, the world watched as George W. Bush was holed up in the Pentagon building and the rebels held the White House.

The coup failed. Yet it signalled the beginning of the end of the capitalist regime, the inevitable fall of the United States. In 1993 a young socialist senator, Hillary Rodham Clinton, was elected as president, ending nearly fifty years of a Cold War and bringing, for the first time, true peace to the entire planet.

I remember watching it, with my grandson in my lap, my grown daughter and her husband on the sofa, my wife in her armchair beside them.

17.

I am old now, but my memory still works. I sleep less and less. My wife passed away a year ago, but I am seldom lonely. My family visits me often, but more and more I find myself going back in time, to that fateful day in London, when I first saw my Anna… when the sky was ripped open and I saw the light of an alien sun. We called that other place Mir, which means both *world*, and *peace*, but it occurs to me that, for the first time, we can give that name to the planet we live on.

JOHN SCALZI
MUSE OF FIRE

The name of this book is *Mash Up*. The idea is that we take first lines of famous pieces of art and then use them for our own stories. The first line that I decided to use is from *Henry V* by William Shakespeare: "O for a muse of fire that would ascend/The brightest heaven of invention." And the reason that I used that particular one is because it always created a very vibrant image for me of an actual muse of fire. Now the story that I write doesn't have much to do with *Henry V* but it certainly does have to do with muses of fire and so I hope you enjoy that. Now one of the things that I also like about this story, and writing short stories in the general sense, is that it allows me to do something different than what I usually do when I write novels. My novels are science fictional, they are often humorous, they have a lot of action, and so on and so forth, and every once in a while it's nice to change things up and try some things that are not necessarily automatically supposed to be in my wheelhouse, as it were. So this was an opportunity to sort of stretch and to do something a little bit different. So when you read it, I hope that you enjoy John Scalzi doing something a little bit unexpected.

MUSE OF FIRE
BY JOHN SCALZI

"O for a Muse of fire, that would ascend
The brightest heaven of invention…"

Well, shit, thought Ben Patton. He shoved his good hand under his leg to keep from reaching for his lighter. He had thought there wouldn't be any triggers at the corporate Christmas party.

A muse of fire…

Closing his eyes, he willed himself to remain still, telling himself he was only imagining the small, subtle weight of the lighter which was in fact in his pocket.

He could usually play it off as a nervous tic, but if he pulled the lighter out here – at a play – there would be a problem. He knew it. Brad Evanson was sitting just three seats over, looking smug, as he so often did. Ben had been on Evanson's shit list nearly as long as the prick had been his boss. Evanson particularly disliked the lighter.

Stupid Brad, Ben thought. *What sort of asshole picks a Shakespeare play for a Christmas party, anyway?* It was just the sort of status-grasping stunt that Evanson would pull. To try to look cultured and suave while everyone else in the company just wanted to drink and laugh and have an *actual* Christmas party. With spiked punch and Christmas cookies and mistletoe and *candles*—

Ben rubbed his hand, slicked with sweat, hard against the plush red velvet of his seat. He'd thought they were just using the lobby of the Lyric Opera. He didn't know he'd be trapped at *Henry V*, with the Chorus intoning *his* word in a plummy baritone.

Fire.

No, Ben had to admit, shaking his head. It wasn't the word *fire*. It was the image.

The *muse* of fire.

He managed to hold out until the end of the scene and then in the brief dimming of the lights, Ben rose and in a half-crouch, stumbled his way past the people sitting beside him. He noted Evanson's displeasure as he scuttled past.

Charlie tapped him as he went by. "You okay?" he asked.

"Something I ate," Ben muttered.

The lights came up as Ben was hurrying up the aisle. The actors started on new lines, but the only words he heard was the first sentence still echoing. *Oh, for a muse of fire…*

He pushed past the heavy red curtain and into the dark vestibule before the lobby. Leaning against the wall, he fumbled his lighter out of his pocket and flicked it open.

The flame danced above it, and inside *she* opened her eyes. Smiled at him.

"Hello, my love," she said.

At home he lay in front of the hearth – the reason why he'd bought the house, which was otherwise far too large for a single man, or at the very least a single man of such limited social activity as he was.

The sprawling three-story Victorian had a fireplace in every room, and a hearth in the living room large enough to cook an entire sheep. The other fireplaces had been converted to gas, which worked, but this one was a real wood fire still. She liked that better. And so he always kept the coals banked so he could keep the window open to *her*.

As soon as he got home from the play, he'd laid the fire with kindling and pieces of dry cedar. The flames licked around the logs, teasing him with glimpses of her, until the wood caught fully.

Hestia sat up amid the flames and stretched. "Feeling better?" she asked him.

"I missed you," Ben said.

She wrinkled her nose at him. "Silly. There were tealights in the foyer. I watched you from there. You should have stayed."

"I can't talk to you when people are there." He rubbed at the tight scars on the remains of his left hand. "It would be easier if the others could see you."

"We've talked about that," Hestia said.

"I know," Ben said. They had. Endlessly.

Ben changed the subject. "Charlie thinks that we have a shot at using the Helmholtz facilities for testing."

Hestia clapped her hands, crackling embers. "Wonderful!" she said. "Oh, Ben. I'm so proud of you. All of your hard work."

"You mean *your* work," Ben said.

"Ours, then," Hestia replied.

He grinned, much of the tension ebbing out of his body as he talked to her. Some part of him was fully aware that the most likely scenario was that he was insane and that she was an expression of that, but he'd given up on meds years ago. What kept him believing in her were the calculations. She was a genius with numbers.

He shifted closer to the fireplace. The heat baked into him and he could imagine her touch flickering over his body. His muse of fire.

"To be fair, I don't know that it'll really come through," Ben said, into the fire. "Helmholtz is notoriously strict around protocols and the parameters you need are on the outside of their safety zone."

"Just show them the Tratorian equation," Hestia said, waving a hand as if to brush away the problem, sparks curling in the air around her fingers. "It directly addresses the thermal variants that Charlie worried about. It should satisfy them at Helmholtz."

Ben grinned at this. The "Tratorian equation" was their personal intimate name for a bit of math fearsome enough that it exhausted both of their talents to describe. It was the sort of things they gave Fields Medals for.

If it worked, that was, and if a medal was what Ben was working for in the first place.

"You were eavesdropping," Ben said to Hestia.

"*You* were playing with your lighter," she replied. Teasing. Then her face sobered and she leaned forward, as far out of the fire as she could go. "I worry about you, Ben. You should have stayed at the play."

He shrugged and flexed the stubs of his left hand. "It wasn't my thing," he said.

"Maybe you should try the medication again," Hestia suggested.

"Not you, too." Conversations like *this* were the ones that worried him. If she was his subconscious, then was she telling him that he was crazy?

Or rather, was he telling himself?

He changed the subject again. "So, I picked up some new books," he said. "Do you want me to read to you?"

Hestia refused to budge. "Ben," she said. "Love. You always dodge this when I bring it up. The medication controls the OCD."

"And it also keeps me from seeing you," Ben pointed out.

"It's okay. I can still see you," she said.

"Well, *that's* healthy," he said. Ben scrubbed his face, trying to press the annoyance out of his skin. What he didn't say, and what he knew that she already knew, was that for him there was no point if he couldn't see her. No point. No spark.

No fire.

His gaze returned to Hestia, in the flames. The fact was that he *should* have stayed for the play. But everything called him to her. He felt guilty when he wasn't there for her. Wasn't there to see her. Wasn't there to distract her from her fate. "I'm sorry," he said.

"Sorry for what?" she asked, soothingly. "It's all right, Ben."

"It is *not* all right." Ben rolled onto his knees. "You're in Hell. I'm supposed to just ignore that?"

She looked away, firelit face blanching white. "I so regret telling you," she said.

"I'll get you out," he promised.

"But at what cost?" She gazed to his left arm, where his hand had been.

He had touched her. Once.

Ben sat in the corporate meeting with the other engineers trying to pretend that he was paying attention to Brad Evanson. Who was droning. Again. Evanson had two modes: droning and ranting. There did not seem to be anything in between them, except the occasional random social bit like "how are you" that he didn't really mean but had read somewhere that you should say, to make it seem like you cared, thus facilitating employee retention. Or *something*. Fact was, for all his pretensions and striving, Evanson was not a people person. He was a numbers man.

Not in the higher math sense, mind you, like Ben and the other engineers. Oh, no. Evanson was all about profit and loss.

This meant that Ben and Evanson used the same

words, but did not speak the same language. Take the word "efficiency." Ben and Evanson both used the word, but did not mean the same thing when they used it. Evanson had zero understanding of the role of efficiency in thermal dynamics. All he cared about was the fact that he thought Ben had invented a force field that the military was very interested in. The reality was more that Ben had to build a plasma window that would function like a force field, if the testing worked.

It amounted to the same thing as far as Evanson was concerned. Money.

Ben had his tablet braced with his bum hand and was drawing on it with the stylus. It could usually pass for taking notes.

His IM popped up a message from Charlie Spencer, silently. LET'S MAKE A DRINKING GAME FROM HOW MANY TIMES HE SAYS SYNERGY, it said.

Ben glanced across the table to where Charlie sat, apparently at full attention. His sandy blonde hair had thinned above the temples and gave him a widow's peak (Charlie's wife Sandra hated the description, with some justification). He kept it a little long on top and could fuzz it up into "Doc Brown" hair when he was escorting investors through the facilities. They loved the authentic scientist look, apparently. He had a pair of black-rimmed spectacles that he put on to look the part, too. Perfect vision, otherwise.

Charlie caught Ben's look and raised his eyebrows just enough to say *Am I right?* without actually breaking his apparent concentration on Evanson's prattle.

As if he'd timed it, Evanson said, "…departments work together in perfect synergy…"

Ben snorted.

In a pause, of course. Evanson turned to him.

Shit.

Ben frowned and rubbed at the scar tissue on his left hand, working really hard at playing the snort off as a sound of pain. "Sorry. Cramp."

His IM flashed. HAVE A DRINK.

Evanson narrowed his gaze at Ben, who returned the gaze calmly, not quite daring his boss to make something of it. Evanson wouldn't, of course: a clueless flub with another disabled employee two years ago had sent Evanson into corporate-ordered sensitivity training. The course was complete bullshit as far as Ben could tell, but as a practical matter it meant he had wiggle room because of the "cripple" status that he occupied in his boss's brain. Ben had no problem exploiting that when necessary, in no small part because he knew Evanson's opinion of him otherwise.

Evanson hummed his disapproval at Ben, but then started up his drone again. "As I was saying... We achieve our best functionality when all departments work together in perfect synergy. Synergy which is perfect."

DRINK! DRINK!

Down the table Rebecca Steuben had a sudden coughing fit. Ben would bet anything that Charlie was IMing her, too. The toad sitting next to her looked actively annoyed, as if anyone wanted to hear more about "synergy."

Evanson droned, "...synergy is the perfect term to use because our work is in energy. Do you see? Synergy and energy? Synergy fans the flames of creativity."

Oh, come on, Ben thought at Evanson. *You're not even trying to sound like an actual human anymore.* He pulled his lighter out and flicked it open. Hestia had to hear this.

He had already brought his finger down on the thumbwheel before his forebrain caught up with him. *Not in a meeting, jackass,* it said. *Don't bring the lighter out in a meeting with Evanson.*

But the flame was lit and she was there. The metal warmed in his palm.

The guy next to him glanced over, then rolled his eyes and looked away. They'd all seen this before – his "nervous tic" – but Evanson hated it. Ben lowered the lighter, but kept his thumb on the wheel.

His IM flashed a message from Charlie: DUDE. PUT THE LIGHTER AWAY.

And, well, Charlie was right, wasn't he? Dude, he definitely *should* put that lighter away. He *was* going to put the lighter away. Evanson wasn't even looking at him. All Ben had to do was lift his finger off the igniter and the flame would extinguish. He just needed to take his thumb off the lighter.

Hestia looked around with curiosity, always wondering where he would take her. Her gaze widened when she realized she was in a meeting. "Ben. Ben!" she said. "Close the lighter." There was an unusual tone of pleading in her voice. "Close the lighter. Do it now."

But he was stuck. He *knew* he was stuck. He even knew what it would take to get unstuck. All he had to do was move his thumb. Move his damn thumb.

As soon as Evanson said "synergy" again, he would. She just needed to hear that.

But Evanson kept droning and came nowhere near the word. The flame danced and now other people at the table had noticed he had it out.

Just close the damn lighter, Ben.

"Is there a problem, Dr. Patton?" Evanson had stopped talking and stared down the table at Ben.

Fuck. Ben spent so much energy thinking about when to close the lighter that he'd stopped paying attention to Evanson himself. Ben didn't see him turn, or see his boss's eye drawn, naturally, to the flame of his lighter.

Ben finally closed the lighter. "Sorry," he said, looking back at Evanson, watching him now.

Which is how he could detect the oh-so-slight change in Evanson's expression; the tiny glint in his boss's eye. Evanson had any number of reasons for disliking Ben; the two of them were pieces in a puzzle that fit into different places, not meant to be jammed together. Evanson didn't *get* Ben, or his work methods, or his tics and twitches. He especially didn't get why he wasn't allowed to just fire Ben; Ben knew Evanson simply didn't have the math to know that what Ben was doing – was doing with Hestia – was putting the company light years ahead of their competition.

Evanson didn't get Ben, and couldn't fire him. But that didn't mean he couldn't make him *uncomfortable*.

"I thought we had discussed the lighter," Evanson said, in a perfectly reasonable tone of voice that immediately made Ben paranoid. "It's a safety hazard. Bringing a flame into an office meeting, in a non-smoking building – what are you thinking?"

"My mistake," Ben said. "It won't happen again."

"No, it won't," Evanson agreed, and held out his hand. "Give it to me."

"Excuse me?" Ben said.

"The lighter," Evanson said. "I want you to give it to me, please. Now."

Sweat beaded on Ben's face and on the back of his hand. "I'm putting it away," he said, of the lighter.

"That is not what I asked for," Evanson said. Ben detected a tone in his voice that he suspected was what it might sound like when a cat addressed a cornered cricket. "Dr. Patton, you've been told about the lighter. You've been told not to bring it to meetings. You've been told it makes others nervous. You've been told it presents a real and present fire hazard. You've been told this again and again, and yet here we are again, with that lighter in your hand. *Putting it away* isn't going to be sufficient this time. I need you to hand it to me now."

"This isn't elementary school," Ben said. "You're not the teacher."

"But I am your superior," Evanson said. "So give me the lighter or I'm going to cite you for a safety violation."

"I'll take the safety violation, thanks." The words were out of Ben's mouth before he realized he'd said them; it took Rebecca Steuben gasping for it to register that he'd said them out loud. He slid the lighter into his pocket.

Evanson gaped; however he expected the conversation to go, this was not that way. "Fine," he said. "Good. Then you can expect that report in your HR file by the end of the day. Along with an additional report for insubordination and for causing a disruption in the workplace. You *do* understand, Dr. Patton, that other people work here, yes? That your attitude and habits make it more difficult for everyone else?"

Ben said nothing to this, waiting.

"Apparently not," Evanson said, after an awkward pause. "Well, then, I am going to make sure you do. And until then, there's a new rule for this department and this building. No open flames of any sort in the building. That means your lighters and your candles, Dr. Patton. They are hazardous materials and you are endangering the life of every person in this building. No more open flames. Anywhere."

Rebecca raised her hand. "What about Bunsen burners?"

"What?" Evanson peered at her with the confusion that he always seemed to have about having a woman scientist on the team. Ben looked over to Rebecca, who had a small and, to Ben, attractively mischievous smile on her face.

"In the lab," Rebecca said. "We have Bunsen burners. Do we have to stop using them?" Ben noticed a strand of her deep brown hair had slipped out of her bun at her temple and curled around her glasses. He was also fairly certain they didn't actually use the Bunsen burners since most of the polymer work they were doing involved much higher temperatures. But Evanson probably wouldn't know that.

Before Evanson could respond Charlie raised his hand as well. "And what about the Meker burners?" he asked. "I'm supposed to show some investors around later today and those always get a good response. The money guys like seeing the old-fashioned burners with the computers. The old-meets-new synergy, you know?"

Ben snorted again. Evanson glared at him and Ben raised his stump. "Sorry," Ben said. "Cramp."

"Yes. The burn victim," Evanson said. "I'm surprised that you carry a lighter since you clearly don't know how to be safe around fire."

This silenced the room as effectively as the air being sucked out into a vacuum. Evanson had just gone someplace he definitely was not supposed to go. Ben couldn't tell whether this meant he'd won the exchange, or lost it. He reached for the lighter and managed to grip the arm of his chair instead.

Evanson glared at Ben, Rebecca and Charlie, in turn. "All right," he said, after a moment. He returned his glare to Ben. "Since we *have* to have flames here, and *you* are not able to follow directions, I want to be certain that you don't have another accident with fire. So you, Dr. Patton, are on medical leave."

"What?" Ben said. "That's completely ridiculous. You can't do that."

"I certainly can," Evanson said. "I can't fire you, but this will keep you out of the building. For your own good. And for everyone else's." Evanson smiled. He was back on top. "Now get out."

* * *

Ben didn't waste time poking up a fire in the hearth at home. He ran up to the library instead, turned on the gas fireplace there. Hestia uncurled with the blue flames and her face wrinkled with concern.

"What happened?" she asked.

Ben paced in front of the fireplace, flicking his lighter open and closed. Open. Closed.

"Ben? You're frightening me."

Open. "Evanson put me on medical leave." Closed. "Won't let me back into the building." Open. Flick.

Hestia turned to look through the small window of flame Ben opened above the lighter. She stared at him from the flame, then shifted to look back through the fireplace. "On what grounds?" she asked.

"Says I'm a danger to myself as long as there are open flames in the building," he said. He held up the stub of his left hand and passed it through the flame on the lighter. The plasma bent around the flesh, heating it but not letting him touch her. He so wanted that, regardless of what it might do to him. What it *would* do.

The line on her brow grew deeper and she didn't contradict him. "How long are you on leave?" she asked.

"It's open-ended. Till I'm *better*, but it's *his* definition of 'better.'" He closed the lighter, stopped pacing and faced the fireplace. "That's not the worst though," he said. "If permission comes through from Helmholtz to do the testing, I'm not going to be on the team."

Plasma was a difficult state of matter to work with. It had to be managed. It had to flow to where you wanted it to go, lead to the places it needed to work, continue to do the work it's needed to do. Ben and his team had been working with plasma for years, using his and Hestia's equations to manipulate the matter. Their latest project manipulated plasma into something approximating a force field – something long possible in theory but too expensive before now to be practical.

If Ben's and Hestia's math worked, then the plasma window could be stabilized and maintained with a minimum of energy. And with it, if their work was correct, he could change the plasma state that Hestia lived in and break her out of Hell.

At least that was the theory. But he had to be there or she couldn't reach the flame.

If he wasn't on the team, he wasn't going to be there. He wasn't going to be there for *her*.

"Oh, Ben," Hestia said. She kneeled and reached toward him. "I'm so sorry. You worked so hard on this. It must be such a disappointment for you."

It was just like her to think about him first. *She* was trapped in eternal flame and yet here she was, more worried that he was disappointed.

He stared at her, struck dumb with the longing to run his hand through her hair or to just put his arms around her. Just to hold her hand. He looked down at the stump. "I can appeal," he said. "I will."

Hestia smiled. "Don't worry, love," she said. "Everything will work out." She gazed at him as the fire burned around and through her.

Ben spent the next day cleaning, candles lit in each room so Hestia could follow him around. It meant the house was spotless when the police detectives came to call.

There were two of them when he opened the door, an Angie Martinez and a Kyle Hanson. As they stood on his porch Ben wondered which one of them was supposed to be the good cop, and which was supposed to be the bad cop, and if they ever changed up the roles just for the fun of it.

"May we come in, Dr. Patton?" Martinez asked.

"Yes, of course," Ben said. He pushed open the screen door to let them in.

"What did Evanson tell you I did?" Ben asked, after he had offered them something to drink, which they refused, and then offered them a seat, which they accepted. They sat in the living room, a fire going. The fire appeared to make the two detectives uneasy. Ben vaguely wondered if one or the other might catch a glimpse of Hestia in there. He doubted it. No one else ever did.

"Why did you bring up Bradley Evanson, Dr. Patton?" Martinez asked.

"Well, that's why you're here, isn't it?" Ben said. "He put me on medical leave yesterday for very specious reasons, and now the two of you are here. I'd guess he told you I set a trash bin on fire, or something ridiculous like that."

"Do you like fires, Dr. Patton?" asked Hanson.

"Well... you know. Occupational hazard." He paused, but they didn't get the joke. "My work is in plasma engineering. Fire is a plasma, so... yeah. I like fires."

"So much so that you were charged with arson in high school," Hanson said.

"Charged, yes," Ben said. "And if you know I was charged then you also know the charges were dropped. It was an accident."

"Was that when *that* happened?" Martinez asked, pointing to his stump.

Ben looked at the two of them. "All right, I'll bite," he said. "What is this about?"

"Dr. Patton, we are here about Bradley Evanson," Martinez said. "But not about him accusing you of setting fire to a trash can."

"Okay," Ben said. "Then what is it?"

"His house burned down last night," Hanson said. "With him in it."

"Oh my God," Ben said, shocked. "Is he all right?"

"He's not *dead*," Hanson said. "But having third-degree burns on eighty percent of your body is not 'all right.'"

"Dr. Patton, where were you last night, between 10pm and 2am?" Martinez asked.

"I was here," Ben said.

"Anyone with you?" Martinez asked.

Not anyone you would believe in, Ben thought.

"No," Ben said, instead. "I was reading until almost eleven, checked e-mail and read news online until about midnight, and then I went to sleep. You could check my web browser history."

"So, no one, then," Martinez said.

"No," Ben repeated. Both detectives made notes.

Ben fought the urge to look over at Hestia, and then remembered what she had said the night before.

Everything will work out.

Ben gave in and looked over to her. She was smiling.

"Sorry, guys," Ben said, turning his attention back to the detectives. "I don't think it's smart for me to talk to you any more without a lawyer present."

"You're probably right about that," Hanson said.

The police investigation into Ben turned up nothing because there was nothing to turn up. Ben had been at home, and he was neither foolish nor crazy enough to hint that he hadn't been alone, because of the nature of whom he had been with. A small but unquiet part of Ben wanted to ask Hestia what she knew of Evanson's fire, but the rest of him overruled that part. The rest of Ben thought it was best to leave certain things unanswered.

A week after Ben was cleared, Charlie, unwillingly thrust into Evanson's vacant role, asked him to come back to work. He did, and then wished he hadn't after the reception his coworkers gave him. Cleared by the police or not, the coincidence of Evanson burning in a fire after confronting Ben was enough to give almost everyone the creeps. Even Charlie avoided him unless there was something directly related to work.

Only Rebecca continued to be openly friendly with Ben; if anything, Ben noted, she seemed friendlier than usual. He assumed it was her compensating for everyone else being a bit of a dick. Even so, Ben spent most of the time shut up in his office, absorbed in paperwork for the tests.

Which is why when Rebecca knocked on his door that afternoon, Ben flinched.

"Sorry," she said. "Didn't mean to startle you." She leaned against the door with a tablet cradled in her arms.

Ben smiled up apologetically. "It's all right," he said. "Just focused. You know." He rubbed his eyes and stood. His back cracked as he straightened. "What's up?"

"Came to give you word that all five of the polymer casings are finished and ready for testing," she said.

"That's great," Ben said. She could have emailed that to him, actually. She must have just gotten the memo as she was on her way to somewhere else.

Rebecca grinned and stepped farther into the room. "I thought a little celebrating was in order," she said.

"Celebrating?" Ben said "Oh. Yeah… that sounds…" His brain finally registered that her hair was down. He'd only ever seen it in a bun at the base of her neck. "Uh. So the team is going out?"

A flicker of disappointment went across her face that even Ben could read. She'd been flirting. With *him*.

Ben could have smacked himself on the forehead. This was his problem; between work and the fact that almost all his attention was given to Hestia, his ability to read women's interest in him was remedial at best.

"Sure. We can get something together with the team," Rebecca said. Her voice was flattened.

Ben opened his mouth to respond and then noticed that his thumb was on the lid of the lighter, which was in his hand. He stared at it for a moment, confused. He had no memory of taking it out.

Do you like fires, Dr. Patton?

Ben set the lighter on the desk.

He stepped away from it.

He stepped *toward* Rebecca.

"It doesn't have to be the whole team," he said. "It could be just the two of us. If that's all right. I mean… Did you have something in mind?"

Rebecca smiled. "I did. There's a new bar. Dante's Inferno."

You have got to be kidding me, Ben thought at the name. He put his hand in his pocket for the lighter.

It wasn't there. A panic went through him and he almost turned to the desk.

Almost.

"That would be… that would be great," he said to Rebecca. She beamed.

"Everything looks stable. Stable is good." Ben scanned the numbers pouring over the console in the Helmholtz control room. They had been prepping for the trial since they arrived in Colorado – since before that, really – and he had the jitters that came from a combination of too much caffeine and straight up nerves.

Rebecca nodded from where she stood by her own bank

of instruments. "Everything's green across the board here, too," she said. "We're a go."

A video feed showed the center of the chamber, where the plasma stabilizer stood. There was a heavy tinted window in the airlock to the test chamber, but Ben had covered it because he didn't want to chance Hestia appearing early. He had to be able to see the glow of the plasma for her to use it. She didn't show up in video, so until he knew he could keep the plasma stabilized, it was all video.

If the plasma stabilized. *If* Hestia even existed.

Ben shook his head to clear it. "Ready infusion on my mark. Three, two, one. Now."

"Infusion commencing," Rebecca said.

The numbers flickered on the screen and the software converted it into a graph that showed pressure and density. Ben shoved his hand in his pocket, running his thumb over the smooth case of his lighter, and watched the video monitor.

Inside the chamber, the plasma flow they were inducing stood between two columns of Rebecca's polymer casing. It almost looked like glass, it was so stable, but glass did not glow like this.

The plasma rippled. A spark caught at the edge of one of the polymer casings. Ben shifted his gaze to the numbers. "Shit," he said. "We're losing stability."

"Got it." Rebecca glared at the screen, where the casing now had an obvious flame in it. "We should shut down."

"It might burn itself out," Ben said. The numbers were starting to trend upward again. "Give it a second."

"I don't think—" Rebecca began, and then was cut off as the entire casing erupted into flame and the plasma spilled outward in a gout of fire. Rebecca slammed a hand down on the shut-off control.

Ben yanked on the suppression switch, and held his

breath as oxygen sucked out of the testing chamber. The plasma writhed, turning the top layer of the heat-resistant tiles inside into bubbling puddles. He cursed and entered a command for a purge cycle. The remaining polymer casing tilted toward the ceiling. The plasma melted the edges of it and the column collapsed inward, plugging the flow.

The last of the air hissed out of the chamber and the flames went out. The floor still glowed red-hot where the plasma had danced.

Ben let out a heavy sigh of relief.

"Okay, so," he said. "That was not good."

Rebecca gave a shaky laugh. "I thought it wasn't going to shut down there for a second," she said.

"No kidding," Ben said. He ran his hand through his hair and was surprised that his scalp was damp with sweat. "Let's get this cleaned up and figure out what went wrong."

"I'll run a check on the numbers while we wait for it to cool," Rebecca said. She leaned against the instrument panel and let her head drop forward. "And then I need a really stiff drink."

"You have the nicest ass," Rebecca whispered in Ben's ear, then her mouth moved to nibble at his ear lobe.

Ben gasped and fumbled with the lock for his hotel room door. Words were not high on his list of abilities at the moment.

He pressed the plastic card to the lock, and twisted the knob as Rebecca ran her hands down his spine to cup his buttocks. She squeezed and he let out a low groan.

Shouldering the door open, he turned and wrapped his left arm around her to pull her close. Rebecca kissed him. She giggled as they collided with the wall, but did not stop kissing him. The door swung shut, leaving the room lit only by the lights from downtown Denver.

Ben slid his good hand up the back of her shirt and paused with his fingers on the bra strap. He pulled back a little to look at her, to be certain she was okay with it.

Looking through her eyelashes, Rebecca said, "Let me know if you need help with that."

He grinned. "I'm pretty good at doing things with one hand," he said. With the long practice of dressing with only one set of working fingers, he undid the catch on her bra. First time he'd done that since high school. Thank God the design hadn't changed any.

She closed her eyes for a moment, tilting her head back to expose her long neck. Ben kissed the hollow at the base of her throat. Her hair smelled of lavender and smoke from the bar.

Rebecca brought her head forward and found his belt buckle. She glanced over his shoulder. "Hey. You have a fireplace. Can we light it?"

Lifting his mouth from her neck, Ben looked back at the fireplace. He'd picked this hotel so that Hestia could travel with him.

"Not now," he said. "I think I've had enough fire for the day."

Ben rolled over, which allowed the morning light to glow redly through his eyelids. And a piece of paper tickled his nose. He opened his eyes to an empty bed and a note. Sitting up, he ran his hand through his hair before picking up the note. A scrawl he had seen in notation on so many of his documents staggered across the back of the room service menu.

> Morning, Ben.
> I needed to go back to my room for clean clothes. See you at the lab? Going over early to check the next casing.

--Rebecca

P.S. Thanks for letting me spank you. Such a nice ass.

His cheeks burned just at the memory, but it also lit other parts. Lord. He should not feel this good considering everything that had gone wrong in the first trial. Rebecca thought it was not a flaw in the polymer itself, but a piece of foreign matter stuck to the casing. That was a huge relief, if it was true. He wouldn't know until the next trial. Speaking of...

Ben crawled out of bed and dragged his pants on. Crouching in front of the fireplace, he flicked the switch to turn it on. With a *whoomp*, the gas caught and Hestia flickered into view.

She lay curled on her side, with her back to him. A livid welt ran down her side and wrapped around to her hip. It looked as though she had been dragged across a floor.

Ben fell forward on his knees. Did *they* know? Did they know that he was trying break her out?

"Hestia?" he called to her.

She lifted her head. With a groan, she pushed herself upright.

"Who did this to you?" he asked.

Hestia turned to face him. Her right eye was blackened. The scrapes on her back covered her arms. "Where have you been?"

"I—" He had been having sex. No more than five feet away from her – except she wasn't really *here*, she was in some other dimension.

She was in Hell.

Ben flushed with an emotion that lay somewhere between shame and regret, immediately leavened by something that was almost defiance. "I was with Rebecca," he said. "The trial didn't—"

"I know!"

"I… Oh, *shit*." Ben shook his head, but all he could see was the plasma writhing in the video. "No. No, you weren't supposed to manifest if *I* couldn't see the fire. That's why I used the video to monitor it."

"Well, I was," Hestia said. Her voice was broken and small.

"I am so sorry," Ben said.

"Why didn't you come to me?" Hestia asked. "Why didn't you call me when it was finished?" Her face crumpled and for the first time since he had known her, Hestia wept. Tears hissed into steam. "I thought something had happened to you," she said. "I thought you had been killed."

"Oh, God… No. I was just…" He wanted so badly to take her into his arms, to hold her the way he had held Rebecca. The only thing he could do was repeat meaningless words to her. "I am so sorry. I didn't think it would affect you."

"This?" She touched the bruising on her face. "It hurts, yes, but—" She stopped, turned away. "You have said good night to me every night since you were old enough to have a candle in your room," she said, voice quiet. "And then, on a day that I know you were working on *our* project, you didn't come for me. And then to be yanked halfway into your world – to *know* the project had misfired. What was I supposed to think? Why didn't you *come* for me?"

A part of Ben's brain pointed out that if he were having guilty feelings about sleeping with a coworker, this would be an excellent manifestation of that.

He pinched the bridge of his nose trying to think. He couldn't just tell Hestia that he'd left her alone because he had a date, but he had to say something.

"I was distracted," he finally said. "It was thoughtless of me and I'm sorry." He lowered his hand. "But the fact that you were almost pulled through is a good sign. It means that we are close to getting the door open, right?"

Hestia slowly turned back to him. "Yes," she said.

"So all we have to do is figure out a way to keep you from manifesting in the plasma while we're getting it stabilized," he said. He looked at his suitcase. He'd packed candles, just in case the fireplace hadn't worked. "When I have multiple flames, do you pick which one you appear in, or are you in all of them?"

"I pick," she said.

"So, if I light a candle in the control room?" Ben asked.

"That should work." Hestia brightened a little. "Plus I can see you work."

"Yeah… That'll be nice," he said.

Except, of course, for Rebecca. And the safety protocols at Helmholtz.

"A candle?" Rebecca raised an eyebrow and then looked pointedly at the smoke detector set in the ceiling.

"Yeah… Maybe it's superstitious, but you know," Ben said, and tapped the lantern. "It's an enclosed flame, away from the equipment."

"Did you get permission?" she asked.

"You know what they say… easier to get forgiveness than permission," he said.

Rebecca said nothing to this, so Ben pulled out his lighter and lit the candle. For a moment, twin Hestias stared at him; then she settled in the tiny flame of the candle. He placed the candle on the work counter, behind their panel.

Rebecca nodded, walked behind him and smacked him on the ass.

"Hey!" Ben straightened abruptly.

Rebecca smirked at him. "Sorry," she said. "Candlelight is an aphrodisiac."

In the candle, Hestia was staring at Rebecca and her mouth was forming a silent *o*. She knew.

"That's fine," Ben said. "But, Rebecca. Not at work, okay?"

Straightening, Rebecca sobered. "Of course. I'm sorry, that was entirely inappropriate. You're right."

"No— I mean… thanks?" Ben rubbed the back of his neck, wanting to explain but also knowing that would be the worst thing he could possibly do. Telling Rebecca that he saw a muse of fire was more than a little crazy.

He rubbed the scar tissue on his bum hand. "I… um… I don't have a lot of practice with girls. Women, I mean." He waved the stub. "This, you know?"

Her face softened, and she crossed the room to him. Rebecca reached out and took the stub, cradling it in both of her hands. "I don't know."

Hestia hissed.

Ben closed his eyes. He had no idea how to process how he was feeling for Rebecca right in that moment. Or for Hestia. Or how the one would apprehend the other.

So he decided not to. He opened his eyes, looked at Rebecca. "So. We should, you know, probably do this thing," he said to her.

"What is it?" she said.

"What?" Ben said.

"There's something going on in your head right now and I want to know what it is," Rebecca said. "And whether I'm in there too."

"You're definitely in there," Ben said. "As for all the rest of it, let's get through this part first and I'll explain the rest of it later."

"All right," Rebecca said. She lifted the stump and kissed each of the three remnants of his fingers. "After work, I want to hear all of it. Now… however. We should get started." She released him and stepped back, a veneer of professionalism slipping over her. "I've checked the casings using UV, infrared, and a magnifying glass. I don't see any contamination on either of them."

Ben had to clear his throat again to knock the longing out of it. "Okay," he said. "If we see signs of a spark again, I'll back off the flow immediately, so there aren't any unexpected flare-ups." He glanced at Hestia to make certain that she understood.

She was glaring at Rebecca with undisguised jealousy.

"Sorry," Ben said, and then realized he had once again said out loud something he'd meant to keep inside.

"What?" Rebecca asked.

"I'm sorry about not listening to you yesterday," Ben said. "About shutting it down sooner."

"You might have been right," Rebecca said. "The foreign matter could have cleared." She began the calibration process for her side of the trial.

Still looking at Hestia, Ben spoke to her, hoping she would understand. "I didn't think things through."

It was Rebecca who responded. "It's hard to think quickly in the moment," she said.

"I'll try to do better next time," he said to them both. Then, before he could drive himself crazier trying to talk to two women at once, he went over to his console. "I'm starting the pressure checks."

For the next few hours, the conversation between Ben and Rebecca stayed in the sphere of science. Ben sank into the comfortable language and looked at Hestia only occasionally. She sat with her knees pulled up in front of her, and her head resting on them. The black eye was a constant reminder that he needed to take his time and get this right.

Finally, Rebecca said, "I'm set on my end."

Ben stretched the kinks out of his back from hunching over the console. "Ditto." He glanced back at Hestia. "Ready for another try?"

Hestia lifted her head, eyes widening.

"Yep," Rebecca said, and grinned. "Have I ever told you that science makes me horny?"

Ben turned away from both women. "Ready infusion on my mark?"

"Yes, sir," Rebecca said, all business.

"Three, two, one. Now," Ben said.

"Infusion commencing," she said.

The numbers began their dance on the screen. Hestia remained in the candle's flame and didn't appear to be affected. Ben opened the shield on the thick, tinted window in the airlock to look inside the chamber. Between the two lines of Rebecca's polymer casing, the plasma flowed into a solid sheet. It glowed red at first, then to blue, then reached a heat so intense that the color passed out of the visible spectrum. Ben stepped back to his instrument console.

The numbers had stabilized. On the monitors, he could see the sheet of plasma holding steady.

Now came the tricky part, which had come from the calculations that Hestia had supplied. If he was crazy, at least it came with ferocious math skills. These skills would allow them to manipulate the flow of the plasma so that it remained stable – even when they stopped pumping fresh plasma into it. If it worked, then they'd have themselves a force field. He pushed the button to start the next sequence in the process.

The numbers stayed steady in pressure and density. Only the power draw dropped, which was what should be happening.

"Ben…" Rebecca said. "Oh, *shit*— Ben!" She sounded completely panicked.

"What?" Ben asked, and then looked up.

Inside the chamber, Hestia stepped out of the plasma.

He swallowed hard and turned to Rebecca. "What's wrong?" he asked

"There's a woman in the chamber." Rebecca reached for the cut-off. "We have to shut down."

"You can see her?" Ben asked, amazed.

She looked at him like he was crazy. "What?" she said. "Yes! Through the window *and* the monitor. I have no fucking clue how she got in there, but if she goes anywhere near the plasma, we're all screwed."

"Wait," Ben said. He had to pause to collect his thoughts.

It had worked. It had really worked. Hestia was out of Hell.

Which meant that she was real.

Which meant that *he* wasn't crazy.

"Rebecca," Ben said. "We should get her out first, in case the shut down destabilizes it." And in case proximity to it during shut down would suck Hestia back into Hell.

Rebecca hesitated and then started to nod. "Right. I'll go," she said.

"No, I'll do it," Ben said. He started for the door.

"She's *naked*, Ben," Rebecca said. "She might be a crazy protestor, but the only thing that will make this worse, aside from her dying in a fire, is if she sues you for sexual harass— What in hell?" She was staring into the room with a growing expression of horror.

Other people were stepping through the plasma window into the chamber.

No. Not people. *Creatures.* Beings with such perfect beauty that it hurt to look at them. All of them carried weapons.

Demons.

Ben took an involuntary step back and his knees almost buckled. They were coming after her.

After Hestia.

Ben screamed her name and ran for the airlock to the chamber.

"Shut it down," he said to Rebecca.

Rebecca continued to stare as the demons kept stepping through the plasma. She shook herself. "Right. Yes."

Ben punched the code to cycle the inner door and yanked his hand back from the controls. It was hot. Heat radiated off the door.

He looked through the thick window set into the outer door. The inner door was open. Hestia stood in the space between them. She put her hand on the outer door. Ripples of heat ran across its surface like the air over a fire.

The door blew open, bringing a Hephaestian stench and a wave of hot, dry air that made it hurt to breathe. Ben backed away, hand to mouth.

Hestia stepped through the door, melting the linoleum under her feet. She looked past Ben to Rebecca and raised her hand as if she were going to wave to the other woman. A ribbon of plasma flowed out of her fingers and wrapped around Rebecca, whose clothes ignited instantly.

Rebecca screamed. She dropped to the floor, rolling. The plasma clung to her like tar. Her hair blazed. She writhed across the tiles.

Ben ran to her, trying to beat the fire out with his hands. Each slap of his hands sent plasma spattering across the room. It burned, but he didn't care.

Rebecca kept screaming, long after there was breath behind it – a high whistling scream that did not belong to anything human. Burning hair and flesh filled the room with their scent.

Ben staggered up, spinning frantically, searching for a fire extinguisher.

The room was filled with demons. More came through

the portal. Awaiting Hestia's command.

Hestia stood between Ben and the fire extinguisher. She put a hand on it and the canister exploded. Ben flinched, ducking as the shrapnel flew across the room.

On the floor, Rebecca had stopped thrashing. The room was quiet except for the sizzle of her muscles cooking.

Ben faced Hestia. She burned, out of Hell.

She walked to him. The heat singed him.

"I loved you," he said.

"Of course you did," she said.

She took hold of him. He was set aflame.

"I rescued you," he whispered.

Hestia set a hand on his cheek, blackening it.

"Oh, love," she said. "Hell was never *my* prison."

She kissed him, his muse of fire.

NANCY KRESS
WRITER'S BLOCK

When Gardner Dozois invited me to write a story which began by ripping off a classic opening line, I had no hesitation over which line to use. No hesitation at all. "It was a dark and stormy night," the opening to Edward Bulwer-Lytton's Victorian novel *Paul Clifford*, has already been stolen over and over again: by Snoopy of the comic strip *Peanuts*, by Madeleine L'Engle for *A Wrinkle in Time*, by Ray Bradbury's novel *Let's All Kill Constance*, and in various forms by Chris Claremont, Terry Pratchett, and singer Joni Mitchell. I wanted to join that august company (especially Snoopy).

Nor did I hesitate about the subject of my story. Writer's block is the dread of every writer: What if one day I sit down at the computer, reach for the words, and they're not there? Even those of us not usually subject to this problem – and I'm one of them – know that it could happen. Wells run dry, crops wither on the vine, Snoopy cannot come up with a good second line. But not, in my story, for Rob Carpenter – or at least, not exactly. So: Here is "Writer's Block."

WRITER'S BLOCK
BY NANCY KRESS

It was a dark and stormy night. But it shouldn't have been.

"What the—" Carson said.

"Too much bloody wind!" Anna bent closer to the screen, as if that might give her a different reading. "You were only supposed to mix the atmospheric layers enough to keep them from separating!"

"I did!" Carson cried. He was an intern and so vulnerable, and this was not helped by a volatile streak that had worried Anna before.

She reached across him and adjusted the air-mixing drafts within the sealed biodome, three miles away on the Scottish moors. The wind inside the biodome did not die down; it increased.

Carson cried, "Something's wrong with the equipment, then!"

Anna shoved him out of the chair and sat at the console, typing rapidly to bring up the system diagnostics. The air-mixture subsystem did not respond, nor did the stored power in the solar heaters. The temperature numbers dropped.

Under the impermeable dome, the dropping temperature brought on condensation. It began to rain.

It was a dark and stormy night. But it shouldn't have been.

"You promised me an evening full fair, and a bright

211

moon," the queen said evenly. Her rosy bottom lip caught lightly between her small, even, very white teeth.

"Your Grace… the portents said…" The astrologer quaked in his bedsocks. He had not had time to pull on boots before the page had wakened him – at midnight! – with a summons to the privy chamber. A bright fire glowed on the hearth, the queen's woman, Emma, waited respectfully in the shadows, and rain pelted against the small-paned windows. Lightning crackled, followed by thunder.

"I had thought, on the promise of your words, to ride out tonight," the queen said, and indeed she wore a riding habit of green velvet, striking with her red hair, and a green velvet hat. "You told me to rely on you."

"I… the portents…" Where could she have been going at midnight?

"I will not forget this, Master Astrologer."

"No, no, Your Grace… I mean, yes…"

He didn't know what he meant. She burned people at the stake.

"You may go," she said, and he skittered from the chamber, but not before he heard her say to the page, "Summon my Master of Horse. I will ride anyway."

More lightning split the clouds.

It was a dark and stormy night, but it shouldn't have been.

"Can he hear us?" Celia whispered.

"I don't know," James said.

Of course I can hear you, you fuckers, Jason thought. He could hear everything his unfaithful wife and his treacherous brother said, even over the storm in the hospital room. He heard the hum of the machinery hooked to him at nose and heart and arm and toes, the rubber wheels of a trolley in the corridor.

"I wish I knew what to do," Celia moaned.

"You must be strong, darling," James said.

Don't pull the plugs, Celia! Jason thought. *I'm in here! I can hear you!*

And then, all at once, he couldn't. All he could hear was wind and rain and the crack! of lightning that shouldn't have been happening, not inside his head.

The storm increased, and then he saw—

What the fuck?

It was a dark and stormy night, but it shouldn't have been.

KZQQ predicted only a ten percent chance of rain, 652 Elm Street sent to 653.

But their accuracy rate is only seventy-three percent, 653 Elm Street sent back.

Two people, both on the facial-recognition approved list, entered 652 and took the elevator to the sixth floor. The Johnsons were having a party. In 3-C, a faucet began to drip and a report went to Human Maintenance.

652 sent, *Even so, if the meteorologists—*

An explosive sound in 6-A. The sound was in the deebee: gunfire. A figure, hooded and masked, ran from the apartment. 652 immediately put itself into lock-down. It made no difference; the running figure held a jammer. In less than a minute, he or she was out the side door and running down the alley. 652 sent an emergency call to 911.

653 sent, *What was that?*

I think it was a murder!

"Which one do you like?" Rob asked his wife. The question came out humble – but, then, what did not when he talked to Karen? His belly clenched and cramped.

She stood with the printouts in her hand, lips pursed, long polished nails holding the pages as if they had just been removed from the bottom of the parrot's cage instead of from Rob's HP. The parrot squawked derisively. The nails were blood red.

"I don't like any of them," she said.

He tried to breathe evenly. "Why not?"

"Oh, Rob, come on – the pathetic fallacy? That weather embodies human feelings? It was old when Wordsworth did it."

"This isn't Wordsworth—"

"Obviously."

"—it's an opening in four different genres to, you know, get my feet wet again. Family drama, science fiction, romance, mystery. The mystery is supposed to be a sort of comedy, kind of. Every possible detective has already been used – butcher, baker, candlestick maker – so these detectives are two buildings who solve murders."

"Buildings?"

"You know, smart-system buildings. They cooperate."

"*Buildings.*"

"Or I might have one building and a side-kick that is a garden shed."

Karen dropped the pages on the floor. "Sure, why not? Even though there are no 'Elm Streets' anymore because there are no elms anymore. They all died of disease. And 'a dark and stormy night'! Maybe you could get Snoopy to blurb the book." She walked out of his study.

Rob picked up his printouts. Was Karen right? She usually was. She was smarter than he was, more decisive, more... *there*.

Too much there.

He squashed the heretical thought – Karen was a wonderful wife! She told him so, often – and laid the pages on his desk, which looked as barren as his imagination. Truth was, he had had these four openings for six months now, which was the last time he'd written anything. But now he was going to get moving again! He was! And he had a secret weapon!

From a drawer he took out the Barnes & Noble bag and drew out the first of a stack of books: *Writing That Best Seller You Know You Have Somewhere In You!* In the index he found "block, writer's" and then the relevant page with advice in big capital letters:

> THE ANSWER TO BEING "STUCK" IS SIMPLE:
> ADD ANOTHER PERSON, COMPLICATION,
> OR IDEA TO YOUR STORY TO GET IT MOVING
> AGAIN! GUARANTEED! SOMETIMES YOU
> CAN EVEN INCORPORATE ELEMENTS FROM
> SOMETHING ELSE YOU'RE WORKING ON!

Rob sat down at the computer. The parrot – it was Karen's parrot but she didn't want it in the main part of the house – squawked and dropped a seed husk on his head. Outside the window, clouds roiled and blew.

It was a dark and stormy night. But it shouldn't have been.

"You promised me an evening full fair, and a bright moon," the queen said evenly. Her rosy bottom lip caught lightly between her small, even, very white teeth.

"Your Grace… the portents said…" The astrologer quaked in his bedsocks. He had not had time to pull on boots before there was a clap of thunder and a vision appeared in the privy chamber: three people strangely dressed, one lying on a bed with tubes and filigree running into his body. Sorcery indeed!

"Don't pull the plug, Celia!" the man on the bed shouted. "I'm in here! I can hear you!" The other two people, a man with his hand on the breast of a woman, did not seem to hear. Behind the vision, the hearth fire crackled, sharp as the lightning outside.

"What evil is this?" cried the queen, drawing back in terror, just as the man rose from the bed and—

Okay, not *those* two stories. Rob hit Delete and tried again.

It was a dark and stormy night. But it shouldn't have been.

"What the—" Carson said.

"Too much bloody wind!" Anna bent closer to the screen, as if that might give her a different reading. "You were only supposed to mix the atmospheric layers enough to keep them from separating!"

"I did!" Carson cried. Under the sealed biodome three miles away on the Scottish moors, two smart buildings swayed in the gale.

Look out! 652 sent. *I'm losing bricks! Warn your people not to—*

A loose brick blew off its eaves and smashed the skull of a man staggering against the wind toward the door. The dropping temperature brought on condensation and it began to rain.

Rob put his head in his hands. His belly hurt again.

Karen was out of town, at yet another academic conference. Lately academia had been holding a lot of conferences. Rob supposed it had something to do with English department politics. Nearly everything did.

While she was gone, he went down to the drugstore to pick up more Maalox. A cleaning crew had invaded the house and were flinging around his grandmother's antiques, scrubbing and polishing. Rob couldn't remember what this set of professional cleaners called themselves; Karen changed companies almost as often as decorators. His trust fund could stand it, of course, but even so…

Sometimes he had dreams of a small cottage with a single chair drawn up before the hearth, a table for his computer, and a narrow bed.

The girl behind the photo counter beckoned to him.

"You Mr. Carpenter?"

"Yes…"

"Well, are you or aren't you? Don't you know?"

"Yes," he said, more firmly. "I'm Mr. Carpenter."

"Yeah, I seen you in here before. Your pictures are ready."

Rob hadn't ordered any pictures. But she was already holding out a white envelope toward him, her expression commanding. How did such a short, young person have so much confidence? She had purple hair, black lipstick, pierced nose, and enough eyeliner to tag the side of a building. Her employee tag said VIOLET. He had never seen anyone less like that shy and delicate flower.

She said, "Why the fuck does anybody still use film?"

"I don't," Rob tried to say, but she talked over him.

"I mean, it has a nostalgic quality and all, but digital gives you the capacity to create *amazing* photographic art."

"I don't—"

"I'm an art major at the university. I know. That's six-forty, please. Did you see the photo exhibit at the gallery on Carrington Street? You should. I can't believe anybody hasn't been yet. Six dollars and forty cents!"

He handed her the money. It seemed easier. She was a gale, an irresistible wind.

In his Lexus (Karen's purchase), he looked at the white envelope. Yes, it said "R Carpenter" – unless that was an "L." Smudging on top of bad penmanship. He slid out the photos.

Karen, naked beneath the hairy back of a man with long blond hair.

Rob sat staring at the photos. A colleague? A graduate student? *"Why the fuck does anybody still use film?"* To control the copies.

Rain streaked the windshield. Carefully, as if they might break, Rob slid the photos back into the white envelope. Fingers trembling, he opened the bottle of Maalox. Some of it spilled onto the envelope and he wiped it off, as panicky as if acid had fallen on a medieval manuscript. He swigged down a quarter bottle of Maalox.

This wasn't a thing he could discuss with Karen on the phone. Unthinkable. It would have to wait until she returned on Tuesday. Yes.

He recognized the feeling that swept over him then: relief. He could put off the confrontation with his cheating wife for a few days; he was temporarily safe. It was such a shaming realization that again he reached for the Maalox, while the rain made long dirty tracks down the window.

It was best to keep busy. Everybody knew that. When anxious or depressed, keep busy.

Rob sat down at his keyboard. He stared at it until his eyes crossed, his vision blurred, and QWERTY became CUE DIX. Other than that advice (Dix who? Cue about what?), his mind was numb, a cold white entity in a blank white room.

The second book in his Barnes & Noble bag, titled *Plot or Die*, had a cover illustration of tombstones fashioned of sagging and failed-looking books. It also had a section on writer's block. He read:

"The secret to never getting stuck on a manuscript is to genuinely inhabit your protagonist. Become him or her. This is akin to Method acting – you must so fully enter into your character's very being that you feel with their fingers, ache with their hearts, be flooded with their thoughts. Then your story will automatically move forward because you will *know* what they do next. You will be in the story, and astonished at how simple this technique is once you fully try it!"

Fully doing anything sounded good to Rob. He had been wandering around the house, picking things up and setting them down, unable to eat or sleep. Maybe it would help to become somebody else.

Of course I can hear you, you fuckers, Jason thought. He could hear everything his unfaithful wife and his treacherous brother said, even over the storm in the hospital room. He heard the hum of the machinery hooked to him at nose and heart and arm and toes, the rubber wheels of a trolley in the corridor. He was trapped in this motionless and unconscious body, but he could—

He was trapped in this motionless and unconscious body. Rob couldn't move his arms, his legs, his eyelids. He was lying on a hospital bed and—

No. He wasn't. He was in his study, and the parrot had somehow pooped through the bars of its cage and onto Rob's shoulder. The bird squawked at a squirrel, which had just leaped from Karen's yew topiary to the windowsill. A squirrel had bitten Rob when he was eight, and he hated them. They were just rats in camouflage.

Downstairs, the front door opened. A suitcase dropped in the hall. Karen was back.

Scenes like this one, Rob discovered, never ended. They started but they didn't finish because even if there were breaks – she goes to work, you go to the bathroom, everybody pretends to go to sleep – the whole miserable thing just resumed again the next time you were together, with no end in sight. It was like the *Rocky* films, or a football game with a clock that never ran out.

"You had no right to open my pictures!" Karen said. She had always been good on offense.

"You're having an affair!" Rob said, trying a play enfeebled by repetition.

"And whose fault is that? If you and I ever had sex, I might not look for it elsewhere!"

"But it was you who—"

"No, it wasn't! You're never here!"

This feint confused Rob. "I'm always here."

"That's what I mean! You never leave the house, don't have any friends – you just wander around living inside your head, always physically present and never emotionally there!"

"But I—"

"Never!"

Rob tried a Hail-Mary pass, his last and most desperate attempt to score. "I should divorce you and take my trust fund with me."

"Go ahead!"

Not the right response – what was in her play book? Karen faced him defiantly, breathing hard, the gleam of triumph in her eyes. Why triumph? He'd always suspected she'd married him mostly for the money, anyway. His head hurt. To his own horror, he was afraid he might cry.

"Karen…"

She saw immediately that she'd defeated him. "Go to bed, Rob. I'm going to sleep in the guest room."

He went, desolate and humiliated and angry. Also confused – what was he missing here?

In the morning, she had left for the university, but in the kitchen were a fresh pot of coffee and his favorite cinnamon rolls, still warm from the oven. What did that mean?

He didn't dare call her at work; she never allowed that. He went to his study and stared at the third book on writing, *Get It Down and Get It Sold!* This one, co-authored by two romance writers, shimmered with motherly concern:

"Writer's block is the feeling that your story simply will not move ahead. It feels terrible, doesn't it? We're not going to offer you easy fixes for this. But there is something that works for us. Go back to the last point in your story where you were excited about it, and start again from that place. That's where your story still had the necessary spark. Delete everything after that."

Rob scrolled back through his story, looking for the last place he was excited about any of his openings. He deleted everything else, then stared at what was left, the part with spark:

It was a dark and—

His stomach hurt.

He ran out of Maalox. All the way to the drugstore, his belly ached and rumbled. Violet had migrated from the photo counter to checkout, where she stood scowling at a magazine. When he approached with the jumbo-sized bottle, she held it out to him accusingly. "Look at that! Just look at that!"

The magazine was *Time*, and the article a report on the art show of someone Rob had never heard of. Facing pages displayed canvasses of stylized street scenes.

"And they call that art!" Violet said. "He should be shot!"

"Just this bottle," Rob said. Pain shot through his stomach.

"That stuff's no good for you, Mr. Carpenter," Violet said. "If you're having indigestion, you need to eat better. Like, what did you have for breakfast?"

"Cinna— God!" Pain so sharp he doubled over in agony. Violet rushed from around the counter.

"Hey! What is it!"

Another lacerating pain, and he fell to the floor. "Call…" he tried to gasp, but she was already there, efficiently talking to 911 on her cell, summoning the manager with a little bell, loosening his belt. As she bent over him, the jewelry in her pierced nose became clear: a filigree moon imposed on a filigree sun imposed on a jagged bolt of lightning, all exquisitely miniature. It was the last thing Rob saw before he fainted.

A hospital room. A stomach pump. Blood in his vomit. Then blessed, artificially induced sleep, and when he woke again, it was to the newly cleansed feeling of a long fast, or of Saturday morning confession as a boy. *Bring it on, God, even unto being hit by a Mack truck – I'm covered.*

Karen sat in a chair by his bed, marking student papers on a clipboard. Before she noticed him, he watched her slash red marks all over some poor chump's efforts. In her severe, rectangular glasses she looked formidable.

"Rob! You're awake!"

Voice sweet and concerned – why? After the first shock, Rob didn't care. Karen was as he remembered from the first days of his courtship. She fluffed his pillow. She laughed at his jokes. She raced down to the cafeteria to bring him a gelatinous mess that called itself chocolate pudding. She kissed him on the lips when she left. So this was what all those Country and Western songs meant! You never did appreciate what you had until you nearly lost it! His bout of illness had reminded Karen that she loved him. As for the photo… Well, anyone could slip once. She had just assured him, with tears in her eyes, that it had been that.

Lying in bed with his arms crossed behind his head, Rob smiled and glowed and watched the sun shine outside his window. He and Karen would weather this. And then they would be stronger together afterward, just like in that song by what's-his-name, the guy with the guitar who—

A doctor came in. "Mr. Carpenter?"

"Yes." He was Mr. Carpenter and Karen – gloriously – was Mrs. Carpenter. Rob smiled at the doctor.

"I'd like to ask you a few questions."

"Sure."

"Are you under a psychiatrist's care?"

"No."

"Have you ever been hospitalized with a psychiatric condition?"

"No!"

"Have you ever been diagnosed at any time with pica disease?"

"No – what's that?" Rob became worried. Was it some weird form of cancer?

"Are you a gardener, Mr. Carpenter?"

"No." He hated yard work and so had hired a gardener. "Why? What is this about?"

"Your blood work and toxin screen turned up a strange substance: yew bark. Do you know how you might have ingested that?" The doctor's eyes were sharp.

"No," Rob said. But all at once he did.

Karen was trying to kill him.

There were cops, but Rob lied to them. He said he'd had childhood episodes of pica disease, once he'd looked it up on his phone ("a medical disorder characterized by an appetite for substances largely non-nutritive: e.g. metal, clay, coal, etc.") Lately, he said, the craving had returned. The cops wrote it down, scowled at him, and clumped off, weighed down by their guns, phones, and disgust.

There was another visit from Karen, sweet as before. Rob laughed along with her and thought, *You want my money.*

Badly enough to kill me for it. So why not turn her in? She obviously deserved it, and it would keep him safe. Why not? He kept that question to mull over after she left.

Before he could do so, he had two more visitors. First came John from next door, who stayed an embarrassed ten minutes and escaped like a man fleeing a tornado. A duty visit. Please, no more like that!

Into the hospital room walked Violet from the drugstore. "Hey, Rob."

Rob blinked, torn between surprise at seeing her and surprise that he was no longer "Mr. Carpenter." Then he understood: illness had demoted him. But why had she come? And she looked different somehow, although he couldn't tell how. The hair was just as purple, the eyeliner just as heavy, the lipstick just as black, nose just as pierced.

"Hi," he said weakly. He didn't feel weak, but maybe lassitude would make her leave. He wanted to be alone to think about Karen.

Violet flopped into the bedside chair. "I came to see how you are. Since you had that attack right there in the store and all, and I was the one who called 911. Wow, you got a private room."

"I'm fine!" Rob said, too brightly. "Going home tomorrow!"

She looked at him steadily. The look became a gaze, the gaze became a lance, piercing right into Rob's skull. It went on and on, and he couldn't look away. Outside the window, thunder sounded.

Finally Violet said, "Okay," and Rob gave a little gasp, as if she'd released him.

She ignored the gasp, but wasn't done with him. "Only you're not okay, are you? You have imagination."

It was the last thing he'd expected her to say, and she pronounced it as if it were a disease, like "pica." Rob must have looked baffled because she added, "Impotent imagination."

Indignation spread through him.

She grinned. "No, not that kind of impotence. I mean, you imagine things, but can't make them come true. Am I right?"

He riposted feebly. "Everybody imagines things they can't make true."

"Not everybody. I can make mine come true," she said complacently. "I'm going to be a great artist."

She was so young. "Well, I… I hope you are."

Violet leaned closer, studying him. "Wow – you really mean it. Most people when they hope good things for you, they really don't mean it because if you fail, they look better."

There was a German word for that, but Rob couldn't remember what it was. Karen would know.

"I like you," Violet said. "I mean, even beyond pity for your stunted imagination."

Rob almost blurted: *My imagination is not stunted!* But then he remembered all those failed novel openings and looked down at his blanket. Thin and white and shabby. Stunted.

"Here," Violet said, with so much unexpected gentleness that he looked up again. "Take this. I want you to have it. But only for a little while – you have to give it back when I come for it. Okay?"

She unscrewed the thing-a-doody from her pierced nose and held it out to him. Rob hesitated – was this sanitary? – but he didn't want to hurt her feelings, and so he took it. "Uh…wow. Thanks."

"You don't know what it is, do you?"

"A piercing… uh, jewelry. But, Violet, I'm not going to get my—"

"Of course not. Just keep it in your pocket and rub it when your imagination fails, okay?"

All at once, she didn't look so young. "Er, okay." At the

moment, in a backless hospital gown, he had no pockets.

"And remember, you have to give it back when I come for it." She pulled a shiny bag from her tote, a huge cloth bag emblazoned with paintbrushes. "Want some fruit gummies?"

"No thanks."

"Okay. I'm glad you're feeling better. Bye now."

"Bye."

She left Rob feeling dazed, and then stuck her head back into the room. "If you lose my talisman," she said cheerfully, "I'll have to kill you."

Which would make two women trying to do that. "I won't lose it!"

"Good. Bye."

Gingerly, Rob examined the nose jewelry, which felt faintly greasy from skin oil or makeup or something. The filigree work really was exquisite, delicate silver tracings of a crescent moon imposed on a rayed sun imposed on a jagged bolt of lightning. Rob put it in the drawer of his bedside table.

He went home the next morning, after promising to see a therapist. Karen went to work each day. Rob spent long hours trying to decide whether she had tried to murder him, whether she might try again, whether he was being paranoid, and why he hadn't spoken about this to the doctor, the police, or Karen herself. The only one of these questions to which he had an answer was the last, and the answer shamed him.

If he accused her – rightly or wrongly – she might leave him. And he could not imagine life without her. With few friends and no occupation except for his failed writing, he had anchored his life to Karen's presence, to Karen's decision-making, to Karen's beauty. Without her, he would be adrift.

Was it really so hard to just shop for and cook all the household food? He had the time.

What if she moved on to a gun or a knife? But she wouldn't. Not her style at all – too messy.

He tried to distract himself by lumbering up to his study. There was still one book left in the B & N bag: *Write It, Sell It, Rake in Royalties!* He read: "The best thing to do for writer's block is…. *nothing*. Just sit at the computer for three hours. Eventually, you will get so bored that you will write."

Nothing. Well, certainly Rob could do that. He had been doing nothing for most of his life.

He sat at the keyboard.

And sat.

And sat.

A squirrel ran across the windowsill.

The furnace in the basement came on, then went off.

A spider inched down the wall and disappeared into the baseboard.

Half of a cracker decomposed quietly under the printer stand.

And, eventually, Rob began to write. Unfortunately, it was exactly what he had written before.

It was a dark and stormy night. But it shouldn't have been.

"You promised me an evening full fair, and a bright moon," the queen said evenly. Her rosy bottom lip caught lightly between her small, even, very white teeth. Her—

Her what? He couldn't remember even his own pathetic words! Frustrated, Rob stood and jammed his hands into his pockets to keep them from pounding on the computer screen. His left fingers rubbed Violet's nose jewelry.

Without hope, he began to type:

—lover burst into the privy chamber, naked except for a helmet, and carrying a sword. Rob would recognize that back anywhere! It was the blond man from Karen's photograph. The queen, in a green velvet riding habit with a velvet hat, stared at Seth and yelled for her Master of Horse. Outside the window, a storm howled.

The naked man turned on Rob. "You promised her an evening full fair!"

"I… I…" Rob stammered. He what? What the fuck was going on?

The naked knight lunged. Rob yelped and ducked behind a heavy trestle table. Frantically he fumbled for Violet's charm. As soon as he rubbed it, he was—

—back in his study, shaking.

"I'm home!" Karen called brightly up the stairs. "You up there, Rob?"

Was he? Where was he? Where had he been? Rob stared at the charm. Karen came up the stairs.

"I thought it might be fun to eat take-out from that new Thai place everybody's raving about, so I picked up some on my way home." She held two white Styrofoam boxes.

Rob stared at the boxes, then at Karen, then again at the boxes. One gaped open slightly at a corner. Had she put—

He fainted. But even as he fell, his fist clutched tightly on Violet's charm.

The next morning, Rob lay in bed as if the sheets were a minefield. Determination stormed through him. Also hunger – he had eaten nothing for a day and a half. ("Must be some sort of stomach flu!" he'd gasped to Karen after his brief faint.) When Karen's car pulled out of the driveway, he leapt out of bed.

One box of take-out, the one with the gaping corner, sat in the refrigerator topped with a post-it note: *Yummmm!* The other box, empty, was in the trash. Rob carried lahb gai upstairs, scraped it onto the windowsill of his study, and waited. In less than five minutes a squirrel dropped from the yew topiary, ate the food, and scampered away. Two hours later he found the animal stiff and dead in the yard.

He felt no compunction, not for a squirrel. But now he knew.

She had always been the most determined woman he ever met.

Back in his study, Violet's charm in his pajama pocket and his entire body trembling, he first researched on the Internet (*Write Your Way to Fame and Glory*: "Know your subject thoroughly!"). Then he rubbed and typed and jumped into places that had never existed before he created them. Banal and clichéd places, maybe, with trite characters – but *his*.

It was a dark and stormy night. But it shouldn't have been.

"What the—" Carson said.

"Too much bloody wind!" Rob bent closer to the screen, as if that might give a different reading. "You were only supposed to mix the atmospheric layers enough to keep them from separating!"

"I did!" Carson cried. He was an intern and so vulnerable, and this was not helped by a volatile streak that had worried Rob before.

Rob reached across him and expertly adjusted the air-mixing drafts within the biodome. He knew just what to do. It was important to keep the atmospheric trace minerals from stratifying at the top of the dome, to keep the trees growing stress wood and thus avoid etiolation, to keep vital free chemicals from locking up. He, Rob, *knew*.

It was a dark and stormy night, but it shouldn't have been.

"Can he hear us?" Celia whispered.

"I don't know," James said.

"I can hear you," Rob said, sitting up in the hospital bed. "And I know what you've been up to!"

Celia screamed. James, no naked blond stud capable of sword play, turned pale and trembled.

It was a dark and stormy night, but it shouldn't have been.

KZQQ predicted only a ten percent chance of rain, 652 Maple Avenue sent to 653.

But their accuracy rate is only seventy-three percent, Rob sent back. It felt odd to be a building, but no odder than his usual life. Just as stationary, just as wind-battered. And when the murderer ran from the lobby, Rob would perform better than 653 Maple Avenue. He'd researched everything the very latest smart tech could do, and he would install it into his story. The killer was toast.

The most important story, however, would have to wait until Karen got home. All the rest of the day, Rob prepared.

She came with more take-out, but without the bright and sweet smile. This was commanding Karen, to whom he had once been so grateful for taking charge of his life. "Sweet Karen," he'd called her during their courtship, and she hadn't even mentioned how hackneyed the endearment was. Not then, anyway.

"Now, Rob, you have to eat. You need to keep your strength up. Look, I brought your very favorite: lemon chicken from Live to Eat."

The chicken smelled wonderful. Rob could picture the crisp slices in their delectable sauce, tart and savory. His mouth watered.

Strong! He must be strong!

He had never been strong. Karen had been the strong one, although now he realized that possibly he had mistaken her indifference for strength. It was easy to remain calm and unemotional when you didn't care much. It wasn't as if his trust fund had ever been threatened.

"It smells great, honey," he told her. "But let me get a bottle of wine from the cellar, to go with it."

Instantly she was suspicious. "What are we celebrating?"

"I wrote part of a story today."

"Oh. That." But she recovered. "Great! Get the wine."

When he returned, she was at his computer: reading, scrolling, smiling derisively. Rob held a bottle of very good Josmeyer Pinot Gris by its slim green neck.

"What do you think?"

"Isn't this the same thing you wrote before?"

"Not exactly," Rob said, peering over her shoulder, pulling the charm from his pocket and transferring it to the same hand that held the wine.

It was a dark and stormy night. But it shouldn't have been.

"You promised me an evening full fair, and a bright moon," the queen said evenly. Her rosy bottom lip caught lightly between her small, even, very white teeth.

"Your Grace... the portents said..." The astrologer quaked in his bedsocks. He had not had time to pull on boots before the page had wakened him – at midnight! – with a summons to the privy chamber. A bright fire glowed on the hearth, the queen's woman, Emma, waited respectfully in the shadows, and outside, rain pelted down and lightning cracked.

"I had thought, on the promise of your words, to ride out tonight," the queen said, and indeed she wore a riding habit of green velvet, striking with her red hair, and a green velvet hat. "You told me to rely on you."

"I... the portents...." Where could she have been going at midnight?

"I will not forget this, Master Astrologer."

"None of us will forget this," Rob said, astonished at his own perfect line of dialogue. Practically Merchant Ivory! He seized Karen from behind, his free hand circling her body and lifting her from the chair. His other fingers rubbed the charm gripped against the wine bottle, and his study vanished.

Karen screamed. The astrologer screamed. The queen screamed. Her woman screamed. Rob, silent, let go of Karen and smashed the wine bottle against the trestle table. Pinot Gris flew everywhere. Quick as a dancer, Rob moved behind the door just as the naked blond man burst into the room, waving his sword. Rob leaped behind him and slashed the jagged edge of the glass across the back of the man's neck. Blood spurted out, mixing with the Pinot Gris.

"Carl!" Karen screamed.

"Don't worry," Rob said. "He's only fictional."

The queen had recovered herself, and so had her woman. Both of them rushed forward, the queen with Carl's fallen sword. But Rob had been writing all afternoon. He held up his hand and said, "Your Grace, stop. He was a traitor come to ravish and slay you, and I have slain him instead. I am the Master Mage foretold in the Prophecy of m'l'Clerabin!"

The queen stopped, uncertain.

"Elizabeth," he said gently, "wasn't I prophesied? In the Book of Prophecy that you were reading only today? Look, I bear the mark!" He lifted his tee-shirt to show the tattoo he'd gotten at the county fair when he was sixteen. It had been a skull but had faded to look more like a piece of Swiss cheese.

The queen had courage (he had written her that way). Her chin lifted and she said, "Have you come for good or evil?"

Oh, this was thrilling! But Rob didn't have much time. Her Master of Horse would be here in moments.

"For good to you, my liege. Your reign will be long and glorious. And I bring you a treasure, my ward, who will serve you long and faithfully. Take care of her well."

Karen, who had been looking dazed, said, "Now wait a minute—"

"Bye, Karen," Rob said, rubbed his charm, and vanished just as the very muscular Master of Horse burst into the privy chamber and Emma, the queen's stalwart woman, rushed forward to throw a chamberpot at him. Rob thought that was a great touch: just the sort of gritty detail that lifted his story above the usual sentimental romance.

The last thing he heard was the crack! of thunder from the storm outside.

In his study, he deleted the story from his files and burned the hard copies in the fireplace, watching the flames dance and flicker like lightning.

There was an inquiry, of course. There were repeated bouts of questions from detectives, a blitz of press coverage, sideways glances from neighbors. But there was no body, no evidence of foul play, and Rob's unshakeable story that he had been asleep when Karen came home, had not seen her, and had no idea what had happened. He was a little surprised that he turned out to be such a good liar. Also pleased – what was fiction, after all, but skillful lying?

"It won't make you a better writer," Violet said when she came for her nose jewelry.

She just appeared in his kitchen as he was making a ham sandwich. Rob gaped at her, and an irrational fear sliced through him. But he had, after all, been expecting her sooner or later, and he'd taken good care not to lose her charm. (*"If you lose my talisman, I'll have to kill you."*) She still wore too much eye makeup, but her hair was now orange and her lipstick cherry-red. She carried a large cloth tote bag with an alternating pattern of butterflies and daggers.

"I—"

"I know," she said, "you want to thank me. But you shouldn't, really. You still have stunted imagination, poor guy."

"I do not!"

She sighed and held out her hand. Rob took her nose jewelry from his pocket and – reluctantly – handed it to her.

Violet sniffed. "Why does it smell funny?"

"I cleaned it for you. With silver polish."

She laughed. "Oh, you poor sad man."

"I don't see why you would say that!"

"No, of course you don't. Is that ham and provolone? Can I have half?"

He gave the sandwich to her. She sat on a high stool at his kitchen counter, talking with her mouth full. "Did you clean my talisman because it had blood and expensive wine on it?"

Rob stared. "Do you… you mean you know…"

"Of course I know. What do you think I am?"

Actually, he had no idea.

"There aren't many of us in any generation," she mused around a mouthful of sandwich. "Geniuses, I mean. People with genuinely powerful imaginations. Will, of course. Isaac. Leonardo."

Rob took another of the kitchen stools. His legs felt a bit wobbly. Shakespeare? Newton? Da Vinci?

Violet continued, "And Albert, who was a *really* interesting case. That's not my field, of course, but he laid bare the main principle. If imagination is big enough – has enough mass and solidity – it can bend reality. Reshape the usually straight-forward nature of it. All kinds of reality – light, art, consciousness."

"Violet…" Now Rob was really afraid.

"You didn't really have writer's block, you know. Writer's block happens to writers who have written and then can't. You just had your poor stunted imagination. Not," she said with an air of scrupulous fairness, "that you weren't justified in what you did. She was a bitch and a half. And you were actually kinder than I thought you'd be. Your trite fantasy queen put together out of old movies and other people's novels – she'll treat Karen just fine. Actually, I thought you'd kill her."

"It—"

"But you're not a killer. I should have seen that." She frowned. "Why didn't I see that?"

"Violet—"

"Well, I'm young yet. Even a genius needs time to grow her talent. Do you have any milk?"

Rob brought the milk from the refrigerator.

"I need a glass," she said patiently.

He brought a glass. She drank the milk and swiped the back of her hand across her lips.

"I like you, Rob Carpenter. I liked you right from the start of this. But I have to protect myself. You're a terrible writer, but you *are* a writer. Writers are the worst gossips in the world. Well, they get paid for it, don't they? Eventually you'll talk about me. I can't have that."

"Violet, don't—"

"Here," she said gently, and pulled a book from her tote. "You'll need this."

A small book, blank cover, with writing so tiny that Rob had to squint to make it out. Names, written in capital letters on the left-hand sides of pages, were easier to read: VIOLA, KENT, ROSALIND, CALIBAN.

"But this is… is…"

"I had it photocopied at twenty-five percent of the size and then bound. A real pain in the ass. Here, you need these, too." From her tote she pulled a clear plastic bag full of crumpled cloth.

"Violet," Rob whispered, "don't—"

"I have to. Real artists are ruthless, don't you know that?

We'd run over our mothers if it would help our art. In fact, I did! Aww... don't cry, Rob. It won't be so bad. You'll be famous, you know. And I promise you it will be interesting. Don't you want interesting? And I *know* you wanted to be a successful writer."

"He's... he's already *there*. The real one! In history! You named him just a minute ago—"

"But this won't be history," Violet said. "This will be a story – your story. A blank page. You were always nervous around a blank page, weren't you? Now you won't have to be. Just copy out the plays in whatever order you like, and ignore all the fuss about who actually wrote them. It would help if you could look enigmatic. Do you think you could practice that?"

"No, but—"

"Too bad. But you'll be fine. It's your story now, Rob."

Violet leaned across the sandwich crumbs on the kitchen counter and looked at Rob steadily. The look became a gaze, the gaze became a lance, piercing right into Rob's skull. It went on and on, and he couldn't look away. His legs tried to run and his hands to clench, but all he could do was clutch more tightly the book and the bag of clothing.

"Oh," she said just before the kitchen vanished, "don't forget to bury the plastic bag. That's the kind of anachronism that bounces a reader right out of the story."

He lay beside a deserted dirt road, at dusk, under a sky of towering black clouds. It was hot. He sat up.

Ruts in the road: wagon wheel tracks. On either side stretched fields of blowing grain bordered by wildflowers, most of which he couldn't name.

Rob put his head in his hands and groaned. How could he do this? There must be a way out, he must be able to go back... But he couldn't see how.

A stunted imagination, she'd said.

But... *some* imagination. A little. Even if she'd pronounced the word like a disease.

He stood and emptied the plastic bag onto a patch of daisies. He wasn't even sure what the items were called – was that velvet thing a doublet? A jerkin? A bodkin? Whatever they were, he stripped and put them on. In the pocket of the silly balloon pants he found a small bag of gold nuggets. Violet had probably gotten the clothing from a costume store or theater back room, but late-sixteenth-century coins were another matter. Gold was good anywhere.

Rob started to dig a hole to bury the plastic bag. All at once he stopped.

"Don't forget to bury the plastic bag. That's the kind of anachronism that bounces a reader right out of the story."

Would it bounce him out, too?

Rob's mood lifted. He had a possible escape hatch, a plot twist that Violet had not foreseen. Well, she was a painter. Rob was the writer. The plastic bag might not wreck his story, but it was something he could try.

He could also try pretending he wrote the plays. *"Interesting,"* she'd said – no arguing with that. And if he really was composing this piece, if he really had control of motivation and plot and all, if he really was free of writer's block...

Well.

In the distance, pale smoke drifted across the darker sky. The cloud rumbled. He would have to reach that cottage, or whatever it was, before full dark.

Rain spattered his head. Hastily, Rob wrapped the little book in the plastic bag and tucked it inside his doublet/ jerkin/bodkin. More thunder, and then lightning forked from sky to ground and rain pelted down. Rob began to run. The road rose and a light gleamed ahead, where the smoke had been. He ran faster.

It was a dark and stormy night.

JACK CAMPBELL
HIGHLAND REEL

I'm best known these days for my *Lost Fleet* series of books. The story I wanted to tell here is set in Scotland, involves supernatural elements, and requires someone to decide what they would do to have what they want. Or, rather, to have what they may think they want. That made it pretty easy to decide on Macbeth as the source for my opening line. I have been wanting to write about the real Highlands for some time, especially since reading the fine books written by John Prebble about Glencoe, Culloden, and the Highland Clearances. We tend to think of history and fantasy as two very different things. History is supposed to be a single, factual narrative, whereas different peoples have different forms of fantasy, and different supernatural things they believe in. Yet the history many people think they know may have far more of fantasy to it than they realize, and those fantasies may have all the power of reality when it comes to the actions of men and women. I hope you enjoy "Highland Reel."

HIGHLAND REEL
BY JACK CAMPBELL

"When shall we three meet again? In thunder, lightning, or in rain?"

Those were the final words I heard my mother say, as storm lashed the rocky coast of Strathglass after we had buried my young brother, he barely ten years of age and now gone from us.

My name is Mary Chisholm, and I am the last. Where my people once lived there is now naught amid the great empty Highlands but the bare stone lines marking where the walls of our homes stood. The lands are empty of people, but not of life, for everywhere stray the sheep our lairds valued more than the people of their clans.

Born in Strathglass north of Loch Ness in the Year of Our Lord seventeen ninety-seven, I lived my first years there in the small stone-walled and turf-roofed home my family shared with our cattle. Springs were fair, summers well and winters ordeals, but we had our small plot held in lease to the laird, whose factor still lived among us even though the laird himself had taken his family to a Lowland city. An unbroken line of twenty-three chiefs of our clan had held Strathglass for the Chisholms, and now the twenty-fourth and his heirs would betray them to bitter exile.

For the sheep came, with the Lowlanders driving them, and our laird took their money in rent for the land where we lived. One day the laird's factor came with agents of the law and told us we must all leave, and before nightfall we stood outside the remnants of our home as the old roof timbers burned from the fires set by the agents. We had heard of other clan lairds expelling their own people but had never believed ours would do us so ill, for by long-held belief the laird was the father, *ceann-cinnidh*, and we the children. What father would treat his children so?

The laird was merciful, my mother said, for though almost all the Chisholms forced from their land were transported to the Americas, we were allowed to lease a couple of acres on the stony coast of Strathglass, the laird's agents bidding us learn to fish and try to grow crops in the thin, tiny patches of soil among the outcrops where salt spray usually killed whatever green managed to sprout. Mother had been strong and clever, but grief for our old home and the awful toil of trying to survive on the coast broke her spirit. She would labor all through the light of days and then sit with empty eyes in the darkness, only repeating that it was the laird's right and God's will and we must obey.

Father, exhausted from working through the days to provide what little he could for us, would slump sipping on illegal whiskey near the small fire in the rude hut we had managed to pile together. He said little, except the one night when I upbraided my mother, demanding to know by what right any man or woman could tear us from the land our ancestors had held.

"Hush, lass," he ordered me, his eyes on the fire. "The Highlanders have always been hated by the Lowlanders. *Mi-run mor nan Gall* we have called that hate since men first walked this land. In the Forty-five, God, too, turned his face from us on the field of Culloden, and since then the Highlanders have been doomed. None can fight the will of

God, girl, and His will was made plain at Culloden, that our race pass from this land."

How to argue with God? Within a month of that my father was swept from the rocks while fishing, drowned and his body lost to the sea. My young brother died that winter, cold, hunger and sickness taking him, and the next day I woke to find my mother gone. A neighbor said he had seen her walking toward the water in the dimness before dawn, but no trace of her ever did I find.

I managed to live through the winter, but as a harsh spring came I faced truth. What hope for a lone girl on the rocky coast? At nearly eighteen years of age I would already have been married but for the lack of suitable men nearby. Perhaps it came from the stubborn independence which had been the despair of both my parents, but I would not now give myself to any man just to survive. I had no future here, and so resolved that I would see my old home again even though we had been ordered not to return. What greater terrors than I had already endured could imprisonment or forced transportation hold for me? So I left the rocks of the coast and walked inland, retracing steps I had never forgotten. I passed a fine new inn built for Lowland visitors and walked a smooth road made to improve the land, the better to serve the trade in wool and mutton.

The Highlanders had beaten back invaders for generations, leaving only graves to mark where the likes of the Norse and more recently the Lowlanders and English had entered the hills at their peril. But the bleating Lowlander Cheviot sheep had defeated the Highlanders. I walked through glens empty but for the flocks of sheep and the rare sight of a distant Lowland shepherd. Of Chisholms, my kin, I saw none.

Finally I reached my goal near the setting of the sun and sank to the ground, my hand touching the line of stones which marked the foundation of a vanished wall. We Highlanders are simple folk, and aside from a blind loyalty to our lairds our greatest weakness may be a love of the land we and our ancestors have known. The cord binding a child to its mother is cut early, but the cord binding a Highlander to the land long endures. Now home, family and the land itself had been taken from me.

Perhaps I swooned. I know not, but as the sun began to flare red near the line of the hills a man's call brought me to my senses. "Lass, are you well?"

He sounded like a Lowlander, but as I rose to my feet I saw a man dressed like no Lowlander, nor like any Highlander. He wore a white shirt of fine fabric and a wondrous garment in place of trousers, something like unto a kilt, but the tartan on it was intricate and finely woven in a pattern I'd never seen. Where the pouch for bullets should have rested in front a great purse of leather hung, trimmed with fur. A gleaming broadsword swung on one hip, the elaborately engraved handle of a dirk rose from a scabbard, and on his head he wore a bonnet as glorious as the rest of his outfit. The man stood tall, his face unlined by sun or weather and his back unbent from labor. To my astonishment the badge on his bonnet bore the hard fern, the sign of my own clan Chisholm.

"Are you well, lass?" the man repeated. With him I saw a young woman, her garments more like those of women I knew but far grander. Though she must have seen more than a score of birthdays, her skin was as fair as that of a newborn and unmarred by worry or work.

This must be a laird and his lady. I looked in vain for the henchman, piper, bard, and gillies I'd been told accompanied such worthies, and curtsied as best I could so they would know my mother had raised me properly. "Thank you, laird, I am well."

Only then did I know who this grand man wearing the badge of my clan must be. He could only be the laird who had betrayed us all to exile.

But before my anger could show itself, the man smiled, revealing teeth so white and straight I wondered at them as well. "Laird? No, lass, not me. I'm but a young man of the Highlands."

A man of the Highlands. "I had not known any young men remained in these parts of the Highlands, except for some of the Lowlander shepherds."

The young woman laughed merrily. "You haven't been in the Highlands, then!"

"Not for years," I admitted.

"And what brings you here now?" the man asked.

"I lived here once." I turned to show him the line of stones, but none were there. All about, the land lay unmarked by any signs that the hand of man had ever rested here. "It's gone," I said, unable to understand.

"Here?" The man laughed in a broad and easy way that held no sting. "Lass, there's no homes here. Down in the village, you mean."

He gestured and I saw such a village as I had only imagined in dreams.

Along wide paths stood houses of stone, some two stories high, and all roofed not with turf but with slate. Lights glimmered in windows of glass such as I had rarely seen, and the lights were those of good candles, not the feeble guttering of lamps fed by poor oil. "No," I whispered. "Such a place is too grand for the likes of me."

"You're obviously sore in need and tired, lass," the lady spoke soothingly. "Come with us, and we will see you fed and rested."

This I understood, for in the Highlands, hospitality is a rule never broken, except for the terrible massacre at Glencoe generations gone. But those were Campbells, and naught good can ever be expected of that clan. These two claimed to be Chisholms like me, and, looking at them, I could not believe them capable of deceit.

I came with them, down to the wondrous village. They took me to a house with stone walls mortared and plastered so no wind came through, windows of rippled glass, finely fitted wooden doors and floors of wood or stone. It was a manse such as I had never set foot within. A great fire warmed the main room, and I sat with the family at a table ringed with chairs. I began eating with my knife and fingers, which was all my family had known, but instead of scorning me those fine people smiled kindly and showed me the use of fork and spoon. We ate mutton, and beef, and oats and barley, such a meal as my memories had dwelt on but far better. The wife brought out pastries, wine, whiskey and ale, and at the end one of the family took up pipes and played.

They gave me afterwards a bed to sleep in with warm blankets. In the gentle dark of night I began to wonder if my swoon at my old home had been the swoon of death. Surely this could only be the heaven of which I had heard. I fell asleep well content if it were so, wondering if my brother and my mother and father would walk over the hill to join me.

Day followed day, each so much like the one before that they ran one into the next. Everyone worked, but not for long and no one seemed fatigued by their labors, yet there was always plenty to be had. I saw no sickness or want. The young men competed at arms and at sports, their brawny muscles rippling in the sun. Some of those handsome young men sought me out. I had little experience with such things and shied from their attentions, but none took it ill. The maidens were equally cheerful, and if any woman among the village had ever suffered in child-birth, it could not be told. Often a story-teller would recite the old tales, of Fionn MacCumhail, also known as Fingal, and his followers the Feinn, still sleeping on every mountain in Scotland, and of the great battle fought by Fingal and the Feinn with the Norse by Laroch, from which but two of the forty Viking ships escaped and they sinking before reaching home. Tales of Ossian the great poet, of King Fergus of Dalriada, and of Columba and Mundus at Loch Leven. Every day seemed a party and a feast, the dancing and the pipes always beckoning.

Truly, if this was not heaven, I knew not what it lacked to be that place.

And yet, as the days passed, unease grew within me. Though they called themselves kin of mine, the people of the village were too strong, too handsome, too merry. I felt crude and ill-matched among them. They used phrases from the Gaelic, but none seemed to speak more than that. I knew the English only because my mother had taught me so, saying that those doomed to serve must know the language of their masters, but here all used the English for common speech. And their dress remained a thing of wonder.

"You call these kilts?" I asked one day of the clothing worn by the men.

"And what else would they be?" The girls with me laughed in the way I was beginning to find too ready and lacking in real feeling.

"A kilt," I explained, "is but a long piece of cloth, wrapped about the man's waist, brought over the shoulder and fastened with a pin. 'Tis well-known that the Highlanders wore the kilt not just by choice but also the necessity of poverty, for we could not afford the trousers of the Lowlanders. Only since the kilt was banned by the English in the Forty-five have rude trousers been seen in the Highlands."

Instead of recent history known to the most ill-learned, I

might have recited a fairy tale. They laughed again. "The kilt banned? Not in the Highlands!"

"Yes, in the Highlands since Culloden! Where else? They wear no kilts in the Lowlands, for it would affront their pride."

"Culloden?" The young man I had first met had been listening and now shook his head with a smile. "I know not that name."

"But the Forty-five," I protested. "Bonnie Prince Charlie and the clans! You cannot have forgotten Culloden, where the swords of the clans failed!"

"The clans endure, as do the Highlands," the young man said. "Our swords will never see defeat. You have been prey to nightmares, lass, and confused their dark visions with the world of light."

I began to wonder if my memories were fancies, for there seemed no place for them here. Yet the longer I stayed, the less I felt at home. I felt as I if had wandered into a tale of Fingal and now lived among the Feinn, yet I wondered if Fingal himself would have felt at home here, or as troubled as I by those like but unlike myself.

Finally one day I went back up the slope to where my home had been and searched in vain for any sign of the stones which had made it. My heart faltered as I again found no trace. If all I thought true was born of dark fancies, then what of my family? Were my memories of them awry as well? They lived now only in me. If those memories were false, what was left of them?

As I stood there irresolute, I became aware of a man on horseback riding up. Why I had not seen him sooner I cannot tell, for his red uniform gleamed, as did the leather of his saddle and tack, and his horse was a fine steed. He wore a sword, too, a long straight blade. I saw the gleam of metal on his collar and knew this must be an officer, for my parents had warned me of such when I was but small.

The officer rode up, dismounted, and inclined his head politely to me. I stared back in wonder, for I had seen but few uniforms in my life.

"I am Lieutenant Calvert of the 21st Foot," the officer stated politely.

"Mary Chisholm, sir," I answered with a curtsey.

"Is that your home?" he asked, pointing to the village.

"Nay, sir. I've been staying there a short while, but my old home is gone. I left my new home along the coast west of Kessock and will not return."

"West of Kessock?" The officer frowned. "I went through there a few days ago. That stretch of coast has nothing but the tumbled remains of a few crude hovels which have been abandoned for decades."

"Perhaps you are mistaken, sir, for I left it not much more than a fortnight ago." He seemed still puzzled, so I dared a question of my own. "What brings you here, sir?"

"I am looking for the Highlanders," the officer answered in a slightly uncomfortable fashion. "My colonel ordered me to undertake the search."

"Highlanders live no more in this land," I said in as steady a voice as I could manage. "Tell your colonel if he seeks soldiers that the only voices heard in these Highlands now are those of the sheep."

"I would have agreed with you until I saw this village," the officer admitted. "But when the queen asked—"

"The queen?" I interrupted, so amazed I forgot my manners to my betters. "Has ought become of King George?"

"King George?" He gave me a puzzled look. "Queen Victoria reigns. The army needs regiments for the fighting in Crimea. Her Majesty asked, 'Where are the Highlanders?' My colonel took that question as a royal command to answer, and so sent me to find them." He swept one hand around. "I've found but few persons in the Highlands, and those not Highlanders. Until now. How came this village to endure while so many others have gone to ruin?"

"I do not know, sir," I told him. "I know not from whence it came. I lived here before we were turned out and sent to the coast." I indicated the unmarred grass near me. "But nothing remains, and a village that I have no memory of sits nearby that has no memory of me."

The officer gazed down at the village. "But it is a Highland town. The men wear kilts."

"Please, sir," I hastened to defend my hosts, "they know nothing of the ban. I know not how, but they know nothing of the Forty-five. Pray do not report them or return with soldiers to take them."

His gaze shifted back to me. "Take them? The ban? Of what?"

"Of... of the kilt."

"But that was long ago. Since then King George IV himself wore a kilt like those I see!"

"George IV?" I felt a strange sensation fill me, as if my whole had filled with icy sea water, and I shivered so I could barely speak. "King George III is dead, then?"

The officer's eyes widened. "For many years. How can someone as young as you be surprised by that? I told you that Queen Victoria rules now. How could you not know?"

"I am lost." I do not know why I said that, but it suddenly felt true.

The officer gave me a sympathetic look, one that felt more real than the habitual kindness of the villagers. "You're distraught. Forgive me. I'm going down into the village. I would feel more at ease if you accompanied me."

Though I wondered at his true motive in asking me

along, I walked beside him while he asked about myself and the village. I answered as best I could, the obedience to the law and authority drilled into me as a child still strong, but this man did not act with the arrogance I had come to expect in those set over me. He actually seemed concerned for me, though I knew not why, but as we spoke more, his worries appeared to lessen.

The people of the village greeted the young officer without surprise, as if his coming had already been known to them. For his part the officer studied the young men and seemed well pleased. "A company of such men would be worth a regiment of ordinary souls."

One man beckoned the officer toward the tavern. "Have a meal and refresh yourself. We'll see to your horse."

The lieutenant went with him. I had not been dismissed and stood unsure for a moment, then followed. When the officer noticed me, he seemed startled, but not displeased.

Inside the tavern, they plied Lieutenant Calvert with platters of food, tankards of ale, and glasses of whiskey. He ate well but drank sparingly, despite their urgings, and asked about the town and the region, the men of the village giving cheerful but vague answers every time.

"The queen needs soldiers for the war in Crimea," Lieutenant Calvert announced. "She has asked for the Highlanders. All able-bodied men of the Highlands are invited to enlist in the queen's service."

"We would not go against the wishes of our queen," a man said in the silence that followed, and I wondered if I had misheard a slight emphasis on the word "our." "But we are loath to leave our homes."

"Yet Highlanders have always done so," the lieutenant challenged him. "Tens of thousands of Highlanders have answered the call, filling dozens of regiments in past wars.

Yet now but three scant regiments of troops can be filled from the Highlands. The queen needs you all."

But though the men applauded the officer's brave talk and the past heroism of regiments from the Highlands, they gave no promises, and the sky grew dark outside. "Stay the night," the villagers urged. The lieutenant agreed cordially enough, and I left for the house where I had been allowed to stay.

The next day, Lieutenant Calvert persisted in seeking volunteers, but the men of the village continued to evade his requests, instead engaging him in their games and competitions. He seemed to enjoy these greatly, and did not appear unhappy when more than one of the village women flirted with him. But he later sought me out. At first he still spoke to me in simple terms; however, as I answered and asked politely of his own self, he seemed gladdened by the form of my replies.

I found myself looking forward to any meeting with the young officer. I knew his station was far above mine, yet silly dreams had long been my only comfort and even now I found solace in them.

Another day went by, and another. Though each day he politely rebuffed the advances of the village women and seemed ever more pleased when with me, Lieutenant Calvert grew steadily less content as the men of the village offered entertainment and delay, but no volunteers for the army. Finally one day, I saw the lieutenant saddle his horse and ride out of the village, face set with determination. My heart fell, but he was back in the evening, seeming perplexed yet also relieved. "Despite all that this village offers, I should not stay," he told me with more than a trace of guilt.

"A man has his duty," I agreed, though I wished I could say other things as well. I had never met a man half so kind or respectful of me as this one.

Lieutenant Calvert looked away and nodded. "Yes. I got

lost today and ended up back here. I need to try to leave once more tomorrow. Will you eat supper with me?" I had unaccountably grown more nervous in his company, not less, but readily assented.

After the meal, the lieutenant smiled at me as if at a friend, taking me aback in a pleasurable way. "Mary Chisholm, though you and I are alike strangers here, can you tell me where the church is?"

"The church?" I sat silent a moment, startled to realize that I knew not the answer. "I have seen no church, sir."

"Where do the folk worship on Sunday?"

I felt myself flushing with embarrassment. "Sir, I cannot say. One day runs into another here, and which one is Sunday I never heard, nor saw any worship services. The plain truth is that I've not thought to ask."

He gave me a curious glance. "You do not seem the sort to not care for her soul."

"I care, sir." I nerved myself to speak the truth. "When the agents came to my people to force us from our homes and our lands, the ministers walked among them, preaching that scripture demanded that we obey those set in authority over us, and warning that the eternal fires awaited any who defied such authority. My soul was troubled less by such fears than the fact that ministers of our good shepherd cared less for His human flocks than for the flocks of Lowlander sheep. Since then, I have placed more stock in the words of the gospels than in the words of ministers."

Lieutenant Calvert smiled again. "You are bold. Do you doubt the authority of those over you?"

I sighed. "Sir, such authority is real and we must obey. Yet I have only seen obligation demanded of those who serve, even though always was I taught that the obligations ran both ways."

"Bold and not unwise," he amended. "I've met few women like you, Mary Chisholm. But isn't it strange to find a village of this size with neither minister nor church?"

"Strange is but a small word for such a thing. Perhaps their minister is away."

"Perhaps. I've asked and received no clear answer. That should be no surprise, because for all this village has, it seems to lack clear answers to anything."

"It has no burial place," I said, only now grasping that nowhere had I seen one. "But perhaps they're like parts of some other clans. The MacDonalds of Glencoe and Stewarts of Ballachulish, I was told, would take their dead to an island in a nearby loch."

"That could be." Lieutenant Calvert shook his head. "I must think."

He rode out again the day after, but was back before the sun had set and sought me out. "Tell me truly. These are your kin, Mary Chisholm?"

"Aye, sir. So they say." I bit my lip then blurted out more. "I do not know these people. I should be happy here, but something feels amiss and I know not what."

"Something *is* amiss," he agreed. "Yes. Will you share an evening meal with me again in the tavern, Mary Chisholm?"

"People will talk," I objected.

"Let them. You help me think and bring me welcome companionship."

"Then I will accept your kind invitation, sir." I expected many a curious glance and whispered comment when we entered the tavern, but the villagers seemed to simply accept things in a way unlike the small places I had known.

Unease built in me through the meal, then I finally spoke of things that sounded absurd to me. "They gossip little here. I have seen no ill will, nor real arguments. The men fight at times, even engaging with dirk and sword or fighting with blows of the fist, yet none ever take lasting injury."

"It is odd," Lieutenant Calvert said in a low voice. "Wonderful and odd, both. This place is what I dreamed to find in the Highlands. I feel as if I have stepped into a novel by Sir Walter Scott."

"I am not unlettered, sir, but my reading is yet weak. I have never heard of this Sir Walter Scott."

"He wrote tales, some of them of the Highlands." Calvert's gesture included the entire great room. "This could be a scene from such a book. Highland warriors like paladins of old and every woman a fair lady. I admit that I feel a strong desire to stay here despite my duty. Have you thought to leave?"

"Where would I go?"

"I understand. But I have tried. There seem to be no boundaries, and yet I cannot ride away, even though duty demands it of me. After hours in the saddle, I find myself turning a hill and see this village before me again. The first day, I thought that I had lost my way. Today, I know I did not turn back here, and yet here I came."

"You rode out each day with no farewells," I said before my better sense could stop me.

He took no offense, instead seeming discomfited. "You could present me with a white feather for that and I would have to accept it. It was very hard to try to leave. I feared that if I had to say farewell to you as well, my resolve would fail me."

I felt a flush rising on my cheeks. "Sir, you are an officer of the army. A gentleman. I am a poor Highland lass."

Lieutenant Calvert shook his head. "But in one of Sir Walter Scott's tales, or others like it, all Highland lasses are ladies as fine as any at the royal court in Westminster. The Highlanders are a noble race in such stories."

"Noble?" I spoke louder than I intended and drew some

glances from the villagers. Casting my voice lower, I spoke with great agitation. "We're a proud people, sir, but we're not fools enough to think the world sees us as *noble*. This Scott is an Englishman despite his name, or a Lowlander? Never did they call Highlanders noble. Savages. Thieves. Idle and slothful. Useless. I have heard all those. But never noble. *Mi-run mor nan Gall*. You have heard of it?" Lieutenant Calvert shook his head again. "The great hatred of the Lowlander for the Highlander. It has always been thus. This writer Scott spoke of others than Highlanders if he used the world noble."

"But if Highlanders are such as these," he said with a tilt of his head to indicate the others in the great room, "they would be seen as noble. Look at them. Every one healthy and strong. It's as if the cholera never came here."

"The cholera?"

"You must know of it." I shook my head and Lieutenant Calvert seemed baffled. "It came before the famines. Between them they killed so many—"

"Famines? In the Highlands? Where?"

This time he took a while to answer, gazing at me as if uncertain of himself. "Everywhere. The last famine started a few years ago and is hardly past as yet. You know nothing of it?"

I felt a chill again and could not speak, but only shook my head like a child.

Lieutenant Calvert spoke very slowly. "You told me when we first met that you had been here about a fortnight."

"About that, yes. It could have been a wee bit longer."

"You believed that George III was still king. I thought you feeble-minded at first and took care with you, though I have since learned that your mind is quick and sharp." Calvert paused as if nerving himself. "What year is it, Mary Chisholm?"

"Eighteen fifteen."

"I left London on August twelfth, eighteen fifty-four. Could you have been here for forty years, Mary Chisholm?"

I stared at him. "No, sir! I haven't even seen twenty winters yet!"

"That's clear enough, and I might wonder at your story, except that you are the only one in this village who gives me answers." As he looked around, his gaze seemed fearful, matching the tight feeling inside me. "It is impossible. How could you have been here forty years, yet not aged? How could this village have kept at bay all the ills which have afflicted this land?"

I took a sudden deep breath as the answer came to me. "Sir, do you know of the Other World? Have you been told of the Second Sight? Of goblins and faeries and witches, and those like *An Duine Mor*, the Big Man who walks at night to herald the coming of great woe? Have you ever heard of the Fair Folk?"

He frowned at me. "I heard tales from my nursemaids as a child, and have read many books that draw on such legends."

"Then tell me, sir, what happens to those who stumble upon the Fair Folk and enjoy their hospitality?"

His frown deepened. "They feast and celebrate for a day or two, but when they leave they find that years have passed—" Lieutenant Calvert's words ceased, then he looked around once more with wonder and fear mingled on his face. "But they're just stories! None of that is real."

"Not real? Who told you such nonsense? Many a soul in Strathglass saw *An Duine Mor* striding through the hills on the nights before we were cast from our homes, and my own mother had the Sight come upon her once. A spark appeared from nowhere to alight on her arm and burned her not, then vanished, and by that she knew that my brother would die that day. Certainly the tales are real." I tapped the table between us. "Real enough for your wine glass to rest upon." Then I grimaced and my voice dropped lower. "But I do not understand. These are not as the Fair Folk were told to me, else I would have known who they were long before now. This village pays homage to the old tales, to Fionn MacCumhail and his like, but neither he nor his Feinn would belong here, I think. These people *know* the old stories, but these people are not *of* the old stories."

"The legends." Lieutenant Calvert gave a pained laugh. "Is that what explains it? Your legends, your land. The Highlanders owned this land, but no more. They're gone in many places and those that are left are being cleared from their hills to make way for more sheep. The Highlanders are gone."

"I have not forgotten."

"Others have." Calvert sighed. "They do remember the ancient and proud fighting reputation of the Highlanders. That's why the queen wants them in her regiments. And they remember your old stories. But once the savages are gone, cleared from their lands, then it's safe to make romances of them, isn't it? Turn them into clean, handsome paragons of virtue and chivalry as well as fighting skill. Turn their hovels to nice homes, turn their rude villages into welcoming towns, turn their threadbare garments into well-tailored fantasies."

"The tartans," I murmured. "These villagers speak of 'clan tartans' supposedly ancient in design and I know nothing of these. By our badges have the clans always been known."

"Yes. There's a new history to go with the emptied Highlands, isn't there? They make paintings of these lands and show Lowland shepherds herding their sheep. They read the books of Scott and think the Highlanders were like King Arthur's knights." He gave me a look of sympathy. "This isn't your faery world, Mary Chisholm. Not the one of your kin. It's *their* dream, the Lowlanders, the English, who now rule the land and have put their mark on more than its surface."

"They have taken my true people from me," I gasped. "These people here, they claim to be my Highland kin, but they're not mine and they're not Highland. They're from this Scott person, and from others of his like."

"I'm afraid so," Calvert agreed. "This village is their fantasy brought to life, not yours, because now this is their land, not yours."

"It is a lie!" I cried, stumbling to my feet, my voice rising. "A lie made by the same people who cleared my kin from the glens and hills of the Highlands! They destroyed us and then they took our lives for their romances! Ah, God, could you not give my people the dignity of their truth? Did who they were have to die with them, replaced by some faery dream of a people and a place that never was?"

The room had fallen silent. Everyone was looking at me and Lieutenant Calvert. The young man who had first greeted me stood up and walked slowly toward us, stopping but an arm's length away, his ready smile finally replaced by grim seriousness. "Mary Chisholm, you have been welcome here. This is what you sought. That is why the door opened. Here is land and kin."

"You stole my people's truth!" I screamed at him. "You are false! I wanted the true land again and my true kin!"

"Truth? No two will ever agree what that is. We're what the new people of this land *want* to remember, lass, the truth they *want* to see. They don't even know your people are gone."

"But I know! You cannot take my past! You cannot take my people! I am the daughter of generations of Highlanders and I do not surrender!"

"Then you will be the last," the young man said icily. "If that is all you want to be. The people of the Lowlands feel nothing for Fingal and his Feinn, just as they know not any love for King Fergus or Ossian. New legends were needed to fill their hearts, and that is what we are."

I answered with heat to match his cold. "Better the last true Highlander than to be lost in a cloud-land built of the dreams and guilt of our enemies!"

"You are a fool, lass. Men and women need dreams, for dreams guide them to greatness. Look around you!" The young man flung one arm wide. "The Highlands need legends as great as the land! Strong men and tall, and women beautiful and brave. Could true Highlanders ever have fitted such an epic? Could your rude hovels ever match the fantasies of a proud and noble peasantry that the new owners of this land need?"

"And what of my people?" I asked, my voice breaking.

"Your people, Mary Chisholm?" The young man shook his head. "In time their own scattered children will take us to heart, because those driven from this land lost everything. What did your father still believe in but cruel fate and certain failure? What could your mother still cling to for hope and pride?"

"Do not name them!" I shouted. "They never gave up!" I felt the lie in my heart as I said it, but I would not admit to that lie, no, not if an angel came before me and demanded it. "I have not forgotten! I still believe! If struggle and pain is my lot, then that I will live with, for I swear before God that I will not accept this false heaven!"

"Do not call on Him a third time or all will be lost to you," the young man warned. "Lieutenant, you have been welcomed as well because you sought this place. This is what you longed to find in the Highlands and could not leave though you pretended to yourself to try. Do you wish to trade it for the grim battlefields of distant lands, to be maimed and die, when you could stay here and be among those who can fight forever, laugh, and lose nothing?"

Lieutenant Calvert had risen to stand beside me, and now he shook his head. "I'm not a perfect man. Perhaps I did seek such a place as this, but not to linger while real life goes on outside it. I have a duty to my comrades. More, I believe that Mary Chisholm is right when she speaks of a duty to truth. This is a falsehood. No man should live in a fantasy world. To be inspired by such is one thing. But to be lost in it? I think that would be wrong, no matter how wonderful the fantasy."

The young man smiled, but now that smile held no trace of humor or warmth. I felt the smile an unearthly thing, born of such knowledge that children of men and women can never share. "Your bones will rest in the mud while we reside happy here in this dream for a thousand, thousand years, a dream better than anything those who once lived here ever knew. Men and women will follow that dream, and the world they will make of it will be a thing others look upon with envy. The Lowlanders and the English will carry that dream to lands far away and some yet unknown, where it will sustain them through hardship and give them pride no matter how hard their lives. What makes such a lie a wrong thing?"

Lieutenant Calvert did not reply.

For a moment, I did not know the answer either, but then it came to me. "For others that may be well enough. But for me to accept it, I must deny all those who came before me, deny those who gave me life and worked themselves to death trying to care for me, and deny them I will not. Dead they may be, but forgotten they will never be. Your dream may give hope to others. Well enough. Let them have their dreams. But the truth should be remembered as well, of who my people were and of the ills done to them!"

To my surprise, Lieutenant Calvert reached to take my hand in his firm grasp. "You're a fine memorial to your people, Mary Chisholm. It's a shame we traded you all for sheep. Shall we deny this lie together?"

The young man and everyone else continued to watch us, their faces cold and pale. The welcome and kindness had vanished, gone like the false front I had increasingly sensed it to be. The fire in the great hearth no longer gave heat, and I felt an edge of ice in the air. Even the colors around us seemed to have faded like a cloth left too long in the sun. "You are fools," the young man said in a voice that already sounded distant, as if he spoke on a far-off snow-laden peak and his voice had been carried down a chill wind.

Lieutenant Calvert nodded. "Yes. We are fools. It's humanity's curse, and perhaps also its hope. Even when truth is harsher than comfortable legend, sometimes we still seek that truth. Please say it for us both, Mary Chisholm."

I raised my chin, fearful to lose this wondrous place, yet thinking of my warrior ancestors and of the Feinn unwavering alongside Fingal at Sgorr nam Fiannaidh. "May God deny this falsehood, for I will not take it as my truth."

Between one eye blink and the next, the inn and everyone within it vanished. Lieutenant Calvert and I stood on a bare field of grass, the bleating of sheep clear in the distance. I knew without looking that up the slope the ruins of my old home would once again be there. Behind us, a bewildered neigh marked the presence of Lieutenant Calvert's horse, who was looking around as if searching for the warm stable where it had been moments before. It had been night in the village, but a morning sun shone upon us in the empty meadow.

Only one thing remained from the faery village, and that was the fine dress I wore. "Why did this not vanish as well?" I wondered, though grateful in truth to still be clothed with Lieutenant Calvert standing close by.

He studied me in a manner that made me blush. "Perhaps you earned it, Mary. There are things you believe in even if you couldn't accept that village, and I think the human dreams which gave form to those who exist there lead them to value our courage even as they scorn our frailties."

I ran one hand down the smooth fabric, so different from the rude garment I had come here wearing, thinking that I wished no gift of those who had displaced the old legends. But if those old beliefs still lived in me... "A gift from the Feinn? Could I call it that?"

"You could. And it suits you well. Your outer seeming should be as fine as who you are inside, Mary Chisholm."

I felt myself blushing again and made no answer, only watching as Lieutenant Calvert saddled his horse. He did not mount, but walked beside me up the slope and to the road. I would have hesitated then, wondering where to go, but he held out his hand to me and so I stayed with him. After some time, we came upon a traveler going the other way, a Lowlander who gazed at us in surprise, as if less at our presence than at our garb.

"Sir," Lieutenant Calvert hailed him. "What news from the Crimea?"

"Crimea?" The traveler sounded baffled.

"The war. How goes the war?"

The traveler looked from the lieutenant to me and then back again. "The war in the Crimea has been over for years now."

I could see Lieutenant Calvert brace himself before he spoke again. "Could you tell me today's date, sir?"

"April the twenty-first."

"And the year?"

"The year?" the traveler asked in astonishment. "Eighteen sixty-one."

Calvert bade the man farewell, then spent a while looking at the road. "I'm going to have a lot to explain. Missing for seven years. My family is not without wealth or influence, but this will not be easy for even them to resolve. All the evidence I have is a horse which has clearly not aged another seven years, and while that will please our stable master, I doubt that the army will accept it as proof." He sighed. "If all else fails I may have to find a home elsewhere, perhaps even in the wilds of America."

He sounded sad and lost, then, and I wished I could bring him comfort. "But your family will be waiting and filled with joy to see you again. For my part, none cared that I was gone, and none will care that I have returned." I felt tears starting and fought them off as I thought of all the years gone from me in faery. "I suppose I should be grateful. I never thought to look so young nearly seventy years after my birth. But there is no place for me now, young or old." The Highlands kept fast the dreams of others and no place in the Lowlands would welcome a true Highlander.

Lieutenant Calvert looked at me and smiled, a real smile, not the false good nature of the faery but a smile full of shared pain and life. "Mary Chisholm, would the last Highlander come with me to London? And wherever life takes me after that?"

What right had I to accept such an offer? "I would shame you, sir."

"I think not. I ask you to be my wife, Mary."

"I am too far beneath you, sir!"

"No. Your outer dress is as fine as any in London and I'd change nothing within you. Without you, without the courage of the last Highlander, I might have stayed there, lost in a dream. Not everyone would have denied the chance for such a paradise, Mary."

"It wasn't even my falsehood," I reminded him. "If I must live with untruths, let them be my own, but I will ever prefer truth."

I am proud and stubborn, yes, and perhaps I am also the fool the faery named me, but I saw a home in this man and a truth in his heart. I placed my hand in his again in answer to him, then we walked onward together, away from the Highlands where tales from the Lowlands had replaced our history just as the Lowland sheep had replaced the Highland people.

My name is Mary Chisholm, I am the last, and no matter what may come, none shall make me forget who and what was once truly here.

PAUL DI FILIPPO
KAREN COXSWAIN, OR, DEATH AS SHE IS TRULY LIVED

I've been writing professionally since 1977, with around thirty books to my credit. When I was approached by editor Gardner Dozois to take part in this fascinating project, I didn't hesitate a moment, either to say yes or to jump at the selection of the first line from Twain's *Huck Finn*. Twain has always been one of my favorite authors, and I believe, as Hemingway maintained, that *Huck Finn* is the true start of modern American literature. Another great admirer of Twain was the writer Philip José Farmer, an author I grew up enjoying. So I layered some of Farmer's themes and tropes into my piece, as a homage to that seminal SF writer. Also, lately I've been watching a number of classic films about the afterlife, such as *Heaven Can Wait* and *Here Comes Mr. Jordan*, so my thoughts were trending in that direction. I hope you all have as much fun reading "Karen Coxswain, Or, Death As She Is Truly Lived" as I had writing it.

KAREN COXSWAIN, OR, DEATH AS SHE IS TRULY LIVED

BY PAUL DI FILIPPO

You don't know about me without you have read a book by the name of *The Adventures of Tom Sawyer*; but that ain't no matter. But of course I ain't talking about that pile of YA puke we all got shoved at us in middle school back on Earth, sometime between our first boy band crush and our first sloppy blowjob. The sappy, corn-fed book that old Mark wrote in 1876. No, the *Adventures* I'm holding up as a not-totally-authentic introduction to my current life—afterlife, really—is the second one that Mark wrote—here in Hell, just a few years back.

You see, at that time, I had taken a lover onboard the *Ship of Shadows*, my first infernal beau, and after our brief honeymoon our carryings-on soon escalated to such hysterical, fucked-up, window-smashing, curses-bellowing, biting, screaming, flailing, lowblow-throwing melees, followed by makeup sex nearly as destructive and outrageous, that I began to acquire a certain seamy reputation in all the cities we regularly visited, from Beetleburg to Crotchrot. Just imagine, said all the righteously and proudly damned infernal citizens, that nice Karen Coxswain, Captain of the *Shadows*, previously such a respectable gal, consorting with a lowlife yeti from Tibet, one who had been moreover the right-hand man and mystical advisor to none other than bloody Kublai Khan hisself, and who was plainly now such a bad influence on the previously serene and pleasant Captain. (Khan hisself doesn't actually figure into my story, since he was then living in the city of Scuzzy Ashenhole about forty thousand miles away downriver, far from my stomping grounds.)

What those scandalized citizens didn't realize, however, was that I had never really been anything like a good girl, back when I was alive. Really, if they had thought about it for even a minute, why else would I've ended up in Hell? I had only appeared docile and meek and mild-mannered for the past ten years, since I had been taking that amount of time to more or less mentally adjust to my death and to process my feelings about my new role in the afterlife, the job of ferrying folks from one side of the Styx to t'other, and up and down its blasted, cindery, jizz-bespattered shores.

I'll never forget my entry interview with the Marquis Decarabia, when the stinking old goat (and he was at least half goat, for along with his naked, brick-red, totally ripped human upper half, big as a Cadillac Escalade SUV, went an actual billygoat-style bottom half, and he stunk of garlic, curry powder, lanolin, and Axe body spray) discovered that when I had been alive, I used to work on a shrimper running out of my hometown, Apalachicola, Florida, often taking the wheel when the Captain got loaded. The *Virgin Berth*, that woulda been, under Skipper Israel Shuby, a fine man, but with a weakness for Jägermeister.

"Why, this is more than splendid!" boomed the Marquis, then belched like a thousand underwater gator-frightening swampgas farts in the deepest Everglades. "Sorry, just had a heavy lunch of banker entrails. Where was I? Oh, yes, your past maritime experience! We're right this minute in need of a cross-Styx pilot, and with the first name of Karen, you're practically destined from birth! We'll get you your 'papers' and you'll be on the water—if you can call that toxic sludge water—before a devil can shake his dick!"

And then, just to illustrate matters, he peed all over me and disposed of the last few droplets across my wet face with a vigorous waggle of his pointy goat member. Luckily, the demon piss tasted just like Kool-Aid. Unluckily, it was the world's worst flavor, Kickin' Kiwi-Lime, endless pitchers of which had been forced on me as a child by a cruel Mama Maybellene at the Home, before the Kool-Aid honchos came to their senses and discontinued the raunchy flavor.

So that's how I found myself in my new Hellish job. As I say, it took some getting used to the notion that I was stuck here for all eternity, cruising these cursed waters under a smoldering sky or canopy or cavern roof that looked exactly like that kind of gray Corrections Department toilet paper made from one hundred percent re-re-recycled older toilet paper, which had then been used to clean up the butts of one million pureed-spinach-and-mashed-bananas-fed babies. But by the time I finally met my yeti man, I was pretty well accommodated to my new position, and ready to have me some fun.

Did I mention yet that the old horny, hot-headed 'bominable called hisself Tom Sawyer? Yup, that he did. Turns out he had met up with Twain a century ago and become good friends with the writer, glomming onto all Twain's books like Holy Scripture. Apparently, there was some kinda simpatico link between Twain's brand of humor and the typical yeti way of looking at life. So whatever my hairy boyfriend's original furriner Tibetan-Mongol name had been, he was now called Tom. And when I met up with him, he used all his borrowed downhome American wit and humor to sweep me plumb off my feet.

And so as that beat-up old steamer, *Ship of Shadows*, with its boilers fired by the catalyzed and condensed screams of succubi, plied its slow way up and down its few thousand assigned miles of the Styx, delivering its motley passengers to such stops as Rat's Alley, Bone Palace, Migraine Gulch, Toadlick, Culo de Sciacallo, Twitterville, Clayface, Vuht, and Hernia House, Tom and I conducted our intense bunk-busting affair that veered all over the emotional map, from whispered sweet-nothings to black eyes and bunged-up heads. When we weren't easing along like two June bugs riding a leaf, all goofy smiles and hand-holding, we just grated on each other like Democrats and Republicans, or weeds and Roundup. I acknowledge I was wound pretty tight and could be kinda demanding, a go-getter with ambitions—whatever that entailed in Hell. Whereas Tom was an easy-going slacker, interested mostly in getting plenty to eat (mostly stray dockside cats, watermelons, Twizzlers, and Rusty Humphries Ol' Southern Style Beef Jerky, which I had introduced him to) and scratching his grapefruit-sized balls en route to a long nap. No way we coulda made a long-term go of our mutual thing, and I guess I knew it all along. If that sugar-tongued, Muppet-furred bastard hadn't featured a bone inside his furry ten-inch cock, I woulda ditched him a year sooner than I eventually did.

But by the time we did finally split, our shenanigans, as I hinted at, had become somewhat notorious along both banks of my route, and somewhat inland, toward the Debatable Territories and the Impossible Zone. And that's when Twain decided to put the two of us, thinly disguised and grossly misrepresented, inside his new *Adventures of Tom Sawyer*. (And why the guy half of the romantic duo should've gotten star billing in the novel, I leave up to you to figure out. Men! If they didn't hang together, we could hang them all separately!)

Mark later confessed to me, half apologetically and all puppy-dog-eyed, that he had been in a bind. He was under contract to Hades House to turn in a new novel in less than a month (having frittered away over the course of the past year his advance of 100,000 chancres, mostly on hookers, cigars, and gambling at billiards), and he was just plumb-dry of ideas. That's when he hit upon fictionalizing the relationship between Tom and me. I must admit, he did a good job, however sensationalized and gossipy it turned out, and he got a bestseller out of the novel, even making enough to gift me a few thousand chancres out of guilt when I needed the dough. (And I mostly always needed the dough.)

So, long story short, that's why I say you probably haven't ever made my acquaintance personally outside the pages of some lurid book. But at the same time, my portrait in those steamy pages being so reality-show, it hardly counts even if you read the thing.

Of course, another way you mighta gotten to know me actually is if you've ridden my scow. But out of all the trillions of creatures in Hell, that number amounts to the tiniest fraction of souls. There's just so many beings in the infernal regions that the chances of any two bumping up against each other is smaller than the odds of me jilling off and cumming just at the exact second a meteor destroys Earth by landing precisely in my busy lap.

Which is why you coulda knocked me over with a feather off the Angel Jegudiel's wings the day I stood at the head of the *Shadows'* boarding plank and saw my big bruiser of an ex-husband, Jad Greenlees, strolling onboard, handsome as a dragon and twice as surly. (And I should know dragons, having had a one-night stand with a Jap one named Uwibami, on the sorrowful rebound from Tom.)

Now, last time I had seen Jad was just about three days before I died. And he had been slightly instrumental in me buying the farm. Maybe even more than slightly. Not that I held it against him anymore, having come to the realization that the fault was truly all mine. Knowing Jad as well as I did back when I was mortal, I shoulda been more careful.

The way it happened was like this.

The *Virgin Berth* was in port for a week, and I had wanted to make a little extra money. My eye was snagged by the Facebook announcement for a Demolition Derby up in Pensacola, at the Five Flags Speedway, just three hours or so down Route 98. I had done Demo Derbies before, and, if I say so, was pretty damn good at them. I figured I had a good shot at taking one of the prizes.

But right that moment, I had no suitable vehicle to enter. So I resolved to get Jad to let me take his old beefed-up Dodge Charger to compete with. It was the least he could do, seeing as how it was my earnings that had paid to kit out the car in the first place. Letting him have the souped-up beater after our divorce had been pure niceness on my part. And I knew he wasn't using it for anything anymore, since he had made some real money and bought hisself a cherry-clean 1985 IROC-Z. So over to Jad's I went.

Standing on the beat-up shady porch of Jad's shack, I could hear a lot of instant frantic rustling around inside, in response to my knocking. Not wanting Jad to flush all his merchandise and then blame me, I hollered out through the ripped screen door, "Hey, shithead, it's just me!" The scrabbling and shuffling stopped, there was a whispered conversation featuring a female voice I didn't recognize and a male one I knew too well, and then my former hubby appeared on the far side of the floppy copper mesh.

Jad looked kinda like Magnum, PI—one reason I had first fallen for him—except for considerable extra inches around his middle, a chewed-up ear from a particularly evil bar fight—the same brawl what left a scar kinda like Harry Potter's on his brow—and a trademark expression of baffled confusion, irritation, and suspicion arising from a far-less-than-Advanced-Placement level of intelligence.

Now he scowled. "So it's you."

"Generally I follow mighty close behind my voice, jerkoff."

"Whatta ya want? I'm busy."

"Yeah, I bet. Cutting your coke, no doubt. You're not still using that de-worming shit you stole from the vet, I hope."

Jad had the grace to look embarrassed. "Not since I lost myself several dead customers, no. Made the skin fall right offen them in hunks."

Jad's ramped-up involvement with drug-dealing had been the primary reason for our splitting up. I just couldn't reconcile even my sketchy set of ethics with the stuff he was pushing. It had been all right when we first married, and he was only selling grass and Scooby Snacks. But I drew the line when he moved into bath salts and all that other deadly junk.

But all that was in the past, and any hurt or loss I felt for what we had had and thrown away was moderated by an equal sense of relief and freedom at being single again.

I explained my errand to Jad, and he brightened up, obviously relieved that I didn't want any weightier favor. For a moment, I could see the fun-loving, easy-going, carefree, considerate guy I had married. Then the woman's voice called out to him to hurry up, and his attitude changed to worry and haste, pissed-offedness, and anxiety. I recognized the voice.

"Is that Scamp the Tramp O'Dell in there?"

"So what if it is?"

I shook my head. "Man, Jad, I thought you had more sense and good taste than that. She is ten kinds of nasty layered on top of a heap of meanness. What can you possibly see in her?"

Jad leered. "She fucks like a cageful of tigers getting their first meat after a week's worth of carrots. And she helps me in my job."

There was nothing I could say to that, except to offer up that they truly deserved each other. Jad took it as a compliment. Then he scooted past the door, opening it just slightly as if afraid I might try to sneak inside. But nothing coulda been further from my desires.

We went out to the side yard where the Charger sat on its cinderblock-chocked trailer, covered in leaves and bird poop. I insisted on spraying the car somewhat clean with the garden hose before I took it.

"What's become of you, Jad? You used to love that car and take good care of it. Don't you give a shit about anything anymore except selling drugs?"

"That and pussy. Except not yours. Now, c'mon and hurry. I got things to do."

Burning mad and biting my tongue, I backed my old Ford Ranger up to the trailer and let Jad hitch them up without even getting out of the cab.

And that was my fatal mistake. I shoulda inspected what Jad had done.

Jad fucked up installing the safety chains. First off, they were too heavy a gauge for the load. Then he secured them not to the rig but to the frigging Charger itself! So a few days later, when I was barreling down Route 98 and the trailer coupling separated from the ball mount on my truck after hitting a bad bump, I suddenly found myself connected to a loose, airborne automobile—the Charger— that had leaped off its runaway trailer, shredding all four tires when it landed. The drag caused my Ranger to careen from lane to lane, sideswipe the Jersey barrier, roll over, hit the pillar of a billboard, and explode in a fiery Hellball, sending me straight to my new job as Captain of the *Ship of Shadows*.

For a time, I would ask myself if Jad had rigged the setup deliberately to cause my death. But ultimately I figured, naw, it was just bad luck and circumstances. That trailer was hauling fine till we hit the bump, and there was no way Jad coulda predicted that. It was just sheer hurried incompetence on his part, and lazy inattention on mine. My death had been just fallout from his lameass haste.

So before too long into my infinite stay in these realms, I forgave Jad Greenlees for my death, and even managed to resurrect a few—very few—happy memories of our time together to comfort me occasionally in my daily rounds.

Which is not to say I did not have some mighty conflicted feelings churning inside me as I watched the big bastard climb that gangplank!

For once, Jad was not swaggering. In fact, he seemed kinda bummed and stomped-down, looking like a dog what had got its boner knot caught between two fence slats. He wasn't dressed in the usual High Ghetto style he favored. In fact, I recognized the suit he wore as the kinda cheap secondhand clothes Hell handed out to newcomers, sorta like the suit prisoners got back on Earth when they were released. His head hung down and he looked only at his shuffling feet. He didn't even do a double take when Humbuzz, my purser, took his ticket. And if you're a human who doesn't jump when you first encounter one of the Bee People of Venus (far as I know, they lived about umpty-ump millions of years before humans even existed), then you're some kinda superman, and Jad was never that.

Once onboard, Jad started to head for the ladder down to steerage, so I knew two things: he was traveling some distance, and he truly had no chancres. Nobody rides steerage if they can help it, it's so dismal and stinking, full of screaming ogre babies and their bone-gnawing parents and ignorant Neolithic shitkickers. And most passengers just crossing from one shore to the next like to stay up top and enjoy the hot, clammy, coal- and sulfur-scented breezes, for whatever relief they offer.

I felt so sorry for the boy I stepped right into his path to halt him. He bumped into me, muttered an apology, and tried to sidestep me. But I hailed him by saying, "Hey, Scarface, dontcha have any time for old friends?"

Jad looked up, and, with no small effort, his expression changed from grim and glum to bogusly boastful. I almost regretted making myself known. But if he was riding any distance, we woulda come face to face sooner or later anyhow.

Jad's voice sounded rough, as if maybe he had spent the past month of Sundays crying in his beer. "Well, sweetcakes, fancy meeting you here! I thought for sure that your holy ass woulda brung you straight to the Other Place."

"Holy ass only next to *your* sinful carcass. How'd you end up here anyhow?"

"My meth lab blew up."

That figured. Jad had trouble remembering not to nuke his tinfoil-wrapped leftovers. Putting potentially explosive chemicals in his hands was asking for disaster.

"Anybody else screw the pooch with you?"

Jad got crestfallen again. "Just Scamp."

"Oh? How come she's not lovingly by your side right now?"

Now Jad looked mad. "One of these high and mighty demons done stole her from me!"

I got the story from Jad in confused bits and pieces. Seemed like he was still in that period of disorientation and disbelief that hits everyone when they first arrive in Hell, and only evaporates when the damned soul has fully reconciled itself to its fate.

Upon their flindersization, Jad and Scamp's joint entry

interview had been conducted by Supreme President and Earl
Rampant Glasya-Labolas, one of the mightier potentates of
Hell, who outranked my own mentor Marquis Decarabia by
about several hundred thousand ass-kissings and ritual face-
in-the-mud abasements. Glasya-Labolas's form was that of a
giant coondog with rainbow griffin's wings, and he loomed
'bout as big as your average Redneck Riviera McMansion.

Turns out that the Earl Rampant had taken a shine to
Scamp the Tramp as new meat, and she had no doubt
encouraged the demon in her slutty fashion, once she saw
which side of the Hell waffle had the molasses. Glasya-
Labolas had done the dirty deed with Scamp right then and
there in front of her outraged boyfriend. (Don't ask how a
sewer-pipe-sized dog dick fits into a normal-sized human
pussy; physics is mighty variable in Hell, not to mention
biology.) Jad had been so enraged he had very foolishly
attacked Glasya-Labolas, all to no avail of course. Except that
Jad had ended up on the demonic shit list.

Glasya-Labolas had flown away with Scamp on his back,
to his castle known as Dark Epcot, about nine thousand miles
downriver from where the *Shadows* was now docked. And
when Jad had recovered himself and tried to fit into the Hell
economy the only way he knew how, by drug-dealing, he had
discovered that the only job any of the established drug lords
would give him was the low-paying one of lookout or mule—
quite a comedown from his mortal rank. A few months of
that treatment and he had got to feeling lower and lower, until
about the only thing he could think to do was to voyage to Dark
Epcot and apologize to Glasya-Labolas and ask to be forgiven.

This was why he had booked steerage passage on my ship.

Telling his story seemed to alleviate some of Jad's funk, as
sharing troubles mostly will, even in Hell. In fact, he began to
act like his old cocky self and presume on our prior connection.

"Christ, Karen, you're looking extra damn hot, like some kinda Hollywood *Pirates of the Caribbean* bitch."

I hadn't even thought twice about my outfit, but I realized after Jad commented that it was indeed pretty piratically smoking. I wore a paisley scarf tied around my hair like Little Steven on tour with Bruce. My boobs were covered with a lurex tube top in red, over which I featured an unbuttoned denim vest. My Daisy Dukes left nothing to the imagination, and I wore Vivienne Westwood ankle-high pirate boots. (A girl's got to splurge now and then.)

"Why, I guess that's about as much of a gentlemanly compliment as I could ever expect from you."

I made the mistake of smiling at Jad then, and so he felt obligated or entitled to grab my ass.

That's when I let him have it in the face with my tail.

You should picture about four feet of thick scarlet scaly garden hose, normally coiled up tight to my butt, that ends in an arrow-shaped knob of flesh about as dense as Mike Tyson's fist. I can unfurl that sucker and whip it around faster than a snake. My tail constituted those "papers" Marquis Decarabia had said he was gonna give me as token of my new job.

Jad flew back about ten feet and landed on his ass against a bulkhead. Several of my crewmembers came running. And most of them, even the humans, looked scarier than Humbuzz. They helped Jad up, but kept his arms pinned. He looked dazed as a manatee in a marina.

"Humbuzz," I said, "how far does his ticket take him?"

"Fishgrunt only."

I turned to Jad. "That's not even halfway to Dark Epcot. How'd you plan on getting the rest of the way?"

Jad acted properly humble, though I knew he'd be burning up underneath. "I dunno… Work at something, I guess…"

"Well, how'd you like a job as stoker on this ship? Join the

Black Gang and work your passage off. I need someone, and the experience might do you good. It's manual labor, but it's not too hard or dirty. And you get to bunk with the crew."

Jad was too dumb to be suspicious of my offer. He musta thought I was just all full of womanly pity.

"Well, okay, I suppose. Gee, thanks, Karen, that's mighty white of you."

"All right then. The boys will take you down and show you the ropes."

As Jad walked off, nursing his jaw, I had to smile again.

The boiler of the *Shadows* ran on condensed succubi screams that came in the form of gleaming silver bricks slick to the touch. Handling one brick was enough to give any male an instant hard-on—and stiffen the clit of many a female too. By the end of each shift, after handling hundreds of those bricks, Jad would ache like somebody was amputating his balls with a butter knife.

His only likely partners in relieving his needs, those willing Neolithic and ogre gals in steerage, were going to have no end of Greenlees loving on this voyage.

With Jad squared away, I turned my attention to my duties. We were docked at Scrope, and due to cast off in the next half hour or so, heading cross-Styx for Halfhead. As you can imagine, schedules drift pretty regularly in Hell— demons ain't concerned with making no trains run on time— and ferry passengers come to resign themselves to reaching their destinations at any old hour, happy and satisfied with the service if arrival occurs on the same day promised.

Now, every ferry on the Styx ran a shoelace pattern: scoot diagonally across the murky waters from one settlement or town, shack or city, to the opposite bank's destination, unload and load, then angle off toward a downriver or upriver dock on the shore you had set off from just prior.

Every straight mile of travel up or down the Styx was attained only by multiple miles of cross-river churning. The necessity to serve every community, however small, in this zigzag fashion meant a leisurely pace.

But that was fine with me. No pressure, no rush, just piloting *Shadows* lazily under the dirty furnace skies, thinking my thoughts, however elevated or gutter-drenched, watching for snags in the form of behemoth corpses or floating war debris, blowing the big horn to alert smaller craft, steering clear of larger ones, aware all the while that at any moment some subaquatic leviathan outta one mythology or another, flashing six heads, each sporting a mouthful of fangs big as my leg, could breach and threaten to swamp us. Every day brought news of one ferry or another stove in and capsized with greater or lesser loss of life. (Where did the dead and damned go when they died? You *really* don't want to know!) But that's why the *Shadows* boasted some sweet honking deck artillery fore and aft. That, and for dealing with local Illustrissimos and Dominions who might've gotten a little too big for their goat bottoms and decided to levy some unfair taxes or cumshaw or fees. My patents from Marquis Decarabia were, document-wise, as powerful as my tail. But some small-pond jokers were just too bag-of-hammers dumb to know when to kowtow without a few hundred 50mm shells from a chaingun upside their heads.

So before much longer we were underway, sluicing through the small floating corpses and frothy fecal scum, plastic soda bottles, and slicks of glowing chemicals, maneuvering just like a bottom-heavy mechanical swan paddling through a tub full of acid-wash and tie-dye colors and jeans.

Darkness never really falls in Hell, but most creatures operate on some kinda wake-and-sleep cycle that approximates Earthly days and nights. So by the time we had gone from

Scrope to Halfhead, and then back across to Shriektown, it was getting on toward the end of my working day. I gave the orders to tie up for the night, made sure a watch was posted, checked that our new cargo of Trojans, gin, pineapples, and roofing nails was secured, and retreated to my cabin.

On the way to my rest, I thought I heard wild yowls betokening sexual release of a mixed appreciative and flinching nature wafting up from steerage. Among the grunts and bellows and hollerings was a certain species of mating call I had come to know intimately, from being pressed beneath their source back in Apalachicola. I think my grin lit up a circle of deck planks around me.

Lying in bed on my belly (I do miss sleeping on my backside), I thought how much fun I could have accompanying Jad all the way down to Dark Epcot and witnessing his meeting with Supreme President and Earl Rampant Glasya-Labolas. My usual run of the Styx didn't extend so far, but us captains were always swapping routes just to liven up infinity a bit, and I had no doubt I could bring the *Shadows* all the way to Dark Epcot. As sleep overtook me, I made the decision to do it.

So the next day I announced my new plans to the crew, and got a variety of reactions ranging from plain old "who-gives-a-fuck-why-are-you-even-bothering-to-tell-me-this?" to "way-awesome-dude!" None of the swabbies objected, since one quiet spot in Hell for their labors was as good as any other to them, they being mostly rootless, non-family types who had chosen this way of life precisely for its permanent migratory nature. And in fact, two thousand of the nine thousand miles to Dark Epcot were familiar territory, my last regular stop being Saliva Tree Hill.

The river beyond that, natch, was an unknown quantity to me. But how different could it be? I thought.

Jad of course stood assembled with the other hands to hear the message, and, having had one taste of my double-edged "favors," mustered up enough wits to look dubious at this large-hearted gesture. He hung back when the crew dispersed, so's he could pester me with his questions. He kept rubbing his crotch like some hip-hop star, and I almost took offense until I realized it was an unconscious reaction to being sore.

"So, uh, Karen, why the change in plans? You figure maybe that once I'm on the good side of that pissant demon canary-dog I can repay you somehow? Is that it?"

"That's exactly it, Jad." Some evil whim shaped my next words—not too uncommon a perverse happening here in Hell. "But I'm actually holding out for even more. I think you can kick Glasya-Labolas's butt and take his place."

This was exactly the kind of impossible ego-boosting bullshit Jad was primed to accept at face value. After all, his default inclination was to picture himself as the magnificent, alpha-dog center of the universe wherever he happened to be, on Earth or in Hell. That notion had just taken a little posthumous beatdown, but it was plainly bubbling under, ready to be stroked and revived.

"You really think so?" The agreeable idea took hold of Jad's whole brain, which was a process like a rising creek spilling over into a shallow ditch. "Yeah, what's that Glassy-assed Labia Lips got that I ain't got! After I learn the ropes here a little more, I can beat him at his own game, and get Scamp back. Gee, thanks, Karen, you showed me the light."

Jad limped off for his stint in the Black Gang, and I shook my head in amazement and took my own place in the pilothouse.

The next several months went by in regular, business-like fashion, as the *Shadows* slipped greasily down the Styx, from one steamy, heaving, maggot-mound burg to another.

Pinchbottom, Gallbreath, Cracked Moon, Furnace Heart, Zezao, Outcast Flats, Gringo Guts, Bloody Albion, Sidereal City, Nopalgarth…

Pardon me if I get downright poetic for a minute. The lack of any kind of weather or heavenly bodies (ha!) contributed to a timeless and uniform existence, filled with an endless cycle of deeds and thoughts, just variable enough to foster some sense of living. The routine daily rituals of piloting. The steady stream of embarking and disembarking weird chittering, crawling, gesticulating passengers, so that the gangplank seemed at times like a conveyor belt with its source in some crazy deity's fevered brain and its outlet in some universal maw of destruction—which pretty much described matters as they actually stood. The occasional bouts of shore leave, when me and my crew gambled, got drunk, got laid, and lost all our chancres, not necessarily in that order. The continuous transshipment of stuff, stuff, stuff, so that sometimes it seemed like the hold of the *Shadows* held merely X number of stationary pallets whose transient contents morphed like a mirage.

Such was life in Hell, a hazy, lazy, crazy, dazed damnation.

About the most you can reliably say is, shit happened.

So before you knew it, we were down to the outpost at the end of my usual reach, Saliva Tree Hill. About the only incident that really stood out in my memory of that time was when we carried two bounty hunters for a few hundred miles, until they caught up with their quarry.

At the dock at Cornhole, two beings came on board and sought me out to present their credentials. They called themselves Coffin Ed and Grave Digger Jones, after two human detectives outta some books by a guy named Hymie or something. Coffin Ed was pretty much a crayfish as big as a man with some kinda helper seaweed and clams attached all over him. He walked upright on his tail somehow. I didn't care to look too closely. Grave Digger Jones looked like some critters I saw in a comic book my nephew Cooter showed me once: stone men from outer space, fighting that long-haired guy with the hammer. Grave Digger did the talking cuz I'm not sure Coffin Ed could.

"Captain Karen, your gentleness, we are seeking a miscreant named Brian Passwater. We have reason to believe he is hiding downriver from Cornhole. Travel by your vessel will allow us to search for him circumspectly and relatively swiftly, as opposed to making arduous and flashy quarry-alerting peregrinations by land, up one shore only. Will you accept payment for our indefinite passage?"

"Well, lemme think a minute. How long you gonna take in each port? I can't screw up my schedule too-too much."

"No time at all, practically speaking. Coffin Ed has very acute and instant remote sensory abilities."

The big crayfish bowed toward me and waggled his antennae significantly.

"Well, okay, I guess. But I can't change my circuit to bring this perp back up here to Cornhole for justice, once you catch him."

"Do not trouble yourself over justice, Captain Karen. We are equipped and authorized to dispense it *in situ*."

Coffin Ed clacked his big serrated claws like castanets. Probably a lotta good eating in those grabbers, I thought, but I for one did not intend to get near enough to learn for sure.

So for a week or three, the two bounty hunters stood like some kinda figureheads at the prow of the *Shadows*, a half-circle of deferential private space always surrounding them, no matter how crowded the ship got, silent and unmoving until we approached land. Then Coffin Ed's antennae would start thrumming and vibrating like Butch Robins's banjo strings. Once or twice, they got an interesting reading and went ashore while I waited, but they always came back empty-handed. Until we hit the metropolis of Crocodile Crater. Then, with Coffin Ed's crayfish deelyboppers vibrating too fast to see, they raced off into the twisty rubbish streets of the city before the gangplank was even firmly lashed down.

They returned just as I was getting ready to leave them behind, and in fact they were done with my services and only wanted to say thank you and goodbye. In his big pebbly paw, Grave Digger Jones was carrying a double-layered paper shopping bag that showed the store logo for the Hell branch of Whole Foods: a radioactively glowing tomacco fruit. The bag was dripping, and one of Coffin Ed's lethal pinchers was smeared the same color as the drippage.

"Captain Karen, we wish to inform you of the success of our venture, and hope that the unutilized chancre-redeemable portion of our tickets will serve as sufficient emblem of our gratitude."

"Uh, sure, right, boys… Happy hunting!"

I never did learn what crime poor Brian Passwater was guilty of. Probably not something really major, like offending one of the Lords of Hell. That would've brought a more vicious supernatural punishment. He musta just got on the wrong side of some powerful Hell citizen, one probably involved in some less savory line of business.

Like I say, that was pretty much the most exciting thing that happened in two thousand miles of travel. And as we pulled into Saliva Tree Hill, I wondered if the rest of the journey would be as boring. But we wouldn't begin to find out until tomorrow, because we had to wait for the arrival of Captain Nance Piebald and his ferry, *Satan's Inglorious Rapture*, in order to swap routes.

That night, I had a confab with Jad. I had to say I was mighty impressed, despite our past track record of mutual hostility and incomprehension, with his new look and attitude. Work in the Black Gang had trimmed off all his excess poundage and muscled him up plenty. He seemed more self-assured and even a whit more considerate of others. I was guessing that maybe some ogre gal had objected to aspects of his callous and selfish lovemaking and undertaken to teach him some manners and perhaps even the meaning of the word "foreplay." In fact, I detected a hickey on his neck exhibiting the unique tusk patterns of that species of female. Half of my objections to Jad as a husband had been to his egotism and unthinking brute ways, and those seem to have been smoothed off, making him a halfway attractive prospect again. Of course, as I soon learned, there had been no alteration in his intelligence or tastes, which were fixed solid as the Mason–Dixon line.

"So, Jad, we've come two thousand miles so far, with another seven to go. You had any change of heart during all that time? Maybe fancy sticking on as a member of my crew? It's not a bad ol' life, is it? Why not give up Scamp and the notion of hitting back at Glasya-Labolas?"

"Nuh-huh! That jumped-up cocker spaniel has it coming to him, and I'm just the bangtail roarer to hand him his head on a platter!"

I pondered telling Jad about some of the more excruciating tortures that the Lords of Hell reserved for upstarts like him, but his next words decided me against handing out such sensible advice.

"Besides, I want Scamp in my arms again. She is the only woman for me. She's always stood by me, and she is the best piece of tail on Earth or in Hell. That girl could peel the skin off a cucumber with that educated pussy of hers."

I blew up. "Stood by you! She ran off with the first demon she saw!"

"I been thinking hard on that. I'm sure she did it just to protect me. After all, the Earl Rampant musta known from my Earthly career how threatening I was gonna be to him, once I got my feet on the ground here. She sensed I was in danger, and so she sacrificed herself to divert him, and now she's just waiting for me to come rescue her."

I threw my hands up into the air. "You're just impossible! Go back to your green-skinned bilge trolls, you asshole!"

Jad grinned. "Sounds to me like somebody's not getting laid regular. Maybe you can get your hands on some incubi ingots."

He left laughing and I went fuming to bed.

Nance Piebald and I had met once before, but his appearance always knocked me out. A pure African black dude from some vanished kingdom called Opar, a smidgen over seven feet tall, he suffered from that disease what Michael Jackson always claimed he had, where his skin was patchy all over, fishbelly against coal. He proudly wore his native costume, which left most of his Appaloosa acreage exposed, so's you could hardly miss his condition.

We shook hands at a grog shop named Ginza Joe's right on the dock at Saliva Tree Hill. Over a regular Johnstown Flood of Mount Etna Lava shots with Black Ram Ale chasers, we caught each other up on our respective beats.

"You'll want to be careful downriver from Dumpster Town," said Nance. "Prince Malphas and Queen Onoskelis are at war again."

I shuddered at that. The domains of Malphas and Onoskelis sat directly opposite each other on the Styx, and the rulers were given to lobbing bundles of flaming typhoid victims and other less pleasant material at each other's burgs, whenever they got their Irish up. Getting past them intact would be a bitch.

"Well," I said, "just have to try some of my best broken-field sailing under a flag of truce."

"Perhaps they will have ceased hostilities by the time you arrive. They are over three thousand miles away from here, after all."

"Anything else I should know?"

"There have been several incidents involving Typhon and Echidna near Hooftscarrow. It is believed the pair were mating on the river bottom—or perhaps just shifting in their sleep. Several ferries lost."

"Oh, well, we all gotta go sometime."

Nance and I clinked glasses, and then parted to assume each other's routes.

Now, to be sure, I'd like to fill up the rest of my story with all the many scary and funny and creepy and boring things that happened to me and the *Shadows* on our seven-thousand-mile journey downriver. But truth be told, none of it was very exceptional or interesting, at least by Hell standards. The voyage had that same kinda not-all-there quality I described earlier, like a dream of a dream. And if I've learned one thing from my friendship with Mark Twain, it's to cut to the chase.

So we steamed past Malphas and Onoskelis with no worse damage than a busted smokestack that intercepted a missile of frozen demon shit, and rode the tsunami caused by Typhon's buggery of Echidna for a quick thousand-mile surfer's shortcut, and dealt with a hundred-hundred other happenings, morbid, dumb, and funny. And before you knew it, we were tying up at Dark Epcot.

Glasya-Labolas had been particularly taken with the philosophizing of Walt Disney when they met, and so had remodeled his domain along the lines of Disney's theme park. But whereas the Earthly Epcot featured pint-sized models of famous landmarks, Dark Epcot boasted recreations of famous Hell landmarks that were even *bigger* than the originals, to testify to the President Supreme's exalted status and cheese off his rivals.

Paimon's Pit of Perverted Passions. The Ninety-Nine Gibbets of Ninurta. Haagenti's Mansion of Horrors. Trump Palace. Stolos's Kitchen. Furfur's Arcade of Screaming Souls. Ziminiar's Car Wash. Okay, I know that last one might not sound so deserving of being immortalized, but take my word for it: the original was one *Hell* of a car wash!

With an enormous frontage, the domain stretched for hundreds of miles backwards from the Styx, like some kind of demonic Washington, D.C.: all monuments, all the time, with thousands of citizens being screwed every minute.

Jad and I walked up to one of the gates of Dark Epcot. I had instructed my second-in-command, Cheb Moussa, to leave with the *Shadows* if I didn't come back in twenty-four hours. I figured my chances as a simple observer of escaping the shit that was gonna fall on Jad's head were slightly better than even. Jad's odds for survival I pegged at about a trillion to one.

My ex carried one of the smaller pieces of artillery from the ferry in his arms, looking like some kinda Redneck Rambo. He kept tripping over the dangling ammunition belt, and eventually I just picked up the end of the sucker and carried it like the train of a bridal gown.

"You sure you wanna go ahead with this now?"

Sweat covered Jad's brow like brine on a freshly netted shrimp. I had to give him points for courage. If only he weren't so damn stupid and self-centered.

"I'm totally sure. What's left for me in Hell if I can't get Scamp and my pride back?"

"Okay, then, it's your second funeral."

I banged on the big riveted iron door, tall as two Nance

Piebalds, one atop the other. In less than a second it swung open, and we marched in.

We were met by the most metrosexual demon I have ever seen. He wore Topsiders, skinny-leg designer jeans and a pink polo shirt that musta cost about seven hundred chancres together. He had even threaded his eyebrows, an elegant look that was marred only by the enormous pus-filled carbuncles covering every inch of his face and neck.

"Welcome to Dark Epcot. My name is Andras, but just call me Andy. You're expected, so if you'll be so good as to just follow me… Oh, you can check your weapon with Shary over there."

A smiling human woman stood behind the counter of a large open booth. Behind her were scores of cubbies, mostly empty but some stuffed with weapons.

"Better do what he says, Jad."

Kinda flustered by this pleasant reception, Jad stowed his gun with Shary and got a claim ticket in return. Shary hoisted the huge weapon with one hand, and I was glad we hadn't messed with her.

Andy walked off at a guide's measured pace, leaving us to follow. The streets of Dark Epcot were filled with bustling minions, imps, and elementals, as well as smiling tourist families. We strolled past one ginormous structure after another. I only recognized a few, chief of which was Vassago's Chamber of Excruciations. Man, you have never *seen* so many Stairmasters in one place!

Eventually we got to what could only be Glasya-Labolas's personal castle, judging by the number of spiked heads adorning its walls. Many of the trophies were still talking and weeping, bitching about their fate.

Andy brought us right inside, past all the minor lords and guards and attendants and plain-clothes security types, and before you could say "The pain of his reign stays mainly in the brain," we were left unaccompanied in the Throne Room.

Glasya-Labolas's Throne Room was about as big as Tropicana Field in St. Pete, where the Devil Rays played. At the center of it loomed the President Supreme and Earl Rampant's mighty chair, a seat made all outta bones and sinews. I could suss out Glasya-Labolas, sitting down with his big griffin's wings enfolding him like a cloak.

Gulping down our scanty spit, Jad and I walked forward.

When we had gotten to within an easy field goal's distance of the Throne, Glasya-Labolas unfolded his wings and stood up, rearing what seemed like miles high above us, and I wondered how he'd gotten so big

Except it wasn't Glasya-Labolas, it was Scamp!

Now I have to admit, all hatred and jealousy aside, back on Earth Scamp the Tramp O'Dell had been one hot mess. Big rack, skinny waist, long legs. Hair black as a crow, heart-shaped face. Eyes that were always daring men to come after her, and challenging women to outclass her. She'd try anything once, then a few more times just to be sure she had the knack of the trick. When I knew her, she was intent on climbing to the top of any heap she happened to find herself in.

Occupying Glasya-Labolas's Throne, a jaybird-naked Scamp at fifty times her standard size looked pretty much the same as she had on Earth. Except that her knobbly skin was a dozen shades of putrid green, like something you'd find at the back of your fridge, and her nipples had eyes. She sported a mouthful of giant fangs, long thick claws on fingers and toes, a tail that put mine to shame, and gnarly bat wings with the span of what you'd expect on a 747.

When she talked it nearly made my ears bleed.

"JAD! YOU LAZY FUCKER! WHAT TOOK YOU SO LONG?"

Jad's jawbone was clacking against his collarbone, and a string of drool crept out one corner of his mouth.

"Uh, I came fast as I could, Scamp. Where—where's Gla-gla-Glasya…?"

Scamp's shriek of laughter made the dome of the Throne Room rain down cement dust.

"OH, I KEEP HIM CLOSE BY SINCE I TOOK OVER! LEMME SHOW YOU!"

I don't get grossed out that easy. But when Scamp reached down into her furry crotch and pulled Glasya-Labolas outta her twat like a tampon, I came nigh to puking.

Scamp swung the soggy comatose demon by his tail like a pendulum.

"COME JOIN ME, JAD! I GOT AN OPENING JUST FOR YOU!"

It's plumb amazing what tricks an abused memory can play on a person. How we got back to the *Shadows* I cannot say, right up to this day. I was bloody, covered with welts and scratches, and had lost most of my clothes. But I was still alive. Or after-alive.

And there was Jad beside me, in a similar condition.

I guess Scamp really couldn't be bothered with such small fry as us, given her new exalted rank.

After we had partially recovered our wits and gotten cleaned up and launched the ferry away from Dark Epcot, with Cheb Moussa at the helm, Jad and I sat on two deck chairs partaking of some well-deserved drinks.

"What next?" asked Jad.

"The Styx is a mighty big river, dude. Let's just see what's round the bend."

MARY ROBINETTE KOWAL
THE LADY ASTRONAUT OF MARS

As I write this, NASA has just landed a robot car on Mars, in the Gale Crater. *Mars*. OMG *Mars*.

I mean. This is science. No, no. This is *Science*. This is why I write science-fiction. Being able to watch this real time was astonishingly moving.

And then… and then I started laughing again because *Curiosity* landed in Gale Crater. Gale.

My story starts with the opening line to *The Wonderful Wizard of Oz*. It's sort of a punchcard punk homage to Ray Bradbury and L. Frank Baum.

Dorothy Gale…

Watching the live feed of *Curiosity* going in was a little like the tornado ride that Dorothy took—an absolutely insane ride that no one should be able to survive. Now Gale Crater is actually named for Walter Frederick Gale, who thought Mars had canals. Those canals gave rise to science-fiction by Wells, Burroughs, Bradbury…

This story is set when I was little, when Bradbury was putting civilizations on Mars, and my dad was programming with punchcards. When we put people on the moon in a craft that looked like it was made from Erector sets wrapped in tin foil. When the entire computing power of the world was less than in your cell phone. This is the story of "The Lady Astronaut of Mars."

THE LADY ASTRONAUT OF MARS
BY MARY ROBINETTE KOWAL

Dorothy lived in the midst of the great Kansas prairies, with Uncle Henry, who was a farmer, and Aunt Em, who was the farmer's wife. She met me, she went on to say, when I was working next door to their farm under the shadow of the rocket gantry for the First Mars Expedition.

I have no memory of this.

She would have been a little girl and, oh lord, there were so many little kids hanging around outside the Fence watching us work. The little girls all wanted to talk to the Lady Astronaut. To me.

I'm sure I spoke to Dorothy because I know I stopped and talked to them every day on my way in and out through the Fence about what it was like. *It* being Mars. There was nothing else it could be.

Mars consumed everyone's conversations. The programmers sitting over their punchcards. The punchcard girls keying in the endless lines of code. The cafeteria ladies ladling out mashed potatoes and green peas. Nathaniel with his calculations… Everyone talked about Mars.

So the fact that I didn't remember a little girl who said I talked to her about Mars… Well. That's not surprising, is it? I tried not to let the confusion show in my face but I know she saw it.

By this point, Dorothy was my doctor. Let me be more

specific. She was the geriatric specialist who was evaluating me. On Mars. I was in for what I thought was a routine check-up to make sure I was still fit to be an astronaut. NASA liked to update its database periodically and I liked to be in that database. Not that I'd flown since I turned fifty, but I kept my name on the list in the faint hope that they would let me back into space again, and I kept going to the darn check-ups.

Our previous doctor had retired back to Earth, and I'd visited Dorothy's offices three times before she mentioned Kansas and the prairie.

She fumbled with the clipboard and cleared her throat. A flush of red colored her cheeks and made her eyes even more blue. "Sorry, Dr. York, I shouldn't have mentioned it."

"Don't 'doctor' me. You're the doctor. I'm just a space jockey. Call me Elma." I waved my hand to calm her down. The flesh under my arm jiggled and I dropped my hand. I hate that feeling and hospital gowns just make it worse. "I'm glad you did. You just took me by surprise, is all. Last I saw you, weren't you knee-high to a grasshopper?"

"So you do remember me?" Oh, that hope. She'd come to Mars because of me. I could see that, clear as anything. Something I'd said or done back in 1952 had brought this girl out to the colony.

"Of course, I remember you. Didn't we talk every time I went through that Fence? Except school days, of course." It seemed a safe bet.

Dorothy nodded, eager. "I still have the eagle you gave me."

"Do you now?" That gave me a pause.

I used to make paper eagles out of old punchcards while I was waiting for Nathaniel. His programs could take hours to run and he liked to babysit them. The eagles were cut paper things with layers of cards pasted together to make a three-dimensional bird. It was usually in flight and I liked to hang them in the window, where the holes from the punch cards would let specks of light through and make the bird seem like it was sparkling. They would take me two or three days to make. You'd think I would remember giving one to a little girl beyond the Fence. "Did you bring it out here with you?"

"It's in my office." She stood as if she'd been waiting for me to ask that since our first session, then looked down at the clipboard in her hands, frowning. "We should finish your tests."

"Fine by me. Putting them off isn't going to make me any more eager." I held out my arm with the wrist up so she could take my pulse. By this point, I knew the drill. "How's your uncle?"

She laid her fingers on my wrist, cool as anything. "He and Aunt Em passed away when *Orion 27* blew."

I swallowed, sick at my lack of memory. So she was *that* little girl. She'd told me all the things I needed and my old brain was just too addled to put the pieces together. I wondered if she would make a note of that and if it would keep me grounded.

Dorothy had lived on a farm in the middle of the Kansas prairie with her Uncle Henry and Aunt Em. When *Orion 27* came down in a ball of fire, it was the middle of a drought. The largest pieces of it had landed on a farm.

No buildings were crushed, but it would have been a blessing if they had been, because that would have saved the folks inside from burning alive.

I closed my eyes and could see her now as the little girl I'd forgotten. Brown pigtails down her back and a pair of dungarees a size too large for her, with the legs cuffed up to show bobby socks and sneakers.

Someone had pointed her out. "The little girl from the Williams farm."

I'd seen her before, but in that way you see the same people every day without noticing them. Even then, with someone pointing to her, she didn't stand out from the crowd. Looking at her, there was nothing to know that she'd just lived through a tragedy. I reckon it hadn't hit her yet.

I had stepped away from the entourage of reporters and consultants that followed me and walked up to her. She had tilted her head back to look up at me. I used to be a tall woman, you know.

[Dorothy as child] "You still going to Mars?"

I had nodded. "Maybe you can go someday too."

She had cocked her head to the side, as if she were considering. I can't remember what she said back. I know she must have said something. I know we must have talked longer because I gave her that darned eagle, but what we said… I couldn't pull it up out of my brain.

As the present-day Dorothy tugged up my sleeve and wrapped the blood pressure cuff around my arm, I studied her. She had the same dark hair as the little girl she had been, but it was cut short now and in the low gravity of Mars it wisped around her head like the down on a baby bird.

The shape of her eyes was the same, but that was about it. The soft roundness of her cheeks was long gone, leaving high cheekbones and a jaw that came to too sharp of a point for beauty. She had a faint white scar just above her left eyebrow.

She smiled at me and unwrapped the cuff. "Your blood pressure is better. You must have been exercising since last time."

"I do what my doctor tells me."

"How's your husband?"

"About the same." I slid away from the subject even though, as his doctor, she had the right to ask, and I squinted at her height. "How old were you when you came here?"

"Sixteen. We were supposed to come before but… well." She shrugged, speaking worlds about why she hadn't.

"Your uncle, right?"

Startled, she shook her head. "Oh, no. Mom and Dad. We were supposed to be on the first colony ship but a logging truck lost its load."

Aghast, I could only stare at her. If they were supposed to have been on the first colony ship, then her parents could not have died long before *Orion 27* crashed. I wet my lips. "Where did you go after your aunt and uncle's?"

"My cousin. Their son." She lifted one of the syringes she'd brought in with her. "I need to take some blood today."

"My left arm has better veins."

While she swabbed the site, I looked away and stared at a chart on the wall reminding people to take their vitamin D supplements. We didn't get enough light here for most humans.

But the stars... When you could see them, the stars were glorious. Was that what had brought Dorothy to Mars?

When I got home from the doctor's—from Dorothy's—the nurse was just finishing up with Nathaniel's sponge bath. Genevieve stuck her head out of the bedroom, hands still dripping.

"Well, hey, Miss Elma. We're having a real good day, aren't we, Mr. Nathaniel?" Her smile could have lit a hangar, it was so bright.

"That we are." Nathaniel sounded hale and hearty, if I didn't look at him. "Genevieve taught me a new joke. How's it go?"

She stepped back into the bedroom. "What did the astronaut see on the stove? An unidentified frying object."

Nathaniel laughed, and there was only a little bit of a wheeze. I slid my shoes off in the dust room to keep out the ever-present Martian grit, and came into the kitchen to lean against the bedroom door. Time was it used to be his office, but we needed a bedroom on the ground floor. "That's a pretty good one."

He sat on a towel at the edge of the bed as Genevieve washed him. With his shirt off, the ribs were starkly visible under his skin. Each bone in his arms poked at the surface and slid under the slack flesh. His hands shook, even just resting beside him on the bed. He grinned at me.

The same grin. The same bright blue eyes that had flashed over the punchcards as he'd worked out the plans for the launch. It was as though someone had pasted his features onto the body of a stranger. "How'd the doctor's visit go?"

"The usual. Only… only it turns out our doctor grew up next to the launch facility in Kansas."

"Dr. Williams?"

"The same. Apparently I met her when she was little."

"Is that right?" Genevieve wrung the sponge out in the wash basin. "Doesn't that just go to show that it's a small solar system?"

"Not that small." Nathaniel reached for his shirt, which lay on the bed next to him. His hands tremored over the fabric.

"I'll get it. You just give me a minute to get this put away." Genevieve bustled out of the room.

[I called after her.] "Don't worry. I can help him."

Nathaniel dipped his head, hiding those beautiful eyes, as I drew a sleeve up over one arm. He favored flannel now. He'd always hated it in the past. Preferred starched white shirts and a nice tie to work in, and a short-sleeved aloha shirt on his days off. At first, I thought that the flannel was because he was cold all the time. Later I realized that the thicker fabric hid some of his frailty. Leaning behind him to pull the shirt around his back, I could count vertebra in his spine.

[Nathaniel cleared his throat.] "So, you met her, hm? Or she met you? There were a lot of little kids watching us."

"Both. I gave her one of my paper eagles."

That made him lift his head. "Really?"

"She was on the Williams farm when the *Orion 27* came down."

He winced. Even after all these years, Nathaniel still felt responsible. He had not programmed the rocket. They'd asked him to, but he'd been too busy with the first Mars expedition and turned the assignment down. It was just a supply rocket for the moon, and there had been no reason to think it needed anything special.

I buttoned the shirt under his chin. The soft wattle of skin hanging from his jaw brushed the back of my hand. "I think she was too shy to mention it at my last visit."

"But she gave you a clean bill of health?"

"There's still some test results to get back." I avoided his gaze, hating the fact that I was healthy and he was… not.

"It must be pretty good. Sheldon called."

A bubble of adrenalin made my heart skip. Sheldon Spender called. The director of operations at the Bradbury Space Center on Mars had not called since— No, that wasn't true. He hadn't called *me* in years, using silence to let me know I wasn't flying anymore. Nathaniel still got called for work. Becoming old didn't stop a programmer from working, but it sure as heck stopped an astronaut from flying. And yet I still had that moment of hope every single time Sheldon called, that this time it would be for me. I smoothed the flannel over Nathaniel's shoulders. "Do they have a new project for you?"

"He called for you. Message is on the counter."

Genevieve breezed back into the room, a bubble of idle chatter preceding her. Something about her cousin and meeting their neighbors on Venus. I stood up and let her finish getting Nathaniel dressed while I went into the kitchen.

Sheldon had called for me? I picked up the note on the counter. It just had Genevieve's round handwriting and a request to meet for lunch. The location told me a lot though.

He'd picked a bar next to the Space Center that *no one* in the industry went to because it was thronged with tourists. It was a good place to talk business without talking business. For the life of me I couldn't figure out what he wanted.

I kept chewing on that question, right till the point when I stepped through the doors of Yuri's Spot. The walls were crowded with memorabilia and signed photos of astronauts. An early publicity still that showed me perched on the edge of Nathaniel's desk hung in the corner next to a dusty ficus tree. My hair fell in perfect soft curls despite the flight suit I had on. My hair would never have survived like that if I'd actually been working. I tended to keep it out of the way in a kerchief, but that wasn't the image publicity had wanted.

Nathaniel was holding up a punchcard, as if he were showing me a crucial piece of programming. Again, it was a staged thing, because the individual cards were meaningless by themselves, but to the general public at the time they meant Science with a capital S. I'm pretty sure that's why we were both laughing in the photo, but they had billed it as "the joy of space flight."

Still gave me a chuckle, thirty years later.

Sheldon stepped away from the wall and mistook my smile. "You look in good spirits."

I nodded to the photo. "Just laughing at old memories."

He glanced over his shoulder, wrinkles bunching at the corner of his eyes in a smile. "How's Nathaniel?"

"About the same, which is all one can ask for at this point."

Sheldon nodded and gestured to a corner booth, leading me past a family with five kids who had clearly come from the Space Center. The youngest girl had her nose buried in a picture book of the early space program. None of them noticed me.

Time was when I couldn't walk anywhere on Mars without being recognized as the Lady Astronaut. Now, thirty years after the First Expedition, I was just another old lady, whose small stature showed my origin on Earth.

We settled in our chairs and ordered, making small talk as we did. I think I got fish and chips because it was the first thing on the menu, and all I could think about was wondering why Sheldon had called.

It was like he wanted to see how long it would take me to crack and ask him what he was up to. It took me a while to realize that he kept bringing the conversation back to Nathaniel. Was he in pain?

Of course.

Did he have trouble sleeping?

Yes.

Even, "How are you holding up?" was about him. I didn't get it until Sheldon paused and pushed his rabbit burger aside, half-eaten, and asked point-blank, "Have they given him a date yet?"

A date. There was only one date that mattered in a string of other milestones on the path to death but I pretended he wasn't being clear, just to make him hurt a little. "You mean for paralyzation, hospice, or death?"

He didn't flinch. "Death."

"We think he's got about a year." I kept my face calm, the way you do when you're talking to Mission Control about a flight that's set to abort. The worse it got, the more even my voice became. "He can still work, if that's what you're asking."

"It's not." Sheldon broke his gaze then, to my surprise, and looked down at his ice water, spinning the glass in its circle of condensation. "What I need to know is if *you* can still work."

In my intake of breath, I wanted to say that God, yes, I

could work and that I would do anything he asked of me if he'd put me back into space. In my exhale, I thought of Nathaniel. I could not say yes. "That's why you asked for the physical."

"Yep."

"I'm sixty-three, Sheldon."

"I know." He turned the glass again. "Did you see the news about LS-579?"

"The extrasolar planet. Yes." I was grounded, but that didn't mean I stopped paying attention to the stars.

"Did you know we think it's habitable?"

I stopped with my mouth open as pieces started to tick like punchcards slotting through a machine. "You're mounting a mission."

"*If* we were, would you be interested in going?"

Back into space? My God, yes. But I couldn't. I couldn't. I— That was why he wanted to know when my husband was going to die. I swallowed everything before speaking. My voice was passive. "I'm sixty-three." Which was my way of asking why he wanted *me* to go.

"It's three years in space." He looked up now, not needing to explain why they wanted an old pilot.

That long in space? It doesn't matter how much shielding you have against radiation, it's going to affect you. The chances of developing cancer within the next fifteen years were huge. You can't ask a young astronaut to do that. "I see."

"We have the resources to send a small craft there. It can't be unmanned because the programming is too complicated. I need an astronaut who can fit in the capsule."

"And you need someone who has a reason to not care about surviving the trip."

"No." He grimaced. "PR tells me that I need an astronaut that the public will adore so that when we finally tell them that we've sent you, they will forgive us for hiding the mission from them." Sheldon cleared his throat and started briefing me on the Longevity Mission.

Should I pause here and explain what the Longevity Mission is? It's possible that you don't know.

There's a habitable planet. An extrasolar one and it's only a few light years away. They've got a slingshot that can launch a ship up to near light speed. A small ship. Big enough for one person.

But that isn't what makes the Longevity Mission possible. *That* is the tesseract field. We can't go faster than light, but we *can* cut corners through the universe. The physicists described it to me like a subway tunnel. The tesseract will bend space and allow a ship to go to the next subway station. The only trick is that you need to get far enough away from a planet before you can bend space and… this is the harder part… you need a tesseract field at the other end. Once that's up, you just need to get into orbit and the trip from Mars to LS-579 can be as short as three weeks.

But you have to get someone to the planet to set up the other end of the tesseract.

And they wanted to hide the plan from the public, in case it failed.

So different from when the first Mars expedition had happened. An asteroid had slammed into Washington, D.C. and obliterated the capital. It made the entire world realize how fragile our hold on Earth was. Nations banded together and when the Secretary of Agriculture, who found himself president through the line of succession, said that we needed to get off the planet, people listened. We rose to the stars. The potential loss of an astronaut was just part of the risk. Now? Now it has been long enough that people are starting to forget that the danger is still there. That the need to explore is necessary.

Sheldon finished talking and just watched me processing it.

"I need to think about this."

"I know."

Then I closed my eyes and realized that I had to say no. It didn't matter how I felt about the trip or the chance to get back into space. The launch date he was talking about meant I'd have to go into training *now*. "I can't." I opened my eyes and stared at the wall where the publicity still of me and Nathaniel hung. "I have to turn it down."

"Talk to Nathaniel."

I grimaced. He would tell me to take it. "I can't."

I left Sheldon feeling more unsettled than I wanted to admit at the time. I stared out the window of the light rail, at the sepia sky. Rose tones were deepening near the horizon with sunset. It was dimmer and ruddier here, but with the dust, sunset could be just as glorious as on Earth.

It's a hard thing to look at something you want and to know that the right choice is to turn it down. Understand me: I wanted to go. Another opportunity like this would never come up for me. I was too old for normal missions. I knew it. Sheldon knew it. And Nathaniel would know it, too. I wish he had been in some other industry so I could lie and talk about "later." He knew the space program too well to be fooled.

And he wouldn't believe me if I said I didn't want to go. He knew how much I missed the stars.

That's the thing that I think none of us were prepared for in coming to Mars. The natural night sky on Mars is spectacular, because the atmosphere is so thin. But where humans live, under the dome, all you can see are the lights of the town reflecting against the dark curve. You can almost believe that they're stars. Almost. If you don't know what you are missing or don't remember the way the sky looked at night on Earth before the asteroid hit.

I wonder if Dorothy remembers the stars. She's young enough that she might not. Children on Earth still look at clouds of dust and stars are just a myth. God. What a bleak sky.

When I got home, Genevieve greeted me with her usual friendly chatter. Nathaniel looked like he wanted to push her out of the house so he could quiz me. I know Genevieve said good bye, and that we chatted, but the details have vanished now.

What I remember next is the rattle and thump of Nathaniel's walker as he pushed it into the kitchen. It slid forward. Stopped. He took two steps, steadied himself, and slid it forward again. Two steps. Steady. Slide.

I pushed away from the counter and straightened. "Do you want to be in the kitchen or the living room?"

"Sit down, Elma." He clenched the walker till the tendons stood out on the back of his hands, but they still trembled. "Tell me about the mission."

"What?" I froze.

"The mission." He stared at the ceiling, not at me. "That's why Sheldon called, right? So, tell me."

"I… All right." I pulled the tall stool out for him and waited until he eased onto it. Then I told him. He stared at the ceiling the whole time I talked. I spent the time watching him and memorizing the line of his cheek, and the shape of the small mole by the corner of his mouth.

When I finished, he nodded. "You should take it."

"What makes you think I want to?"

He lowered his head then, eyes just as piercing as they had always been. "How long have we been married?"

"I can't."

Nathaniel snorted. "I called Dr. Williams while you were out, figuring it would be something like this. I asked for a date when we could get a hospice." He held up his hand to stop the words forming on my lips. "She's not willing to tell me that. She did give me the date when the paralysis is likely to become total. Three months. Give or take a week."

We'd known this was coming, since he was diagnosed, but I still had to bite the inside of my lip to keep from sobbing. He didn't need to see me break down.

"So… I think you should tell them yes."

"Three months is not a lot of time, they can—"

"They can what? Wait for me to die? Jesus Christ, Elma. We know that's coming." He scowled at the floor. "Go. For the love of God, just take the mission."

I wanted to. I wanted to get off the planet and back into space and not have to watch him die. Not have to watch him lose control of his body piece by piece.

And I wanted to stay here and be with him and steal every moment left that he had breath in his body.

One of my favorite restaurants in Landing was Elmore's. The New Orleans-style café sat tucked back behind Thompson's Grocers on a little rise that lifted the dining room just high enough to see out to the edge of town and the dome's wall. They had a crawfish etouffee that would make you think you were back on Earth. The crawfish were raised in a tank and a little bigger than the ones I'd grown up with, but the spices came all the way from Louisiana on the mail runs twice a year.

Sheldon Spender knew it was my favorite and was taking ruthless advantage of that. And yet I came anyway. He sat across the table from me, with his back to the picture window that framed the view. His thinning hair was almost invisible against the sky. He didn't say a word. Just watched me, as the fellow to my right talked.

Garrett Biggs. I'd seen him at the Bradbury Space Center,

but we'd exchanged maybe five words before today. My work was mostly done before his time. They just trotted me out for the occasional holiday. Now, the man would not stop talking. He gestured with his fork as he spoke, punctuating the phrases he thought I needed to hear most. "Need some photos of you so we can exploit— I know it sounds ugly but we're all friends here, right? We can be honest, right? So, we can exploit your sacrifice to get the public really behind the Longevity Mission."

I watched the lettuce tremble on the end of his fork. It was pallid compared to my memory of lettuce on Earth. "I thought the public didn't know about the mission."

"They will. That's the key. Someone will leak it and we need to be ready." He waved the lettuce at me. "And that's why you are a brilliant choice for pilot. Octogenarian Grandmother Paves Way for Humanity."

"You can't pave the stars. I'm not a grandmother. And I'm sixty-three not eighty."

"It's a figure of speech. The point is that you're a PR goldmine."

I had known that they asked me to helm this mission because of my age—it would be a lot to ask of someone who had a full life ahead of them. Maybe I was naive to think that my experience in establishing the Mars colony was considered valuable.

How can I explain the degree to which I resented being used for publicity? This wasn't a new thing by a long shot. My entire career has been about exploitation for publicity. I had known it, and exploited it too, once I'd realized the power of having my uniform tailored to show my shape a little more clearly. You think they would have sent me to Mars if it weren't intended to be a colony? I was there to show all the lady housewives that they could go to space too. Posing in my flight suit, with my lips painted red, I had smiled at more cameras than my colleagues.

I stared at Garrett Biggs and his fork. "For someone in PR, you are awfully blunt."

"I'm honest. To you. If you were the public, I'd have you spinning so fast you'd generate your own gravity."

Sheldon cleared his throat. "Elma, the fact is that we're getting some pressure from a group of senators. They want to cut the budget for the project and we need to take steps or it won't happen."

I looked down and separated the tail from one of my crawfish. "Why?"

"The usual nonsense. People arguing that if we just wait, then ships will become fast enough to render the mission pointless. That includes a couple of serious misunderstandings of physics, but, be that as it may…" Sheldon paused and tilted his head, looking at me. He changed what he was about to say and leaned forward. "Is Nathaniel worse?"

"He's not better."

He winced at the edge in my voice. "I'm sorry. I know I strong-armed you into it, but I can find someone else."

"He thinks I should go." My chest hurt even considering it. But I couldn't stop thinking about the mission. "He knows it's the only way I'll get back into space."

Garrett Biggs frowned like I'd said the sky was green, instead of the pale Martian amber. "You're in space."

"I'm on Mars. It's still a planet."

I woke out of half-sleep, aware that I must have heard Nathaniel's bell, without being able to actually recall it. I pulled myself to my feet, putting a hand against the nightstand until I was steady. My right hip had stiffened again in the night. Arthritis is not something I approve of.

Turning on the hall light, I made my way down the stairs. The door at the bottom stood open so I could hear Nathaniel if he called. I couldn't sleep with him anymore, for fear of breaking him.

I went through into his room. It was full of gray shadows and the dark rectangle of his bed. In one corner, the silver arm of his walker caught the light.

"I'm sorry." [His voice cracked with sleep.]

"It's all right. I was awake anyway."

"Liar."

"Now, is that a nice thing to say?" I put my hand on the light switch. "Watch your eyes."

Every night we followed the same ritual and even though I knew the light would be painfully bright, I still winced as it came on. Squinting against the glare, I threw the covers back for him. The weight of them trapped him sometimes. He held his hands up, waiting for me to take them. I braced myself and let Nathaniel pull himself into a sitting position. On Earth, he'd have been bedridden long since. Of course, on Earth, his bone density would probably not have deteriorated so fast.

As gently as I could, I swung his legs to the side of the bed. Even allowing for the gravity, I was appalled anew by how light he was. His legs were like kindling wrapped in tissue. Where his pajamas had ridden up, purple bruises mottled his calf.

As soon as he was sitting up on the edge of the bed, I gave him the walker. He wrapped his shaking hands around the bars and tried to stand. He rose only a little before dropping back to the bed. I stayed where I was, though I ached to help. He sometimes took more than one try to stand at night, and didn't want help. Not until it became absolutely necessary. Even then, he wouldn't want it. I just hoped he'd let me help him when we got to that point.

On the second try, he got his feet under him and stood, shaking. With a nod, he pushed forward. "Let's go."

I followed him to the bathroom in case he lost his balance in there, which he did sometimes. The first time, I hadn't been home. We had hired Genevieve not long after that to sit with him when I needed to be out.

He stopped in the kitchen and bent a little at the waist with a sort of grunt.

"Are you all right?"

He shook his head and started again, moving faster. "I'm not—" He leaned forward, clenching his jaw. "I can't—"

The bathroom was so close.

"Oh, God. Elma..." A dark, fetid smell filled the kitchen. Nathaniel groaned. "I couldn't—"

I put my hand on his back. "Hush. We're almost there. We'll get you cleaned up."

"I'm sorry, I'm sorry." He pushed the walker forward, head hanging. A trail of damp footsteps followed him. The ammonia stink of urine joined the scent of his bowels.

I helped him lower his pajamas. The weight of them had made them sag on his hips. Dark streaks ran down his legs and dripped onto the bathmat. I eased him onto the toilet.

My husband bent his head forward, and he wept.

I remember wetting a washcloth and running it over his legs. I know that I must have tossed his soiled pajamas into the cleaner, and that I wiped up the floor, but those details have mercifully vanished. But what I can't forget, and I wish to God that I could, is Nathaniel sitting there crying.

I asked Genevieve to bring adult diapers to us the next day. The strange thing was how familiar the package felt. I'd used them on launches when we had to sit in the capsule for hours and there was no option to get out of our space suit. It's one of the many glamorous details of being an astronaut that the publicity department does *not* share with the public.

There is a difference, however, from being required to wear one for work and what Nathaniel faced. He could not put them on by himself without losing his balance. Every time I had to change the diaper, he stared at the wall with his face slack and hopeless.

Nathaniel and I'd made the decision not to have children. They aren't conducive to a life in space, you know? I mean there's the radiation, and the weightlessness, but more it was that I was gone all the time. I couldn't give up the stars... but I found myself wishing that we hadn't made that decision. Part of it was wishing that I had some connection to the next generation. More of it was wanting someone to share the burden of decision with me.

What happens after Nathaniel dies? What do I have left here? More specifically, how much will I regret not going on the mission?

And if I'm in space, how much will I regret abandoning my husband to die alone?

You see why I was starting to wish that we had children?

In the afternoon, we were sitting in the living room, pretending to work. Nathaniel sat with his pencil poised over the paper and stared out the window as though he were working. I'm pretty sure he wasn't but I gave him what privacy I could and started on one of my eagles.

The phone rang and gave us both something of a relief, I think, to have a distraction. The phone sat on a table by Nathaniel's chair so he could reach it easily if I wasn't in the room. With my eyes averted, his voice sounded as strong as ever as he answered.

"Hang on, Sheldon. Let me get Elma for— Oh. Oh, I see."

I snipped another feather but it was more as a way to

avoid making eye contact than because I really wanted to keep working.

"Of course I've got a few minutes. I have nothing but time these days." He ran his hand through his hair and let it rest at the back of his neck. "I find it hard to believe that you don't have programmers on staff who can't handle this."

He was quiet then as Sheldon spoke; I could hear only the distorted tinny sound of his voice rising and falling. At a certain point, Nathaniel picked up his pencil again and started making notes. Whatever Sheldon was asking him to do, *that* was the moment when Nathaniel decided to say "yes."

I set my eagle aside and went into the kitchen. My first reaction—God. It shames me but my first reaction was anger. How dare he? How dare he take a job without consulting with me when I was turning down this thing I so desperately wanted because of *him*. I had the urge to snatch up the phone and tell Sheldon that I would go.

I pushed that down carefully and looked at it.

Nathaniel had been urging me to go. No deliberate action of his was keeping me from accepting. Only my own upbringing and loyalty and… and I loved him. If I did not want to be alone after he passed, how could I leave him to face the end alone?

The decision would be easier if I knew when he would die.

I still hate myself for thinking that.

I heard the conversation end and Nathaniel hung up the phone. I filled a glass with water to give myself an excuse for lingering in the kitchen. I carried it back into the living room and sat down on the couch.

Nathaniel had his lower lip between his teeth and was scowling at the page on top of his notepad. He jotted a number in the margin with a pencil before he looked up.

"That was Sheldon." He glanced back at the page.

I settled in my chair and fidgeted with the wedding band on my finger. It had gotten loose in the last year. "I'm going to turn them down."

"What— But, Elma." His gaze flattened and he gave me a small frown. "Are you… are you sure it's not depression? That's making you want to stay, I mean."

[snorts] "Now what do I have to be depressed about?"

"Please." He ran his hands through his hair and knit them together at the back of his neck. "I want you to go so you won't be here when… It's just going to get worse from here."

The devil of it was that he wasn't wrong. That didn't mean he was right, either, but I couldn't flat out tell him he was wrong. I set down my scissors and pushed the magnifier out of the way. "It's not just depression."

"I don't understand. There's a chance to go back into space." He dropped his hands and sat forward. "I mean… if I die before the mission leaves and you're grounded here. How would you feel?"

I looked away. My gaze was pointed to the window and the view of the house across the lane. But I did not see the windows or the red brick walls. All I saw was a black and gray cloth made of despair. "I had a life that I enjoyed before this opportunity came up. There's no reason I shouldn't keep on enjoying it. I enjoy teaching. There are a hundred reasons to enjoy life here."

He pointed his pencil at me the way he used to do when he spotted a flaw in reasoning at a meeting, but the pencil quivered in his grip now. "If that's true, then why haven't you told them no yet?"

The answer to that was not easy. Because I *wanted* to be in the sky, weightless, and watching the impossibly bright stars. Because I didn't want to watch Nathaniel die. "What did Sheldon ask you to do?"

"NASA wants more information about LS-579."

"I imagine they do." I twisted that wedding band around as if it were a control that I could use. "I would... I would hate... As much as I miss being in space, I would hate myself if I left you here. To have and to hold, in sickness and in health. Till death do us part and all that. I just can't."

"Well... just don't tell him no. Not yet. Let me talk to Dr. Williams and see if she can give us a clearer date. Maybe there won't be a schedule conflict after al—"

"Stop it! Just *stop*. This is my decision. I'm the one who has to live with the consequences. Not you. So, stop trying to put your guilt off onto me because the devil of it is, one of us is going to feel guilty here, but I'm the one who will have to live with it."

I stormed out of the room before he could answer me or I could say anything worse. And yes—I knew that he couldn't follow me and for once I was glad.

Dorothy came not long after that. To say that I was flummoxed when I opened the door wouldn't do justice to my surprise. She had her medical bag with her and I think that's the only thing that gave me the power of speech. "Since when do you make house calls?"

She paused, mouth partially open, and frowned. "Weren't you told I was coming?"

"No." I remembered my manners and stepped back so she could enter. "Sorry. You just surprised me is all."

"I'm sorry. Mr. Spender asked me to come out. He thought you'd be more comfortable if I stayed with Mr. York while you were gone." She shucked off her shoes in the dust room.

I looked back through the kitchen to the living room, where Nathaniel sat just out of sight. "That's right kind and all, but I don't have any appointments today."

"Do I have the date wrong?"

The rattle and thump of Nathaniel's walker started. I abandoned Dorothy and ran through the kitchen. He shouldn't be getting up without me. If he lost his balance again— What? It might kill him if he fell? Or it might not kill him fast enough so that his last days were in even more pain.

He met me at the door and looked past me. "Nice to see you, Doc."

Dorothy had trailed after me into the kitchen. "Sir."

"You bring that eagle to show me?"

She nodded and I could see the little girl she had been in the shyness of it. She lifted her medical bag to the kitchen table and pulled out a battered shoe box of the sort that we don't see up here much. No sense sending up packaging when it just takes up room on the rocket. She lifted the lid off and pulled out tissue that had once been pink and had faded to almost white. Unwrapping it, she pulled out my eagle.

It's strange seeing something that you made that long ago. This one was in flight, but had its head turned to the side as though it were looking back over its shoulder. It had an egg clutched in its talons.

Symbolism a little blunt, but clear. Seeing it I remembered when I had made it. I remembered the conversation that I had had with Dorothy when she was a little girl.

I picked it up, turning it over in my hands. The edges of the paper had become soft with handling over the years so it felt more like corduroy than cardstock. Some of the smaller feathers were torn loose showing that this had been much-loved. The fact that so few were missing said more about the place it had held for Dorothy.

She had asked me, standing outside the fence in the shadow of the rocket gantry, if I was still going to Mars. I had said yes.

Then she had said, "You going to have kids on Mars?"

What she could not have known—what she likely still did not know—was that I had just come from a conversation with Nathaniel when we decided that we would not have children. It had been a long discussion over the course of two years and it did not rest easy on me. I was still grieving for the choice, even though I knew it was the right one.

The radiation, the travel… the stars were always going to call me and I could ask *him* to be patient with that, but it was not fair to a child. We had talked and talked and I had built that eagle while I tried to grapple with the conflicts between my desires. I made the eagle looking back, holding an egg, at the choices behind it.

And when Dorothy had asked me if I would have kids on Mars, I put the regulation smile on, the one you learn to give while wearing 160 pounds of space suit in Earth gravity while a photographer takes just one more photo. I've learned to smile through pain, thank you. "Yes, honey. Every child born on Mars will be there because of me."

"What about the ones born here?"

The child of tragedy, the double-orphan. I had knelt in front of her and pulled the eagle out of my bag. "Those most of all."

Standing in my kitchen, I lifted my head to look at Nathaniel. His eyes were bright. It took a try or two before I could find my voice again. "Did you know? Did you know which one she had?"

"I guessed." He pushed into the kitchen, the walker sliding and rattling until he stood next to me. "The thing is, Elma, I'm going to be gone in a year either way. We decided not to have children because of your career."

"We made that decision together."

"I know." He raised a hand off the walker and put it on my

arm. "I'm not saying we didn't. What I'm asking is that you make this career decision for *me*. I want you to go."

I set the eagle back in its nest of tissue and wiped my eyes. "So you tricked her into coming out just to show me that?"

Nathaniel laughed, sounding a little embarrassed. "Nope. Talked to Sheldon. There's a training session this afternoon that I want you to go to."

"I don't want to leave you."

"You won't. Not completely." He gave a sideways grin and I could see the young man he'd been. "My program will be flying with you."

"That's not the same."

"It's the best I can offer."

I looked away and caught Dorothy staring at us with a look of both wonder and horror on her face. She blushed when I met her gaze. "I'll stay with him."

"I know and it was kind of Sheldon to ask but—"

"No, I mean. If you go… I'll make sure he's not alone."

Dorothy lived in the middle of the great Mars plains in the home of Elma, who was an astronaut, and Nathaniel, who was an astronaut's husband. I live in the middle of space in a tiny capsule filled with punchcards and magnetic tape. I am not alone, though someone who doesn't know me might think I appear to be.

I have the stars.

I have my memories.

And I have Nathaniel's last program. After it runs, I will make an eagle and let my husband fly.

TAD WILLIAMS
EVERY FUZZY BEAST OF THE EARTH,
EVERY PINK FOWL OF THE AIR

Ever since my childhood, when my father helped install the 40-watt light bulb that represented baby Jesus in the local congregational church's Christmas play, I have been deeply interested in religion. My parents never gave me one of my own, which is probably why when the Virgin Mary appeared to me on a piece of toast, I buttered it and ate it instead of sharing the blessed visitation with other people. (That may also explain why I spent my adolescence following girls who smelled like wheat.)

The Bible is a bit like a jukebox full of familiar songs – everybody knows the first words to lots of it. You say, "Blessed are," and most people can immediately answer, "the peacemakers" (or "cheesemakers" if they grew up with Monty Python), but they get a little fuzzier after that. It's just like how everyone can sing, "I get knocked down! But I get up again!" when Chumbawamba comes on, but after that they kind of have to go, "Hmmm, something the night away, hmmm, hmmm," because the "knocked down" bit is the only part they actually know.

And like an old jukebox at a seldom-visited pizza parlor, the Bible's full of all-time classics like "Let there be light!" Everybody knows that one – in fact, admit it, you've probably said that once or twice yourself while switching on a lamp. But do they remember all the words to the rest of that part, all that "And Samuel begat Barnabas, who married Sadie, and they begat Caleb and Tyler, who although only fraternal twins, later each begat at least one child named Zebedee…"? Do they? I think not.

So anyway, when I was thinking about a famous literary first line to use for this anthology (and after editor Gardner Dozois politely informed me that "This is the city. Los Angeles, California. I work here. I carry a badge," was from the TV show *Dragnet* and had nothing to do with Charles Dickens at all) of course Genesis popped into my mind, due to my lifelong interest in religion. Then Gardner reminded me that "Something In The Air Tonight" was actually from Phil Collins's solo work, so I nimbly changed my opening line to the famous "And in the beginning God created…" bit (which I'm told by Bible readers is kind of the "My Heart Will Go On" of the Old Testament).

The rest, if not actually history, will at least fill the next two or three minutes of your life with the kind of concentrated, Tad-related enjoyment that only my own family and neighbors get to experience all day, every day. You need not thank me, just absorb this story and let the high-quality spirituality wash right over you. Your immortal soul will thank you. So will Phil Collins. Chumbawamba, however, still think you're a bourgeois pig, and if they ever see you trying to play any Flock of Seagulls on their jukebox again, they'll give you a good kicking. Here's my story, "Every Fuzzy Beast of the Earth, Every Pink Fowl of the Air."

EVERY FUZZY BEAST OF THE EARTH, EVERY PINK FOWL OF THE AIR

BY TAD WILLIAMS

"First God made heaven and earth. The earth was without form and void, and darkness was upon the face of the deep; and the Spirit of God was moving over the face of the waters. And God said, 'Let there be light'; and there was—' Oh, bother, what now?"

"Sorry? Didn't get that last bit, Gabriel, sir."

"That wasn't supposed to be part of it. Bugger. Now I'll have to start all over. It doesn't work right without the proper dramatic rhythm." He peered down at the new Earth, gleaming like a blue and white pearl. "What *is* going on down there, Metatron?"

"Couldn't say, sir." The junior angel squinted. "Looks like someone's wandered onto the work site."

"Lovely." Gabriel shook out his wings with a discontented rattle of plumage. "Just lovely. Schedule already shot to pieces, supposed to be finished already, Himself resting but we're still building and the overtime is through the roof. *Now* what?" He pushed back his halo, which had begun to sag a little. "Might as well find out. You coming?"

Metatron nodded. "Yes, sir. Just sweeping a little star dust off the firmament, then I'm right with you."

"We spread the stardust there on purpose," Gabriel said, frowning. "Atmosphere, you know."

"Atmosphere? But we don't have any out here…"

Gabriel sighed. "All right, 'ambience' – is that better? We put it there for ambience, so stop sweeping it up. Remember, we want this universe to have that lived-in look. That's what they're going for nowadays."

"Hey, there!" Gabriel said as they entered the Garden, "who are you and what are you doing here? This area is off-limits to non-essential personnel." He stopped, blinking. "What are you, anyway?"

"I'm a little girl," said the little girl. "More specifically, I'm Sophia."

"Hi, Sophia," said Metatron, who was one of the friendlier angels, and was constantly bringing home stray comets.

Gabriel sighed. "I'm sure it's all very nice, you having a name and all – you're way ahead of all the other Earth-dwellers that way, so good for you – but you really can't be here, little girl. This is a very, very important project, and God Himself wants us…"

"…to finish everything up in time for when He comes back to work tomorrow. I know." Even standing straight, she was still only as high as where Metatron's belly button might be (if such things existed, which of course they didn't. Not yet). "And I'm going to help you finish it…"

"You most certainly are not…!" Gabriel began.

"…because God is my daddy."

Gabriel stared. "What did you just say?"

"That God is my daddy? He is. And He said I could do anything I wanted to help, and that you had to let me, Gabriel, or else He'd put you back on supernova-extinguishing duty, and you know how *that* was. That's what He said."

The archangel stared for a long moment at the little girl. She stared back. Gabriel looked away first. "Metatron," he said, "may I speak to you for a moment in private?"

"It's your duty to keep her out of trouble, Metatron," the archangel said when they had moved away from the girl. He peered out from the shadow of the Don't-Eat-This-Fruit Tree that God had insisted on planting despite there being several more attractive alternatives, including a very nice flowering Tree of Moral Relativity. "Look at her! Why on my shift? Why not when Michael's on duty? He gets all the breaks. No wonder he's the Big Guy's favorite."

The girl was examining a tiny winged creature that she held in careful hands, her small face solemn. After a moment she tossed it up into the air. It rose, then dropped, and hit the ground with a quiet *thump*. The little creature gave Sophia a mistrustful look as it limped away.

"What do you call those things?" she asked.

"Birds," Gabriel called. "Some of your father's favorite creatures."

"Why do they have wings but they don't fly?"

"Fly?" Gabriel shuddered. "Do you hear her, Metatron?" he said in a quiet but panicky voice. "She wants the birds to fly! What next? She'll be yanking the fishes out of the ground and throwing them in the river! Just... just take care of it. And keep her away from me."

"Ummm," said Metatron. He watched the girl beginning to unearth frightened carp from their burrows. "Do I have to...?"

But Gabriel had already hurried back to Heaven to finish some important paperwork that he had ignored for several days.

"What is it now, Metatron?"

The angel was wringing his hands in a very guilty way. "I think you'd better come down."

Gabriel closed his eyes, searching for the patience he was certain he'd had when the morning began. "What is it now? The girl?"

"It'll be easier if you just come."

There was a great deal of confusion down in the Garden when they arrived, but no sign of Sophia.

"Where is she? He'll kill us if we lose His daughter!"

"She's around somewhere. But to be honest, sir, it's getting a bit much for me to handle all by my—"

"What in the name of our boss did she do to the *trees*?" Gabriel stared in horror. "She's turned every one of them upside down!"

"I know, I know! I told her not to, but she insisted. She said that the roots looked… *icky* just sticking up into the air."

"Icky? What does that mean?"

"I think it means she didn't like it. Anyway, she said that the leaves and branches would look better in the air and the roots in the ground, then she just, well, turned them all upside down, as you can see."

"It's so… green, now."

"Exactly. But she claims it looks nicer."

"This is a nightmare, Metatron. And what's that horrible noise?"

"Another of her little ideas, sir. She thought that the water splashing in the streams and rivers should make a different noise."

"What's wrong with growling?" Gabriel hiked up his robe and stepped closer to the stream. "That's a very strange sound it makes now, kind of… musical. Soft and lyrical, plink, plink, plink – what is that about? Completely spoils the point of warning people not to fall in the water."

"She says we can use the old, loud noise for something like fast-moving, dangerous water, like waterfalls and rapids. This would be just for shallow streams and dripping snowmelt and things like that."

"Snowmelt? She wants the snow to *melt*?"

"Sometimes, yes." Metatron nodded, shamefaced. "You

have no idea what she wants, sir. Some of it is just terrifying."

"Well, wait until I catch up with her, *I'll* tell her – oh, sweet Employer, what is *that*? That's the most horrible thing I've ever seen! They're… they're all *pink*."

"Sorry, sir, but she said the old gray flamingos were yucky and boring."

"Yucky?" Gabriel could hear his own voice getting shrill.

"It's like icky, I think." Metatron shook his head sorrowfully as the squadron of rose-colored birds suddenly took to the air. Meanwhile, Gabriel was struggling not to scream.

"They *fly*?"

"All the birds do now. And there's more…"

Metatron broke off because Sophia had appeared at the other side of the Garden, her hands full of small, furry animals. "There you are, Gabriel. I had a really good idea. See these? I call them 'bunnies'."

"They're already called 'rabbits', young lady. We tested it on a focus group and they liked 'rabbits' just fine."

"'Bunnies' is better. Anyway, I had another idea. Our bunnies would be a lot cuter if you got rid of these long, naked tails which are really gross and gave them little fluffy tails instead. That would be much cuter."

Gabriel blinked. "But all the rodents have long, skinny, naked tails, Miss Sophia – the mice, the rats…"

"They can keep them. But the bunnies and the squirrels need fluffy ones. Give the squirrels *long* fluffy ones, though, because they like to jump through the air from branch to branch and it looks pretty."

"How are they going to jump from branch to branch at the bottom of ponds?"

"Squirrels live in trees now." She set the rabbits down; they quickly scattered into the grass with little flicks of their tiny new tails. "With the birds."

It was all Gabriel could do not to fall to his knees, moaning. "My Lord, what have You done to Your servant…?" he muttered.

"I don't know how you ever got along without me." The girl walked through the sun-warmed Garden. "A lot of this is really stupid and gross. I mean, look. What's this?" She bent, then lifted a large ovoid object from the grass.

"It's an egg," said Gabriel, but his confidence was a bit shaken and he turned to Metatron for confirmation. "It's an egg, isn't it?"

She frowned. "I *know* it's an egg. But what kind?"

"That's a lion egg. Big, fierce creature. Top of the food chain. Has a loud, impressive roar…" Gabriel blanched. "You're not going to make it go 'splashy-splashy-splashy' like you did with the stream, are you?"

"Don't be stupid. I'm talking about the egg part. Have you even seen a baby lion?" She cracked open the egg and let the tiny bundle of fur roll out into her hand. "Look! It's adorable! All fuzzy-wuzzy!" She leaned closer. "Yes, who's fuzzy-wuzzy – is it you? Is it you, little lion? Are you my widdle cutie-wootie?" She stroked the tiny cat's belly until it wriggled and purred.

"Miss Sophia, I hardly think…"

"Cute little furry guys like this shouldn't hatch out of *eggs*. Eggs are icky. They're for lizards and snakes and bugs and gross things like that. Which reminds me, all the bugs and spiders and snakes are going to live in holes and under rocks now. Because they're gross."

Gabriel was now wondering whether God would accept his transfer request if he pretended he had suddenly become allergic to Earth.

"So all the fuzzy ones are going to be born without using eggs?" asked Metatron, who seemed to be trying to keep up with this nonsense, and was in fact making a note.

"Yeah." She lifted up a very strange creature Gabriel had never seen before, an unlikely mix. "Maybe this one could keep using eggs because he's part bird. See, I put a duck's bill on a beaver! I call it a platypus!"

"How do you spell that?" asked Metatron, still making notes.

"But if the furry ones can't have eggs," Gabriel asked, "then how will they be born? Just... fall out of the sky or something?" The archangel paled and looked upward. "I didn't mean that..."

"I don't care." Sophia dismissed the problem with a wave of her little hand. "*You* think of something. Because now I need to fix something else. It's super important."

She beckoned for the angels to follow her, which they did. The Garden really was extremely green now, Gabriel couldn't help noticing, and the new splashing noise of the stream gave it a peaceful air in the late-afternoon sun. For a few seconds he found himself wondering if maybe one or two of the child's suggestions might not be acceptable, as long as nobody examined the whole thing too carefully. All the different-colored birds were impossibly garish, of course, and she seemed to have gone out of her way to daub the butterflies with shades never imagined on any angelic drawing-board, but still, as long as she didn't mess about with any of the Lord's favorite creations...

"That," she said, stopping and pointing. "That has got to go."

Gabriel suddenly went queasy. "You mean...?"

"Yes, that stupid hairless monkey-thing. It's ugly and it's stupid and it smells."

It was Adam, of course, the apple of the Lord's eye, the only one of the new creatures made more or less in God's own image.

"But… what's wrong with it, Miss Sophia?" Gabriel didn't really want to know, since it was bound to upset him, but he was desperate to stall her. "Your father was very, very specific about wanting…"

"Well, *look* at it."

"That's exactly what he's supposed to do. He's supposed to have dominion over the beasts of the Earth, and use them to feed himself," Gabriel said.

Adam heard them talking and looked up from where he had been repeatedly spearing a tomato, and waved. "Hi, Gabe! Hi, Metty! What's up?"

"Well, for one thing, he's totally stupid," said Sophia, not hiding the scorn. "He just goes around spearing everything. He's been killing that tomato for about ten minutes and there's nothing left of it to eat. He needs someone to tell him how to know which things to stab and which things to harvest. Someone like me."

Gabriel drew himself to his full angelic height. A line had to be drawn. "I feel quite sure that your father is not going to let you follow his favorite creation around and give him orders all day…"

"Okay, fine, fine. Sheesh." Sophia rolled her eyes. She watched as Adam climbed a tall tree and began enthusiastically spearing a beehive. A moment later, surrounded now by irritated bees, he began to screech and wave his arms, then fell off the branch and plummeted to the ground. "Look, part of him popped out," the girl said, interested. "That's gross… but also kind of cool."

Gabriel sighed. "Go fix him back up, will you, Metatron? I admit it would be nice if he'd quit doing things like that."

"I've got a better idea." The girl hurried over, and before Gabriel or Metatron could stop her, she had lifted up the curve of shining bone that had popped out of Adam when he hit the ground. She examined it thoughtfully, then set it back on the ground. After a momentary shimmer of light, the rib was gone and in its place lay another fully formed Adam creature. This one, though, had subtle differences.

"What is that supposed to be?" Gabriel demanded. "It's lumpy. And it hasn't got a nozzle!"

"It's a more sophisticated design," said the girl. "You won't see this one always tripping and hitting himself in the plums like the old one. In fact, I don't even want to call it 'him'. It's named 'Eve', and it's a 'her'."

Gabriel was considering an immediate transfer. Somebody must be mortaring up the walls of Hell, and that suddenly sounded like a very comfortable, safe job compared to his current occupation.

"I don't get it," said Metatron. "Why do we need a second one? Won't they fight?"

Sophia stuck her tongue out at him. "You're just grumpy 'cause mine is *better*. They'll get along fine. They can make babies together, like the animals do."

"We already took care of that! He's full of eggs!"

"Eeewww!" Sophia shook her head in disgust. "No. Do something different. They can make babies some other way."

"But what…?"

"I don't care. Just take care of it." She looked around in satisfaction, but when she turned her eyes to the sky, reddened now with light of the setting sun, her expression soured. "I just thought of one more thing that's really dumb that I have to fix."

Gabriel fought down panic. God was going to have a screaming fit about the lumpy new Adam. What now? "Honestly, Sophia – Miss – it's getting late. I mean, it's going to be dark soon, so maybe you should…"

"That's what I'm talking about. Watch." She pointed to the sky.

"I don't see anything." Gabriel turned helplessly to Metatron. "Do you see anything?"

"Sssshhh. Just watch." She waited as the sun disappeared behind the west end of the Garden.

"I forgot to tell you," Metatron whispered. "She got rid of one of the directions…"

"What? You mean there's only *four* now?" Gabriel gasped. "We're going to have to redo all the winds and everything…!"

"Now look," said Sophia. "Don't you see?"

Gabriel looked up at the sky. With the disappearance of the sun, the stars sparkled against the dark sky like jewels. "See what? It's lovely. Your father said that was some of our best work…"

"It's boring. And it's really *dumb*, too. I mean, you've got the sun up there all day long when everything's already perfectly bright, but as soon as it gets dark and you really need it, boom, the sun goes away! How stupid is that?"

"But… but that was always your father's plan…"

"No, see, what you need is a nice bright sun for the night-time, too." She clearly was not going to accept disagreement. "I'm going to make one."

"No!" As soon as he saw Sophia's expression, Gabriel immediately realized he should have spoken more courteously – after all, what if God's daughter decided the universe didn't need archangels, either? "I mean, yes! Grand idea! But if it's sunny all the time…" – he cast about for an excuse – "then… then the cute, furry, iddy-widdy bunnies and kitties won't get any sleep. Yes. Because the light will keep them awake."

"Kitties will sleep in the daytime," she said, scowling.

"Okay, but bunnies! They *love* to sleep! And just think of all the fish up in the trees getting sunburned…"

Metatron leaned toward him. "They're in the water now,

sir, remember?" said the junior angel, sotto voce.

"…I mean the birds, yes, the birds, high up in the trees. If the sun's out all day, the cute colorful little birdie-wirdies will all get sunburned and they'll be so sad!"

Sophia gave him a withering look. "'Birdie-wirdies'? My dad must really like you, to let you keep this job." She shook her head. "Okay, then not a regular sun. Just a little one that doesn't shine so bright."

And before Gabriel could invent another excuse, she raised her hands and suddenly a vast ivory disk hung in the night sky. As Sophia stood admiring it, several unsuspecting birds and even a butterfly or two banged into it, leaving pockmarks on the pearly surface.

"Stupid birds," she said. "Guess I'll have to put it up higher."

The first day of the new week had already come once before, but this time it had a name – Monday. The Lord God showed up in the morning with his coffee in a travel-cup, looking relaxed and fit.

"Good to be back, good to be back," He said. "Ready to get to work, boys. Still have to figure out how Adam is going to lay those eggs – I mean, any way that we do it, it's going to look funny…"

"Uh, now that you mention it, Lord," said Gabriel, "we wanted to talk to you about that and… and some other things. See, a few changes got made yesterday, while you were gone. Your daughter came and rearranged a few things."

"My who?"

"Your daughter, sir. Your daughter Sophia."

God lifted one of His great, bushy brows. "Daughter. Sophia. Mine, you say? But I don't have a daughter."

Gabriel was suddenly grateful that God had not seen fit to give the archangel a nozzle like Adam's, because Gabriel felt certain he would have wet himself. "You… you don't? But she said she was your daughter."

"Impossible. I mean, really, Gabriel, where would I come up with a kid? Just… I don't know, impregnate a virgin human or something?" He frowned. "Which would mean Adam, since he's the only one, and he's not really my idea of…" The Lord God trailed off, staring at the Garden. "What's going on down there? Why are there two Adams?"

Gabriel swallowed. "I'll go get Metatron. He was in charge of the whole thing."

His master was barely listening. "And what's with the trees? Why is it so Me-blessed *green*?"

When Metatron arrived he quickly realized that Gabriel was planning to throw him under the celestial chariot. To his credit, he did not attempt to return the favor. "But, Lord, she was *here*," he said. "She told us she was your daughter and that her name was Sophia. Why would we make that up?"

God frowned. "Well, in a few billion years Sophia is going to mean 'wisdom' – so maybe you're telling the truth at that."

"We are, Lord. We really are," said Metatron.

"I don't understand," Gabriel said. "What do you mean, her name's going to mean 'wisdom'?"

"Simple. I was sleeping most of the day yesterday – all that parting the darkness from the face of the waters and whatnot turns out to be surprisingly tiring – and suddenly she just… shows up here. Holy Wisdom. I suspect she was a part of *me*."

"Wow." Gabriel had heard his boss say some weird things, but this was right up there. "That's deep, Lord. Part of you? You really think so?"

"Maybe." God set his coffee down. "Can't be positive, of course – My ways are mysterious, right?"

"They sure are, Lord," said Metatron.

"They sure are." God laughed and clapped the junior angel on the back, which set a few feathers flying. "So let's forget about all this for now and get back to work, guys – maybe see if we can get that whole ozone-layer thing cracked before we break for lunch. What do you say?"

"You're the boss," said Gabriel.

"Yes, for My sins, I am." God laughed.

Gabriel hoped He'd still be in a good mood after He saw His first platypus.

JAMES PATRICK KELLY
DECLARATION

I'm mostly known for my short fiction and have been fortunate to have earned some lovely recognition from both the Hugo and Nebula Awards voters. The story you are about to read, "Declaration," arose out of my frustration with a famous science fiction movie trilogy.

One of my biggest problems with the *Matrix* franchise isn't the way the Wachowskis undercut the achievement of the first film with two redundant and imaginatively impoverished sequels. Rather it was that they let their story default to the standard Evil Computer plot. Recall that Agent Smith asks Neo in the first movie, "Did you know that the first Matrix was designed to be a perfect human world? Where none suffered, where everyone would be happy. It was a disaster. No one would accept the program."

Really? Really? When I peer through my computer screen, I see a world in which the video game industry made twice as much money as the recorded music industry last year and threatens to out-earn the film industry in the not too distant future. We love virtuality! Some people are even getting addicted to it. Look, if someone managed to build a virtual world "where none suffered, where everyone would be happy" buyers would be busting down the doors of unreal estate agents. Reality snobs might argue that any simulation would be just a shadow of reality – like *The Matrix* with its cheapjack 1999 simulation. No! That was just the Wachowskis putting their thumbs on the scale. Why would you furnish a simulated reality from the Dollar Store?

I know, it's just a movie, a seventeen-year-old movie. But it is also the culture beginning to think about its future, which is why it's worth interrogating the assumptions here. What if the snoozing population in *The Matrix* was fed a nice nutritionally complete vegan broth? What if virtuality made them happy, in the same way that interacting with today's intricate video games gives so many millions pleasure? And would it really be so terrible if they never smelled a real rose again? Yes, that last would be a loss, no question. But how many people in our real world have access to gardens and the leisure to sniff flowers?

Anyway, rant over. But that's why my first line comes from an oddball source. The Declaration of Independence is our most famous political document – America's birth announcement. I think it likely that someday, some community of cyberfolk may actually want to assert their independence from reality. Here then, is "Declaration."

DECLARATION
BY JAMES PATRICK KELLY

"When in the course of human events…"

As Silk spoke, fluffy clouds formed the phrase in a Magritte sky, which was simultaneously noon and dusk. While Remeny could appreciate the control Silk had over his softtime domain, she wished he wouldn't steer their meeting in an artsy direction. They had work to do.

"Wait," said Botão, "what about *we the people*?"

"That's the other one." Silk shot her a (.1) anger blip fading to (.7) irritation. "The Constitution."

"But we're the people we're talking about." Botão ignored Silk's blippage. "That's the whole point."

"Human events," said Silk. "If you'd wait just a second, I'm getting to the people part."

Botão had only been assigned to their school coop team for a month now and Remeny knew what she did not: Silk didn't like to be challenged, especially not in his own domain. They had chosen his corner of virtuality because Silk had enough excess capacity to host them all, but his was not the ideal place to plot their pretend revolution. The opening words of the Declaration of Independence were going wispy above them.

"Get on with it then," said Sturm. "And skip the special effects."

"When in the course of human events," Silk said, "it becomes necessary for one *people* to dissolve the political bands which have connected them with another…"

"Okay," said Botão.

"…and to assume among the powers of the earth, the separate and equal station to which the Laws of Nature and of Nature's God entitle them, a decent respect to the opinions of mankind requires that they should declare the causes which impel them to the separation."

The four others – Remeny, Sturm, Botão and Toybox – scanned each other and then turned on Silk. They had agreed to close all private channels and keep their avatars emotionally transparent, so the air filled with blips of confusion and disapproval.

"Laws of Nature?" said Toybox. "What the hell is that about?"

"Maybe relativity." Sturm's scorn blip started at (.3) and climbed.

"They didn't even have relativity back then."

"They did, they were just too stupid to realize it."

"Mankind? What about the other fifty-two percent?" Botão was laughing now. "And who is Nature's God?"

"Exactly," said Sturm. "I call bullshit. Crusty oldschool bullshit."

Remeny kept quiet; she focused on Silk, who was waiting for them to calm down. "Agreed," he said. "But it will mean something to the old people because Thomas Jefferson wrote this stuff."

"Who's he and so what?" said Toybox.

"Jefferson as in Jefferson County," said Remeny. "As in where we live."

"I live in softtime." At (.9+), Toybox's rage was nearly unreadable – but then he was always shouting. "That's where I live."

Silk waved a hand in front of his face, as if the blip was

a bad smell. "History is important to reality snobs," he said. "This gets their attention."

Remeny noticed that he was keeping his temper in check. She was definitely interested in Silk; poise was something she looked for in a boyfriend.

"So will making their lights flicker," said Toybox. This was why he had flunked one coop already. "Crashing their flix."

"We're not talking about anything like that," said Botão. "We're students, not terrorists."

"Speak for yourself." Sturm spread his hands and between them appeared an oldschool clock. "Revolutions don't play by the rules." Its face showed two minutes to midnight.

Remeny couldn't believe Sturm, of all people, aligning himself with terrorists. She agreed with Botão; she didn't really care about the revolution. All she wanted was to get a grade for her senior cooperative, graduate and never log on to the Jefferson County Educational Oversight Service again. The problem was that a third of her grade for coop was for contribution to the team's cooperative culture. The senior coop was supposed to demonstrate to the EOS that students had the social skills to succeed in softtime by coming together anonymously to plan and execute a project that had hardtime outcomes.

Of course, anonymity wasn't easy in a county like Jefferson. Students spent hours in soft and hardtime trying to figure out who was who. Botão, for example, was one of the refugees from Brazil and probably lived in Tugatown. Remeny had first met her two years ago in the EOS playgrounds, mostly ForSquare and Sanctuary. Now Botão was Sturm's friend too – maybe even his girlfriend. Toybox defied the rules of anonymnity by dressing his avatar in clothes that pointed to hardtime identity. Everyone knew that he was the Jason Day whose body was stashed in bin 334 of the Komfort Kare body stack on Route 127 in Pikeville. Unfortunately for him, no one cared. Bad luck to have him on the team – if he was going to be such a shithead, they might all flunk. Good luck, though, to get Silk – whoever he was. The avatar was new to the senior class, but Silk didn't act new. She thought maybe he was a duplicate of some rich kid they already knew. It cost to be in two places at once and considering how crush his domain was, Remeny guessed Silk had serious money. Probably lived in that gated community at the lake. She wondered what he looked like in hardtime. His avatar was certainly hot in his leathers and tanker boots. Sturm's identity, obviously, was no secret to her, although she hoped that she was the only one on the team who knew that he was her twin brother.

It took them most of a prickly afternoon to rewrite the second paragraph of the Declaration of Independence; they were being as cooperative as cats. Sturm and Silk took the revolution too seriously, in Remeny's opinion, as if it might happen next Wednesday. Silk argued for making as few changes as possible to their version; Sturm said their demands should be clear.

"Unalienable?" said Sturm. "There's no such word."

"There was back then."

"Well, this is now."

Botão seemed nervous about advocating the overthrow of anything. She was probably worried about being deported. "I like life, liberty, and the pursuit of happiness." Botão was standing so close to Sturm that their avatars were practically merging. "We should keep that part. Someday I'm going to own my own domain, move in and never get real again."

"What's in your domain?" Sturm's blippage went all flirty.

"You mean who?" She pushed away from him and poked a finger into his chest. "Maybe you wish it was you?" She smirked. "Not yet, Mystery Boy. Earn it."

"Focus please," said Silk.

Later....

"No, governments are supposed to serve us, not the other way around."

Silk had created a rectangular glass conference table with himself at the head. The draft of the declaration glowed on its surface. "We can't change 'consent of the governed.'"

"What is consent, anyway?"

"Like permission, only more legal."

"I never gave no consent for some bullshit EOS to ruin my life."

Much later...

"So that means we have the right to overthrow the EOS?" Botão sounded doubtful.

Toybox was lighting his fingertips on fire. "Overthrow the oldschool and be done with all the bullshit." The longer they talked, the higher the numbers on his boredom blip climbed. It was like watching a cartoon fuse burn.

"I don't see how they give us an 'A' for overthrowing them," said Remeny.

"If we prove they're unjust—"

"But that's why we have to keep 'alter' and 'abolish,'" Silk interrupted Sturm for the hundreth time. "Means the same as overthrow, only Jefferson wrote it. So we hide behind his language."

Much, much later...

Sturm had changed the conference table from rectangular to round. "If we get rid of the old government, then we need a new one," he said.

"I'm not making up a whole new government," said

Botão. "My job starts in half an hour."

"So then no government," Sturm said. "Everyone for themselves. Law of the jungle."

Before she could stop it, a (.2) shock blip flashed above Remeny's avatar. This wasn't like him.

Eventually, after arguments and much blippage, they persuaded Silk to yield the power of the keyboard to Remeny, since she was willing to take other people's suggestions. While Silk brooded, they agreed on a draft of the crucial second paragraph.

"*We hold these truths to be self-evident, that all realities, hard and soft, old and new, are equal, and so are we the people who live in them, whichever reality we choose. All people, no matter whether they live in bodies or avatars, are endowed with certain inalienable rights, and among these are life, liberty, and the pursuit of happiness. To guarantee our rights governments are supposed to serve we the people and not the other way around. They derive their powers from the consent of the governed. If a government goes off, it is the right of we the people to alter or to abolish it, and to make up some new government that will do the right thing.*"

"Okay." Remeny checked the time on her overlord; she too would have to get real soon. "So now what?"

"List everything the government is doing wrong." Silk broke his grim silence.

Toybox groaned. "Not today."

"No," said Remeny. Save that for next time. "Anything else?"

"We need to think about making something happen in hardtime," said Sturm. "Take the revolution to the streets."

"Then you're talking homework," said Botão. "I've got to be at work in ten minutes."

"What if we speed this up to double time?" said Silk.

Botão's embarrassment shot immediately to (.4). "Umm… I'm not allowed."

"Not allowed?" said Toybox. "Everybody's supposed to get some double time. They just don't let you have enough."

"It's my mother." Now the blip was (.6). "She—"

"Makes no difference," Sturm interrupted her. "I already used up this month's overclocking allotment."

Remeny knew this wasn't true, but she approved of the lie and decided to join in. "Me too."

"See, that's why we need a revolution," said Toybox, "so we can overclock whenever we want."

"Yeah," said Botão, "and then we can ask Santa to bring us diamond trees so we can feed the unicorns."

Remeny ignored them. "We're talking about getting real. You were saying, Sturm?"

"We need a message." He considered. "What do we say to the oldschool?"

"That EOS sucks." Toybox's avatar got up from the table and created a door in Silk's domain with a huge glowing red EXIT sign above it.

"That's our complaint." Sturm shook his head. "But what do we want?"

Nobody spoke for a moment.

"How about life, liberty, and the pursuit of happiness?" said Botão.

"Sure," said Sturm. "But those are just words until we explain what they mean."

"No," Silk leaned forward on his seat. "She's right. We make that our slogan, put it out there, get people talking about it." He poked the table top. "Posters, tee shirts…"

"Graffiti."

"Timed-erase only," said Remeny. "Okay, there's your homework. Life, liberty, and the pursuit of happiness – ten times each."

"Ten?" Toybox had his hand on the knob of his door.

"How am I supposed to make ten hardtime changes from a stack?"

"I don't know," she said. "Send your friends ten letters…"

"He doesn't have ten friends."

"…print stickies."

"Write a song and record it." Botão warbled tunelessly. "*Life for me needs liberty*… umm… *something something happiness.*"

"That's it," said Remeny. "Next meeting at 1300 on Tuesday the 12th." She saved a transcript of their meeting to her student folder. "Got to go. Out of time."

The biggest grievance that Remeny had against the government was that her Health Oversight Manager, aka her overlord, was too bossy. It forced her to exercise and monitored her diet. It required daily minimum times for being alone and for family interaction. Worst of all, if she didn't meet these goals, it could limit how long she could spend in softtime. Even after she turned twenty-one and could make her own decisions, it would still be watching her. It wasn't fair. Stash like Toybox and Sturm never had to wander around smelling the damn roses.

She owed her overlord another hour and a half of family interaction and needed to burn three hundred calories exercising. It was now 1717. They had a family dinner scheduled softtime for 1930; that would kill an hour. If she jogged her five-kilometer course at a decent pace between now and then, that would take care of her workout. But she still had to squeeze in at least another half hour of family time now, because Silk had said he might stop by ForSquare around 2100. She stripped off the NeuroSky 3100 interface that Dad had given her as a pre-graduation gift. She'd only had it a week and while she definitely liked it better than her old Deveau interface, the 3100's electrode array was sensitive to stubble.

That meant she had to shave her head every other morning. Once she pulled her nose plugs and peeled off her haptic gloves, she was once again Johanna Daugherty, age 18, of 7 Forest Ridge Road. She liked herself better as Remeny. She had chosen the name because it meant *hope* in Hungarian, but that was a secret. Nobody she knew spoke Hungarian.

"*Mom.*" She stuck her head out of her bedroom door and called down the hall. "I'm home."

"Hi, honey. I made a banana smoothie. Some for you in the blender."

Remeny put on her headset, positioned its glass over her left eye and pressed the mic to her jaw, where it stuck. Headsets lacked cranial input so there was no softtime immersion, but at least she could monitor what was happening online. "How many calories?"

"I don't know. Three hundred? Four? Ask the fridge."

The fridge reported that Mom had added a tablespoon of peanut butter to her usual recipe, which boosted the smoothie to four hundred and thirty calories. She decided to save it for dinner. Instead she got an Ice Cherry Zero out of the freezer.

Mom was at her desk – wearing a glass headset. She had a Deveau interface for full immersion that she didn't use much. She was more comfortable with the oldschool interfaces. And reality. She sat in the late-afternoon gloom, her face lit from below by the windows on her desktop. When Remeny snicked on the overhead lights, Rachel Daugherty glanced up, blinking.

"Thanks," she said.

Mom's office was like a museum with its antique paper books on wooden shelves and family pix that didn't move. Hanging on the wall was an embroidered baby blanket in the Úrihímzés style that had belonged to Remeny's Hungarian great-grandmother. A trophy case held the tennis trophies that Mom had won in high school and college. The rubber plant in the window needed dusting.

"So what's up, Mom?"

"Work."

Remeny leaned against the door frame and twirled the Cherry Zero in her mouth. "Work?"

Mom sighed and waved a hand over the desktop, closing half the windows. "The health budget. We're running a surplus and I need to move some of it to building maintenance."

"The people are in better shape than the buildings?" Remeny's lips tingled from the cold.

"Buildings live in snow and rain and sleet and hail. People, not so much." A window flashed blue. "Speaking of being outside," she said, expanding it, "didn't I get an EOS advisory a couple of days ago? Something about your Phys Ed status?"

"Took care of it." Remeny wished Mom would stop nagging her. "I already have an overlord, Rachel. I don't need an overmom too."

"Sorry." Mom frowned; she didn't like it when her kids called her Rachel. "Look, I'm sorry, sweetie, but I'm really busy just now. You need some family time, is that it? Could you maybe go talk to your brother?"

"I just spent two hours with him in coop."

"Good." Mom's attention drifted back to her budgets. "How's that going?"

"Okay, I guess. We gave ourselves homework. We're making it real."

"That's nice."

Silence.

"Aren't you going to ask what our project is?"

"Sure," said Mom, but then she started shuffling windows.

"We're writing a declaration of independence," Remeny said.

"Really?"

Remeny dropped the empty Zero sleeve into the trash and waited. Then waited some more.

"A declaration," she said, finally. "Of independence."

"Umm… didn't somebody already write that?"

Too bad there were no blips in real life.

"I guess I'll talk to Robby then."

"You're a good sister." Mom nodded but did not look up. "Do a favor and turn him, would you?"

Maybe it was best that Mom didn't know about their project. Rachel Daugherty was Bedford's Town Manager. She was part of the government they were declaring independence from.

Robert Daugherty Junior's entire room was a deep twilight blue: walls, floor, ceiling; even the two painted-over windows that no longer looked onto Forest Ridge Road. When Remeny closed the door, shutting out the hallway light, the monotone color skewed the geometry of the space, erased the corners and curved the walls. Robby had just three glowworms and he kept them dimmed because of his photosensitivity; their slow crawl over the room's surfaces cast a changing pattern of dreamy radiance and midnight shadows. The only thing in the room that seemed solid was the carebot, which had tucked itself into a corner. Its eyestalk tilted toward her briefly to note her arrival, then returned its gaze to monitor her brother's naked, twitching body, suspended in its protective mesh. Robby had a state-of-the-art stash; Mom had spent a boatload of Dad's money on her injured son after the attack. His intracranial interface was implanted directly into his cerebral cortex, which also helped relieve the worst of his dyskinetic thrashing. Robby could never have managed his avatar with an ordinary interface;

his control over his movements had been so compromised by the neurotoxins in the DV gas that the True Patriots had used that he could barely feed himself. That was the carebot's job, as was cleaning up after him. Once, before the carebot, he had worn diapers. That hadn't worked out for anybody.

=*Oh, Sturmy.*= She pinged him on their private channel. =*Reality calling.*=

=*Go away.*= His reply scrolled across her glass.

"Mom sent me to check up on you." She switched to speaking aloud and the mic on her headset reformatted for messaging. "Time for some sweet family togetherness."

=*Go online then.*=

"Nope. I need some hardtime." She queried her glass and opened his overlord account; they had each other's access. "And so do you."

Even though they were twins, Robby's disabilities meant that he had different overlord quotas. He couldn't exercise and the carebot controlled his diet. He only owed an hour of hardtime a day, all of which was currently due. Remeny had never understood how waking up in a dark room to thrash around like a fish caught in a net could be good for anyone.

"*Blaaagh.*" Robby never re-entered hardtime in a good mood. "Shit."

"Hello to you, too. Mom said something about a turning. You want?"

"No." He coughed up a wad of phlegm and spat onto the floor. The carebot whirred out of its corner to clean it up. "I don't need... oh, go ahead."

Robby's smartsilk net was the only furniture in the room. He rarely left it, even when he logged off, because of the fibromyalgia. His skin was sensitive to the slightest touch and the mesh distributed pressure points. It was suspended from the walls and ceiling so that its shape could be thermally reconfigured to roll him from one side to another, even from his back to his belly, to prevent bedsores.

She swiped her finger halfway across the control screen and then up. Parts of the net stretched while others shrank.

"Ow, ow, *oww*." His fingers caught at the net while he kicked at the air. "Okay, enough. *Stop*."

"Sorry."

He came to rest facing her, eyes slits, eyelids gummy, curled into a fetal position as if to protect his erection. Seeing his cock didn't faze Remeny anymore. After helping to nurse him for the last couple of years, she had developed a high tolerance for brotherly ick.

"I was fine, you know," Robby croaked at the carebot's eyestalk; he was talking to Mom. "You just turned me this morning, Rachel." Then he nodded at Remeny. "I'm three screens on her desktop. Can't even fart without setting off alarms."

"I told her she was turning into the overmom."

A head jerk scattered his smile.

"So," she said, "think we can carry that loser Toybox?"

"Sure.' He sucked in a raspy breath. "Jason isn't so bad."

"Jason, is it? He's a moron."

Robby swallowed twice in rapid succession. "*Ahhh.*"

"Pain?" she said.

"No."

"You want a gun?" Ever since the attack, he'd had a fascination with the old handguns in the house. As if having a real one might have saved him. Still, handling them seemed to relieve his stress, which then calmed the spasms.

"*No.*"

She waited for him to say something else. This was her day to be ignored by her family.

"You were getting pretty weird on me in coop," she said at last.

"Weird?"

"Everyone for themselves. I've got the transcript in my folder. Revolutions don't play by the rules." She exaggerated a Sturm imitation, made his edges sharp enough to cut. "'Speak for yourself, Botão. Maybe I am a terrorist.' Come on, Sturm. A *terrorist*? You're going to do other people like you were done?"

"Right wing scum," he muttered. "Assholes."

"Right wing, left wing – they're all assholes."

"Revolution." He didn't seem very interested in the conversation.

"What revolution?" She felt like he was pushing her toward a cliff. "What the hell are you talking about?" Then she noticed the edge of his overlord window in her glass. He wasn't getting hardtime credit for their conversation. "Wait a minute," she said. "You're still running your avatar?"

"Huh?" He was confused. "What?"

"This is me," she said. "Your sister." Remeny was at once impressed and insulted. It took supreme concentration to run an avatar in softtime while carrying on a conversation in hardtime. "You thought I wouldn't notice?" Then she guessed why he hadn't logged off. "You're with someone."

"No."

"I bet it's your little Button Bright."

He writhed and his right arm flung itself up, grazing the top of his head. "What makes you say that?"

"For one thing," she said, "you've got a bone like a dinosaur."

"A second. Give me a second." He closed his eyes and his body went slack. Then with a shudder, he was back. The clock was ticking. She had his full attention.

"Kind of a pervy thing to say to your brother." He gave her a grimace which she knew was a grin.

"We share the perv gene, Sturmy." She grinned back.

"So Botão is your girlfriend now?"

"No one is my girlfriend." His voice was like sandpaper. "She's a reality snob like the rest of them. I mean, suppose we really wanted to get together. Eventually she'd want to come over here for a visit, see me for herself. You know how that goes. Imagine her standing there, staring at this twitchy sack of meat. Romantic or what?"

Remeny wanted to say something but couldn't think what.

"I'll take a gun now," Robby said. "Kent's Glock."

Dad kept his memorabilia in a study at the far end of the house. He had been in flat movies way back, but had made the transition to flix and adventures and sims and even some impersonations. Although he had been cast in all kinds of parts, Jeffrey Daugherty was mostly known for playing bad guys: serial killers, drug lords, CEOs, stalkers, and, yes, terrorists. He had won a Golden Globe and an Appie for playing Kent Crill on *The Revenger*, which was where he had acquired most of the collection of prop weapons displayed behind his desk. Kent had used the Glock to take down his arch-nemesis, the vampire Sir Koko Mawatu, in the Season Five finale. Of course, it was just a prop that didn't really fire silver bullets, but it had the heft of a real gun.

Remeny parted the ultra-smooth strands of the mesh and offered him the pistol, grip first. He swiped at it and missed the first time but nabbed it on the second try. He settled back, rubbing the steel barrel lengthwise across her cheek. She'd seen his gun fetish many times but it was still something about her brother that she didn't get.

"It's not Toybox I'm worried about," he said. "Who is this Silk?"

"I don't know, some rich kid." She shrugged. "I kind of like him."

"I don't."

"Why? Because he wants to run the show? So do you. So does Toybox. All you boys doing your alpha male thing – it's kind of cute in an annoying way."

"He's already got slogans out. A dozen floaties around town – they have to be his. No one else has the money. One keeps circling the town office."

That *was* interesting. "Fast work." She called up the satellite image on her glass and zoomed. "Hey, that's some serious signage. Maybe he needs extra credit."

"It was his idea. Doesn't that seem suspicious?"

She leaned against the wall and wished once again that he would let her bring a chair when she visited. "No, it wasn't. Botão came up with life, liberty, and…"

"Just words." He aimed the gun at the carebot and stared down the sights. "The slogan was his idea."

"So he's smart. So?" She jiggled the net. "Did you tell Botão who you are?"

"Nuh-uh." He held the gun steady and Remeny could see him mouth the word *bang*. "But she knows I'm stashed."

"She knows and she's still interested?"

"She just thinks she is."

"Then maybe you're wrong about her. You've got a crush setup here, pal. What if you were stashed in a body stack, like Toybox? Think she'd go all melty over whatever is behind the doors at the Komfort Kare?"

"She'll still want…"

"What she wants is Sturm and that's who you are, twenty-three out of every twenty-four hours. Your body is just leftovers."

His laugh was bitter. "Rah, rah, rah." He waved the Glock in a circle. "Too bad cheerleading doesn't kill the pain anymore."

Robby *was* getting weird on her. "I've got to go for a run

– overlord orders." She couldn't handle him when he was like this. "You going to stay real for a while?"

"Sure."

"Want me to leave Kent's gun? You never know when your arch-nemesis is going to show."

"No, take it." He thrust the pistol through the mesh. "I'll find some other way to thwart Silk's evil plan." His hand was steady now.

"He's not your problem." She leaned in close and blew on his face. "See you at dinner then." It was as close to kissing as they got.

"Something's got to change," he said.

"Yeah, yeah," she said. "Come the revolution."

As Remeny jogged up Forest Ridge Road, the spray can of Sez in her fanny pack bounced against her back. She had queried her glass for places she could tag that would have the highest foot traffic. The list was short and most of the choices were in Bedford's modest downtown, a couple of kilometers away. That would mean her graffiti would overlap with Silk's floating ads, but that was okay.

She began to see bots on errands: delivery bots from Foodmaster and Amazon and Express-It, a McDonald's dinerbot reeking of yesterday's fries, an empty taxi idling on Little Oak. The first pedestrian she passed was an old man in a breather walking his dog. She saw Officer Shubin's motorcycle parked at the Cocamoca but no Officer Shubin. She slowed to a stop when she spotted the floaty bobbing down Third Street toward her. The squat barrel shape floated at eye level and the slogan scrawled continually around its circumference. *Life, Liberty, and the Pursuit of Happiness Life, Liberty, and…*

"Stop," she commanded. Its top propeller rotated one

hundred and eighty degrees until it faced in the opposite direction from its bottom propeller. "I have a question."

"I will try to answer," it said.

"Who paid for you?"

"I was hired by PROS, which stands for Protect the Rights of the Occupants of Softtime." It played a short musical flourish.

"Never heard of it."

"The organization is less than two hours old."

Her overlord nagged that her metabolic rate was falling. She began to jog in place. "Who's in it?"

"Membership information is confidential."

"How long are you contracted for?"

"I will be proclaiming the new world order in this area through Tuesday."

New world order? Silk was having delusions of grandeur. "What do you mean: Life, Liberty, and the Pursuit of Happiness?"

"What does it mean to *you*?"

"I don't know. Nothing."

"PROS would like to change that. If you were to google it…"

Remeny stopped paying attention and pinged Silk instead. When she got no reply, she queried her glass about floaty rentals. Rates ran between two and three hundred dollars a day depending on the size of the floaty, the sophistication of the pitch and the choice of sales route. She was impressed. Rich was rich, but what teenager would spend two thousand dollars a day on a coop project?

"Do you have any other questions?" said the floaty.

On an impulse she reached into her fanny pack, grabbed the Sez can and sprayed *call me* on the floaty. As it tried to dodge away, it jiggled her "e" into looking like a mutant "p."

"At 1753," the floaty said, "I identify you as Johanna

Daugherty of 7 Forest Ridge Road. Per the Defacement Clause of Bedford's Commercial Speech Ordinance, you will now be charged the standard rate for use of this device for as long as your unauthorized commentary persists."

Remeny wasn't worried; the Sez had been in draft mode. "Make sure Silk gets my message."

"What is Silk?"

Her graffiti was already fading, so she brushed by the floaty and jogged up Third Street.

"Your total charge is sixty-seven cents," it called. "Have a nice day."

More than half of the stores facing Memorial Square had gone out of business. To keep the downtown from looking like a mouthful of broken teeth, the town had paid to have the buildings torn down but had preserved and restored the facades. Behind these were empty lots converted to lawns, gardens, and patios with picnic tables, all tended by bots, all deserted. There were spaces downtown designated for civic tagging as long as the message conformed to font, color, and content guidelines. She sprayed slats of the benches that faced the Civil War monument, the windows on the facade of the Post Office and the abutments of the pedestrian bridge that crossed Sperry Creek. She set the Sez can to a 158 point Engravers font, which she thought looked suitably historic, and set the duration for Tuesday. Same as Silk. *Life, Liberty and the Pursuit of Happiness* fit nicely alongside *silence is golden but duct tape is silver*, *We are not a bot*, and *Think More About Working Less*.

On the way home, she took the shortcut through the grounds of the Gates Early Learning Center since there were designated tagging surfaces at its playground. A handful of little kids milled about in their bulky, augmented reality helmets, pulling up grass, tripping over the balance boosters, hitting trees with sticks. One of them came up to Remeny while she was spray-painting the slide.

"What's your name?" The girl had an annoying squeaky voice.

She didn't have time for this – where was the teacher? "Ask your helmet to look me up."

"Why? You could just tell me."

Remeny glanced over and saw black curls framing a face pale as a mushroom. She was five or maybe six, wearing a Dotty Karate tee shirt. "Johanna."

"I'm Meesha, but my real name is Amisha." She pointed at the tag. "What does that say?"

"Read it yourself." The kid was breaking her concentration.

"Don't know how."

"Your helmet does."

She put her hand over her mouth and whispered the query as if she didn't want Remeny to hear. "I don't know pursuit," she said at last.

"Your helmet could..." Remeny looked around for help and saw Joan deJean headed her way. "It means to chase after."

Meesha considered this. "Is that why you're all sweaty? 'Cause you're pursuiting happiness?"

"Hi, Johanna." Ms. deJean had been Johanna's teacher when she was a kid. "I see you've met Meesha." She put a hand on the girl's shoulder.

"Hi, Ms. deJean. Yeah, she's not exactly shy."

"You can say that again." Ms. deJean turned the girl gently and aimed her back toward the other kids. "This is learning time, Meesha. Not chatting time."

"Chatting can be learning," the girl said.

"Scoot." She gave her a nudge back toward the center, but Meesha squirmed and skipped away in a different direction. "So what's this?" Ms. DeJean bent over the slide and read.

Remeny slipped the Sez into her fanny pack. "Coop."

"Already?" Her old teacher sighed. "Seems like yesterday you were toddling around here, talking back like Meesha." She lit up with the memory. "You and your brother. How is Robby?"

"He doesn't get out much."

"No." Her light dimmed. "The Declaration of Independence? You breaking away from something?"

"I don't know," said Remeny, then she laughed. "Maybe the EOS."

"Good for you." Joan deJean laughed with her. "It's a train wreck, if you ask me. All software and no people."

Remeny usually walked Forest Ridge Road to cool down at the end of a run but when she saw her mother and Emily Banerjee sitting on the Banerjees' lawn, she broke into a sprint. Her mother had her arm around Mrs. Banerjee's shoulder and was speaking softly to her.

"Everything okay?" Remeny pulled up in front of them.

"Emily isn't feeling well," said Mom. "She's confused."

The Banerjees had been antiques when the Daughertys had moved in, crinkly and cute as Remeny and Robby grew up. Sadhir Banerjee had died in March and his wife had been lost ever since. Mom had called the son Prahlad last month when she had found Mrs. Banerjee sorting through the Daugherty's garbage at night.

"I am not confused," said Mrs. Banerjee, "and I will never lie in those coffins."

"Nobody wants you to, Emily."

"I watched it on the teevee – just now. Those coffins are small." She spread her palms. "This wide, maybe. And not much longer even." The way her hands shook reminded Remeny of Robby. "They lie awake in the coffin so they can always call other people on the Internet but there is no room.

Not for everyone. The Internet is too small, too, even for an old woman."

Teevee? The Internet? Remeny didn't want to laugh because this was sad. But talk about oldschool.

"Don't worry, Emily," said Mom. "Prahlad is coming soon."

"Yeah, it's okay, Mrs. Banerjee," said Remeny. "You don't have to call people if you don't want."

Mrs. Banerjee glanced up at Remeny. "You're the girl. Rachel's child. Isn't there a brother?" She pointed a finger as if in accusation. "We never see you kids playing anymore."

"Johanna, that's right. We're all grown up now."

"You know in those coffins? The people?" Mrs. Banerjee leaned toward her. "Do you know what they call them?" Her voice was low. "Trash. I swear it; Sadhir was with me, he heard too."

Remeny and Mom exchanged glances.

"You mean stash?" said Remeny.

"Stash?" Mrs. Banerjee rocked back and gazed up at the darkening sky for a moment. "Yes. That was it." She nodded at them. "Stash." Her mouth puckered as if she could taste the word.

The Daughertys gathered for their weekly family dinners in softtime because Dad was so often on location and Robby couldn't leave his room, much less sit at the table. Besides, her brother's two-thousand-calorie high-bulk liquid diet looked to Remeny like just-mixed cement. Not appetizing. Mom had paid for a space in the family domain that recreated the actual dining room at 7 Forest Ridge Road. A buffet with a marble top matched a china closet with glass doors. Its dining room table could seat ten comfortably but had just the four upholstered chairs gathered around one end. The furniture was all dark maple in some crazy oldschool style that featured arabesque inlays, fleur-de-lis, and Corinthian columns. The meal that nobody was going to eat was straight out of the darkest twentieth century: a platter of roast chicken – with *bones* – bowls of mashed potatoes and green beans with pearl onions, a basket of rolls. Remeny thought the whole show a waste of processing power; in softtime you were supposed to challenge reality, not just fake it. But this was what Mom wanted and Dad always humored her. Robby and Remeny didn't have a vote.

"The kids were working on their coop today," said Mom.

"They're on the same team?" Dad liked to sit at these meals with a knife in one hand and a fork in the other, even though all they did was stare at the virtual food. The kids could have made their avatars appear to eat, but their parents, Mom especially, had yet to master the tricks of full immersion. "How does that happen?"

"Just lucky, I guess." Remeny's dinner was the leftover smoothie and snap peas out of the bag. She ate in her room.

"So what's it about?"

"It's kind of boring actually." After talking to Robby that afternoon, Remeny had been hoping coop wouldn't come up.

"No, it isn't." Her brother opened their private channel with a (.4) impatience blip. =*We should have this conversation now.*=
=*They'll want to talk about it all night. I'm going out later.*=

"Something to do with the Declaration of Independence?" Apparently Mom had been paying attention after all.

=*With Silk?*=
=*None of your business.*=

"Oh, right," said Dad. "We the people blah blah in order to form a more perfect union of whatever." Remeny had been hoping that Dad would take the conversation over, as he usually did. "I've always wondered how you get to be more perfect. I played James Madison once, you know; he was a shrimp, five feet four – what's that in meters?"

"A hundred and sixty-two centimeters." Even though Robby was using his parent-friendly version of Sturm – no scars, no iridescence – she could tell he was mad.

"Just about Johanna's size." Dad's avatar was wearing a Hawaiian shirt with a sailboat motif. As usual, he looked like his hardtime self, handsome as surgery and juv treatments could make an eighty-three-year old, but then his image was part of his actor's brand. "No, wait. That's not right." He pointed his knife at Remeny, as if she were thinking of correcting him. "More perfect union is the Constitution. The Declaration was Jefferson. He was a tall one, him and Washington. Never played Washington. Wanted to, never did, even though we're about the same size."

"We're declaring our independence," said Robby.

=*Sturm, no.*=

That stopped Dad. "Who?" He frowned. "Teenagers?"

"Everybody who's stashed. We're giving up on hardtime – reality. We want to live as avatars."

"Cool." It was exactly the wrong thing to say. Remeny wondered if he'd been biting into a slice of pizza wherever he was and hadn't been paying attention to the conversation.

"And how do you propose to do this?" Mom's avatar looked like she had swallowed a brick.

"Just do it. Stay stashed." Robby gave them a (.6) impatience blip. "Never log off."

"No blips at the table, please." Mom had strange ideas about manners. "Never come back – *ever*?"

Remeny started to say, "Only when we want…" but Robby talked over her. "Never." He pushed back his chair and stood up, which seemed to Remeny more disrespectful than a blip. "And we want to be able to overclock as much as we want. Live double time. Triple. Whatever."

"Now you're talking nonsense," said Mom. "Your brain is not a computer, Robert. Overclocking causes seizures. And being stashed is hard on the body. The mortality rate for—"

"That's why we overclock," he shouted. "We can burn through subjective years while the meat rots."

Mom looked shocked that he would use the m-word at the table. Remeny couldn't believe it herself.

"Sit down, Robby." Dad didn't seem angry. He just scratched his chin with the fork while he waited for Robby to subside. Robby obeyed but sulked. "Funny this should come up. So I'm in Vermont with Spencer this morning…"

"*Jeff.*" Mom sounded betrayed.

"Pirates in Vermont?" said Remeny.

=*Don't encourage him.*= Robby was on Mom's side in this one. =*Let's finish this.*=

"I was done early at the *Treasure Ship* shoot." Dad shook his head. "Bastards cut half of my part. So, there I am at Steve Spencer's summer place in Vermont and he pitches me an idea about how people want to do exactly what Robby is talking about. He's got a script ready to go and everything. Financing no problem, sixty mill starter money he says. Sixty million dollars kind of gets my attention. The idea is that there are people who want to live in virtual reality…"

Remeny raised her hand to correct him. "Softtime."

"Sure. And they never want to come out. It's wild stuff. They're cutting off arms and legs and whatever, body parts they claim they don't need, and I say it sounds like horror, which isn't what I do, but Steve says no. The script plays it straight. It's a damned issue piece! Apparently there are people who believe this is a good thing. People who can raise sixty million no problem. Do you know about this, Rachel?"

She shook her head.

"How do we not know about this?"

"Because we're still only *some* people," said Robby. "Not *enough* people yet."

"And you're going to do it," said Mom. Remeny wondered who she was talking to. Dad? Robby? Both of them? It almost looked as if she had calmed down except that just then her avatar went completely still. Remeny searched the house cams and found her at the real dining-room table with a plate of tortellini in front of her. She had pushed her Deveau back onto her head. She was crying.

"Sweet part for me." Dad hadn't noticed that Mom had logged off. "I'm a senator and I'm against it. I've never actually played a senator before. President, yes. Mayor. It's only a supporting, but still Frederick Nooney is attached, Gonsalves to direct. I told Steve I'd give him an answer tomorrow, but this… is this some coincidence or what?"

"You should do it," said Robby. "Absolutely. What's it called?"

"Title on the script is *Declaration*, but that will never fly."

Remeny almost choked on a snap pea. Robby started to laugh.

Then Dad did something that Remeny didn't think that an oldschool eighty-three-year- old could. He opened a private channel to Robby in softtime.

=*You there, son?*=

=*Maybe.*=

Unfortunately he didn't know how to close Remeny's private channel with her brother, so she was able to eavesdrop.
=*Look, Robby, if this is what you want, I'm for it. I know you're in pain and miserable.*=

=*Only when I'm stuck in hardtime.*=

=*I get that. Ever since that day, all we've wanted is to help.*= His sympathy blip was (.8). =*I know it's hard for you but it's hard for us, too. Your mother blames herself because she sent you…*=

=Dad, stop. I love you but stop. You want to help me then take the damn part. It'll be good for the cause. My cause, Dad. But what I really want is for you to come home and help me with Mom. Because reality sucks and I'm giving up on it. We need to make Mom understand. All of us, face to face. Oldschool.=

"Stop saying you're sorry." Sturm was trying for stern but his blippage read embarrassed.

"I just didn't want Mom to freak," said Remeny.

"Well, she did and nobody was killed. I call that a win for our side."

"Think Dad can convince her?"

"He's an actor." Sturm scanned the crowd around the dance floor for Silk. "He'll give a performance."

The music twanged and couples began to take their places.

"Nine minutes after," said Sturm. "He's not coming."

"There's no schedule." Remeny's irritation climbed to (.3). "He's not a train."

"*Bow to the partner, now bow to the corner, all join hands and circle to the left, please don't step on her, now circle to the right, and we go round and round.*"

Now that she was old enough to know better, Remeny was sick of square dancing. When she was twelve, ForSquare had been one of her favorite EOS playgrounds. She had loved the movement, the color and the concentration it took to remember and execute all of the calls. When she was sixteen, she had come in second in the Jefferson County Challenge. There had been more than twenty calls that day that involved changing avatars on the fly, on top of two hundred more traditional calls. A hell of a lot of remembering, but what was the point? It was all about teaching kids how to use their interfaces while they pretended to have fun.

"*Promenade now, full promenade.*" Crystal stalactites rose at random from the dance floor and the dancers weaved around them.

Another thing: the music was so loud that you had to shout to be heard. Okay for these kids, so young that they had nothing to say. But now that she was eighteen, Remeny preferred a quiet place like Sanctuary. It was better for flirting.

Remeny spotted Botão and waved. She skirted the dancers to join them.

"I'm here but I can't stay. I'm babysitting my sisters." Her avatar was wearing a *Life Liberty and the Pursuit of Happiness* tee shirt.

"I like this." Remeny brushed a hand down the sleeve.

"Yeah." She tugged at the hem, stretching the front of the tee so she could admire it too. "My mom and I designed them and then I printed out ten on our home fab, sizes six and seven. I'll bring them to the Gates Center tomorrow and have the teachers send them home with the kids. Cost less than ten bucks."

"I was just there today myself."

"Oh my God, what if we had met?" She clutched her throat in mock horror. "You ask me, I say the whole secret identity thing is dumb. The oldschool is just trying to keep us from ganging up on them." She brushed up against Sturm. "What do you think, Sturm, or are you ignoring me on purpose?"

"You forgot the commas," he said, "and I wasn't ignoring you. I was looking for Silk."

"Asshole." She was stunned. "Be that way then." She pushed away from him.

"What do you know about Silk?" he said.

=*What are you doing?*= Remeny sent Robby a private message.

=*I think she's in on it.*=

=*In on what*?=

"Why should I tell you?" said Botão.

"Because Silk isn't who we think he is."

Botão's anger blip had a sarcastic edge. "Nobody here is who I think they are."

"Did he tell you to come up with that slogan?"

"Oh, I get it. I'm not smart enough to come up with an idea on my own. Let's see now, is it because I'm a girl? Because I am *uma Brasileira*?"

"There." Remeny pointed. Silk had entered with a couple of avatars new to her.

"*All roll now, and spin those wheels, easy now and boys form a star...*" Some of the avatars on the dance floor morphed their shoes into roller blades; the others grew casters in their legs. "*Now be our stars, and keep it rolling.*" One of the boys in the star formation slipped and toppled into the boy next to him. The girl dancers clapped and giggled, but the caller didn't pause. "*That's all right, no time for regrets, head back home and into your sets.*"

Silk appeared beside Remeny. "Our meeting isn't until Tuesday," he said, "but as long as we're here... I don't see Toybox."

"Leave him out of this," said Sturm.

"Oh, and are you giving the orders now?" His amusement blip barely registered.

"I think there is some kind of conspiracy going on and you're part of it. You're manipulating me. Us."

"Speak for yourself," said Botão.

"How can it be manipulation..." Silk spread his hands. "...if you're doing what you wanted to do anyway? You believe, Sturm. I know you do."

"But I don't," said Botão, "and you can take your conspiracy or revolution or whatever the hell it is and shove it." As Botão tore her tee shirt off and hurled it at Silk, she generated a replacement Seleção Brasileira soccer jersey. "I'll find another coop. Remeny? You with me?"

With a shock, Remeny realized that she wanted to say yes, that she was actually afraid of what Silk and Sturm were trying to do to themselves. She liked being an avatar, sure, but this wasn't how she wanted to live the rest of her life. Not if it meant getting stashed. She started toward Botão.

=*Wait*.= Sturm was desperate.

Silk didn't wait. "You can't quit," he said. "Don't you want to live your life in softtime? You're the one who wanted to make your own domain and never get real again."

"No." Botão glared at the three of them, and Remeny was ashamed to be lumped with the boys. "I was just saying that I like the real world *and* VR." She had to raise her voice to be heard over the music and now people were eavesdropping. That only made her talk louder. "I don't know about you jerkoffs, but I like sex, oldschool sex, the kind you probably can't get; you know with touching and kissing and… and sweetness." Her anger blip soared. "And I'm going to have my own kids someday."

In her room, Remeny felt tears come. She agreed with everything Botão was saying – except maybe the part about having kids. But it would hurt Robby if she spoke up and he had been hurt so much already. Not fair, *not fair*, but then nothing in her life was fair. She had been so busy being Robby's sister that she had forgotten how to be herself.

"But we're doing your kids a favor," said Silk. "And your grandchildren."

The caller had stopped and the music shut down. Now the entire playground was listening to them. Remeny was pretty sure they were about to be kicked out. Or worse.

"We've got nine billion people crowded onto this planet," he continued. "Most of us stashed aren't ever going to have kids. We say that's a good thing. And the stashed don't burn through scarce resources like you and your kids. We're saving the planet. All we ask is that we get to live the life we want."

"*Avatars Silk and Botão, you are disrupting this playground.*" The caller's warning pierced the argument like a fire alarm. "*Stop now or there will be consequences.*"

"Okay." Botão raised her hands in surrender. "So you have some ideas. But a revolution? No. You haven't seen what evil a revolution does. I have." Then she brought her hands together with a sharp clap and her avatar popped.

Everyone but Silk seemed to be holding their breath. He knelt, picked up her discarded tee shirt and held it up. "Life, liberty, and the pursuit of happiness," he said. "Someday. That's all. In the meantime, I apologize."

The music started again. The crowd in the playground buzzed.

"Please." A kid in a foolish wizard's hat touched Sturm's elbow. "What was that all about?"

Sturm waved him off and snatched the tee shirt out of Silk's hands. "You and I still have something to settle."

"We do. But what about your sister?"

Sturm froze. "What did you say?" A blip shimmered but he suppressed it.

"We don't play by the rules, remember? That's how revolutions work." Was Silk smirking? "But we should really take this elsewhere. I have a place."

"You smug bastard. Why should we trust you?"

"Because you're smart? Because you need us?" He was ignoring Remeny. "We can leave her behind if you want."

"I'm right here," said Remeny, although she felt like she was in someone else's dream. "Don't pretend I'm not." She poked Sturm. "Either of you."

"Fine," said Silk. "Now, we should go."

Remeny was surprised that Toybox could afford a domain, although his taste in decoration was about what she would have imagined. The floor of his space was bone, the walls fire, the ceiling smoke. His temporarily abandoned avatar, dressed in garish vestments, perched at the edge of a gilt Baroque throne, obviously a copy of something. Remeny queried and it turned out to be the Chair of Saint Peter from St. Peter's Basilica, part of some altar designed by Bernini. It didn't seem like Toybox's taste until she found the sublink: some people called it Satan's Throne. In front of the throne were couches and chairs that seemed to have been made from writhing bodies. These gathered around a glass coffin, on top of which were an open bottle of absinthe, a crystal decanter of water, four matching goblets with slotted absinthe spoons, and a dish of sugar cubes. Inside the coffin was the stashed body of Jason Day, or at least what she assumed was a fairly accurate copy. It wasn't too hard to look at: the breathing mask and feeding tube hid most of the face and the body had not degenerated as much as some of the stashed she had seen images of. He still had all his arms and legs, but then Jason Day was underage and would have to log off and leave his coffin for several hours a week. This meant he wasn't yet eligible for an intercranial interface like Sturm's. His Deveau had a larger array of sensors than her Neurosky 3100 and it was connected to the body sock which monitored his vital signs.

"Where is he?" Sturm flicked a finger against Toybox's idle avatar.

"Don't know," said Silk. "Wobbling around hardtime? I'm sure he'll show up before long. Meanwhile, you need to promise that you won't rat us out."

"Rules?" said Remeny. "Wasn't there something about revolutions not having any?"

"Sorry, but either you promise or we're done."

"Sure, sure. We promise." Sturm bent and pretended to examine the Chair of Saint Peter. "Just get on with it."

"Johanna?"

"Remeny to you. How do you know I'll keep my word?"

"We've done our homework." He tried a smile on her. "Which means I trust you more than you trust me." She was embarrassed that, just a few hours ago, it would have worked.

She morphed one of Toybox's repulsive couches into a park bench and sat. "Promise."

"Thank you. The first thing to know is that there are a lot of us. Not enough, but more all the time. Did you know that when Jefferson wrote that first declaration, only about a third of the colonists favored independence? A third were loyal to the King and another third were on the fence. The point is that we don't need to convince everybody, okay?"

Toybox jerked on his throne and opened his eyes. "What did I miss?"

Remeny swallowed her blip of chagrin.

"We just started." Silk seemed annoyed at the interruption. "The contact went well?"

"About what we expected. Botão bailed."

"But these two bit after all." Toybox rubbed his hands together. "I wanted to be there but the damn overlord... well, you know. Besides, Silk says I'm not quite ready for a contact. I need to work on my issues." He came off his throne to the coffin. "Absinthe?"

Remeny scooted away from him on her bench. She opened the private channel with Robby. =*Does he have to talk*?=

=*Humor them. They're taking a risk.*= Sturm joined him. "I'll have some." He laid a sugar cube on one of the slotted spoons and set it on a glass.

"Could we please get to the point?" said Remeny. It felt

good to close her hands into fists, like she had control of *something* at least. "What are you asking us to do?"

"Recruit," said Silk. "What we were doing in coop – that's what we're doing all across the entire county. You talk to kids. Make friends. Get our point across."

"I signed on last month," said Toybox. "Easiest thing I ever did."

"Okay," said Sturm. "But we're graduating."

"Are we?"

Remeny and Sturm stared at one another. =*Oh shit*.=

"We flunk coop." Toybox's glee was (.7). "On purpose. Isn't that crush?"

Remeny couldn't help herself. "Shouldn't be hard for you."

Sturm drained his virtual absinthe at a gulp. "So we're stuck in EOS hell forever."

"There are only so many times you can repeat coop," said Silk, "although we can help you extend your time here. We can arrange it so that most of the kids assigned to your teams are sympathetic to the stashed. Changing avatars can buy time. Eventually you *will* have to graduate. There will be another assignment waiting, if you want."

Remeny was stunned by the enormity of what Silk was saying. And who was he, really? How old? Did he even live in Jefferson County?

"All of this is voluntary, understand, drop out any time. But you won't want to. We're busy everywhere, working in every demographic group. Lots of us are overclocked and can think rings around those who lived the majority of their lives in hardtime. And, Remeny, we're not all stashed. There are lots of us out and about in the real world. Maybe they have brothers or sisters or mothers or fathers…"

"Wait," Remeny said. "Aren't our parents going to get suspicious if we keep flunking coop?"

"Some do." Silk nodded.

"My parents don't give a shit," said Toybox. "They're stashed too."

"Sometimes kids convert their parents," continued Silk.

"Let me guess." Robby held up a hand to stop him. "And sometimes you try for entire families at once."

Toybox chuckled.

"Special families get special consideration."

Remeny thought about Steve Spencer in his house in Vermont and a sixty-million-dollar Vincente Gonsalves flix and Robby's ultimatum. Which was more important to Dad, the part or his son's pursuit of happiness? Wondering about it made her head ache.

"So that's pretty much the deal," said Silk. "I'm happy to tell you more, but I'd like to hear what's on your mind now."

The silence stretched. Remeny couldn't look at Robby. She closed their private channel. She felt like curling up into a ball. He had to speak first. But she knew. He was her brother. She *knew*.

"I'm interested."

"Good man." Silk came over and sat on the couch beside her. "Remeny?" What had she seen in him? "We definitely want you too." She thought that if he tried to touch her, she would slap his hand away.

On an impulse, she pulled the Neurosky off her head and Silk, Toybox, and Sturm disappeared. It was almost midnight. She was going to owe her overlord big time for this night. She stood and stretched in the dark of her room. Her home. She didn't bother with lights or a headset. Mom and Dad were almost certainly asleep but she opened the hall door as if it were made of glass and slunk down to Robby's room. She was glad now that she hadn't left ForSquare with Botão. It was important that she understood what Silk was

375

offering Robby. The pursuit of his happiness. As Sturm.

But his happiness wasn't hers, and that was okay. Silk had given her something, even though she couldn't accept his offer. She would have life and her liberty from her brother's pain.

Johanna leaned close to Robby and blew on his face.

Goodbye.

He stirred but did not wake.

ABOUT THE EDITOR

Gardner Dozois has won fifteen Hugo Awards and thirty-two Locus Awards for his editing work, plus two Nebula Awards for his own writing. He was the editor of *Asimov's Science Fiction* for twenty years, and is the author or editor of more than a hundred books. He is the founding editor of *The Year's Best Science Fiction* anthologies (1984-present), and has co-edited several anthologies with George R.R. Martin. He was inducted into the Science Fiction Hall of Fame in June 2011.

WASTELANDS 2
MORE STORIES OF THE APOCALYPSE

EDITED BY JOHN JOSEPH ADAMS

Famine. Death. War. Pestilence. Harbingers of the biblical apocalypse—Armageddon, The End of the World. John Joseph Adams returns with a second anthology of post-apocalyptic short stories from masters of their craft.

GEORGE R.R. MARTIN • ORSON SCOTT CARD • PAOLO BACIGALUPI • HUGH HOWEY

JACK MCDEVITT • CORY DOCTOROW • LAUREN BEUKES

RUDY RUCKER & BRUCE STERLING • ANN AGUIRRE • CHRISTOPHER BARZAK

NANCY KRESS • GENEVIEVE VALENTINE • D. THOMAS MINTON • JACK MCDEVITT

RAMSEY SHEHADEH • ROBERT SILVERBERG • MIRA GRANT • JOE R. LANSDALE

MARIA DAHVANA HEADLEY • JUNOT DIAZ • JAKE KERR • MAUREEN F. MCHUGH

TOIYA KRISTEN FINLEY • MILO JAMES FOWLER • TANANARIVE DUE

MEGAN ARKENBERG • JAMES VAN PELT • CHRISTIE YANT • SEANAN MCGUIRE

"A magnificent collection" *SF Crowsnest*

"A super bumper fun book of nightmarish dystopia" *Starburst*

"One of the best post-apocalyptic anthologies you will find this side of the big crunch" *SF Book*

TITANBOOKS.COM

DEAD MAN'S HAND
AN ANTHOLOGY OF THE WEIRD WEST

EDITED BY JOHN JOSEPH ADAMS

From a kill-or-be-killed gunfight with a vampire to an encounter in a steampunk bordello, the weird western is a dark, gritty tale where the protagonist might be playing poker with a sorcerous deck of cards, or facing an alien on the streets of a dusty frontier town. Here are twenty-three original tales—stories of the Old West infused with elements of the fantastic—produced specifically for this volume by many of today's finest writers. Included are Orson Scott Card's first "Alvin Maker" story in a decade, and an original adventure by Fred Van Lente, writer of *Cowboys & Aliens*.

KELLEY ARMSTRONG • ELIZABETH BEAR • TOBIAS S. BUCKNELL
ORSON SCOTT CARD • HUGH HOWEY • DAVID FARLAND • JEFFREY FORD
ALAN DEAN FOSTER • LAURA ANN GILMAN • RAJAN KHANNA • JOE R. LANSDALE
KEN LIU • JONATHAN MABERRY • SEANAN MCGUIRE • MIKE RESNICK
BETH REVIS • ALASTAIR REYNOLDS • FRED VAN LENTE • WALTER JOHN WILLIAMS
TAD WILLIAMS • BEN H. WINTERS • CHRISTIE YANT • CHARLES YU

"One wild weird west ride" *The Book Plank*

"A colourful, memorable and, above all, imaginative collection of fiction" *Bookbag*

"Gloriously weird" *Kirkus*

TITANBOOKS.COM

ENCOUNTERS OF SHERLOCK HOLMES

EDITED BY GEORGE MANN

A brand-new collection of Sherlock Holmes stories from a variety of exciting voices in modern horror and steampunk, including James Lovegrove, Paul Magrs and Mark Hodder. Edited by respected anthologist George Mann, and including a story by Mann himself.

**MARK HODDER • MAGS L HALLIDAY • CAVAN SCOTT • NICK KYME • PAUL MAGRS •
GEORGE MANN • STUART DOUGLAS • ERIC BROWN • RICHARD DINNICK • KELLY HALE
STEVE LOCKLEY • MARK WRIGHT • DAVID BARNETT • JAMES LOVEGROVE**

"Some of the most exciting upcoming genre fiction talent in the UK today" *Starburst*

"As you might guess, most of these tales involve the outré, the recherché, the improbable, and the downright fantastic" *The Sherlock Holmes Journal*

"A Delightful escape" *Celebrity Matters*

For more fantastic fiction, author events,
competitions, limited editions and more

Visit our website
titanbooks.com

Like us on Facebook
facebook.com/titanbooks

Follow us on Twitter
@TitanBooks

Email us
readerfeedback@titanemail.com